Praise for Patricia Hummingbird

1999 National Book Award Fiฺ.....t in Fiction

The New Yorker Book Awards
Best Fiction 1999, Finalist

" . . . passionate. . . . " —**Book Magazine**

" . . .[an] accomplished first novel. . . . Henley guides her
readers through this tale one graceful and slicing sentence
at a time, calling up both despair and wonder,
outrage and hope." —**Hungry Mind Review**

". . . deeply-felt. . . ." —**John Sayles**

"It is impossible to read *Hummingbird House* . . .
without thinking of Hemingway; and, with due respect for
his mastery of the craft, thinking less well of him."
—**Dan Carpenter,** *Indianapolis Star*

" . . . Kate's tale rings true in her realistic conclusion
that gross injustice calls for more than merely sorrow,
but also rage, sacrifice and the ability to simultaneously
love and lose." —**Publishers Weekly**

" . . . a moving story of love and injustice."
—**Independent Publisher Magazine**

" . . . I loved the book."
—**Caeli Wolfson, Missoula Independent**

"Henley is a gifted writer with a poignant and important
story to tell. . . . " —**Rocky Mountain News**

HUMMINGBIRD HOUSE

Also by Patricia Henley

Back Roads (poetry)
The Secret of Cartwheels (stories)
Friday Night at Silver Star (stories)
Learning to Die (poetry)

HUMMINGBIRD HOUSE

PATRICIA HENLEY

MacMurray & Beck
Denver

Printed and bound in the United States of America

2   3   4   5   6   7   8   9   10

Library of Congress Cataloging-in-Publication Data
Henley, Patricia.
Hummingbird house : a novel / by Patricia Henley.
p.   cm.
ISBN 1-878448-87-0 (cloth)
ISBN 1-878448-98-6 (paper)
I. Title.
PS3558.E49633H86   1999
813'.54—dc21   98-31274
CIP

MacMurray & Beck Fiction: General Editor, Greg Michalson
Hummingbird House cover design by Laurie Dolphin.
The text was set in Janson by Chris Davis, Mulberry Tree Enterprises.

ACKNOWLEDGMENTS

I thank the many people who contributed to the writing of this book: the refugees in Chiapas who took the risk of sharing their experiences; Nancy Makransky, a midwife in Guatemala; the men and women of Guatemala who opened their hearts to me; Susan Hawkins, the friend with whom I first ventured to Central America; Wandy Toro-Zambrana, David Flory and Elizabeth Corbett for the advice on the Spanish translations; Charlotte Sheedy and Fred Ramey for their editorial comments; Victor Perera, whose book *Unfinished Conquest: The Guatemalan Tragedy* informed me and corroborated what I had observed; and my husband and son for discussing the story with me and reading and rereading the manuscript.

I am grateful to the School of Liberal Arts at Purdue University for its support during the completion of this manuscript.

I would also like to acknowledge a debt to the following sources: the publications of the Robert Kennedy Memorial Center for Human Rights; the publications of Human Rights Watch, Americas; *Ixil Country* by Benjamin Colby and Pierre L. Van Den Berghe; *Life Stories of the Nicaraguan Revolution* by Denis Lynn Daly Heyck; *Granddaughters of Corn* by Marilyn Anderson and Jonathan Garlock; *Guatemala* by Jean-Marie Simon; *Where There Is No Doctor* by David Werner; and *Spiritual Midwifery* by Ina May Gaskin.

There are probably people whose contributions I have neglected to mention; if so, my apologies. I owe a great debt to many.

Short excerpts of this manuscript have appeared in *Arts Indiana* and *Indiana Review*.

for S. K. R.

. . . there will be no high days and no bright praise for our work, our design, until the rise of the human work, the human design.

Mayan creation myth
Popol Vuh
translated by Dennis Tedlock

Father Dixie Ryan got off the bus on a wide boulevard in Zone 2, Guatemala City, carrying a soft-sided suitcase patched with duct tape. Sunlight slashed here and there into the shady street where traffic stood nearly still in black waves of exhaust. He imagined the oily mix coating his lungs. The orphanage, a gas station fenced on three sides with tall blue planks: these were familiar landmarks.

A Cherokee, its windows glossy black, crept out from an alley clotted with houseware vendors. The priest turned—his neck hair bristling—and maneuvered in an oxbow through the people on the street. At the gas station he asked the attendant if he could use the restroom. "Sí, sí, padre," the man said, wiping his hands on a rag. "The night watchman lives back there." The priest slipped through the blue gate and into a dirt yard where there stood a brand-new cement-block toilet stall with grainy newspaper photos of Michael Jordan plastered above a basin. Inside he relieved himself. Then he leaned his head against the cement wall. His vision swam. He took out the scrap of paper with Sunny's address. El Pacífico Sueño.

He waited as long as he could manage without arousing suspicion before slipping back into the street and the neighborhood, through the park where trash drifted, where street kids congregated, sucking on brown paper bags of cobbler's glue, past bakeries, past market stalls with radios on and mothers combing out the hair of little ones or men waiting for customers to make the smallest affordable purchase, a cigarette or two, a box of Black Cat matches, a cup of white rice. The Cherokee did not reappear. At El Pacífico Sueño—the peaceful sleep, the peaceful dream—he knocked on the red front door. A wooden sign creaked above him; a star the size of a butter cookie had been carved after the word *Sueño*.

Sunny answered his knock.

"Dix." She took his hand, drew him inside.

A blinking fluorescent tube lit the foyer. Child-sized coffins stacked against two stucco walls were dusty, though he could still detect their piney smell. A three-year-old picture calendar of churches—turned to November 1985—hung over a desk in whose many open cubbyholes lay the yellowing invoices of funerals past.

He said, "I might have been followed."

Sunny turned to the desk and plucked a tiny manila envelope from a drawer.

"Here it is," she said. She took his arm, kissed his cheek. "Make yourself at home."

He pocketed the key and left at once.

He found a café in the same block and settled into its dim cool interior, his Roman collar and Panama hat on the table. The last bus would leave a little after seven. He could be at Sunny and Ben's Antigua house by eight o'clock. He'd do as the Canadian doctor advised: rest until the breakbone fever gave up its hold on him.

Waiting for dusk, he drank limonada and read *Twenty Love Poems and a Song of Despair*. Out on the street a vendor hawked toy skeletons for Day of the Dead and an old woman scattered flowers on the sidewalk: golden *flores del muerto*. So that the dead may find their way home

"Go on now. I can't keep you anymore."

The man on the motor scooter lifted Marta by her wrist and Eduardo caught his little sister. They stood in sunshine at the edge of a park scruffy with trash and tree limbs blown down by wind. Flocks of children loitered, squatting, poking each other, hunching head to head.

"Es Guate, Marta," Eduardo said, taking her hand in his. "El capital!" He fingered the wrinkled dollar bill the gringo had given him. He kept it in a secret pocket inside his shirt, a patch pocket his mother had sewn for him so that he could run errands for her without being robbed.

Marta said nothing. Her hair tangled in permanent greasy knots. She was eight years old, Eduardo twelve. The sun was bleached like straw where an animal slept.

In the park they watched the beggar who shared their bench. With his white beard, his gray hair thatchy, his trousers rolled to the knees, his legs streaked with dirt, his feet—Eduardo had never seen such feet. Big, thick-skinned, with toenails as black as tortilla blisters. His dusty bolsa had been crocheted in a design familiar to Eduardo: purple and green stripes with the plumed quetzal worked in. It was a design from the village nearest the village where Eduardo and Marta had been born in the highlands above the Chixoy River. A similar bolsa hung in front of the statue of the Virgin in the village church; his mother had sometimes filled it with corn as an offering.

Tall trees shaded their park bench. The smell of rotting fruit nearby. Marta perched primly beside Eduardo, her eyes wide, her red corte tattered along its folds. She had to be vigilant about adjusting the folds and retying her sash; the fabric was soft and worn and if she did not watch, her corte would slip down. It was her one last piece of clothing. Her grandmother had made this corte. Her grandmother had woven her sash on a backstrap loom; the sash was gray and red and black: sturdy stripes. When the sash and the corte had been brand new, she had worn a red glass-bead necklace tied in a knot against her chest. The necklace had been long lost. Trucks and cars and bicycles dodged and swerved, bright and ramshackle, horns blurting. She had never before seen the capital, the traffic and the big advertisements and the capitalistas in glistening bloody lipstick, their spiky leather shoes. The gringo with the motor scooter was a man so tall that Marta had to tilt her head back to see his long horsey face. He had peanut butter in his backpack and he had bought them hot-from-the-griddle tortillas in Los Encuentros. Early in the morning, before daylight.

Go on now. I can't keep you anymore.

They had ridden, clinging to him, clinging to each other, in the dust, in the oily exhaust, in the itchy vibration of the worn-out tires against the washboard roads, all the way from Chichi.

The beggar reached into his bolsa. He glanced around guardedly and pulled out part of a loaf of brown sugar. He took a bite. Eduardo salivated. Marta squeezed his kneecap. Their mother had nearly always kept a piece of such sugar in a tin on the shelf. She had shaved curls of the coarse brown stuff on their hot cereal or rice. Eduardo did not like to think about his mother but she and his father were never far from his thoughts. He had last seen his father at the municipal hall in the center of the village. A rainy night, a night of fiesta. Eduardo had peeked through the loose fenceboards and there he had seen his father dancing like a marionette to marimba in a line of drunken men. The courtyard of the municipal hall had been slick with mud and the birds-of-paradise had been coated with mud and the mud had soaked up the striped trousers of the drunken men who shouted and slurred the monotonous and mournful songs. They danced and laughed, although they looked as though they cried, with the whites of their eyes sore and red. Rain and clouds bled like ink over everything. After the fiesta the military had come. Soldiers with hard eyes. Shiny bayonets. Steel-toed boots. Helicopters had chopped like razor wings above the village.

With his dirty thumb the beggar pressed out two hunks of sugar from the loaf and offered them to Eduardo and Marta. They hurried down the concrete bench, hovered over his open hand. The beggar shrugged. Eduardo plucked the sugar—hunks the size of small bird eggs—from the old man's hand and ate. And Marta ate. The sugar melted on their tongues, at once rough and velvety; the palm trees swayed, their palm leaves clacking; the scent and oil of oranges burst in invisible clouds nearby where a man unloaded oranges in red net bags from a flatbed; and the capital was for that moment a place of generosity.

A boy swaggered up to the bench. His knuckles were bony, his skeleton visible under his ashy dark skin. "Give it to me," he said.

The beggar crammed the sugar into his bolsa, hugged the bolsa to his chest. Eduardo and Marta scrambled to the end of the long bench.

"For—my—boys." The intruder called his boys forward with a chop of his hand. His flat cheeks were chalky, his eyes devoid of light. Busy people passed by. They swarmed along the sidewalks. No one took notice.

One of the boys—a little older, perhaps fourteen, in a plaid shirt that had all its buttons—stared with malevolent eyes at Eduardo and Marta. "Are you with the old one?"

The first boy hit the beggar's face with a stick.

Eduardo said, "No lo conocemos a él."

He grabbed Marta's trembling hand and slipped away to a palm tree behind a fruit vendor's stand. They squatted at the base of the palm tree, stealing glances, watching but not watching the beggar and the boys, their hearts beating hard within the spark and boom of the strange city. The fruit vendor's plywood stand had been painted to resemble a bunch of bananas. Beneath the stand was a bodega. Eduardo imagined sleeping under there. That was on his mind, finding a safe place to sleep.

"Piña y mango, piña y mango," called the fruit vendor. "Piña, piña."

The beggar folded his body over his bolsa. The gang of boys pounced, kicked the beggar's ribs. Eduardo could see only the back of the beggar's brown coat puffing out like a bird's feathers.

One boy jerked the bolsa from its strap and sprinted into a straggly grove, a lean shadow among the white-barked trees. The others kicked the beggar again and again. They kicked, cursed, grunted, laughed. Dust as fine as incense rose around them.

"I have it," shouted the boy in the trees.

"Get out of here," the fruit vendor growled at Eduardo. "You are like animals. Animals! Mierda! Get out of here." He pitched a mango pit and it landed in dirt at their feet.

A morsel of fruit clung to the pit. Sunlight shone on the fleck of mango as it flew but it was dusty now, wasted. The molasses taste of the brown sugar had made Eduardo's stomach growl. He pulled Marta by the hand and walked across the street, walked away from trouble, thinking, We are in the capital now and we must never carry a bolsa.

The Nicaraguan National Cathedral in Managua was not a sacred place. Kate Banner ventured inside despite that; she wanted to see the damage for herself. Weeds had taken over the sanctuary; statues had fallen out of their niches, their porcelain fragments long since ground into dust. Piss and shit everywhere, broken glass winking, black streaks from mortar fire staining the columns.

She picked her way to the foot of the altar. Some evenings, on her way home from the clinic, she glimpsed men playing softball inside the cathedral. Still, it was not hard to imagine that it had once given refuge to women, women tired of babies crying and children pulling and men reaching into their blouses. Christ loved women and they love Him. She pictured the Nicaraguan women in the cathedral praying for their men to quit drinking or praying for Somoza's plane to crash, whatever they had prayed for. She thought of the quiet of the cathedral, the peace of it, the gratitude of the women.

And then a witchlike voice spoke. "Brigadista!"

Kate's heart sped up. "Qué pasa?" she asked, startled, peering around.

An old man broke cover from behind a marble column. Sunshine half hid his face, sunshine pouring through the caved-in roof. "Brigadista, brigadista, brigadista," sing-songy like a bully, he said, "You do not belong here." A few steps above her, his hands clutching weeds. Dancing wickedly in rags. Skin and bones. Kate thought that she could smell him, smegma, sweat, piss and all.

She ran from the altar, tripped, stumbled to the entry.

"Go home, brigadista. Go home." He fired a bit of gravel and cackled.

On the street the people waited endlessly for a bus. There weren't enough buses; because of the embargo, vehicles had been abandoned all over Nicaragua. Sweat ran down her sides. She sweated all the way to the apartment.

After that the Cathedral Man penetrated her dreams. Whenever she did not sleep at Deaver's she would catch herself waiting, the way you wait for the bogeyman when you're a child—with such dread.

Harm's Way

A black chicken skittered under the red tables. Kate swept palm fronds across the patio floor and down the stairs. Somehow the hurricane had left untouched this second-floor open-air comedor and the red chairs were every which way as though left there by sweethearts in a hurry to get home. Lupita had been evacuated to the capital, over two hundred kilometers away. Beyond the comedor the brackish streets—brown rivers, salty rivers—flowed sluggishly into buildings. Shreds of clothing, skirts or aprons, clung to banisters and broken lumber. A bicycle twisted, half in, half out of a shattered window across the street. On October 22 the mad Atlantic Ocean had spilled into four hundred miles of coastline and crews were cleaning up and would be cleaning up for months. Seagulls swooped in, scavenging, cawing, from wherever they had taken refuge during the storm. There was no electricity.

The water was not as deep as it had been. Down on the street Kate could see the high-water mud line on every wall. The heat had to be worked through; it was a soup they lived in, a substance that changed your metabolism. Not unlike the heat at home.

She investigated the casa. The first floor was open to the weather and had come very close to being flooded, but not quite; it was built up on pilings of cinder blocks; water lapped at the third

step down into the street. Not much was on the first floor. A padlocked freezer. A high greasy table for cleaning fish. Bamboo walls.
A floor laid with warped planks. Beyond a gate of wrought iron, a
steep stairway led up to the comedor with its thatched-roof shelters
over the tables, a pine bar and galley, and a tiled patio crisscrossed
with clothesline. A fragile balcony gave onto a view of the town and
the river.

Lupita's bedroom was a windowless cell. Kate peeked inside; in
the shadows a picture frame lay face down on the floor. Purely out
of curiosity about María—about her intimate life with Lupita—
Kate went in and picked it up. The glass was cracked. María as a
girl in her first communion dress smiled across the years; someone
had cut a lock of her black hair and pressed the hair under the glass.
Kate slipped the photo under Lupita's pillow for safekeeping and
nearly skulked out, a little ashamed of prying.

In the comedor a lipstick-red hibiscus had been tipped over.
Above the bar hung a framed picture of César Sandino, the revolu-
tionary martyr for whom the Sandinistas were named. César
Sandino, wild-eyed, a little man in a big hat and a floppy bow tie.

She discovered beer in a round-cornered refrigerator. Cerveza
Victoria. Warm beer. What a gloating surprise that would be for
Maggie and María when they returned. They'd gone out looking
for more bottled water. It was rumored that an evangelical church
was giving away stockpiled water on the other side of town.

Kate's old Wellingtons had let in squishes of water; she imagined her feet were shriveling. She had an ammo box of medicines—
chloroquine for malaria, metronidazole for giardia, some antibi-
otics—and a waterproof bag of sterile supplies. They had heard
that the town's clinic had been swept away. Her midwifery kit she
kept in a fanny pack; it contained a few basic tools of her trade, a
fetoscope and a syringe, clamps and sterile gloves. She was rarely
without the fanny pack. María and Maggie had taken turns carrying a rucksack with whatever else they thought they might want for
a few days: changes of bikini underwear, shampoo, black market
chocolate bars, a sewing kit, a half kilo of rice. They had ridden out

to the coast in a transport truck full of Sandinista soldiers, soldiers with rifles and strong singing voices. They had turned the trip into a cautious lark in spite of whatever danger lay in the campo. Contra troops, the soldiers' own brothers and sisters and cousins, might be lying in ambush. A peace pact had been signed at Sopoá but that had not stopped the fighting. The Sandinista soldiers had sung anyway, in the rumble of the difficult road.

Night was coming on. With finality she chucked the broom into a corner and watched the night. The sky was clearing; orange bolts of cloud blew away and away, out to sea, like a bandage being removed from a sensitive scar. Copper-faced men went by in boats, rescuing people from trees and housetops. Most had gone to escape the storm but some had stayed. The men laughed, giddy with surviving.

From the balcony railing she could see La Iglesia de Santa Clara, its bell tower, its red roof. She shucked off her Wellingtons, peeled away her wet socks, and wiggled her toes. Her skinny feet looked leeched of blood. It was sunset and they had left Managua at dawn the day before and had slept that first night in the back of the transport truck. Then she had been on her feet all day, treating whatever minor ailments or injuries came her way: headaches, abrasions, and a puncture wound. A boy had stepped on a nail. Sleep muddied Kate's thoughts. She could feel sleep begging.

She patted her pants pocket. Her Swiss army knife was there and with it she could open the beer bottles. The beer would dry them out, she knew, but still, drinking beer would be festive. They could balance each beer with water, if they found water. Across the street the priest on his balcony was giving communion, the paper-thin wafers homing into the mouths of the people—mostly women—who knelt before him. Someone was up in the bell tower ringing the bell, a cheerful, tinny, and not quite grating tune. Kate closed her eyes drowsily.

"Kate!"

"Catarina—ayuda! Pronto, pronto!"

She roused herself from dozing.

Breathing hard, Maggie appeared at the top of the stairs, her kerchief askew on her head, her curly hair tucked up under. "We found a woman—she's been—in labor—since last night—she thought she was going to die—"

Kate straightened her glasses. "I'm out of it . . . truly . . ."

"I know that, sweetie, I know," Maggie said. "This gal is terrified. She's just a kid."

Kate pulled on her boots. "Why don't you bring her in?"

Maggie made a face. "I doubt she can make it." At Kate's feet she placed a gallon of water in a plastic jug. "She's in the boat."

Kate strode to the counter behind the bar, the jug of water in hand. A long cockroach, with a shiny black shell like a button, stared at her from below the water faucet. "Try the propane burner," she said.

Maggie hurried over to the stove, dripping muddy water from her pantlegs. She lit the burner, and a blue ring of flame leaped from the jets. She opened a cupboard and pulled out an aluminum soup pan.

"That'll do. Boil about half that water. Boil these," Kate said, depositing chrome clamps and needles and hemostats into the soup pan. In a bowl she scrubbed her hands with Betadine and drinking water. She liked the disinfectant odor. It made her feel capable. She said, "Where's her family?"

"Drowned, I think." Maggie looked out toward the sea though the sea was not visible to them; it was many miles beyond the town. "She said she lost them."

On the clothesline behind the bar hung several flowered towels. Kate sniffed them without touching them. They were musty, damp, but beneath that was the smell of detergent, something lemony, and Kate guessed that the towels had been just washed before the hurricane hit. She snatched two towels from the clothesline.

The priest leaned on his balcony railing, watching.

The boat rocked where the water met the steps. It had once been blue and white but now the paint was worn away and re-

mained only in the swollen splinters of the gunwales. The woman
lay in the bottom, curled up. Her dress indistinguishable from the
blue-black night.

María stood on the steps holding a flashlight. The humidity
had curled her hair until it seemed nearly tangled. Her blouse and
slacks were streaked with mud. She shook her head and met Kate's
glance. The look on her face told Kate that she had little hope, little despair. She was waiting to see what would happen. "El sacer-
dote está rezando. The priest is praying," she said to Kate, who
could not tell if there was an edge of sarcasm in María's voice or
not. She had tied the boat to a porch pillar.

Kate waded into the water. The water came up above her knees.
She reached into the boat, touched the woman's feverish forehead.
The woman's eyes flew open. Her cheeks were planes, Miskito
cheeks, but her skin was creamy brown. Mestizo, Kate surmised,
Spanish-speaking. A birthmark, a mole, marked her temple.

"Buenas noches, buenas noches," Kate said, doubling the towels. "I'm going to put these under you." The floor of the boat
curved like the inside of a ribcage. A scum of dirty water and bits of
indeterminate refuse littered the floor.

The salt air blew in a swirl. From afar a rooster crowed. María
aimed the flashlight toward Kate's work. The woman howled.

"She's all right," Kate said, "if she can holler like that." To the
woman she said tenderly, "Cómo se llama?"

"Consuela," the woman said, wincing. "Consuela María."

"Consuela," Kate said, "I want you to turn over and let me see
what is happening to your baby. I am a nurse. I won't hurt you."

"Me duele!" Consuela cried.

How young she was, fourteen or fifteen. "You look very brave
to me," Kate said. From her fanny pack she pulled a sterile white
washcloth wrapped in brown paper. She waited.

Consuela shifted her weight, reared up on her elbows, and
opened her legs. Kate flung her dress above her knees. She said,
"Levante el trasero. Raise your bottom." She slipped the towels
under Consuela and the towels soaked up water and a little blood.

Her thighs were slick.

The baby was coming.

Kate washed the woman as best she could. She barely had time to pluck waxy thin surgical gloves over her hands. The malleable head of the baby, gray and reddish with a thatch of wet black hair, swelled—regressed—then popped out. The face was puckered. The shoulders did not want to come.

"You've got a big baby here," Kate said. "You're going to have to get up on your knees. Can you do that?"

"No puedo, señorita, no puedo!"

"Oh, sí, puedes hacerlo sí lo intentas, oh, yes, you can do it if you try," Kate said. "You can do it. Hold the gunwales. We'll keep you steady. Grab on, now. Just get up on your knees. I'm holding on, you've got a baby who wants to be born, hold on to the gunwales—"

María set the flashlight down on the top step. Its beam shone into the muddy water. She braced one foot against the bottom step and kept the boat steady. Kate supported the baby's head. Consuela rose up on her knees, moaning and grunting. Maggie came and set a bowl of steaming water on the top step. She lit a lantern and its wick was long; the flame blackened the globe.

"You're doing fine," Kate said. "Easy does it."

Maggie fiddled with the lantern; a smudged shimmer lit them up. The priest on the balcony turned away.

The baby came, a quick and slippery squirm.

Consuela collapsed, groaning. The boat pitched.

"Yahoo," Maggie whooped. Then, "Incredible, it's always incredible."

"That's fine, that's fine," Kate said. "Baby girl," she said. "Big baby girl, big shoulders, football player."

She held the baby. "Thanks for the light. Now suction, that's it, let's get a breath—" And Maggie did as she was told. The baby coughed a puny wet cough, then cried.

The cord was a luminous green and lavender. They watched it pulsing. They waited. Maggie hummed a muted song. María said,

"You are fine now, you are fine now. To know that a baby was born here would make my mother happy. That would make her very happy. It's a happy night."

"Tengo sed," Consuela breathed.

María gave her sips of water from a cup.

Slowly, slowly, the cord changed color. It drained of blood, turned white and thin. "Now—right here," Kate said. Maggie plucked a clamp from the bowl of water and clamped the baby's curling cord. "Way to go. One more, por favor." Then, "Time for the razor."

Maggie unwrapped a sterile razor blade, cut the cord, and laid the razor beside the lantern. She took the baby from Kate and wrapped her in a sweatshirt she'd found on the clothesline.

Kate sweated. Her glasses slipped down her nose and she pushed them back up. María leaned into the boat, holding Consuela's head in her arms. "Can you move?" she said.

"No, no," Consuela whimpered. "Madre—de Dios—no."

"Está bien, está bien," María hushed. Her voice was not always the voice of an officer. She was a merciful woman. Before she started the clinic in Managua, María had been a Sandinista officer for five years, in starched khakis, a pistol at her waist. She had lost her only brother in the war.

"Not yet," Kate said. "Let's wait for the afterbirth."

Consuela turned over, sighing a river-long sigh. She unbuttoned her bodice and they put the baby at her breast.

Her dress was not so dirty, Kate decided. She stood in the water beside the boat, holding her hands up to keep them clean. Clean was a relative term. "María, you can help here—massage her uterus—let's get this out of there."

María took off her blouse and padded Consuela's head with it. In her honey-colored camisole she waded to the side of the boat and made soothing noises and kneaded Consuela's belly.

"Most of them look like Winston Churchill," Maggie said, smiling at the baby, "but this one's a beauty. In the pink."

You just get high—

You just get high—

You just get high delivering babies, Deaver would say. I almost believed him. Eight years have passed since Hurricane Joan but I still remember the way his voice would come to me when I least expected it and it would come when I needed strength but for some perverse reason I'd pick up his signal instead. You don't really care about what's happening here. You just get high delivering babies.

I had to fight his voice.

Lightweight. Spoiled North American woman.

His voice was like the earthquake tremors I knew were always there beneath the pavement, about to happen. Little shifts in what I had thought was certain, the ground beneath my feet.

We left the afterbirth in the bottom of the boat. Upstairs we had hammocks and a trundle-bed mattress and the beer and a pot of leftover red beans and rice. We wanted to take Consuela upstairs with us but she couldn't make it and we couldn't carry her, not without hurting her. We moved the mattress downstairs, set it up on the fish table. We put Consuela on the table. Lupita had a drawer full of table linens. That was all we could find. We looked high and low but we could not find any bedsheets, so we made the

18

mattress up with table linens. Fine tablecloths. Yellowing with age. Tablecloths with crocheted trim. Someone had once eaten grand dinners on them. I can't get that out of my mind, the way we wrapped her in those tablecloths. Ironed smooth as glass to the touch. Consuela was worn out and she drank one half of a cerveza and she slept. Her fever had gone down. We had cleaned her up and I was sure there was no excessive bleeding, no lacerations, nothing to worry about. We put the silver nitrate drops in the baby's eyes and syringed the mucus from her nose and we gave her sterilized water from an eye dropper. We checked her over and decided she was all right. Un milagro. We laid the baby in a dresser drawer nearby on one of the red tables. The three of us watched over her and we took turns going down to check on Consuela. We offered her drinking water, a bite or two of beans, whatever she wanted, which wasn't much. We ate the beans and rice and drank the beer and we felt lucky to have a tank of propane for the burner, lucky to have matches. We were happy. Oddly enough. I thought we had come to the ends of the earth. Hurricane Joan.

Sometime after ten, Maggie came up the stairs and said, "My friends. Consuela has died." Her face looked old with shock.

María cried out.

"Sweet Jesus," Kate said. "What—"

"I know," Maggie said. "I know." She picked up the baby. "Come on."

They gathered downstairs around the dead woman. Maggie swaddled the baby in the gray sweatshirt. María held the lantern high. Lantern light wavered on the bamboo walls. Kate checked Consuela's pulse.

"Mierda!" María cried. She stamped her foot. "Jesus, Mary, and Joseph!" She crossed herself. She crossed herself again.

With a trembling hand Kate closed Consuela's eyes. Someone had placed a row of chipped sand dollars on a shelf above the table. Kate laid gritty sand dollars on Consuela's eyelids. She straightened her arms and legs. It had not been twenty minutes since she'd gone down to check on her. She cursed under her breath.

A striped cat with huge green eyes went slinking into the boat and nosed the afterbirth. Here and there in broken windows they could see lantern light or candlelight or the bluish beam of a flashlight. Clouds of breeding mosquitoes hovered above the muddy water of the street. They stood there for what seemed like a long time. Kate did not have the heart to say anything.

Finally Maggie said, "What'll we do with her?"

"What're they doing with all the others?" Kate said bitterly. She had no idea what had killed Consuela. She was tired of bodies, the broken ones, the way the dead sprawled gracelessly.

María said, "Not so many died, Kate."

No one said anything.

María went on, "We had excellent evacuation procedures. In case we were invaded by your Uncle Sam."

Kate said in a quiet voice, "He's not my Uncle Sam." She wondered why Maggie was exempt from her barb; perhaps because she held the baby. She did not think María intended to make her feel bad.

Kate said, "Jesus. Poor kid."

Maggie said, "I mean what will we do with the baby."

María set down the lantern and cupped one hand under the baby's head. "My mother will take her."

Kate looked skeptical.

"She was born on her steps," María said. "She'll take her." She kissed the baby's forehead. "My mother might know her family."

Maggie said, "What do you think happened?"

Kate grimaced apologetically.

A rash of gunfire startled them, from a few blocks away. That might have been soldiers after looters or it might have been a Contra skirmish or it might have been a drunk. Kate's heart leaped, not knowing.

"We're better off upstairs," Maggie said.

"Should we get the priest?" Kate said.

María said, "Please, no."

They looked questioningly at her.

"Let it wait. Let's just be together without him."

They plodded upstairs. The joy had gone out of their steps. The comedor had lost its gleam, its safety. The stars had been visible before, and now the sky was like a sponge squeezed of sour rain. They sat under the thatched roof sheltering the bar and watched the rain stipple the water pockets on the floor.

Kate said, "She's got to learn to suck. A pinkie or a nipple."

"Don't look at me," Maggie said.

A small plane flew over, an abrasion on the silky air.

María held up her little finger. "Mine's small."

"Scrub it first," Kate said. "She can do without milk for a day. We can feed her with a dropper. Until . . ."

"Until what?" Maggie said.

Kate sighed. "Until we can find a woman with milk who wants to nurse her. Or until we can get our hands on bottles and formula."

"We'd better go back," María said. "To the clinic."

Their clinic in Managua was a renovated brothel with a gigantic mural painted on the front stucco wall: a smiling compañera nursing a babe in arms and carrying a rifle. María had made the clinic come into being. After the Revolution she had wanted a place where women could stay healthy and learn to read and children could play on a playground without being blown to bits of blood and bone by the National Guard as they had been during the final days of the Somocista regime.

"We can't be much use here," Maggie said. "With her."

No one said, Let's split up for a few days. Kate was glad of that. Internationals weren't supposed to be anywhere near a potential combat zone but they had gotten permits and taken their chances in order to help after the storm. She made a mental plan to leave the ammo box of medicine and the supplies with the priest. They did not talk about the dead woman. Kate felt the failure of it like a foul lump in her chest, more freight to carry.

María took the baby to sleep with her in a hammock.

Once during the night Kate stood on the balcony where she could see the empty boat. She had slept a little and had been awakened by her old dream of the Cathedral Man. The black chicken slept on a stool that had floated by and become lodged between the boat and the steps as the water receded. There was no escaping the

baneful mildew and drizzle. They had wrapped the body with a
canvas tarp weighted with bricks to keep out vultures and dogs. She
hoped a relief worker would come by, collecting bodies. Consuela's
dying made her feel green, caught short. She chastised herself for
that. Chain of ego. Palm trees swaying belied the fury of the storm
that had passed through.

She wept, a surprise. She wept copiously, dreamily, with no
force behind the weeping. She did not know what she wept for.
Mark Deaver was on her mind. The little comedor was a place they
might have come on holiday. They might have whiled away an afternoon in the salt air, drinking beer and flirting. They might have
kissed across the table. At one time they might have done those
things. She was not so sure about now. Deaver was back in
Managua and she was not sorry they were going back.

Maggie crept out of her hammock and sidled up to Kate on the
balcony. She hugged her. "Sweetie, aren't you sleepy?" she said.

"I am sleepy," Kate said, wiping her tears away with the tail of
her shirt. She put her head on Maggie's shoulder. She smelled the
coconut fragrance of her hair, still there, after all their dirty work.
"But I can't give in to it."

They patted each other, easing away. Kate leaned on the railing
gingerly, as though it might give way beneath her weight. Maggie
wore a short nightgown and stood there waiflike, tired. Not at all
her usual robust self. They watched the street and the town, the
crooked tin roofs, the sky.

"It wasn't your fault," Maggie said.

Kate shook her head, pursed her lips, and almost wept again at
Maggie's kindness, holding back her self-pity, her fear of the
Cathedral Man, the secret strategies she worked over, her desire for
Deaver and the sweet wool of sleeping next to him that could quell
her nightmare.

"You need rest for the trip back."

Kate said, "You don't know how young you are in your thirties,
but you are."

"That thought's occurred to me."

A hush of wind and water was all they heard. Kate said, "How could we have stayed so long?"

Maggie sighed. "I see we're into the big questions."

"I think I want to go home."

"We will."

Kate said, "I mean *home* home."

"What are you thinking?"

Kate stared down the street. The water was going down; where the street was high the cobblestones were visible. You don't necessarily notice little safe rises, higher ground, until there's flooding. Until you're desperate. A long half minute passed. She said, "I don't know—"

Maggie stifled a yawn. She took Kate's hand, rubbed the palm with her thumb.

Kate said, "I can't go back to Indiana."

"That's a given," Maggie said.

"I am forty-two years old."

"Don't remind me, sweetie."

Kate said, "I'm restless."

"Let's talk about it. Okay? Not tonight, but soon." Maggie yawned again. "I have a wee headache." She begged off, saying coaxingly, "It's the middle of the night. I'm sleepy."

She went into the bodega, where they had set up a temporary chamberpot. Kate could hear her peeing into the pot. She watched her go back to a hammock and settle herself.

In the early hours of the morning the sky was streaked with a pink and pearly light. Once she saw the priest across the way, an insomniac too, and she waved at him halfheartedly. He waved back and cut a gentle cross in the air, blessing her.

Any one of them could nurse the baby at her breast. Eventually milk would come. Kate tried to imagine it, the way a baby owned you. Kate and Maggie's resistance to such a tie was strong. Tied down, that's how they thought of it. All of their work had been about helping women who were tied down in a way they never wanted to be. The baby rocked in a hammock with María. Each time the baby stirred or cried, the sound comforted Kate, in spite of what ran in her blood, what she called restlessness.

Somewhere along the line she had lost her bearings. What landmarks, what cairns had guided her?

Watching black children on television fire-hosed in Alabama in 1964 when she and Maggie were girls themselves. The aftermath of the bombing of the 16th Street Baptist Church in Birmingham. Being called nigger lovers in high school. The thirteen seconds of gunfire at Kent State in 1970. The gospel verses they memorized on the railroad trestle when they weren't reading movie magazines, verses down in their bone marrow, no matter what dark side of desire they'd known, the perils of the flesh the nuns had warned them against. Remember that you have been called to live in freedom. You shall love your neighbor as yourself. Let it be the narrow gate through which you make your entry. For the love of money is the root of all evil. Photos of Vietnamese children screaming with napalm burning their backs. Children with rifles, trained to go to war. Images that scarred her. You could think of those as landmarks. Incident after incident that had pushed her, like a birthing, like giving birth in hard labor to what she would become, to ask, How can I help? You could only pack it all up and move on, bearings or no.

The way was not so obvious from here. The ends of the earth. Time out is what I need, she bargained—with whom she did not know. Just a little time out. She half smiled when María sleepily stuck her pinkie in the baby's rosy mouth.

This is what I learned in Mexico.

A Mayan woman gives birth kneeling. She holds on to a post. Like this. Her husband is right there kneeling behind her. Her husband holds her. Her mother tends the fire and waits. She wears her traje, her traditional clothes. She won't undress, no matter what. Her clothes are taboo for forty days after the birth and there's a washerwoman whose job it is to wash the clothes of the mother and the baby. No one else is allowed to touch those clothes. When her time comes she digs a pit in the dirt beside the post and she lines the pit with plastic or nylon and she kneels there. A young one might cry out but an older one might not. She'll just wait. She'll just surrender. Though some would say that crying out is part of the surrender. The husband might give her black pepper to make the baby come. They wait for the placenta before they cut the cord and if the placenta is slow to come, her mother tickles the back of her throat with her long black hair and that will make her gag and the gagging stresses the abdominal muscles and that pushes out the placenta. If the placenta is slow to come, the mother ties a corncob to her daughter's end of the cord to keep the placenta from pulling back up into the womb, you never want that, the cervix closing up too soon. They use corn for that, they believe they're made from

corn, that God breathed life into corn to make men and women. I
have heard of them cutting the cord with a machete but I always
use a sterile razor blade. If possible, a man builds his woman a special bed and she stays in bed for thirty days after the birth. The babies' toes and ears were always soft and brown and their hair was
either fine or coarse but always the blackest black and they were
often perfect babies. When the father would say, un milagro, I
would agree, un milagro, yes indeed. Imagine the woman walking
all that way through the jungle and running from the soldiers and
eating only wild greens and with her tongue feeling a tooth rotting
away and knowing the baby grew bones with the calcium from that
tooth. Imagine the bad water they drank, when they had water. A
miracle. Un milagro. And there was a baby born every week or so
in Casa Buena, the refugee camp near the border where I learned
these things.

Amazing how life keeps pressing itself upon us. I have heard
that in Rwanda doctors went on a rampage through a hospital,
stabbing—slaughtering—women in labor, women of an enemy
tribe. Doctors did this. We have come that far, we kill the goddess,
source of life. We're not astonished either way, now, are we?
Astonished at the mystery, astonished at the killing.

Sometimes the babies had problems I'd never encountered before. I could feel a hard time like that coming on, I could feel it in
my own body, my jaw would clench up, I would prepare myself for
the worst. Though there is no way to prepare yourself for that. A
baby might be bleeding from his anus or a baby might have feces in
his mouth and nose or he might be jaundiced or she might be blue,
milky blue, grave blue, or she might not be able to suck.

And there was a baby very sick or dying every week or so. They
died from infections or measles or dehydration from diarrhea. The
diarrhea might be caused by not eating right or the flu or food poi-
soning or allergies or worms. Roundworms can enter the blood-
stream and the intestines. If the child has a fever the roundworms
might crawl out through his nose or mouth. Whipworms can make
the rectum prolapse and hookworms can reach the lungs through

the blood. And diarrhea from all of this can cause extreme dehydration. We tried to catch the dehydration in time. Whenever I went to San Cristóbal for a couple of days, I would leave two gallons of rehydration drink. I'd mix the drink of boiled water and sugar and salt and soda and I would give the instructions to a curandera. I would go to town to see Deaver and that was my reward for all I had been doing. Deaver was my reward. I would walk around his bedroom naked and feel his eyes on me. His eyes could make me want him then. This was another life, a period of accruing regrets. From June until December 1982, I left the refugee camp ten times and went to town for my reward. And only one baby died of dehydration while I was away with Deaver. Only one. Deaver never wanted to hear about the babies.

Fourteen years ago. Now Paul Byrne has come a long way to my highland kitchen, where sunlight falls across the table, across the maps he brought from the States. The door is open to the mountains. Los flores del muerto grow in a golden curve beside the barn. A neighbor woman sits back on her heels in dirt, a wooden shuttle zinging through the warp on her backstrap loom. The caramel-colored goat named Wabash lays her chin upon our porch to see what she can see. Hummingbirds weave intricate nests of meadowsweet and insect silk, bits of bark and lichen, minute twigs and fibers of hemp stolen from a hammock.

Kate, come home with me, he says.

So that's why you came, I tell him. I can't keep the lilt from my voice. Flirtation. A bad habit I thought I'd left behind. I rest my hips against the kitchen counter.

It'd be good for Marta too.

He's the same, the same. Blond hair glinting in the morning light. A patch of sunburn where his collar is open. Strong arms. A pale yellow golfing shirt. Once I borrowed such a shirt for sleep or sex.

He says, I remember everything. About you. He turns me around to face the window, hugs me from behind. His arms across my collarbones. Lips at my ear. In the distance near the white-washed clinica, a man unloads green pineapples from a lorry.

Paul's maps depict land claims and new world exploration, colonial administrative organization, and what little remains of once exuberant tropical forests. The maps do not tell you that the forests of Belize and Honduras were cut down to rebuild London after the Great Fires of 1666. They do not show you the scars of Nicaraguan children who lost their arms and legs when their school bus struck a Contra mine buried in the road. Nor do the maps delineate the precise number of Mayan cornfields soaked in gasoline and set afire by Guatemalan government soldiers. And they cannot tell you the exact words of the sermon given by Oscar Arnulfo Romero, the archbishop of San Salvador, before his murder at his own altar.

You don't know me now, I say. In a voice as kind as I can muster.

Consuela's baby still had no name at ten days old. They were calling her Bebé de la Tormenta, Baby of the Storm. Or La Pequeñita, Little One. She thrived in their care. Lupita dealt in black market goods—petty quantities of staples and luxuries—and she provided the baby with snowy cotton diapers and undershirts and talcum powder. They made a bed for the baby in a plastic laundry basket; she slept first in María's room with Lupita and María and then in the dining room with Kate and Maggie.

Once part of a wealthy house, all of the rooms in their apartment opened onto what had been the back courtyard, where someone, a servant Kate guessed, had kept a cutting garden and an herb garden. They entered through a narrow oak door, now splintered with neglect, where once vendedoras had knocked with pyramids of crusty loaves of white bread for sale or rosy mangoes in a net, close to the kitchen. The dining room, the largest room, had a high-beamed ceiling, a big opaque window with a transom that opened by turning a long brass crank, a creaking table at which they could seat ten, and two daybeds, where Maggie and Kate slept. Each morning they would tuck their sheets and blankets in the closet, though sometimes Kate slept at Deaver's house, two kilometers away. There was about the apartment the feel of homey improvisation, everything threadbare and makeshift; they had shared it for five years. Upstairs two men lived in one room with a kitchenette; Maggie and Kate and María could hear everything that happened up there—horseplay, arguments—and that could be a comfort or an aggravation.

The evenings when La Pequeñita was her responsibility, Kate would lay out a beach towel on the long table, a terry towel with ACAPULCO printed in rows in all the colors of the rainbow. She would place the baby on the towel and lean over her in the woody evening sunlight, bathe her, change her diaper, test her reflexes, check her pulse, and call her sweet names, endearments she drew from some unending unknown well, a deep place over which she laid a veil if someone else walked in the room. She played a cassette tape, what she thought babies ought to hear, Vivaldi or Bach. Gentle music. Plenty of flutes. Meadow music, she called it. The baby's skin was an elixir as she held her cheek to cheek.

Lupita had been trying to find a relative for the baby among the others who had been evacuated from her town, to no avail. She knew many people; she knew their needs: what cigarettes they preferred; who had to have insulin; in whose home dried beans were stockpiled; who had rock-and-roll tapes still in their shrinkwrap to trade. Lupita never held on to stock for long. She moved it through her house out near the coast or through the streets of Managua, sometimes without ever touching it herself. She had young girls who worked for her, girls whose innocence was beyond reproach.

"Lo pasan mejor conmigo. They are better off," she would say. "With me."

And María would say, "Individually, yes, Mamá, but the people—in general—are not better off. You and people like you make it hard for the state to recover."

"The state!" Lupita would sneer. "Mira lo que pasa a puertas cerradas. Look what happens behind closed doors. The state took my son from me." Here she would pat the shoebox of memorial cards she gave away for her dead boy. "Él está presente, está presente. He is present." The boy's picture was on one side, the date of his death, July 15, 1979, beneath the picture, and on the other side, a prayer to Jesus the Revolutionary.

María loved her mother and did not want to see her suffer. Whenever Lupita stayed in Managua they would share a glass of Russian vodka after dinner and work through their grief, month by month, year by year. Lupita had lost her husband to tuberculosis before María was born.

They had decided to have a naming party for the baby. They expected Frank, who worked as a freelance contractor with the American embassy, providing holiday excursions and dinners: roast turkeys for Thanksgiving, dive trips to Roatán. It was his job, he said, to keep the embassy personnel from living too mired in the third world. It wasn't what they'd bargained for. Frank knew all about sport fishing and diving. He knew where the resorts were going up from Rio to Baja. And they had invited Deaver, who had spent the day in his studio building puppets prized by puppeteers for their educational performances in the campo. It was seven o'clock and the men had not yet arrived. A light rain fell in the courtyard among the squash blooms and tomato plants.

María said, "Now that the baby is here, Mamá, you must smoke in the courtyard." She had told Lupita this every day.

"I have made this party," Lupita said, "and you banish me." She went to the doorway between the dining room and the courtyard; she leaned against the doorframe and smoked. Her face had a handsome bulk to it. She had once been beautiful before she gained weight. She carried her weight around her middle and she was still proud of her legs—her ropy calves, her shapely thighs—and wore clothes and shoes that showed them off. Shiny pumps with open toes, short skirts or tight jeans. Her toenails were misshapen from her tight shoes and painted a fiery orange, the orange of flame-tree blossoms.

The others sat at the table, drinking rum and eating peanuts sprinkled with lime juice. Six novena candles lit the room and shadows flickered on the walls. Smells of dinner in the kitchen, hot peppers and garlic, the steam of rice, came to them on a wedge of light from down the hall.

Kate held the baby.

"La Pequeñita, La Pequeñita, La Pequeñita . . ."

"Rosa," Lupita said from the doorway. "I vote—we are a democracy, we can vote, sí?—I vote for Rosa." She blew smoke toward the courtyard.

"Too common," María said.

"It's good, it's for Saint Rosa," Lupita insisted. "She never wanted to marry."

They laughed.

"Still, we need more than just one to choose from," Kate said. "How about Elizabeth? Saint Elizabeth liked to build sand castles."

"How do you know this?" Lupita said.

Kate smiled. "Once a Catholic, always a Catholic."

"You girls are my fallen angels, my lapsed Catholics, no liberation theology for you, no theology, period, you are sensualists, where did I go wrong. . . ."

"Mamá."

"María, María—no es un secreto. It's not hush-hush. Where is your sense of humor? The Sandinistas have robbed you of it."

"I am celibate," Maggie said, "since 1985. Three and a half years of virtue. Can a celibate be a sensualist?"

"If possible, you are," María said.

Someone tapped at the front door. "That might be Deaver," Kate said. María went to the door at one end of the courtyard.

"Everybody wants to see you, don't they?" Kate said to the baby.

They heard María say, "Buenas noches, San Francisco."

"Please, you flatter me," Frank said, sweeping into the dining room. "Hola, buenas noches, hola." He bore packages, which he unceremoniously dumped on the table. His baggy Hawaiian shirt shimmied with hot pink flowers and vines. "I'm just a professional fun hog—" Here he rummaged through the packages until he came up with a bundle of orange No. 2 pencils, slightly used. He presented them to Maggie. "And trash picker. Or to put a better spin on it—recycler extraordinaire. I found those in the trash at the embassy," he said. "Thought you could use 'em."

"You're a sweetie," Maggie said.

Maggie had come to rely on Frank's finds. He brought her paperback novels in Spanish and English that his clients discarded in Cabo San Lucas or Miami. He brought her scrap paper by the ream. All for the students in her literacy classes.

"Likewise," Frank said.

Frank took the drink Maggie offered him, warm rum in a glass tumbler. They never had ice. He plopped down in an easy chair at one end of the table. His hair was still damp from his shower, his skin leathery. He had just shaved. Frank's face had the agreeable lines of a man who smiled more often than not. Once in a while, out of the blue, Maggie would say, Why doesn't one of us fall for Frank? He loves us, he plies us with questions—how many men will ask you questions?

"So, what else did you bring?" María said, eyeing the packages he had set on the table.

"Baby stuff." He sipped his drink. "Open 'em."

Maggie and María opened the presents. Kate brought the baby over to Frank's chair. She knelt down beside him. "Want to hold her?" she said.

"Sure, yeah," he said. "I—wow, she's little." He set his drink down on the floor and Kate transferred the baby to his arms. She did not wake up. "She's in dreamland, I'd say. Baby Margaritaville."

Lupita crushed out her cigarette butt in an ashtray. She strode purposefully to the kitchen, singing under her breath. Her heels clicked on the tile floor.

Frank said, "What'll you call her?"

"Got any ideas?" Kate said. She had retrieved her drink and come back to sit on a stool beside him.

"Maude?"

Kate frowned.

Frank tugged at her braids. "That's my grandmother's name."

The baby was a tidy yellow bundle in his arms. "Okay, not trendy, I know—how 'bout—Cecelia? Like the song."

Kate said, "Patron saint of music."

Maggie and María looked up and considered the name. "I like it," María said. "Cecelia."

"My friends, we might be reaching consensus already," Maggie said.

"About what?" Deaver said from the courtyard doorway. Lupita had let him in. They could hear her singing along to the radio in the kitchen.

Kate said, "Hola," in a voice reserved for him, a notch low, muted.

Mark Deaver's face was as sharp as a spade. His hair was long and pulled into a ponytail, his jeans spattered with old paint and wood stain. He walked over to Kate, put his hand on her shoulder. She turned her face up to him. He planted a light-as-rain kiss on her forehead. Indifferent as rain. Such judgment haunted her.

Everyone said hello. Kate took his hand, squeezed it. He headed for the rum on the table.

"You were saying?" he said, pouring a long drink.

"We're naming her," Kate said. "Cecelia."

"Someone else'll name her after you," Deaver said. He went to Kate's daybed and sat on the edge. He wore huaraches and tapped one foot incessantly.

"Lupita might end up with her," Maggie said.

"Then Lupita should name her," Deaver said.

Maggie and María carefully folded and put away the gifts Frank had brought. For a minute no one said anything. Rain fell in the courtyard, a windless ethereal rain, shutting them away. Not unpleasant, Kate thought, the way the rain buffers you.

"How's tricks?" Frank said to Deaver, lifting his glass.

Deaver shrugged. "I've missed her," he said.

"Kate, you mean?" Frank said. "Kate's missable."

Kate smiled at that.

Deaver went on, "But she's got baby-itis."

"Not true," Kate said, pretending to pout.

"Teasing, only teasing," he said. "Here's to . . . Cecelia."

Maggie and María began a murmurous private chat. They took their drinks and moved to the doorway and faced the courtyard, side by side. Maggie was taller than María by almost a foot. María was mighty—with round tight biceps revealed by her short sleeves—and petite, with narrow hips; she wore a light pink cotton dress and a flower in her hair. Maggie seemed statuesque in worn-out silk pants and a silk shirt—rusty brown and soft as suede—clothes she had owned for as long as Kate could remember. There was still something of coltish elegance in Maggie's physicality. She leaned down toward María, their long hair brushing each other. Kate was not able to make out what they said. Deaver and Frank talked about the Contras, about Reagan, rumor over rumor. Kate did not pay close attention to what they said. She considered going out to the kitchen. But the soft light wavering, the rain, the baby sleeping in Frank's arms, and Deaver's presence, his smell, some clean spicy soap he used: these kept her right where she was.

Deaver took out a pack of Payasos, tapped a cigarette on the table, flipped the lid on his lighter.

"Ah, ah, ah," María said, shaking her finger at him but smiling. "No smoking near the baby."

He said nothing. He put the cigarettes away. Abruptly he downed his rum. He set his glass on the table and said to Kate, "How 'bout a walk?"

"It's almost time," she said with a nod toward the kitchen.

His voice a coax and a goad, he said, "We won't be gone long."

She got up and took a black umbrella from a ceramic stand.

"It's raining," María said, as though to say, You're crazy. "Pero, adiós."

"Hurry back," Maggie said. "Adiós."

They parted to make way for them. Deaver went on to the back door at the end of the narrow courtyard and waited. A pale veneer of light lay over the courtyard, light issuing from the dining room and kitchen windows. He did not look back. Kate opened the umbrella partway and held it out in front of her. "Cecelia," Kate said, calling toward the dining room. "Adiós, Cecelia!"

Out on the dark street she lifted the umbrella high enough for Deaver to get under. He shook his head no, pulled up the collar on his shirt. Kate wore her usual clothes, a man's shirt and khakis. A woven yellow belt was her only color, that and the lipstick, presented as a gift from Lupita, which was nearly worn away. Its greasy taste felt foreign on her lips. She wished she hadn't brought the umbrella—it was in their way. Between them.

"Where to?" she said.

"A stroll," Deaver said sarcastically. "Let's just find a dry place. For a smoke."

"Is everything all right?"

He stopped at a corner under a streetlight. "Why're you upset?" he said. Kindly. He was making an effort.

She shut the umbrella. He put his arms around her, reminded her of the way their bodies fit. Then Deaver carefully took off Kate's glasses, folded the temples, and handed them to her. "I've been thinking about your idea," he said. He kissed her nose. He kissed her mouth.

Kate shook out her braids and reared back. His arms were still around her. "And?" She thought every word mattered; you could not be too careful in the dissonance of talking with Deaver.

"It might work out," he said. "We might be able to find a place that suits us both. You always have your nursing, right? And I could start over. I've been here so long. But we could find a place." He seemed to warm to his subject. He started walking again. She went along. "Austin's an easy place to live. But there might be a better place. The States"—He stood still again. "It's a big country, right? There's bound to be a place we could stake out as our own."

Kate breathed out, "Okay . . ."

"It might be time to go back."

It had been a week since she had mentioned it. An ordinary life, that's what I want for just a little while, she had said. Is that too much to ask? Her stipend from the sister-city clinic in Indiana was about to end. His stipend would never end; his mother faithfully sent him a thousand dollars a month. Someday he would inherit the house in Merida and the house in San Cristóbal.

"I'm thinking about it." He kissed her temple. "I'm thinking about work I could do from Texas. Things I could acquire there and move to Guatemala. People there are in dire straits."

She knew what that meant. She didn't want to dwell on that: the heavy wooden Mausers left over from World War I, the pistols. What a glutton for risk he was. Once she had admired that about him. She said, "We'd get our own place?"

He nuzzled her throat. His voice was barely audible, a murmur. "We could work toward that."

Kate remembered other versions of this conversation. It did not take much for those memories to rise like buried pot shards to the surface of their mutual landscape. It was just dawning on her what a bad habit it was, all that talk about living together.

He said, "We could see about it. After we've had a chance to adjust."

"I see," she said. She remembered what Sunny had once said, remembered it like a hat blown off in the wind that you chase for a minute but then let go. The thought was that fleeting: One lover always knows before the other that it's over.

She pulled back and put on her glasses.

"Don't be like that."

"Like what?"

"You know. Don't pressure me."

They walked to a trashy lot where once there had been a bandstand in a park. Mud she imagined always there grew more liquescent with each hour of rain. A streetlight gloomed dimly over them. At least the electricity was on; they had not had a blackout for a week or more. There was a boarded-up tienda, perhaps six by six, with an overhanging roof where they stood sheltered while Deaver smoked two cigarettes. Paper advertisements for soft drinks and candy peeled from the wall of the tienda. All that was left of the bandstand was the crawl space, the wood foundation upon which it had been built, and a partial floor. The gray-green light of the drizzle, like fuzz on fruit, enveloped them, enveloped the city.

"Dinner's probably on the table," Kate said.

"What's your rush?"

"It's a party."

"Frank and I don't really get along."

Since when? Times they'd all sat drinking until midnight. Days they'd spent in borrowed boats on the lake. She thought they'd all gotten along just fine.

"He's good to us."

"Be good to me," Deaver said. He took a mock bite of her neck. He wrapped one hand in her braids.

Kate laughed, though she did not know from what source the laugh arose. There was always the anticipation and the letdown, seeing Deaver. She thought, What's left of us? But she said, "Let me."

Just then a naked child emerged from beneath the bandstand crawl space. Kate thought she saw a hand push the child out. A boy about five years old, his hair black and raggedly cut, his legs muddy. With one hand he pulled at his penis. His other hand hung limply; there was something wrong with it. He looked around. Puzzled. Frowning.

Someone—a sister or mother—reached out from under the bandstand and swatted his bottom. She said, "Andele!"

He let go of his penis. He padded over to Kate and Deaver.

"Fuck," Deaver said under his breath.

"Compañero, señorita," he said. "Tienen un poco de dinero?" He held out his hand timidly.

"No," Deaver said. "No money."

Kate patted her pants pocket. "You have money, don't you?" she said to Deaver.

The boy remained there. Hand out, eyes blank. The dim streetlight shone on his dark belly.

"Jesus," Deaver said.

"Lend it to me," Kate said.

Deaver took out his money roll and peeled off a wrinkled thousand-cordoba note, worth about twenty cents U.S. Inside that money roll were dollars; Deaver always had dollars.

"Give him a dollar," Kate said.

"I'm not."

"Dea—"

"Kate, don't push."

He gave the cordoba note to the boy, who did not say a word. He ran back to the crawl space, his bare feet sucking in the mud.

They walked the quiet streets where here and there a dog barked, a horse neighed, a taxi stopped and started in a fit of trying to find an address in the mess that had become Managua after the earthquake: no street signs, no major landmarks.

Finally Deaver said, "When will you ever learn?"

"I guess I don't understand you," Kate said. Hard to admit. After all this time.

"How so?" He waited.

"I don't want to get into it." She was not angry.

"You don't want to get into it."

"That's right."

Suddenly he softened. He said, "You don't have to protect yourself from me."

His voice confused her, a ghost of caring she thought she could remember from their early days.

At her door he said, "I think I'll go home."

"Come on," she said, tugging at his hand.

"No, no. You go on. Come over later if you want."

"It's our night with the baby."

"That's fine," he said. "Whatever you need to do."

"Well, give me a kiss, you—" Kate said.

He kissed her, what might have been a sweet probe that even after all those years could arouse her. This time it felt aggressive.

She watched him go. Head down, he hunched his shoulders against the night as though it searched him out. He whistled; that was the one indicator she had of his mood. Or what he wanted her to believe was his mood. He whistled some old Grateful Dead song. His gait or the situation, saying good-night to him reluctantly, reminded her of Paul—

She did not want to cry; the loss of a mutual history cut into her, the loss of a longtime love. You think you have plenty of time to have a longtime love, but you do not understand time when you are young, the way it compresses. She wanted to be able to turn to a loved one and say, Remember when?

She went in. She could hear the others in the dining room. Right at that moment she wanted to lay hold of time and make it stand still. Music was on upstairs, a mournful Nicaraguan folk song: "Luna." "It lets itself be seen in the shadows, breaks the silence with its indifferent light, traps my senses without warning, defeats the mystery of the night. . . ." Cecelia was crying, a scratchy high-pitched baby cry. Irritated and hungry. When Kate got as far as the dining room doorway she saw their fiesta, the table strewn with leftovers in bright clay bowls, the half-filled glasses of golden rum still quivering in the candlelight. Maggie bent over the baby, changing her diaper. María held a four-ounce baby bottle in her hand, waiting. Frank confided something to Lupita, leaning companionably toward her, speaking low into her ear.

Lupita looked up and said, "That man's not good for you." She shook her head, her earrings tinkling. She pursed her lips. "Es un amor triste. Sad love."

"Mamá," María warned.

Kate laughed ruefully. She said, "It's a little late for that."

Maggie scooped Cecelia up into her arms and murmured, as though to the baby, "Remember when we told her that? Hmm?" Cecelia seemed to float, her sweet head still wobbly.

"Come," Lupita said. "Eat." Lupita dished her up a plate of food; she set a round basket of fragrant rolls beside her plate.

Kate lifted the checked napkin covering the rolls. She thought of the boy in the mud. Begging had been outlawed. As if that made a difference to the beggars.

By six months Cecelia had learned to crawl and had tough skin on her little knees; Kate had received and spent the last installment of her stipend; the rainy season was about to begin again; they could feel the waiting in the air, the heaviness, the moisture-laden wind, the rainy season embossed on the cloudy sky. The televisions and VCRs for their clinics in the campo had not arrived. Frank had heard that the caravan from northern Indiana had broken down near Guatemala City and they were waiting for truck parts to come in. The drivers were Quakers. Not one of them had been any farther south than Houston. Kate watched the map on the wall in the clinic, tracing the route of the Quakers, imagining what they must be going through to bring the truckloads of donated school supplies, clothing, medicine, bicycles, tractor parts, whatever odds and ends people were willing to get rid of or had an abundance of. She hadn't been back to the States in a long time but she could still imagine that abundance, the cornucopia of shopping malls, the grocery carts piled high, the accretion of things and more things in the garages and basements of North America. What she steeled herself to face: the culture shock.

She and Maggie would go back and face all that together.

Kate had been crying; she cried when she and Deaver made love or whatever it was, tears wetting her face when she came. She could still come. Sometimes the body wants to know nothing of the heart; the body seeks its own experience. The bed was damp with humidity and their sweat. Semen trickled vexingly between her thighs. A knot of tension bloomed in her muscled upper back. She was exhausted. She had wanted to leave Managua months before; the waiting had been a burden, a daily task. Cecelia's baby smiles, the way she matched whatever she was given, were love and loss all in the same moment. Kate had borrowed a little money from Deaver to live on until she installed the televisions and trained a woman in each clinic to use the videos. After that, she had planned—hoped—that she and Maggie and Deaver would travel to Antigua, Guatemala, where they had Sunny and Ben, where they could simply relax before going on to the States. A parrot screamed from the house next door. Not far away, the crow of roosters. The grind of bus gears.

Deaver leaned in the doorway, smoking a Payaso and tapping the red cigarette package with its smiling clown face against his leg. Shirtless. Lean and dark-skinned. His back looked still—after everything, perhaps more than ever now that they were nearly finished talking out the end—like luxury, what she might never have again. She thought, You just don't know. In your forties passion is not a predictable possibility. The light was gray-blue in the room, his studio and bedroom, a light that could have been fading day as well as morning before sunrise. A pile of smooth hairless puppet heads lay on the dresser. Liter cans of paint were stacked against one wall. The house smelled like mildew and pine and mahogany chips, carpenter's glue and felt, marijuana and yeast bread rising. No matter where Deaver lived—Merida, San Cristóbal, or Managua—his house smelled the same. Behind high street walls, all the rooms opened onto a bleak little sunless courtyard and that is what Deaver stared into, with his jeans barely pulled over his buttocks.

"You have never," he said flatly, "never really cared about what was happening here." He did not turn around.

"How can you say that?" Kate said. She sat up abruptly, the sticky sheet tangling around her legs.

He said, "Don't whine at me."

"Don't accuse me."

"You don't really have any politics."

He flicked his cigarette butt into the courtyard.

Silence. They'd been over all this before.

Kate said, "That's not what matters now."

"What does matter?"

"What matters to me," Kate said, a knot of tears clotted in her throat, "is what we were going to do. And that now we're not. And finding a way to get through the beginning of that. I'll be fine once I get through the beginning." She said that but she did not know if it was true.

A rooster crowed again. Deaver walked to the bed and knelt down beside her. He tucked her hair behind one ear and lifted her chin. He wanted her to look into his eyes. She would not.

"I've loved you," he said. "You know that, don't you?"

Kate did not answer.

Very softly he spoke again. "Don't you see I can't?" His voice was weary from saying it. "I played it out. I imagined it."

"It's not like moving to the moon."

"To me it is."

"I need to be alone," she said, "to work it out." Out on the patio a woman went by, a boarder in the house, a woman who left bottles of scent, massage oil, gels, perfumes on the shelves in the bathroom. "I'm sad is all. It's another piece of my life."

Deaver stood up abruptly. He grabbed his leather belt and began sliding it through his belt loops. "I know that. You think I don't understand that. But I do."

Her skin felt raw. Kate pulled the rough sheet away from herself, sat up, feeling with her feet for her sandals on the floor, pushed back her hair, looked around for her glasses, her clothes.

Only habit made her say, "I've got to go now." As though it were any other morning; as though they had slept the night together and she had to go to work; as though they would sleep the night together again soon.

"I'll be in the kitchen," Deaver said. He plucked his black T-shirt from a wad of clothes at the foot of the bed. He hesitated, took one step closer, touched her shoulder and fingered her dark hair.

"Please—don't—touch me—anymore," Kate whispered, rocking slightly on the edge of the bed.

He punched his arms into the T-shirt sleeves, jerked it over his head on the way out the door. An athletic anger surrounded his body, a violent light.

Kate put on her glasses, shivered, and got dressed. Her clothes comforted her oddly: her rumpled khakis, her cotton shirt.

She couldn't remember the new boarder's name. She could hear her singing in the kitchen. Deaver said she had a revolutionary's heart. There would be a moment when they would hold their gaze ten seconds longer than usual. Like a flower opening. If not her, someone else, and soon. Perhaps it had happened already. Deaver would say, Christ, we're erotic animals, aren't we?

Before Deaver there was Paul.

Maggie's brother. You could mark a life that way. By the men in it. Which story do you want to hear?

Paul was my first love.

We were kids.

We lived on the same road.

I got my first kiss from Paul, and toward the end he wanted me more than I wanted him. There's always that inequity. Lupita would have said, Be with the one who wants you most. If only I had the benefit of Lupita's wisdom now. Paul makes his offers. Tangible offers. He says he has forgiven me for what happened to Maggie.

Paul and Maggie and I were inseparable, in the woods, under the railroad trestle, at the bookmobile, at the creek, among the flickering blue gills. We measured ourselves by the mayapples like green tents sheltering the morels. That first time, Paul and I kissed out of curiosity. We were just about the same size, I was sixteen, he was fourteen. We would dance in their attic, that's how it started, the attic with its barnboard walls. It comes back to me, I can remember that, those are powerful memories, the first time. It's too bad you can't feel the same way just remembering. All that fades, doesn't it, the intensity fades, but the memory can be conjured up like a home movie, the dusty Oriental carpet with a wide thread-bare patch in the center, the floor lamp with the orange shade and on the shade black silhouettes of Egyptian dancers, and the window under the long slant of the roof letting in a low breeze. I could feel that breeze under my skirt, when I wore a skirt. We had a boxy record player, left over from when we were little, and we had to Scotch-tape a penny to the needle's arm for weight and we had a stack of forty-fives. Gladys Knight and the Pips. Smokey Robinson and the Miracles. Johnny Mathis. You really got a hold on me. That kind of music. Paul sighed sweetly, he kissed nervously. Those honey voices pushed many a boy and girl into kissing, I bet it must be the same, the first time's the same for everyone. Paul gripped my bottom, he was guileless and silent, only unspoken desire between us, desire of kids, and I could feel the perk of his cock just bloom-ing, just finding its own way between us—

What poet said, We learn the lessons of the flesh and then we move on?

Mark Deaver and I met in San Cristóbal de las Casas when I was visiting Maggie for three weeks. I'd come for three weeks. An ob-gyn nurse on vacation.

Maggie swore she had been in love only once, with Flory. Who was bold and strong and fearless. And I was jealous, I'll admit it, I felt shut out, I'd come all that way to see her, she was the only per-son I knew in all of Mexico. She'd been working at a museum in San Cristóbal and it was almost time for her to come home when she wrote and said that she had fallen in love with a woman. Flory was away in El Salvador when I arrived. But she came back, late one night, my third night there. Maggie and I'd been drinking wine and talking. I'd brought her presents, things I knew she loved, a certain brand of lemon hand cream, licorice buttons, and our reunion had been good. She'd always been the friend I could pick up with right where we'd left off, but that time there was this little rub, that she had gotten involved with a woman and I'd been startled by that.

When Flory knocked on the door and they were together and I was confronted with them—their physical closeness—it was hard for me, though I could not have articulated it then, I could only react. I wish that I had learned earlier in my life to watch myself without reacting, to watch the daily ebb and flow of ugliness and beauty. Inside, I'm talking about what's inside, hidden. Hindsight's better than foresight, my mother always says.

My leaving caused a rift between us—Maggie and me—and I do not know to this day whether we ever healed that rift or whether we simply stopped discussing it. Flory was a photographer and eventually she photographed too many atrocities for her own good. Her father was a commandante in the Guatemalan army and here his daughter was a player in the resistance. She'd gone to good schools, something she said he sorely regetted. Tall, almost Maggie's match, unusually tall for a Guatemalan, in high boots and black jeans and a saffron-colored silk shirt, Flory had a pock-marked, worried, pretty face and a long black ponytail. Their bodies fit. A visible luminosity, a lovers' sheen, separated them from me. That sheen wears thin with time and if you're lucky it becomes an ease you trust, but I did not know that then, none of us did. We lived in the dream of perpetual falling in love. They settled themselves before our little fire—the night was cold—and they talked about the trouble in Guatemala.

This was 1982. One hundred thousand Mayans had fled their ancestral homelands in the mountains. They had come on foot to Mexico. The trails were like a sieve, the old trading trails, centuries old. Flory had seen a Guatemalan woman burying her dead baby in a ditch. That was not what I had expected to hear. But in that part of Mexico you could not avoid these things. People passed the word in the cafés, they gossiped in hotel lobbies.

I listened to Flory and Maggie and the wine crept up on me. I went into the bathroom and put on a nightgown and I remember the bed was damp and cold and the covers felt inadequate. I listened to them talking. Their voices sounded like a habit just forming. I never did fall asleep, not even after they changed their clothes and

went to bed in the single bed next to mine, not even after they settled down in what I imagined was a warm bed of skin they made for
each other, not even after the roosters crowed at dawn. As soon as
I could call it day, I showered and dressed and packed and left them
asleep in each other's arms.

I did not want to know what would happen next in my life.
With a little Spanish, I thought I could get by. I checked into another hotel, attracted to the hefty spray of bougainvillea on its
wrought iron gate. Blooms as bright as hummingbirds. My white-
washed wall was neat and pure, my new bed big and empty. I had a
kitchenette there. I remember the clay bowls, the chickens painted
on them.

I hadn't been to mass in years but when I heard the church bells
ringing something led me there, to the church where the priest
spoke the liturgy in Tzotzil. I got pressed up against a covey of
kneeling Indian women in blue shawls and black skirts, their
muddy bare soles upturned on the stone floor. Gold and rubies
glinted in the sanctuary and at the altar. There was a cross, a chalice, a tabernacle. Familiar things. That's where I first saw Mark
Deaver. He leaned against one wall. His hair was long then. He had
been warned, everyone had been warned, that the authorities
frowned on men with long hair, but a warning like that was a chal-
lenge to Deaver. He wore a chamois shirt. Sulky he was, and dark
and wound tight. I saw something of myself in him. I went out after
mass and sat on a bench in the park beside the church. I remember
the few minutes before he entered my life. The pigeons fluttering
into palm trees whose fronds were dusted with sunlight, the glads
and mums for sale in buckets, long pine needles strewn on the
church steps, ice cream vendors hawking, some Nilsson song in
Spanish, teenage boys cruising by in a red Trans-Am with *Super-
Mex* in silver letters on the bumper, German backpackers unfold-
ing a map, the forested hills turning bluish, smoky, with oncoming
rain, the smell of the rain preceding the rain itself, mingling with
the dust. Just as the taste buds of babies are concentrated on the tips
of their tongues and they taste everything more sharply, sweets are

sweeter, sour more tart, I tasted everything more sharply then. It doesn't seem so long ago, but it was, it was. Deaver came and sat beside me on the concrete bench and our body chemistry changed.

I wanted him. My cunt—he taught me that—my cunt felt like a being of its own, men don't know this, the way we feel. I let him take me over. Drug of desire. Like never before.

On the street she felt weak. In the sun's metallic glare. People in pastel clothes spilled, blurred, around her. Deaver's van, the one they'd come to Nicaragua in, a rusted sea-blue Chevy— that van was slowly rotting into the street for lack of a fuel pump, a carburetor. She stood there staring at it, searching with one hand in her purse for her prescription sunglasses. They had crouched by a night fire with the van as a windbreak. Drinking from a canteen of cane rum. Talking, once they'd talked for hours. About what they believed in. They had crawled on top of sleeping bags in the back, the desert an arcane furnace just beyond the rolled-down windows. They had tested each other, raking fingernails, probing, locked in sex, Deaver coaxing her, You can come again, sure you can, you're up there; and the sun flattened out white and hard and gritty in that arid grassless place.

She shoved on the sunglasses and put her others in her purse. She had routines that could shore up a day; she had the clinic and people who needed her. This day would be a long day but she could get through it. First she would go home to Maggie. She could count on Maggie. To see her through the worst of what was happening.

At the corner snack stand she bought a half slice of pineapple. A helicopter chopped overhead. A bus with bald tires went by, tightly packed, with riders on the steps and in the aisles and crammed six to a seat. The ayudante in a starched yellow shirt listed precariously on the bottom step, gripping the chrome pole just inside the open door, gesturing to her, absurdly waving her aboard the jammed bus, with its hologram photo of the Sacred Heart flashing out the wide front window: a gargoyle of sorts. She shook her head no. She couldn't bear to be that close to strangers.

Walking home, she passed two soldiers in berets buying candy bars from a pretty girl, thirteen or fourteen years old, in a slippery black miniskirt, flirting, looking for love, what love could be had in a time of war. She passed store clerks sweeping sidewalks, burned-out buildings and more abandoned cars, vacant lots grown high with wildflowers about to bloom, crumbling walls collaged with layers of posters. *We will not sell ourselves. A free country or death—*

Her legs were shaky. She sucked on the pineapple without tasting it, then tossed the rind in the weeds. She thought about the threat of passion; she thought about a hot shower and hoped that the water would be on.

Three beggar children lay in wait for her in front of her apartment, two sisters with uncombed hair and their clubfooted brother. In big black shoes, heavy as bricks. His crutch made of a tree branch. Kate gave each of them a thousand-cordoba note, squatted down to place the note in each brown palm. She had a nurturing word with each child.

Inside, Maggie was in the shower; the kettle whistled cheerily. Kate turned off the flame and set the kettle on another burner.

"It's me," she called. Humidity seemed dense as wet smoke in the courtyard. Cherry tomatoes dangled from the plants in the garden. The bathroom door was open; Kate leaned against the wall outside the bathroom.

"Have I got some news for you," Maggie said, stepping out of the shower. She wrapped herself in a beach towel. "Frank heard from the convoy again—it'll be another week at least, more likely ten days." She fingered gel into her hair, combed it through. "I met a guy. A real sweetheart. He's from New Mexico, and he's been here for three months, working on a potable water system—he's an engineer—just my luck to meet him when we're both on our way out of here, but—" She looked up and said, "What's wrong, sweetie?"

Kate hung her head. She took off her glasses and set them on the bookcase, on a pile of moldy magazines no one had read for a year.

"Oh dear, what's going on? Come and sit down," Maggie said. "Let me make us a cup of tea. Come and sit down." She led Kate into the dining room. She sat her down on the daybed and plumped a pillow behind her. "You sit there and tell me what happened. I'll make some tea." Maggie dropped the towel and slipped into her robe, cinching tight the belt. She went into the kitchen and propped the door open with a conch shell so she could maintain eye contact with Kate. She opened a cupboard and over her shoulder said, "So?"

Kate said, "I'm all right. Really." She wiped her eyes with the back of her hand, tried to smile. "I'm a mess," she said. "Where is everybody?"

"María's at work. Lupita left with the baby last night. She caught a ride out."

Maggie turned around, leaned against the counter, and waited, her arms folded. "What's going on?"

"He's not going. That's all."

Maggie shook her head. "Why doesn't this surprise me?"

"I'm not even sure I love him anymore."

"I can tell that, sweetie."

"You can?"

Maggie nodded reluctantly. "It shows."

She poured the boiling water over tea bags in a porcelain teapot. She set a tray: spoons, mugs, sugar in a Chinese bowl. She brought the tray into the dining room and set it down on the low table at one end of the daybed. "Scoot over, now," she said. "I'll serve you."

Kate said, "And—even if I stayed—which I can't, I just can't— I don't know. My brain is fucking scrambled, I feel crazy, how could

I have thought—" She shook her head as though to dislodge confusion.

"Thought what?"

"I can't think."

"Did he ask you to stay?"

"Not exactly."

"What did he say?"

"*You* thought he was coming, didn't you?"

Maggie bobbed her head evasively. She squinted. "Well . . ."

"Well?"

Maggie set her mug down, rearranged her robe. She fiddled with her belt. "Do you want to get into what I think?"

"Tell me."

"Don't you see? You're leaving him."

"I'm . . . not so sure about that."

"Come on."

"I don't see it that way."

"Why not see it that way?"

Kate begged, "Please don't start. I'm leaving . . . the situation—I'm worn down."

Maggie got up. She paced the room, her robe switching around her legs. "I have an idea."

Kate looked up. Her eyes ached. She felt her tears drying on her face. Upstairs a toilet flushed; sandals scuffed across the floor.

Maggie sat beside her. "You go. Go on to Antigua. To Sunny and Ben's. Just as we planned. You wait there for me. It'd be good to see Sunny, wouldn't it? I'll go out to Ruinas with Bob. When we get back the TVs'll be here. I'll finish up everything—"

"I don't think I can go alone."

"What? Get on a bus and leave? Don't think he won't wonder, don't think he won't come around. He'll come around just to see how you are. You won't be here and neither will I, and at least—"

Kate said, "I don't even care about that. You don't know how exhausted I am."

"You need a couple good nights' sleep. That's all."

Patricia Henley

They sat silently. Maggie watched the clock. Their tea grew lukewarm in the mugs. Morning sunlight had moved in a sheet across the floor and up the daybed, a drowsy cue. Somewhere in the neighborhood rowdy music blurted from a radio.

"You have to go, don't you?"

Maggie said, "I sort of do."

"He must be something."

"He's . . ." She got up, opened a duffel, and began tucking clothes inside it. "Nice. He's a no-bullshit kind of guy. He's kind. I just want to be with him for a little while." She held up a T-shirt, eyed it, tossed it aside.

"I'm not going to go without you," Kate said sleepily. She had lain down on the daybed. "I'll wait for you."

"That's fine," Maggie said. She took off her robe and slipped quickly into her underwear, cotton panties and a bra. She squirmed into a black cotton dress. "That's fine with me."

She knelt down, kissed Kate's forehead, and went into the bathroom. Kate was vaguely aware of that, Maggie's lips, then the jangle of her bracelets, before she drifted into irresistible sleep.

When she woke up there was a note on the kitchen table. It was noon; she had slept for hours. "I needed this, you know what I mean," Maggie wrote. Kate read the note again. She knew what she meant. She could remember Maggie sleeping in one of Flory's shirts for weeks after Flory died.

She sat down at the table. Someone had left the refrigerator door slightly ajar and roaches were making their way up the rubber gasket inside the door. There were two browning plantains in the fruit basket on the counter and one brown egg in a plastic egg carton. The place looked as though no one had come home to it in a long time; somehow she hadn't noticed that while Maggie was with her.

Upstairs there was music, some saxophone on a boombox that distorted the sound. She wanted to cry at its soulful tug, but she didn't. She felt a wolfish appetite for strength, or the pretense of strength.

55

She had never been to Antigua. Sunny and Ben had sent photos. A courtyard with a pastel mural and a steer's head. Elephant
ears growing lush. A volcano you could see the cap of above their
walls. At night, Ben said, the moon would pass over the courtyard
and shine on the volcano. There would be mountain weather, cool
nights and warm days. And plentiful markets. In Guatemala, Ben
promised paella and gin and tonics. Sunny promised long walks and
conversation she was hungry for. She could imagine it: the shrimp
and chicken and rice in a big black cast-iron skillet, the lime and
ice, the pungent gin; Sunny in what she called her schoolmarm
clothes—denim skirts and cotton sweaters—being vulgar, making
her laugh. Calling her a trollop. Saying, You've got to laugh to keep
from crying. Her imagination had failed her whenever she thought
of Deaver talking with Ben. Ben was a pacifist through and
through. Never mind, never mind. That dream was over. What she
felt was not akin to waking up; it felt like falling in a nightmare. It
was not about Deaver; it was about where she was in time, what
time she had left.

She went into the bathroom and turned on the tap. Nothing
came out. "Fucking son of a bitch," she hissed. She checked the
mirror above the basin and she had not even braided her hair.
"Fuck, fuck, fuck," she said, striking her hand on the edge of the
basin with each word.

"What's going on down there?"

She looked up; one of the men upstairs eyed her through a cutout place around the pipes, which ran through their bathroom as
well as hers. She recalled this much about him: he was from
Tuscaloosa; he loved humidity. Once she had shared a half pint of
aquavit with him on his stairway.

"Mind your own business," Kate said.

"Do you all have any oregano?"

"You can have whatever's left."

"I'll come down," he said.

She opened the door for him. He had saved her in a way,
brought her back to the mundane, the need for oregano. She told

him she was leaving Nicaragua. She was leaving right away. She tried that out on him. He wished her luck and said that he would relay any messages she had for Maggie or María. Kate stood there in the kitchen, a tin of oregano in one hand, and she knew she was seeing that room, that neighbor, for the last time. Maggie would take care of everything; she'd be high; she'd be riding the wave you ride when you've been fucking your brains out. How vulgar we've become, she thought. Once they would have said sleep with, get next to.

"Where is she, by the way?"

"Who?"

"Maggie." He put out his hand for the oregano.

"With some guy."

"Lucky guy," he said.

Kate gave him the tin. "There's not much left," she said.

"I wish I was goin' with you," he said.

"What's to stop you?"

"I haven't done all I intended."

"I think I have," Kate said. "And then some."

When he'd gone she pulled two bricks away from the kitchen wall; hidden there she and Maggie had a credit card and money, three hundred U.S. dollars in a beige nylon money belt and, in a blue envelope, many thousand cordobas, worth very little. They had not talked about the money. She took half of it. Packing did not take long; once she began, packing felt like a chore she had practiced mentally for a long time. Upstairs the men made a grocery list out loud—rice, beer, toilet paper—while she wrote the letter on a sheet of yellow legal-sized paper. She detailed a plan to meet Maggie in Antigua. She begged María to understand. She could not bear going to the clinic to say good-bye; she felt emptied out, graceless. "Give my medical books and fetoscopes to the midwives at the clinics. Divide everything as you see fit," she wrote to Maggie and María. Her hand trembled and her handwriting sprawled—ungainly—on the page. "I will miss Cecelia and Lupita. Miss them dearly. Many hugs to them. I'm so sorry—"

She found a man on their street with a mule and cart. He agreed to take her to the bus station. She lifted a cardboard box and a duffel into the cart, and from the corner of her eye she caught the bright bounce of María's red shirt in the next block. María stopped to speak to someone. Kate wiped her hands—dusty from packing—on the seat of her khakis, climbed into the cart, and said, "Pronto, por favor." The man clicked his tongue and the mule jerked awake and began the trudge through the deep cocoa-colored dust, away from the Managua apartment, away from María, away from all she had been for seven years. She had loved María and she believed that María had loved her; their struggles had been many but they had cut through their differences to do the work that mattered: for the women. In emergencies you found out what others were made of. Now she inhabited a private emergency. She could not think about what she might regret. What she might feel ashamed of. Privilege was like skin; you live in it, no matter how eroded your attachment to it. She would think about that later.

At the bus station she waited only forty minutes for the Pullman to the Honduran border. She waited on a broken-down car seat in the shade of the oily-floored bus garage. No one tried to speak with her. She braided her hair while she sat there, a rucksack between her knees. A drunk man mutely tried to beg from her, but she kept her eyes averted. From a vendedora she bought a bag of rice bread.

On the bus she thought of all the people she could have said good-bye to, the embraces she'd denied herself; passing the cane fields and mountain roads not traveled, she was lucid enough to know that part of her had to die, and that endurance was required for the long bus ride, border crossings, nights on steep mountain-sides, in order to stop enduring, to rest at Ben and Sunny's.

A rotund woman slept in the next seat. The woman's hair was long and silvery, the braids crisscrossed with cotton rags, her wrinkled face date-brown and framed by pendulous turquoise earrings. Kate was plain beside her, a wisp of wiry woman in a pink shirt, a shirt she'd borrowed from Paul long ago and never returned. She had rolled the sleeves above her elbows and she wore wire-rimmed glasses repaired at the temple with a dull bluish pinch of solder. Deaver had repaired them for her. He was handy that way.

A pliancy entered her like a taproot. Not budding yet. Tenderness of old love. Love past. She might—someday—think well of him because she didn't have to fight him anymore. The commonplace kind deeds. The moment waking from a nightmare, the hand on her shoulder. She and the old woman leaned against each other as the bus lumbered along.

On the Threshold
of the Dead

"Guate! Guate! Guate!" Ayudantes waving straw hats leaned from the steps, hawking a last seat or two on the buses heading out of Antigua. On May 6, at the market, across a dusty boulevard from the post office, Kate descended the worn-to-the-metal steps of the chicken bus. The trip had taken three days. Greasy exhaust fumes could not quite extinguish the ashy sweet smell of tortillas on a griddle.

She kept watch. The ayudante climbed the back ladder and shunted down her belongings—a duffel bag and a cardboard liquor box in which she'd packed odds and ends she couldn't bear to leave behind, stupid sentimental things. A brown clay pig with flowers painted on his back. Her journal from the first months with Deaver, filled with page after raving page. Photographs still in their envelopes from the printer. Photographs from the Bay Islands. Underwear in which she'd felt like a courtesan. A dress she hadn't worn in years: rayon, printed with the tropics, palm trees and coconuts. Had she ever been the Kate of such a dress? The belt tied at her waist and the bodice gathered under her breasts, flattering her. She had been so full of herself in that dress. She flushed hotly, remembering. All the long bus ride from Managua to Antigua she had held that box in her mind, visualizing it on the luggage rack, clinging to it, and only upon alighting from the bus in Antigua did she admit the waste of carting the box across entire countries. She would joke about that with Sunny. Sunny would force her to laugh at herself. One thing you could count on in life was the laughter of women friends cutting through the ways you fooled yourself.

The ayudante grinned down at her. Ragtime piano tinkled from an ice cream vendor's truck.

"Taxi?"

"Taxi? A dónde va?"

Arabesque of music, market haggling, young boys wrestling, gears grinding, chickens cackling, fireworks popping and fizzling, all this swept around her; she braced herself to sort out a new place. A little girl who had been on the bus stared at Kate curiously. Perhaps six or seven years old, delicate, shy, in a stained corte tattered along the hem, the girl sucked on a plastic bag of lime soda. Her eye was giving her trouble, encrusted with a greenish discharge, the lid inflamed and swollen like a boil, almost shut, probably pinkeye. Her mother and she had sold Cokes from a plaid shopping bag to the people on the bus. Now the girl and her mother squatted before the curandera's blanket, which was laid with worn glassine envelopes of grasses and seeds and powders.

Kate picked up her duffel and kick-pushed the box in their direction. Orange peel littered the ground. She knelt down beside the girl's mother.

"Buenas tardes, compañera—lo siento—senora—"

The woman peered up, her face wrinkling, a net of fright. The side seam of her huipil unraveling.

"Soy enfermera," Kate said. "I have medicine that will help that eye."

The two women—the mother and the curandera—discussed Kate in their indigenous tongue. Blunt assessments.

"No es ne-ce-sar-i-o," the curandera said, the lilt of the highlands in her voice, her black eyes indifferent when she looked at Kate. On the ground beside her lay a string bag. Stuffed with a dried hummingbird, a deck of holy cards. Slim tallowy candles, velvet ribbons. She waited, and with her thumb she counted by twos a stack of tortillas half wrapped in brown paper.

The mother hesitated, frowning. She adjusted her headdress: thick handwoven bands of blue cotton, wound up with her hair like a nest and trimmed with pom-poms.

Still kneeling on the pavement, Kate rummaged in the top pouch of her rucksack. She brought out a skimpy tube of antibiotic ointment, deeply creased, nearly used up. She offered the tube to the woman.

The mother stared at the ointment. The squatting girl inched closer to Kate in a duck walk; she reached out and with her plump brown hand almost touched the ointment, then flinched. Kate smiled at her, nodding, saying, "You can use both."

The curandera spoke again, a sullen remark, in language that seemed to fill up her mouth like bread.

"No, no, gracias," the mother said. "Pero, si Dios quiere, if God is willing, estará bien." She snugged her little girl near and turned her back to Kate.

Kate stood up, slipped the tube of ointment into the pocket of her khakis.

Maybe the girl would be cured by the curandera. Maybe, as Deaver would have said, in the vast scheme of things it didn't matter. He was big on the vast scheme of things. Thinking that way, Deaver's way, shriveled your heart. She didn't want to think that way and there was no reason to think that way anymore. Kate had heard that an eyewash of purple coneflower might help pinkeye. She had never learned more than the occasional bit of lore about herbal remedies. At one young and boundless time she had thought that she might apprentice herself to an indigenous curandera and practice healing with herbs and roots, but that urge had been added to the inventory of all that she would never master or even explore. When she had begun such an inventory she could not recall.

"Taxi?"

"You want taxi?"

Yes, yes. She didn't even ask the price of the ride to Sunny and Ben's. She took the directions from her pants pocket and said, "On the way to Jocotenango. The house next to the Hungarian's garage." The yellow taxi, a Volkswagen bug, was cool inside, parked in the shade of a jacaranda tree. A black-and-white soccer ball rolled around the back seat.

The driver swerved into traffic with veteran abandon. He said, "It's okay? I will practice my English with you?"

"Sure," Kate said. A frame cut from a tin can hung on the dash; his family photo had been glued inside the frame: the driver, a woman in a white huipil, and three children—boys—in dress shirts and clip-on bowties. In the photo he smiled proudly, his arms around them all.

"You have been to Antigua before?" he said, watching her in the rearview mirror.

"No, never." The girl with pinkeye infected her thoughts; where Kate had come from, no one had turned down medical attention.

"Antigua is beautiful, sí?"

"Sí."

"The rainy season is just beginning. You have come for the rainy season, though it is not so bad here." He stuck his head out the window and glanced at the sky; with one hand he waved at the sky. "A few clouds, little ones, in the afternoon, a little later, rain. Not for long. Enough for a rest, enough for la comida—" He laughed. "There are worse things than the rainy season, I—assure—you. I assure you." He rolled the phrase pleasurably around in his mouth. "It is not so bad you cannot—" He searched for the word. "Endure." He flung his baseball cap on the seat.

At a bank, a soldier in dappled camouflage stood at the ready. His stare hostile. Bored. His black rifle like a prosthesis. Kate looked the other way.

They passed a church. Under an archway, a bride in a creamy satin gown adjusted her slip straps, surrounded by fluttering women in jewel-colored dresses. The taxi driver crossed himself, kissed his fingers. "Where are you from, señorita?"

Kate slipped on her sunglasses. She wasn't sure about that anymore. She stared out the window. In front of a juice bar, two tall blond men pored over a map, their kerchiefs twisted through their uncombed hair.

"Señorita?"

"I have been living in Nicaragua."

"Sí, pues. But Guatemala is better?"

"Claro," she agreed.

She had not thought about the country she was entering; this visit was to Sunny and Ben, to a place akin to home since friends were there, a suspended place on her way to somewhere else. She nursed a fragile optimism. A very private stance that had to do with the two travelers with the map, the sunlight on the terra-cotta roof tiles, the volcano, greenish-black and giant. Peripheral perceptions. Denial engendered by flowers perpetually blooming over slum decay. In spite of the killing eyes of the soldier, she hoped that the rough life she had been living was over. It was a choice she made, like the mother turning to the curandera to heal her daughter's pinkeye.

"Your English—it's great," Kate said.

He smiled in the rearview mirror, revealing a gold eyetooth. "I am a teacher. Y tambien, I am a fútbol player. I played fútbol for my country."

In front of the taxi, the driver of a lead-blue pickup tooted his horn; just ahead, traffic was blocked by a riderless mule loaded with kindling, his ribs achingly visible, his wooden saddle splintered and rain-swollen. Someone had spray-painted graffiti on the splotchy pink wall: *Campesinos! La union hace la fuerza. CUC.* She saw the address two doors down: El Petén #3. Her hands trembled; her smile seemed to rise from deep in her chest. Her heart pounded Sunny's name.

"This is good," she said. "I'll get out here. This is fine."

"Buenidea," he said. "Buenidea."

"Gracias, muchas gracias, señor." She scrambled to get out, find the money, shoulder her duffel and rucksack, all at once.

The taxi driver set her box on the sidewalk with a flourish. He stuck out his hand. He said, "You need me, my name is Alberto Diego Quevado. I am usually at the park. Near the cathedral."

She shook his hand vigorously. Paid him. Smiled. "I am Catarina," she said. All the while with her eye on El Petén #3.

At the door she banged the brass lionhead knocker. No one answered. Fireworks exploded up the street. Cuetes, bombas, cachinflins—all fireworks made her jumpy, made her heart speed up, echoes of gunfire. She knocked again, harder. Sweat dribbled from under her arm, down her side. Her knees felt weak.

The wooden door swung wide, opened by a stranger, a young woman in a striped bandeau and jeans worn almost white. Her fine red hair fidgeting, swinging, around big chrome crucifix earrings. She was heavily freckled; in her eyes was the muddled look of someone abruptly awakened.

"Buenas tardes. I'm Kate Banner. Sunny's friend."

The young woman's puggish face looked suddenly flat and uncluttered as a dinner plate. "Buenas," she said, chewing gum. She made no welcoming gesture.

Kate said, "Are they home?"

"Who?"

Kate raised her voice over hissing skyrockets. "Sunny. And Ben."

"Oh, yeah yeah yeah. They said you'd be here. Whyn't you come in."

The courtyard, at first glance, was a relief. There were the things from Sunny's photos. The burbling fountain. The cement statue of a boy peeing in the fountain. The hibiscus and roses. The steer skull. Ben's mural—

"I'm Ginger," the young woman said. "And they're like, not here."

"Did they say when they'll be back?"

"Nope."

Road weary down to her bones, Kate sank into a canvas sling chair. She wondered how long she would have to wait. After waiting so long already. After seeing that first moment with Sunny and Ben in her mind's eye over and over. Maybe she'd have time for a shower and a nap.

The long narrow house shared high walls with neighbors. There was an open-to-the-sky courtyard, and to its south a colonnade tiled in mismatched tile, squares and diamonds, blue and brown and gold, and off the colonnade were the rooms all in a row. She counted them; it looked like five bedrooms, a kitchen, and a bath. One door was padlocked. A dwarfish green parrot shrieked. He perched on the rim of a potted fern hanging not far from the kitchen door.

Ginger went on, "Ben's gone to the States. For art supplies. He took the van. Sunny stays in the capital now. To avoid the commute."

"You mean they're really gone?"

"Right."

"Since when? Since when are they gone?"

Ginger closed her eyes, thought for a moment, yawned. "Ben— he left over a week ago. I haven't seen Sunny in over a month. She swoops in, takes her clothes—adiós."

Kate frowned. "I thought . . . they were settled."

"Things change," Ginger said.

She went into the kitchen and left Kate in the courtyard. Skeleton puppets, grinning darkly, hung poised to dance on either side of the kitchen door. In pots too far from the courtyard to catch the rain, geraniums had been neglected.

The green parrot called from his perch to Kate. She heard, What now? What now? She felt the disappointment in her body: a clamp. How naive she'd been to be caught with expectations. If only Maggie were there, none of the changes would matter.

Ginger peeked out of the kitchen and said, "You want something to drink?" She had turned cordial, eager.

Kate hauled herself up. In the kitchen roses drooped in a vase on the table. Dishes filled the sink.

Ginger offered her an orange Fanta soda. "It's warm, but—"

"Thanks."

"—you need water. Of some kind. D'you think this counts as water? You burn more fat if you drink lots of water. And your skin and like your internal organs stay hydrated."

"Is that Posh?" Kate said. "Ben's parrot?"

"Uh-huh. He doesn't like me."

"How can you tell?"

"He pecks at me." She made a scrunched-up face, then bit a sliver of cuticle from her thumbnail. "He likes Dixie. Dixie says he likes to be petted. Same as any old pet."

"Dixie?"

"Father Ryan. He lives here. Temporarily." She lowered her voice. "He's recovering. From breakbone fever." She raised two fingers. "Also, his sib's here sometimes."

"His sib?"

"Sister Judith Ryan. She goes by Jude. We are talking one big Catholic family. They're from New Orleans. And Lino. He's becoming a catechist, I think they call it. He doesn't actually live here, but he's here every day." She fiddled with the tap on the five-gallon agua puro bottle, turning it on and off, on and off. On and off. It was empty. "Nobody's home right now. But me. I been here by myself for a week."

"I want to ask you—so many things—" Kate said, sighing. She slipped down into a chair at the kitchen table.

"Fire away." Ginger leaned against the sink and lit a cigarette. Her toenails were lacquered cranberry red; her ankle bracelet of filigree charms tinkled when she moved her foot. Kate slowly averted her eyes when she saw that Ginger had an extra little toe, but she was too late. Ginger had noticed her noticing and stared back, almost smirking, biting her lower lip.

"How can I get in touch with Sunny? I really need to see her."

"Join the club."

"Pardon me?"

"People want to see Sunny. But—" Ginger blew smoke toward the ceiling, then plucked open her bandeau and stared inside for just two seconds. "I'm monitoring my tan," she said.

"But what?"

"Sunny's secretive about where she's staying. Some people have been able to catch her after school. I heard that. Overheard that."

"What's the big secret?" Kate's throat contracted. She thought of the trip back to Guatemala City, twenty-six miles on the cramped bus, the hellish smog when she got there.

"Beats me."

Kate drank from her soda; she took a deep breath. "I don't know what I'm going to do. I really don't know."

"Oh, you can stay here." She blew smoke toward the ceiling. "Ben did say you were coming."

"Where were they putting me?"

"In the front room. It's kind of noisy." Ginger stubbed out her cigarette on the tile floor, then tucked the butt into her jeans pocket. She said, "Soon I'm out of here. I'm not getting anywhere. You could have my room. Eventually."

"What're you doing here, Ginger?"

"I live here."

"Guatemala, I mean."

"I'm not just hanging out."

"No?"

"I'm only twenty. I'm supposed to be learning Ixil and doing research. I go to Evergreen—ever heard of it?"

"I've heard of it."

"You design your own course. My parents have this thing about freedom—they like to give me enough rope to hang myself, my dad says." She snorted, a halfhearted, failed laugh. She looked away. "My dad says a lot of things. Anyways—my Ixil lessons are all in Spanish." She fingered her pack of cigarettes. "And, of course, there's, like, a guy in the picture."

"There usually is," Kate said. She plunked her soda bottle down on the table. Toast crumbs were scattered in front of her. She rolled the crumbs between one thumb and forefinger.

"For you too?"

Kate could hear and recognize the longing in Ginger's voice to confess her history, to obsess with another woman. I can't be your friend, she thought. For a moment she wondered if she had said it out loud. "Sometimes," Kate said. Then, "Where's your phone?"

"We don't have one. You go to GUATEL. By the park."

Ah, yes. How hard it had been to communicate with Sunny and Ben. Letters took a long time. She sought out the kitchen clock. Two forty-five. If she hurried she could catch Sunny at the American School. Ginger gave her a key to the front door.

Kate went out into the strange street, thinking, Concern yourself with basics: changing money, calling Sunny, learning the way from here to there. She had nothing to tell Ginger.

Kate always, whenever she tried to tell her story, circled back to certain peripheral perceptions, a private code. The refugee girl crying, Catarina, Catarina. The baby boy in Comitán, his toe cut off by the soldiers. Flory arriving that night in Chiapas, Kate's third night, naive night, in Mexico. A sunflower bending in the rain at Mark Deaver's mother's house when Kate and Deaver first made love. A tall sunflower like a songstress in the rain. As though her life might have turned out differently if it had not been raining. If the flowers had been hibiscus. Regret is a kind of aggression against yourself. Torment. One way of staying alive.

I have crossed so many borders. At border crossings you know without doubt how little you control your own destiny.

You surrender your passport and that alone feels naked and you are in between identities and usually there are men with guns nearby and you must pay some money and you must wait. You give up or take on power, depending. I always have the feeling that things could get out of control. The money changers, that's a muddy purgatory they work in. They wear gold rings and watches and their fingers are dirty with money and when they see you coming—North American woman—they rearrange their testicles because they can. Men are allowed to touch their bodies in public any way they want to. I can pass if I am quiet, I'm that dark. My maternal grandmother was Syrian and my father was half Bohemian, first-generation American. My mother called him Gypsy. I have seen his photo from during the war, a tinted photo, with rosy cheeks, and my mother always said the color's all wrong, that's not the way he was. I harbor no memories of him, good or bad. My skin takes on the sun and stays brown, not the maple sugar brown I always craved as a girl but a kind of muddy tan, and sometimes, sometimes, if I'm obsequious enough, only the man who takes my passport knows that I am Katherine Jean Banner, born June 9,

1947, in the state of Indiana in the United States of America. When I cross borders I am grateful to my father for his skin. Rock and roll is usually playing. A child might be about, a bored boy teasing a parrot with a stick. Some countries will not let you in if you have a visa from Cuba or Nicaragua. There's so much fear, you can breathe it in, you have to, there's no choice. Crossing borders, I thought I could go through fear, get to the other side of it. I wanted to be ready for emergencies. To know the worst. They'll probably put that on my gravestone, if I have a gravestone. Pauper graves don't have them, and now I almost qualify, don't I?

When I left Nicaragua I'd been in harm's way too long.

All those borders I crossed with Deaver, the memories kill me. I entered his country, lived under his laws. You might say I had been assimilated. I knew women's bodies, the blood and mess, the way the veins are never the same, the scars, the infections. Once near Los Manos I found a raped woman miscarrying in a stinking latrine. But Deaver took me back into his country to pleasure before all that, to pleasure that left me quaking, dying. I can't stand it, I can't. I'll make you, he would say. I'll make you do whatever I want, he would whisper. He could whisper that and make a woman say, yes, yes, whatever you want. I'll make you.

On a long bus ride or a walk across town there was too much time to think.

Aversion is a stumbling block and stumbling blocks are all that are worth examining. Delight and love you just enjoy. Sin calls your attention to itself. Sin requires your attention. The memories, the little manipulations, the lies. What I did for him. What I did to him.

I always thought Deaver and I would leave Nicaragua together just as we had come together. Before we left San Cristóbal for Nicaragua I'd been working in the refugee camp—Casa Buena— with the Guatemalan refugees. I'd had to lie twice to soldiers, but after that they let me pass and I lived out there under a tarp, de-livering babies and making do with what little I could scrounge from hospitals in the nearby towns. We hadn't planned to leave together. He was traveling to Huehuetenango in the highlands of Guatemala, not too far across the border, and he'd offered me a ride back to the dirt road that led to the camp. I always liked being dropped at that inconspicuous place on the Pan-American Highway. I could walk in, carrying a load, past the cornfields, past the cypress trees, and soon the children would run out to greet me. His van was packed with woodworking tools and three bicycles and clothes in a leather suitcase and weapons and cartridge boxes and books. The weapons made me nervous and I asked him what he was going to tell them at the border and he said, Household goods. As though the trouble he risked was slight. At that time I had not yet developed a loathing for weapons, they only made me nervous. I still felt slightly bruised between my legs from our night together, a soreness I always relished days later. I wondered when he would return but I didn't want to ask. I knew a French doctor in Comitán and we stopped there to see if I could beg some measles vaccine. Already that month three children had died from measles in Casa Buena.

Outside the Comitán hospital a crowd had gathered. I thought I recognized an Indian woman who cried and cried on the sidewalk. Her skirt was torn, her bare feet blackened with blood. She held up her baby boy, screaming, Mire, mire, look what they have done to him. He is all I have. And even from a distance I could see that her boy's little toe had been cut off. A girl ran up to me and squealed. Like a hurt animal. Catarina, Catarina, the soldiers came across the frontier, they killed our people, they came from Guatemala, she leaned toward me, her arms out. I knew her. Her huipil, her blouse, was sky blue and dirty and turned inside out, revealing the wispy ends of embroidery knots and stitches. I hugged her, but Deaver grabbed my arm, his fingers digging in, and he said, No you don't, you can't stay here, let's get the hell out of here. He pulled me away, I let him pull me away. The girl kept calling, Catarina, Catarina. Just come with me, Deaver said, they need nurses everywhere. A boy knelt nearby, playing jacks with a pitted rubber ball. A fruit vendor sold his mangoes half a block away.

I had very little with me in the way of personal possessions when I left Mexico with Deaver that day in 1982, thinking we were on a mission together. And I would hear the girl calling Catarina in the nights we spent in poor hotels. I'd hear her calling in that soft fold of time right before falling asleep. Waking dreams are sometimes worse than sleeping dreams. I knew that then. Nothing unnerved me more until the Cathedral Man.

Brigadista, brigadista.

His rags, his smell. His delight in my fear.

Crossing borders, I longed to divest myself of dreams.

Kate charged out into the afternoon, into the cobblestone street ripe with exhaust and the odors of commerce and excrement and animals. Women carrying bundles on their heads slapped barefooted on the stone sidewalks. Men cycled by with pickaxes or shovels slung over their shoulders. How narrow was the street, how difficult for traffic: the motorbikes and cars and pickup trucks. She hadn't expected to see so many running vehicles. Children were about, some of them ragged and selling a quetzal's worth of this or that to make enough for dinner and some of them on their way home from school, dressed in school uniforms with knife-pressed pleats and hair plaited precisely by a sister or a grandmother with a strict sense of how hair should be plaited. It was a twenty-minute walk to the center of town. She retraced the way Alberto had driven.

The late afternoon sun struck the volcano's upper slopes. The trees there looked all of one piece, a brass shield, while the lower slopes were blackish green and mysterious. At the Church of the Merced, two Mayan women knelt on a tapete under a palm tree, combing out their hair. In red cortes with the tiniest thread of yellow running through the fabric. Their cortes had the rumpled look of clothes slept in.

She passed a tavern. The sourish smell of stale beer clouded out from the open door. Farther down the street a man in muddy clothes lay drunk and sleeping on the sidewalk, one arm flung out, his mouth shriveled and his lips cracked. She skirted him and walked the street beside the central park: a square of fountains and roses and concrete benches. With a pocketknife a vendor popped the twine on a knee-high bundle of newspapers.

GUATEL was at the next corner. A soldier in army fatigues stood outside smoking a cigarette, his sleeves rolled above his elbow, his rifle slanted toward the sidewalk. Kate stepped up into the GUATEL office and a chill rose around her. It was dim inside and she took a half minute to let her eyes adjust, to let the brown shapes become distinct.

"Denis! Número cuatro!" the woman behind the metal grate harped over a loudspeaker. A thin man in red cowboy boots leaped up, charged to one of the wooden booths, and slammed the door. "Hello, lover!" he barked into the receiver.

Kate went to the metal grate and gave the woman her name and the phone number of Sunny's school. She sat down on a sofa. The seat had been replaced with a splintery sheet of plywood.

The lights were shut off in the far side of the room. A couple hunched there on a car seat, waiting. The woman smoked, squinching up her face with each puff. "How could you let this happen?" she said. "How?" The man set his jaw and blew up at his greasy blond bangs. He said nothing. Kate gathered that they had been robbed in Guate. She thought of Maggie's favorite toast: Salud y dinero y amor—major concerns.

"Catarina! Número uno!"

Kate rushed to the booth and pulled the door tight, though she knew there was no reason for that; she knew everyone could hear if they strained to hear. The Plexiglas window of the booth was smudged with fingerprints. She picked up the receiver; it felt dirty with sweat and snot and belches; she overcame her initial repulsion because Sunny would soon be on the line.

The secretary of the school answered. "Hold please," she said. And Kate said, "Yes, yes, of course," and she waited there for four minutes. The secretary came back on the line. She was not sure whether Sunny had left for the day.

"Please try to find her," Kate said.

She waited again, through the rough and tumble of students at the other end, laughter, books slamming down, questions flying. Someone moved the receiver—it clunked—and she feared whoever it was might hang up.

"Hola! Sunny Hires here."

"Sunny. It's Kate."

"You're here."

"Well, I'm in Antigua. Maggie didn't come along. That is, I left without her."

Sunny lowered her voice. "Is everything all right?"

"Everything's all right. Maggie's coming in a couple weeks, and then we'll go to Mexico City and then—home, I think. Home to the States."

Sunny was silent.

"So what's going on? I thought you'd be here."

"Didn't Ben leave a note?"

"Not that I know of."

"Kate—I'm sorry. This isn't a very good time to talk."

"I should have asked you if this was an okay time to call. When is it okay?"

"Don't call me here. I'll get in touch with you."

"When can we get together?"

"Not right now."

"Well, when?"

"You'll be hearing from me."

Kate sighed. "All right. I get it. I'll wait to hear from you."

And then Sunny said, "What about your beau?"

And Kate was quiet for a moment. Then she said, "That's all over."

"Oh dear." Sunny sighed.

Kate said nothing.

"I'm sorry. Sorry you're having to deal with that."

Obdurately Kate said, "I'll get over it."

A tunnel of silence. Then a grating "Número siete!" from the clerk.

"I'd like to talk."

"I can't, hon. Not right now."

Kate could not speak with any degree of coherency after that. Her throat felt tight. She knew they laughed once, a clipped, cynical laugh—about what she wasn't sure—and they said good-bye. But all she could think was, Fuck your busy life and your secrets, come back, Sunny. She went up to the metal window to pay for the call. The clerk was tall and wore dark liver-colored lipstick and a black wool skirt. She was signing a birthday card for someone, a Garfield card, and she made Kate wait until she had signed her name with a flourish. Then she took Kate's money without looking her in the eye.

Impulsively Kate placed another call: to her mother. It was May in Indiana too. There would be lilacs, wisteria. Her mother and her aunts would welcome her when she got home, she was sure of that, even though there had been hard feelings between them. She was bad about keeping in touch. She had deprived them of a life they could live through her. So far.

"Catarina! Número cinco!"

She got her mother's machine. "We've gone to the lake to open the cottage. We're painting the porch! You know what to do. Dodie or I will return your call." The lake. Lake Michigan. Kate pictured the white rattan chairs, the dark green porch floor, the endless steely blue lake. The cottage at the lake had been their dream and they had made their dream come true. They lived in a place that still felt so safe to them that they would announce on the machine that they were away. Her voice was simply the voice of a woman in her sixties, not the voice of a mother. Her voice changed whenever she spoke to Kate, those few and far-between times in the past decade.

"It's me," she said to the machine. "I'm safe and sound. I wish I could help you paint the porch." She hadn't expected to say that. "I'll call you in a week or so."

Sunlight slanted on the sidewalk and roses scented the heart of the park; a fountain plashed and whirled cold air. The concrete nymphs around the fountain held up their breasts; water spouted from them. A man with a flute, his graying hair in a short ponytail, set up an amplifier and plugged his flute into it. He leaned a cardboard sign against the side of the amp; he collected money in a coffee tin for handicapped children. University students carrying satchels streamed across the park, heading home.

Kate sat down. The sun angled away and cold accumulated in the bench. She did not think she could sit there long. How odd it was to be without Maggie. Had Maggie felt the same all the nights Kate had stolen through the Managua streets to be with Deaver?

Across the street a woman came out of the wooden double doors of the Palace of the Captains-General. She leaned against the door frame, wiped her hair from her eyes, and peered into the colonnade shadows. Kate registered that the woman was hurt. A soldier came up behind the woman, nudging her lower back with his rifle butt. At the next corner a man slopped water from a zinc bucket onto the stones of the sidewalk. The woman stepped into the little sunlight left on the street. Fresh blood stained her mouth. Her blouse hung out of her slacks.

Kate watched her limp away and turn down a side street. She waited a few minutes. The soldier across the street had put on dark glasses. The tourist office at the end of the block was closing for the day, its enormous wooden doors creaking shut. The music of the flute wavered like flower petals lightly gusting. Kate resolutely strode back to GUATEL and down the street it was on, away from the central park. She circled back around the block, past a hospital with a SILENCIO, POR FAVOR sign, past a bakery with its hot sugar odors. People lined up at the bakery to buy their evening bread.

She found the injured woman at the west end of a narrow park, sitting on a bench under a palm tree, crying. Kate sat down.

"Señorita," she said.

The woman laced and unlaced her fingers in her lap. "Sí?"

At the wide pila nearby, ten women washed their clothes. Pila life went on around them. Children eating on the ground, women washing and combing out their hair, piles of twisted wet laundry.

"Con permiso. Can I help you?"

The woman shivered. Her hands and wrists were red and abraded.

"Yo—tengo—miedo," she said, cringing, glancing over her shoulder in the direction from which she had come.

"I can see that," Kate said softly.

The woman's slacks were worn and expensive, raw umber–colored silk, and her blouse pocket had been embroidered: LHR. She wore scuffed gold flats. She was a Mayan, short and compact and dark, and her eyes suggested delicate wings on her round face. What Kate had thought was blood on her mouth was a mix of blood and lipstick. Someone had painted her mouth and chin with shiny lipstick.

She did not look at Kate. She plucked at her blouse. "These are not my clothes," she cried. "They took my traje. I have never worn clothes like these in my life." She bent over and wiped the lipstick on the hem of the blouse.

"Do you want to come with me?" Kate said. "To a comedor? Maybe it would be good to get off the street."

"I am afraid."

"I know."

"They have my husband. I don't want to leave him." Her face was streaked with tears. A puffy blue bruise had risen on her temple.

Nearby Mayan children sat in a circle on a blanket, eating tortillas. The domestic music of the pila rose beside them—water rinsing, clothes slap-slapping, women talking.

"They let me go," she said, her voice subdued, puzzled. "They let me go."

"Who?"

"Soldiers."

"Soldiers?" Kate whispered.

"They have my husband."

"Let me give you a cup of coffee. Or una comida. Por favor. Let me."

The tinning of church bells followed them away from the pila.

They went into a small café, not a place for travelers but a neighborhood café for the people who lived on that street. A dark and simple place, each table with a milk-glass vase of plastic flowers. The big woman behind the counter smelled like woodsmoke and wore a spotless apron over her dress, house slippers on her feet. Kate ordered cafés con leche. They waited. Chickens clucked in the proprietor's dirt courtyard. The aluminum coffeepot scraped against the gas stove burner behind the counter.

The proprietor brought the coffee in cups on saucers. Thin paper napkins and tarnished spoons. A bowl of yellowish sugar. Then she took her post behind the counter and began chopping onions.

"What is your name?" Kate said.

The woman turned to Kate and said, "I am Vidalúz, and I am a dangerous person." She wiped at her mouth with a napkin; the lipstick made a stain like berry juice. "A soldier bit me. He bit my mouth."

Under her breath Kate said, "God in heaven." She shrank from what the woman told her. "Lo siento, lo siento." She held her cup like a mug, for warmth.

"Cómo se llama?"

"My name is Catarina," Kate said. "I am sorry we are meeting this way."

"Yo también. Yo también."

"Do you want someone to know?"

Vidalúz began to cry. "I could hear my husband groaning. I . . . heard him. They kept him in another room. I tried not to—" She bit her lip.

Kate patted her arm. "Vidalúz," she said quietly, "only tell me what you want to tell me."

"Don't tell anyone. Por favor."

The two women sat in the smoky café, whispering and drinking coffee. The coffee tasted very bitter even with the creamy milk. After a little while, the proprietor lit a novena candle at each end of a row of family photographs on the counter. She turned on the radio. Then she picked up the cat and stood there watching them, the calico cat in her arms.

Lightweight.

Spoiled.

Needy.

Kate woke up hearing Deaver's voice, not sure where she was. He had been a master of the one-word put-down. And short seductions. Pet. Love. Sweet cheeks. She remembered where she was in layers: girls chattering and scuffing along the sidewalk outside her shuttered window; Ginger's extra toe; Sunny! All the loss came seeping into her as she awoke, all the poison. Vidalúz and all that she had told her.

A blue bar of street light across the tile floor. A door slamming, vibrating.

They had parted without a mention of meeting again; Kate wished she had given Vidalúz her address, in Antigua and in the States. Maggie would have. Maggie kept track of everyone she met; she sent regular care packages; she wrote postcards and letters. An undersong echoed back and forth across her aloneness: it won't be long, soon, soon. She imagined in one brief flash Maggie arriving, all laughter and teasing, flushed and excited by her adventure and love life. Ready for the next go-round.

She turned on the lamp beside the bed, sat up, and ran her hands through her hair. She had come back from the park, taken down her braid, and slipped stealthily into her bedroom, that cool dark cave, the windows shuttered, the darkness more a substance than the absence of light. She remembered nudging off her sneakers without untying them and easing onto the double bed. The bedspread of thin cotton; the pillow smelling like bleach. She'd remembered a green paisley cotton bedspread hanging on a wall in a college dormitory; how the smell of India, the sizing they used in the dye, had remained in the bedspread; the music they had listened to then, the Beatles or Bob Dylan; and the boys, the boys at the window, bringing them a pizza and begging them to sneak out of the dorm and make them men.

And then she'd slept. Dreamless. Until Deaver's voice.

Things were not turning out; she would have to dredge up resources to deal with the changes. Her head hurt, a pinch between her eyes. Her mouth felt parched.

She went out to the courtyard. Jazz played in the kitchen. She placed it. Billie Holiday. Night was coming on. A golden light from the kitchen lay in a blurry rectangle on the twilit courtyard. There were good smells: roses, moist wind, cardamom and raisins. She heard voices; she prepared herself to have to meet people and be sociable. She felt she was in no condition to have to give—anything to anybody. In English or Spanish. And she dreaded more of those conversations in which you detail your history, the high points, just enough to give form to the shadow of your presence.

At the kitchen door she said, "Buenas noches."

There stood Dixie. And others, but Kate focused on him. She recognized him.

He was stir-frying vegetables in a cast-iron skillet. Billie sang, "Pennies from heaven." He was tall, with a sweet boyish face; you could see the boy he'd been in his face. In his forties, handsome, in a way that made Kate think, Handsome is as handsome does: her mother's words. Not classic but with a kind smile, a strong hooked nose, abundant gray-blond hair curling over his collar, clean-shaven.

The shadow under his eyes bespoke the illness, the fever: he didn't look frail, only fatigued. He wore a chambray shirt and chinos; his clothes inspired comfort in her; they were a mirror of her own.

"Hola, where y'at?" Dixie said. Then, "I remember you. It was the rainy season, wasn't it. When we met in San Cristóbal?"

Kate said, "Are you sure?"

"Cool," Ginger said. "Déjà vu." She hunched over her bitten fingernails, polishing them with lavender nail polish. She had put on a flannel shirt to ward off the night's chill.

"Not exactly," Kate said.

She stood there slack-jawed, still waking up, with the wilted disoriented sensation induced by afternoon naps that stretch into evening. Dixie bore down on a manual can opener, opened a tin of shrimp, dumped the shrimp into the stir-fry.

"This is Lino," Dixie said, pointing with a wooden spoon.

Lino was not quite a man, a boy still, seventeen or so, in a white shirt and pressed black slacks, with a gold cross on a gold chain around his neck. His face was dark and smooth like oiled wood. A notebook lay open before him on the table, filled with pencil script. A Spanish-English dictionary at his elbow. A softcover Bible on the chair next to his. "Buenas," Lino said, smiling broadly.

"Kate, right?" Dixie said.

Kate folded her arms and nodded. "Is there . . . water?"

"They'll deliver tomorrow," Dixie said. "Hows about an agua mineral? Fetch her one, Ginger."

And Ginger did as she was told.

"Things have kind of gone to hell in a handbasket, but we've got Victoria and Juanita coming to clean tomorrow. Dixie. Dixie Ryan," he said to Kate. He wiped his hand on his pants and reached out to her.

She let his hand hang there for a split second before she took it. He was solid. There. A man who attended to whatever was right in front of him. She saw a question in his eyes. He wore glasses but they weren't thick and you could read his eyes perfectly. Blue as a night sky two shades before you call it black.

She shook his hand. "I think I do remember you," she said. "You were on your way here."

"Been and gone and been again," he said. "I can't stay away."

Steam and a sweet smell rose from the stir-fry. Kate took the mineral water from Ginger, thanked her, and sat down in a cane-bottom chair. The music went on, "Who loves you, ask yourself the question." Ginger hovered over her nails. Lino took up his pencil and wrote in his notebook.

That May evening, eating Dixie's stir-fry in the kitchen in Antigua, she was not sure what made her shy. She gave him one-word answers to questions.

When she finished her meal Ginger went to the sink, rinsed off her plate, said good-night. "I'm out of here," she said. "They're showing *Something Wild* at the video bar." Lino too rinsed his plate, put away his books and papers, and said he would go with her. Ginger shrugged. In that offhand gesture Kate could see that certainly Lino was not the guy Ginger had mentioned.

Kate thanked Dixie for the meal. She picked up a leather foot-stool, went out to the courtyard, and sat down near the fountain. The light from the kitchen shone in ribbons on the water. The night felt silky and plush, a place to relax into, but Kate guarded against that. She and Maggie always liked to say that they landed on their feet, wherever. She had landed all right, in this unexpected household in an unfamiliar town. Things could be worse; that seemed like the best take; she could convince herself of that.

She thought of Maggie in her tent with her new lover. She wished them all good outcomes. Maggie had been alone for a long time while Kate had been able to garner consolation with Deaver. Such as it was. Maggie had loved Flory and their love had struck them in the middle of la violencia and they had never had a simple romance; fear and desperation had colored every kiss. Flory had maintained a darkroom in Guate, in a friend's house, and finally that darkroom had been broken into and all of the equipment smashed. When that had not stopped Flory from taking photographs and sending them to newspapers in the States, she had been murdered. Her Renault had been forced off a switchback one slick and rainy night on the Pan-American Highway. The night she found out the news Maggie had hitched a ride all the way from San Cristóbal to the refugee camp to be with Kate. They had sat up all night under a tarp, feeding a fire and drinking gin straight from the bottle in manageable sips. Salud y amor, Maggie.

"May I join you?" Dixie said.

Kate nodded and with her open palm gestured toward the canvas slingback chair nearby. It was a niggardly response, she knew. Barely polite. Better be nice, she warned herself. He's all you've got.

Dixie settled down, spreading a gray-and-white blanket over his lap. His eyes were merely blue smudges in the dark but his feet in sandals rested near the kitchen light shining on the tiles. He told her about his illness, the dengue fever, what they called breakbone fever. He said that in the first phase of the disease his temperature had gone up to one hundred and four. He told her about Lino, what a good soul he was, how he dreamed of teaching his people to read the Bible and understand its call to justice.

Kate said nothing. She had for years skirted around religious talk, though it was hard to avoid in Central America.

All the while she kept looking at his ankles and his feet in sandals. They were slender and perfectly formed, the feet of a statue. There was something graceful about the hollow of his ankle around the anklebone. The Billie Holliday kept on scratchily from the kitchen, too intimate, too sly, too bold. She would have liked listening to it with Sunny.

"Where've you been?" Dixie asked.

"Managua mostly," Kate said.

He waited. When she said nothing more, he said, "Doing?"

"Delivering babies."

"So—what's it like there now?"

"Poor. It's very poor."

"And the people, how're they holding up?"

Kate pursed her lips, tried to formulate what she could say that would be true. "They're very tired. Worn out." She shivered.

Dixie reached for an afghan that lay folded on the back of his chair. He handed the afghan to Kate. "Here."

She said, "That's okay."

"Take it."

She wrapped the afghan around her shoulders.

She said, "I talked to Sunny this afternoon."

"Oh?"

"What's going on with them?"

"Did you expect them to be here?"

"Months ago—they said come on. We—my friend Maggie and I—we didn't know . . . their circumstances had changed."

He waited until she met his gaze. "I'm sorry."

A racket on the street, traffic, the kinky haul of a truck across the cobblestones, gave her pause. And then she asked, "How well do you know them?"

"It's been a couple of years."

"Where's she living?"

"She didn't tell you?"

"She . . . was in a hurry."

"I don't feel at liberty to talk about them."

"I thought Ben was in the States."

He frowned. "That's right."

"Didn't Sunny say we were coming?"

"I believe she did. A while back."

The parrot toddled across the patio, cocked his head, and seemed to squint up at Dixie. Dixie bent down and stuck out his index finger. The parrot stepped up on his finger. "Hey, Posh, hey, Posh," he soothed. He drew the parrot in close to his chest and petted him behind his head in a gentle circular motion. Posh's feathers were the green of an unripe mango. "She wasn't quite sure. When you were coming."

"We couldn't get away." She was tempted to tell him about Vidalúz. But she'd promised.

"I like to cook," Dixie said.

Kate said nothing.

"You're welcome to eat with us. We chip in to a kitty—five Qs a day. We take turns marketing."

"Could I play it by ear?" Kate said, standing up and folding the afghan. "I'm kind of an erratic eater." She put the afghan on her chair and said, "But thanks for tonight. For the stir-fry." She didn't want to get involved in domestic arrangements.

"My pleasure."

He did not scrutinize her; she felt grateful for that; she was not at her best. Posh chirked quietly under Dixie's stroking.

They heeded the click of a key in the front door. Out of the shadow of the foyer came Jude.

"Hello," Dixie said, reluctantly it seemed.

"I see you have company," Jude said. She walked over to them. She wore a wooden rosary around her neck. Its crucifix hung between her breasts. Her jeans were baggy, her sweater patched.

"This is Kate Banner," Dixie said. "A friend of Sunny and Ben's. Maybe you remember her from San Cristóbal? She's passing through. Kate, this is my sister. Jude Ryan."

Kate and Jude shook hands. Kate remembered her. Jude had eradicated any nooks and crannies of New Orleans from her voice. She had been in the capital; the jeep she and Dixie shared had gotten a flat tire halfway back to Antigua and two men had stopped to help her change it.

"I'm tired," she said. She fingered the crucifix on her rosary. Then, "We need to talk."

"We will," Dixie said. "Have your dinner. I saved you some veggies and rice."

"This is important," Jude said.

"I was . . . ah . . . just going to take a shower and turn in," Kate said. "Do you have hot water?"

"Hey, we're uptown," Dixie said. "It's one of those electric gizmos. On the showerhead. Don't touch it or the pipes or you'll get a shockeroo."

"Good-night, now," Kate said.

"Pasa buena noche," Dixie said. "God bless."

"Yes, goodnight," Jude said.

And Kate walked across the courtyard, trying not to stalk. Or run. The impulse to run, to hide, was strong in her. She got a towel and a kimono from her room and went to the bathroom to shower. They sat very still in the dark as she walked by again. As she shut the door she heard Jude say urgently, "Why didn't you tell me?"

In the shower she masturbated standing under the warm water. To come she thought of a woman Deaver had desired and she had known. She could imagine the woman opening her blouse—a sleeveless white cotton blouse with a pointed collar—and Deaver's breath coming ragged, almost imperceptibly. That was enough to make her come this time though sometimes she had to go further. She made herself sick with the fantasies she had shared with him.

Afterward she leaned against the mildewy wall—a yellow tile wall with a pink flamingo on each tile and faint green swirls like grass or a dream of grass. Then she turned the water on as hot as it would go, curved her back to its pulse, and tried to shut out everything else. She thought these things would make her sleep.

She went back to her room, passing the open door to the kitchen, where Dixie and Jude talked. Jude said, ". . . but you're arrogant. In the worst way."

Kate stopped at her own bedroom door. She listened.

"That's mine to confront, not yours to point out."

Their voices were raised but controlled. They did not want anyone to hear.

Jude said aggressively, "I don't want what happened to Sam to happen to you."

And Dixie said, "Sam's happy, Jude. He went to seminary when he was only seventeen. Leaving—that had to happen. And now he's happy. Why in the world do you begrudge him that?"

Get out of here, Kate warned herself, get out. Wait for Maggie. Find Sunny if you can. Put out your hand to no one. Suddenly Billie sang again: "I can't give you anything but love." She could not hear Jude and Dixie anymore. It did not matter anyway. She had her own concerns. She slept a light and irritable sleep.

Where y'at?

I knew him, yes. No one else I'd met in Central America had New Orleans in his blood.

He had a history of rabble-rousing and he was proud of that.

His first three parishes were working class. Never far from an industrial center in northern Ohio. Places where the laid-off men would drink all winter in VFWs, squat brick buildings lit by neon beer signs. Places where the streets were gray with slush. Where the women knew when to lie low and ask for nothing and when to go to morning mass and offer prayers and novenas to get them through the winter. Where the girls wore tube tops under jean jackets until Thanksgiving and that skin goose-pimpled with cold, that tease, was their power and their only power. They did not know the prayers, but they tried to pray along anyway, the boys too, they mumbled, they were embarrassed by prayer or worship and no one held hands during the Our Father. That was their one chance to break out of their isolation and Dixie could not get them to hold hands. I could picture it. He told me more than he'd told anyone. More, sometimes, than I was ready to know.

His eyes were an unusual blue, darker than most Irish eyes. His hands were calm. Sure of cooking or whatever he did. When he cooked, that was all that mattered in the world. He had a way of doing each and every act that way, mindfully. You felt blessed being around him. Even when he was gruff. He wasn't a saint, especially with Lino and Ginger—he was like their dad. They needed that. I think of his eyes when I'm able to remember him, though it's sad to say that these things fade too, yes—

That May in 1989 wasn't the first time we'd met.

The first time was in San Cristóbal de las Casas, Chiapas, Mexico, in 1982. We danced together, oddly enough. That isn't what you expected to hear, is it? A dancing priest.

We were in a coffeehouse or bar across from the city palace. There were big windows, and we could see out into the zócalo. It had been raining for days. The Exquisito hot-dog vendor huddled under a sheet of plastic. There were always kids there selling things, Chiclets and clay pigs and pulseras. It was a cold rain. In the mountains you can see your breath when it rains, even that close to the equator, and the kids squatted and shivered under the bandstand. But we were snug inside. I was keenly aware of that at first, the way I could buy shelter for myself, a drink at a bar or a hotel room. I stopped thinking about that eventually, I got past that by sleeping under a tarp in the refugee camp for six months. In that particular bar there was always music that made you think it was the '60s again, protest songs, folk music. We had been invited to a meeting about the refugees from Guatemala.

Maggie was there. And Flory. Deaver too. And Jude—she's a Maryknoll. Suffice it to say my motives were mixed. We were sitting around a long wooden table, drinking Coronas and coffees with brandy. Flory smoked and kept one hand on Maggie's thigh and Maggie was beautiful in a sea-green sweater, her cheeks in the high color of love. There was another man there—Gonzalo. A high-strung Mexican who kept time to the music on the table edge. Jude had driven a truck from Austin filled with plastic tarps and buckets and old clothes and rice and beans. She was intense. Tall. Angular. She wasn't much older than Dix. Dressed seriously. No nonsense. In hiking boots and a ragg sweater. She wore a diver's watch and a Saint Chris medal and she refused coffee and told the waiter, Export crops keep indigenous people down, and Dixie said, Boycotting's not the solution, Jude. It's a meaningless gesture. I said, What's your solution? And he said, Give the Indians back their land. Work for that. He was on his way to work with Father Cantillo, the one who leads the marches to the capital. Dixie was about thirty-two or -three, he liked tequila, he'd been in some trouble at his last parish. But I didn't know that then. I remember he gave some money to a boy or bought some postcards from him.

There was tension between him and Jude—maybe it was the drinking. He had given up drinking by the time we met in Antigua. He had become more pure, in ways that most of us cannot imagine. I remember the music changed to reggae and Jude said, Kate! Why don't you dance with my brother, he deserves a dance, doesn't he, before he flies into the eye of the storm? Jude never would've done that later. We were young, our positions hadn't yet calcified. Guatemala at that time was a dangerous place for Catholic clergy, they had been accused of working to stir up the rebels. Dixie always said that he was teaching people to read and perhaps that does stir people up more than anything else. He was scared, he told me he was scared when I asked him. Every day, he said. Deaver had gotten up to talk with a woman who sat at the piano, a redheaded white woman with a brown baby. He'd gotten up to remove himself from the discussion. Deaver was bored by talk of Father Cantillo, he was bored by talk of nonviolent means. He and the redhead leaned toward each other and laughed in a way that sent a shock of jealousy through me. Rain pounded on the skylights. There was always this odd light when it rained. An eerie light. Deaver's white shirt glowed bottle-green beside the baby grand. Dixie and I got up to dance on the tile dance floor. It was in the shape of a pineapple. Some things you never forget, and some you wish you could. Dixie was a good dancer, and I will not forget his gentle hand on the small of my back, guiding me back to the table.

Where y'at?

Those first few weeks in Antigua while I waited, while I adjusted to the phones not working and the terror Vidalúz brought into my life, I wasn't sure what Dix remembered of me. Had I done that night in San Cristóbal, as I had often done, things to regret?

Catarina, Catarina!

She awakened abruptly, her mouth cottony, her throat locked up with thirst. Her room deathly quiet and dark. Smelling of damp plaster and strangely stale unfamiliar sweat. Spice and incense, smoky and pungent.

Catarina!

The bedsheet roped around her thighs and she struggled to free herself. Then she remembered that she had moved just for the night into Ginger's room, that this was Ginger's smell, Ginger's cardomom chewing gum. Ginger had not been home for a week. Every night Kate had been kept awake by street noise, and finally, the night before about midnight, she had tugged her linens off her bed and gone to find quiet. Waking up was a relief, palpable, a discovery that erased the panic she was edging near. Catarina.

"Y'all okay in there?" Dixie said from beyond her closed door.

A hairline crack of yellow light split the panels of her door. Daytime. And her room was black as a well. She was sick of other people's ruins. The National Cathedral in Managua briefly filled her mind.

"You cried out," Dixie said.

She had slept in the nude, the warmth of her own body assuasive. "I'm okay," she said.

"Time to rise and shine, anyhoo."

"What time is it?" She got up and pulled on a long T-shirt she'd left on the foot of the bed.

"Nineish."

She opened the doors: Posh emitted what she had come to think of as his happy song, a chipper gobble; sunlight waved like a banner into her room. Dixie stood before her, his prayer book open in one hand, his glasses in the other, a folded newspaper tucked under one arm.

"Good morning, merry sunshine." He arched one eyebrow—blond, bushy, interwoven with iron-gray—and half smiled. "You're taking over Ginger's room?"

"I was desperate for silence."

"She won't mind. Though I wish she'd come by. I wish she'd let us know."

The floor was cool against her bare feet but she could discern the promise of a hot day. "I'm dying of thirst."

"There's company in there."

"Company?"

"Sort of. Lino. And two friends—"

Kate whisked past the kitchen to her own room. She went to her clothes rack, stripped off the long T-shirt, and pulled a caftan from its hanger. Billowy and past her ankles, the creamy cotton caftan lent her an air of modesty. She'd wear it for the pope himself.

Dixie sat in the shade of the colonnade reading the newspaper. When Kate emerged from her room he said, "Look at this." He held up the front page of the *Miami Herald*.

Kate stood behind his chair, adjusted her glasses, and took the paper from him. A black smear of ink came off on her left hand. He wiped his face with a yellow bandanna. The fountain tinkled and light glistened on the water.

The *Herald* carried a large grainy photograph of a collapsed Chinese student wearing sweatpants and muddy court shoes, with an IV taped to his hand and forearm. Two men supported him clumsily. One raised the drip in a clear plastic bottle above his head. *One of twelve students from the Central Drama Academy who refused even water during the hunger strike.*

"What's it about?" Kate said.

With a flutter, Posh half flew, half glided from his fern down to the courtyard floor.

"There are thousands of them. Demonstrating for democratic reforms."

Posh scurried to Dixie, his talons scratching on the tile.

Kate said, "In China?"

Dixie put down his hand and Posh climbed up on one finger. "Yessiree. China."

Kate dropped the newspaper on his lap. "Fat chance."

"Nothing like this has ever happened there."

"You know someone there?"

"I'm just moved by it."

Kate said, "They're not armed."

Dixie said, "That's the beauty of it."

Kate shook her head. She did not agree but without a strong cup of coffee like a transfusion she did not think she could refute him. The desire for coffee first thing every morning had convinced her to pay her daily five Qs.

The kitchen smelled of toast and honey. Two children sat bunched together on a cane-bottom chair.

"Catarina," Lino said. "Buenos, buenos." He stood and smiled and shook her hand.

"Buenos días. Welcome back," she said.

They'd been eating oatmeal. There was honey in a Johnny Walker Red bottle on the table, a chipped porcelain teapot, and two red boxes of raisins open before the children.

"These are my friends," Lino said. "Eduardo—"

Kate said, "Mucho gusto," and nodded to Eduardo, who with his teeth tore at a hunk of bread.

"—and Marta."

Marta's eyes were big, dark; she stared anxiously at no one, squeezing her little fists open and closed.

"Buenos días, buenos días," Kate said. She went to the refrigerator, got out a carton of orange juice, poured the juice into a glass, and drank. Her dry throat stung as the orange juice went down.

"Café?" Lino said, and he was up again, pouring coffee into a big mug.

She took the coffee gratefully and sat down.

The girl's hair was black and matted; she had yellow crusty sores around her mouth.

"Como está?" Kate said to Marta.

"Ella no habla," Eduardo said.

"Nada?" Kate said.

"Nada," Lino said.

"Porqúe?"

"She don't want to," Eduardo said in English. He eyed the honey; he eyed the bread; his appetite was there in his eyes. Lino pushed the bottle of honey and the bread in Eduardo's direction; he reached for it and focused on that, on eating.

"I found them in the capital," Lino said above their heads. "Sí, pues, maybe they found me. Their mother and father—" He opened his hands skyward.

"You found them?" Kate took off her glasses. She pressed the mug of hot coffee against her forehead.

"In the park."

"Tu no-vi-a?" Eduardo said, smiling, nodding maniacally.

Lino frowned. "No, mijo."

The boy grunted, half laughter.

"Lo del padre?"

Kate stood up. "He makes up for the other one, doesn't he?"

"They live on the street."

She put on her glasses, picked up her mug, and said, "I've got something for those sores."

Lino said, "Gracias, Catarina."

"She'll have to let me wash the sores. Do you think she'll let me?"

"Here?"

"Yes, here's okay. We have to boil some water."

When Dixie came into the kitchen a half hour later, he found them still there: Eduardo eating, Lino watching, and Kate sitting at the table washing Marta's impetigo gently, gently, with a square of gauze. Marta stood passively, penned between Kate's legs. She wore molded transluscent Mary Janes—lime green, with torn straps. Nothing about Marta was clean and Kate wondered what it would take to get her to bathe. Her sweet arms were ashen. Eduardo had coaxed her into the treatment. Kate steadied Marta's fragile head in one hand. Her bones seemed like the bones of a bird.

"They'll stay with us?" Dixie said.

"Okay?" Lino said.

"You're the boss," Kate said to Dixie.

Eduardo got up from the table and wandered around the room, poking into shelves, checking out everything. He hitched up his pants; the rope belt he wore did not keep them up around his waist. His shirt was torn at one shoulder and without buttons. He said, "Ah, matches, candles. Oatmeal, mucho oatmeal. Azúcar! You are rich, Lino."

"He'll be a tough one," Kate said.

"Like a brother," Lino said. And he play-punched Eduardo in the arm; they wrestled.

Dixie's eyes met Kate's for an instant. He thanked her silently. She looked away.

When she finished washing Marta's mouth, Kate scrubbed her hands thoroughly. She poured another mug of coffee. In the courtyard the sun lay like gold leaf on everything, inviting her among the hibiscus and elephant ears. Posh groomed himself, feather by feather, on the rim of the fountain. It was a nice day. She sat down near the fountain. It could be that Maggie would arrive; it could be that in the cosmic scheme of things, the children arriving meant that Maggie would arrive and that she, Kate, would go back to the

States and leave her room to the children and that balance would be restored.

"You want a pastry?" Dixie said.

He was right there with a plastic bag of cinnamon swirls and raisin buns. "Maybe later."

He sat down in the chair next to hers, the bag of pastries on his lap, his face up to the sun. Their chairs were turned in the same direction, toward the kitchen, and they sat side by side that way, not looking at each other. Kate wished she had her sunglasses. He had his and he could hide behind them, though that was not his style, to hide. Still, she felt exposed—her face unwashed, her long hair unbraided, unbrushed, kinking just slightly from the humidity, the sleep still in her eyes, that bit of rot in the corner behind her thick lenses—and he was not. He'd been up for hours, said his prayers, showered, read whatever he read, had his coffee by himself the way he liked it. She knew how he fixed it. She'd watched him one morning: he heated the milk in an enamel saucepan and poured the very black coffee and the steamed milk simultaneously into a specific mug he preferred, a wide blue mug. He wore a pair of putty-colored shorts and a polo shirt. His Birkenstocks needed repair; their soles were worn down nearly to the cork. There was the grace of chosen poverty about him, of practical clothes treasured. Kate liked the hair on his body, the spring of it, the way the sun brought out the different colors, blond, strawberry blond, red. She admitted that to herself while he sat there, kindly talking bird-talk to Posh as the parrot climbed up on his finger.

"I don't know how much I can give," Kate finally said.

"What do you mean?"

She nodded toward the kitchen. "You know."

"Look how thin they are."

"I see that."

"They've been using cobbler's glue. To ward off hunger."

"How do you know?"

"He told us. It's no secret. Street kids live like that." He set Posh down.

Marta came to the kitchen door. She watched them. Her muddy corte had not been washed in a long time. Kate could barely make out its color.

"There're ten thousand more like them."

Kate said nothing.

"Lino wants to return them to their village."

"To who?"

"Someone'll take them in. He'll find someone."

She said, "Meanwhile—"

Lino had turned on the radio; music racketed forth, horns and drums, with whooping and trills of marimba.

Dixie said, "There's a cot in the bodega. Or there's the front room."

Marta came shyly out into the courtyard. She circled indirectly over to Kate and laid her head on Kate's lap, a feral gesture, like an animal eliciting petting. Kate tucked the girl's hair behind one ear. At that angle she could see that Marta's nose was swollen inside, the membranes red and puffy from the glue.

Quietly, almost inaudibly, Dixie said, "You have wonderful hands."

"Come on," Kate said. "Sometime I'll show you my scars."

"That's part of it."

Kate gave him a look intended to silence him.

Dixie said, "You two look alike."

Kate laughed. "Like ragamuffins?"

"That's not what I meant."

"She's going to have to have a bath before I'll accept that."

"Give it a go."

"Quiere bañar?" Kate said to Marta.

Marta lay very still, her eyes shut. She had grabbed a fistful of Kate's caftan.

Kate thought of Mayan women she had seen posing for tourists. They would insist that the photographer wait while they combed out their long and shining indigo hair. She whispered, "Your hair is very pretty. We can wash it and make it smell good."

Marta stood up straight and placed her hand in Kate's.

"How old do you think she is?" Kate said.

"Ten, Eduardo says. But he seemed uncertain. Tiene diez años, sí, Marta?"

Marta waited, ignoring him.

Kate said, "She's small."

Just how small, Kate discovered in the bathroom. Without her clothes Marta looked as though she were about seven years old. Her legs thin at the thigh. Her hair dry and brittle. Her toenails ragged and long. Kate coaxed her to sit in a plastic laundry tub and that was a heartening sight, the steam rising around Marta in the yellow tub. Kate sang to her, just murmurous repetitive songs, "Row, Row, Row Your Boat," and "Intsy, Wintsy Spider." She soaped her all over with a lavender-scented soap. She washed her hair and conditioned it. She wrapped her afterward in a beach towel, sat her on the toilet lid, and trimmed her toenails. Kate's scattered self concentrated, pulled together, as she knelt beside the toilet.

Now I have cared for many children.

To do that you have to cut off pieces of your heart. You have to stop thinking about them and just keep on bandaging or keep on cleaning sores that fill again with pus the minute you are through or keep on watching, sometimes watching and waiting is all you are capable of. When a baby wants to be born but something is stopping that baby and the crown of his head keeps blooming from her, bloody crown, so soft, you can't imagine how soft it all is at the beginning, the bones, the head, the skin, and in many cases there is little I can do but wait, and it won't do me any good to be caught up in the emotion of the moment whether we are talking about a birth or whether we are talking about a death or worse, a maimed child, someone in the way of the war. Children are in the way of the butchers. We always give the butchers a wide berth, don't we. The children are whole when they are born, whole and perfect, los milagros, and then they are not. Think of their bodies, the skin still fine as baby skin, the ease with which they smile, but they have had their temples blown away or their facial bones crushed or their eardrums ruptured. Their teeth may be blocking their throats; blood clots or a tongue may keep them from breathing. The portion of the brain that stimulates breathing may have been damaged and I can think only of stopping the bleeding and keeping the airways open. I am telling you about medical emergencies. I cannot think in that moment of all the music they will never hear or all the concepts they will never understand or all the wonder lost to them, no, no, I can never think of that, the exchange of wonder for terror and sorrow in just a flash. What kind of animals are we that we do this to our young?

But Marta was still whole. That was a miracle to me. She caught me off guard and I felt such tenderness for her as I knelt there, trimming each petite toenail and rubbing lotion into her tough feet and I can recall the smell of that lotion, just telling you reminds me, it is a smell that brings to mind Maggie, a verbena lotion, a little like lemon, and Marta loved that. I forgot myself while serving her. For a few moments. That can happen once in a rare while, the self disappears and that is a relief and perhaps some people serve for that very reason, to get beyond their puny selves. Still, I thought of not having a daughter and a sentimentality like a sickness came over me. I remembered hearing Maggie quoting Carl Jung when he said every woman extends backward into her mother and forward into her daughter and without a daughter I would never extend forward and I remember feeling that more deeply at that moment, the loss of that, for I was certain that I never would have children, though of course I was perplexed by that, even then, because I'd been taught by my mother and my aunts that having children was what one did with a life and with Marta there in the bathroom my heart hurt knowing that, so stupid, thinking I would never hear someone say, look, she has your eyes or listen, her voice sounds just like yours and because I would never have a daughter I would always be only a daughter and I would always be extending backward and I would always be ripe with old lessons, repeating the inevitable past instead of finding my way through whatever lay ahead. I would never completely grow up.

All of this occurred to me while I was cutting Marta's toenails and I felt she sensed this because she stayed right by my side and she never spoke but she stayed right by my side. That night she crept into my room and I raised the sheet and blanket and let her into bed with me. We slept curled together and I could imagine that I felt the way a new mother might feel, for just that night.

Sometime early the next morning, before daylight, Marta left Kate's bed. She and Eduardo stole out of the house as everyone slept. From the kitchen counter they took a cupful of coins—the kitty for Cokes and eggs and other odds and ends. Like a trickle Marta and Eduardo joined the river of orphan children flowing down to Guatemala City from the homeland of the Maya.

"Kate?" Dixie said.

"Mm. Yes," Kate said without opening her eyes.

"You have a hankering for anything special from the market?"

She watched him from behind her sunglasses. In his Panama hat. They'd had a few hours to overcome the thwart of the children stealing out at dawn. Now she felt a strange concoction of loss and violation. Lino had already left for the capital to see if he could find them. She wanted most of all to tell Maggie.

Jude lingered at the front door, a straw basket on her arm. She unbolted the door and held it open. Cars rumbled by, and a white bus with its windows down. "We'd better get going," she said genially, forcefully.

Kate said to Dixie, "Whatever you get is fine."

"Well, do you want to come along?"

She shook her head. "I have to go to GUATEL later."

"Jude says the phones were down this morning."

"What's going on?"

"There were tanks on the streets in Guate. Yesterday. But that's all over."

"So I can't call out."

"That's what I hear. But maybe by now—"

"Well, I just don't feel up to dealing with the market."

"Are you all right?"

She lifted her sunglasses to her forehead and met his gaze. She thought of Cecelia, her baby skin against her cheek.

"Do you want to beat the rain," Jude said, "or not?"

Kate said, "Lino looking is a lost cause. Isn't it?"

Dixie didn't answer. He glanced toward Jude, started to speak, then hesitated.

Kate said, "Maybe you can tell me. When's Ginger actually moving out?"

"She's pretty unpredictable. I hope she hasn't done anything irrevocable. You're after her room?"

"It might not be worthwhile to move," Kate said, sliding her sunglasses on again and looking away. "I'm not going to be here very long."

"I left five Qs on the kitchen counter. For the water man, if he comes." He went over to a hook on the wall, took down two mesh bags, and joined Jude, who had stepped out into the street. The bolt on the door ka-chunked when he shut it. Then—the glorious emptiness.

Posh squawked from the fern, his home under the colonnade.

She liked being there alone. With Posh. And the skeletons dancing on either side of the kitchen door. The fountain water prisming. Next door someone was building an addition; even the hammering did not bother her.

Her eyes were drawn over and over to Sunny and Ben's padlocked bedroom door. She kept going back to the padlock the way your tongue goes back to a canker sore. Somewhere there was a key to that lock. She pictured the wafer-thin key on a keychain that Sunny would keep in her skirt pocket. Or maybe Ben would place it in his wallet. She thought that if she could go into their bedroom she would know the reason why they weren't there.

She would go to GUATEL and wait and see. She wanted to know about the televisions, the clinic, Maggie's time in Ruinas with Bob

Elliott, and Cecelia; she wanted, craved, news of Cecelia, her baby tricks. Maggie's voice, no matter what she said, would be an abiding and familiar reassurance. That was the point in time she looked forward to, the only point in time.

Time had expanded in her idleness.

For dinner she sometimes ate black beans and tortillas and rice at a neighborhood café that smelled of grilled meat and lard and methane from sewage decomposing and passing through a cracked pipe in the patio. She tried to avoid the smells by sitting at a table close to the street. Then she would walk back to Sunny and Ben's along the darkening road. Once inside the house she counted it a good sign if there was no one about and she had to speak to no one. She could simply go to the bathroom and then go in her room and close up the shutters. Drink. And read. And mull over all that had happened to her. Almost every night in her room, the rain would cross over the tile roof like cats' paws. She had a fifth of gin and a quart can of grapefruit juice and a glass that felt good in her hand, pebbled and weighty.

She had eavesdropped on Jude and Dixie on more than one occasion. Their struggle persisted, a struggle Jude picked up whenever they had a spare moment.

"Don't do this," Jude had said. "The longer you stay away, the harder it'll be to come back."

"That's not the way I see it."

"I'm almost afraid to ask again—how do you see it?"

"The longer I have to consider," Dixie said, "the more I learn about why."

"Talking's not getting us anywhere."

Or once—

"I don't want to hear about your dialogue. You've got fancy terms for all of it. It's very seductive."

"I'm sorry, Jude. We each must go where we're led."

"You're kidding yourself."

Kate pieced together their conflict: Dixie's bishop had asked him to spend the time in Antigua with a discerning heart. Did he want to be a priest or not? Jude didn't like Kate, she was sure of that. Simply because Dixie did.

Maybe the phones had been down but by two o'clock the GUATEL office was packed and functioning. A string of Japanese students chatted in the long line. A Mayan woman with a newborn sat on the edge of the sofa. An older man—with white hair and a goatee and liver spots on his hands and face—stood by himself near the front door. A slick boyish man in a pinstripe suit cracked his knuckles and waited. You could taste the waiting in the room—like something sweet that might turn bitter without warning.

Kate gave the clerk the number of the clinic in Managua. She decided to stand rather than perch on the edge of the sofa. Immediately she felt a blister on the ball of her foot, a burning she hadn't noticed until that moment of standing still. Her sneakers had worn out and she thought of buying new ones, of what they would cost, of how much money she had left, of the credit card she had left for Maggie. Maggie—she could picture so many things about her. A bandanna and a long cotton skirt. Her jewelry box, a Japanese tea box. All the bracelets and earrings and necklaces tangled there. African trading beads. Silver and copper. Brass and gold. Leather and amethyst and turquoise and jade. Love of Maggie: this was a good thought. She held that thought. Or tried to hold that thought. She's wild. A wild woman. I like that, Deaver had said. That wasn't love, Kate determined. That was desire and not even the fullness of desire, its full potential. Deaver thought desire was contained in the experience of penetration. Discrete units of pleasure. A locked box you left behind once you came. Or had she been the one who saw it that way? Had Deaver been an accomplice to her own misconceptions about desire, that storm, working change in all it touched? She'd never thought of it that way before. She'd been too much in the path of it.

"Juanita! No contesta."

"Akihiko! Número siete!"

"Luis! Está ocupado."

She waited. Ten minutes passed. The blister nagged.

"Catarina! Número ocho!"

In the wooden booth Kate picked up the dirty receiver.

Maggie said, "Hola," Kate said, "Hola," at the very same moment.

"Am I glad to hear from you," Maggie said. "How are you?"

"I'm sort of in a holding pattern."

"The TVs came!"

"That's a relief." A momentary silence, then Kate said, "How were you—when you found out I was gone?"

"I was okay."

"Are you sure?"

"If you're doing what you want."

"I had to. It felt like I had to."

"So what's it like there? How're Sunny and Ben?"

"Well. There's plenty of everything. Food and shampoo and hot water. But Sunny and Ben aren't here."

"Oh?"

"Sunny's in Guate. Ben's still in the States."

"That must've been a disappointment. Getting there to find them gone."

"Sort of. Yeah. It was. But when you get here . . ."

Silence. Kate waited.

Maggie finally said, "Sweetie, it's going to be a bit longer. I need some leeway."

Kate didn't say anything. She felt a knot in her throat.

"Are you all right?"

"Mm-huh."

"So, Kate—ask me about Bob Elliott."

"How's Bob Elliott?"

"Kate—he's a nice man. I mean, really a nice man. I'm going back out to Ruinas with him while he finishes up his work. I'm actually learning some things."

Kate laughed.

"About water systems, goofball. He wants to finish up soon. It's harder than ever. Anywhere near the conflict."

"How's the baby?"

"I've only seen her once. She's sweet as sugar pie."

"Did she get her last shot?"

"María's handling that."

"How did María take my leaving?"

"Well. She took it well. She knows—you know—she knows we can't stay forever."

"Are you bringing this guy here?"

"Maybe. What would you think of that?"

"Do whatever makes you happy."

"I've been happy." She paused. "I really have been."

They were quiet again. Then Maggie said, "I'm sorry . . . about what happened to you. With Deaver."

"I don't want to talk about that."

"Do you have someone there to talk to?"

"Not about that."

Maggie was silent. A buzz eddied in the phone line.

"When's the soonest you can come?" Kate said. "Pack up old Bob Elliott and get over here."

Maggie hesitated; Kate could feel her hesitating. "It might be as long as a month."

Mid-June. A whole livelong month.

"Call Paul, would you," Maggie said, "and ask him to send us a bank draft. To you. There. That can take forever. Tell him we're coming home. With bells on."

"Will do."

"Are you all right?"

"Better than I might've imagined I'd be. Under the circumstances. I feel free."

"Do you want me to come sooner?"

"That wouldn't be fair, now, would it?"

"Thank you, Kate. We all miss you. Love you."

She said, "Love you too. Should I call again? Maybe that's not necessary. It's muy caro."

"Kate—please don't go without me."

"I won't."

"And baby yourself," Maggie said.

Baby yourself. An imperative they used in times of stress. It was permissible to baby yourself. If you didn't do it, who would?

She stepped down into the street and nearly tripped over a young girl selling pulseras from a basket. Then she remembered Marta. She'd forgotten to tell Maggie; she had completely forgotten. It had not been that kind of phone call. Intimacy did not come easily at a public telephone.

She had not pressed Maggie about Deaver. It did not matter now. Though later it would matter and she would save those questions until Maggie arrived. She didn't want to care and by the time Maggie arrived she wouldn't care so much anymore. She hadn't been required to go through the loss of a love in a long time. She'd been grieving already, before, while she and Deaver were still together. That had given her a head start. She'd been experiencing the gradual loss, the way you can lose some physical ability imperceptibly over time, night sight or strength in your hands. And then you wake up one day and realize what's no longer there for you. And the grieving has been going on under the surface for a while. Things you thought were crucial peel away, until one day you give up life itself. She'd seen old people do that. If not with grace, with courage they hadn't a choice about.

Kate did not have the patience to stand in line to call Paul. Tomorrow would be soon enough.

She went home; she had begun to call El Petén #3 home. This was the beginning of waiting all over again. But progress had been made. The televisions had arrived. Maggie was in good spirits. She consoled herself with all of that and she consoled herself with gin. And sleep. Even the gin did not disrupt her sleep. She would come to her door and look out to the courtyard about ten in the morning to check out the weather. She would yawn and stretch and brush her hair and she would be wearing sweats or a long blue cotton nightgown. Posh would squawk at her and Dixie would say, Good morning, merry sunshine. What makes you wake so soon? You scare the little stars away and frighten away the moon. She would be a little hungover, her skin a little raw, her head achy, and she would laugh, an ironic laugh at herself.

Lino returned from Guate without Eduardo and Marta. "Es impossible," he said to Kate. "You should go and see for yourself. The streets are full of children."

Kate did not know if she could stand to see for herself.

Dixie wore a red kitchen mitt and was shifting a hot skillet from the stovetop to the table when the lights went out. Music from the radio died. The refrigerator ceased humming with a spiraling whine like air being let from a balloon. There was no window in the kitchen and Kate noticed that fully for the first time. Darkness bloomed around them.

Lino said, his words measured, "There was talk of this."

"Sure," Ginger said, exasperated. She'd come back, but she hadn't said for how long.

He lowered his voice still more, ducked his head. "My friends who are friends of los subversivos—they say this will happen."

"You don't know that," Ginger said.

Dixie slid the skillet onto an iron trivet, turned on one of the stove's burners so that for a minute—while he felt around in the cupboard for candles—the kitchen was lit by the blue fire ring of gas. He lit a candle and turned off the stove. Their eyes adjusted to the grainy skirt of candlelight. Steam rose from the skillet. In the dark, Kate's sense of smell intensified. Moist rice, redolent cumin, the candle wax, the gas of the stove just extinguished.

"No biggie," Dixie said. "Let's eat."

"The frigging lights are out," Ginger said. She had been bouncing a green ball on the floor and the ball had veered off toward the counter into a pile of newsprint wrappers and bags from the market. "How can we eat?"

"Give-us-a-break, Gin-ger," Lino said.

"Very good," Kate said. "Very good English. Muy apropriado."

"You're hungry, aren't you?" Dixie said. He sat down and with a snap opened his cloth napkin.

Ginger stamped her foot churlishly.

Lino laughed and waited. When they'd all bowed their heads, he exhaled slowly, as though to rid himself of his search for the children, his irritation at Ginger. Then he said grace.

Kate watched curiously, surreptitiously. She couldn't quite bring herself to fold her hands, though she remembered doing that as a girl at holiday meals when her grandfather would endure her grandmother's blessing. Kate's own mother did not say grace, though every evening she had made them kneel on their beds and say an Our Father and a Hail Mary while she listened.

Dixie made the sign of the cross. Candlelight flashed on the stucco walls.

Kate felt the brief ease of the moment: a day took so much boring care; it was hard to hold to gratitude. Dixie paused, with his hand on the wooden spoon handle beside the skillet. He smiled tentatively at Kate. She gazed away from those eyes.

"Do you ever, like, wonder if you're going to survive being here?" Ginger said to no one in particular. Her sulk was prominent and obvious, her mouth pinched, her eyes downcast.

Lino lifted his plate and Dixie spooned the rice and vegetables onto it. Then Kate, then Ginger. He served himself last.

Kate got up and took her plate out to the courtyard and set it on the edge of the fountain. In Managua she had lived without electricity many evenings. To her it was nothing new. She shuffled to

her room—a gait intended to belie her impatience with Ginger—
and found two candles in a drawer. Back at the fountain she lit the
candles, dripped wax onto the rough concrete of the fountain's rim,
and ground the candles into the soft wax to secure them. She eased
down into the slingback chair, relaxed. She could hear the others
talking in the kitchen. There were no sounds in the neighborhood,
no radios, no fireworks. She ate alone, a chore. It had been the
same almost every night except for the smell of Dixie's cooking,
which varied: cinnamon from a mango pie, sauteed onions, basily
tomato sauce. She had allowed herself to eat communally only once
or twice a week. She would stay in her room or in the shadowed
courtyard while they took their meals. She was wounded and she
tended her wound; she both punished and fed herself with solitude.

Just as she finished and set her plate on the cement floor, the
lights came on again. A sigh throughout the town was nearly audible. The kitchen light glowed; a yellow lightbulb lit the back of the
courtyard near the bodega where the cleaning supplies were kept.
Where Kate sat it was pleasantly dim.

Dixie came out. His eyebrows drooped, flecked with gray. He
still napped every day, still became fatigued easily. His face was getting back its color, though, a ruddiness Kate associated with living
in the mountains. He put his hands in his pants pockets and jingled
his change.

"Kate—we're here. Wouldn't you like to just talk sometime?"

Kate sighed. "I'm not sure I'm up to it."

"You might feel better for it."

She crossed her arms. A chill like cool fingers went up her back.
In the kitchen Lino and Ginger ran dishwater and tried out different radio stations. Ginger said, "It's not my turn. I'm not here
enough to take a turn."

Kate said, "I don't think you have any idea how much I feel like
running away."

"What're you running from?"

"Don't. Please."

"Skip it." He turned to go.

Kate blurted, "Do you have the key to Sunny's bedroom?"

Dixie faced her and folded his arms. He had long athletic arms. "The key?"

Before she could answer, there was a knock on the front door. He went to answer. She watched him go: his walk, his jaunt, the way he rolled energetically on the balls of his feet, his sweater dark and square like his strong back; he still had strength in spite of the damage done by his illness. Posh on his fern chittered for Dixie's attention as he walked by.

"Buenas noches. Come in, come in. I've been wondering where you were," she heard him say, but she could not see—from where she sat—who was invited in. A murmuring female voice. Dixie and whoever it was huddled just inside the door, in the shadow of the foyer. He shut the door and locked it. He said, "No, no, it's fine, está bien, Vidalúz," and just as Kate heard her name Vidalúz emerged from the shadows into the light of the courtyard.

"Vidalúz!"

"B· enas noches, Catarina!"

Dixie stood beside Vidalúz, his hand on her elbow. She was dressed in her traditional clothes. Nearly emanating light. Great care had been taken with everything she wore: a starched white cotton blouse with a square neckline embroidered in red and blue stitches; a bright red skirt, not gathered, but instead a folded length of fabric wound around her hips and secured with a handwoven sash. Her hair was thick and black and pinned up in a loose knot. Her headpiece wove within the coils of her hair—a multicolored sash with pom-poms at either end, like a soft crown. Her complexion was scrubbed clean and dusky, pure. She held herself with regal bearing.

"Pues, se conocen?" Dixie said.

Vidalúz was learning English. "Sí, God brought us together," she said.

Dixie guided her to a director's chair beside Kate. Vidalúz sat with her spine quite straight, her hands patiently cupped in her lap. Dixie sat down again on the fountain rim.

120

"Are you all right?" Kate said.

"I am better," Vidalúz said. To Dixie she said, "We met under very bad circumstances. Dangerous circumstances. Father Ryan, Hector is in custody." She said this and waited for the news to sink in. "It has been nine days."

"Why have you waited to tell me?"

"I was afraid. I went home. To dress properly. To see my people."

"Are you sure they still have him?"

"He would come home." Vidalúz paused. "He would." She glanced at Kate, then Dixie, qualmishly.

"It's all right," he said. And then to Kate, "She and Hector have been working to stop the civil patrols. You've heard of them?"

Kate said, "Is it forced conscription?"

"In a manner of speaking. It's not the army. These are civil patrols. Neighbors—all men over fifteen—are required to serve several shifts a week guarding each village. The farmers aren't able to provide for their families—they spend so much time on civil patrol. They're not paid for it. Many have died while on patrol. And the constitution says that the patrols are voluntary. But of course—"

"How can you stop them?" Kate said.

"I'll tell you, I'll tell you," he said. "But first, Vidalúz, por favor, tell us what happened."

Vidalúz sighed. In Spanish she began her story. "We had been in the capital for a meeting," she said.

Kate drew her chair near.

"It was not a good meeting. They smiled at us and went behind our backs. They would not touch us in the capital because Shannon—"

Dixie put up his hand to interrupt her. "Shannon's a North American woman," he said in English to Kate, "who usually stays with them as a witness."

Vidalúz went on. "Shannon was with us. Shannon was not feeling well. She wanted to go to the doctor here, in Antigua. She wanted to go to the Canadian doctor. They kept her at the hospital—she has asthma. And we were picked up near the market. They shoved us into a car—" She began to cry. "Hector begged them to let me go."

Dixie hunched forward, frowning.

"First they separated us. But I could hear Hector groaning. They took my traje. They gave me ladino clothes to put on. They made me undress—" Her face fell into a fragile state. The woman she had prepared, her public self, disappeared. She cried out again and pressed her hand against her mouth.

They waited while she cried. Dixie attended to her, acknowledged her, by waiting. Then he took her hand and offered, "You don't have to."

"Someone should know," she said, her voice trembling. "You should know—"

Lino and Ginger were singing along to the radio, some Madonna song. Their spat was over. The golden light poured forth from the convivial kitchen. They laughed within.

"Where did they take you?" Dixie said.

"It was here. In Antigua!"

"But where?"

"No sé, Father. No sé. When they let me go they took me through many hallways. They let me out on the park.

"You are communist, they said to me. They made me drink water. Many glasses. They would not allow me to relieve myself. They said there were no toilets for communists. I stood before them, Father, wetting myself in front of the soldiers."

Kate closed her eyes as though to keep from seeing.

"They smeared my mouth with lipstick. One soldier bit me—"

"Vidalúz—"

"He bit my mouth until I bled."

No one said anything. Dixie held her hand.

Finally he said, "What did they want?"

"Names . . . they wanted names."

"How long were you there?"

"The next afternoon they let me go. That is when we met, Catarina."

Kate nodded. It was all she could do—nod along to Vidalúz's story.

Dixie said, "Why did they let you go?" Implicit in his words were, Why did they keep Hector?

"Pues, they want the others to know. They want me to do what I am doing. Telling you. And our friends in the highlands. They want to terrify us. They want us to crawl into our houses and never come out. They want us to lie down like dogs."

She sat up very straight in her chair. "I am useful this way. But Father, they want to be rid of Hector.

"I have been back to my village. I needed my clothes. The governor of my province sent me a bag of corn and a bag of beans. I sent a letter asking him if he would go on giving me food and he sent word to me, Yes, he said, if you can prove that your husband is dead."

Under his breath Dixie said, "How many more times can they get away with this?"

"Now I wait for a new witness. Shannon has gone home to California. I will wait for Hector. I am not going back to my village until they let Hector go. I am staying at a hotel—where the tipico vendors stay. Los Arboles Grande. You know the one? It is not expensive."

"You could stay here!" Kate cried.

"That's probably not wise," Dixie said. "Though I know a safe place you could stay. Two places. One here in Antigua. One at Lake Atitlán."

"We could protect her," Kate insisted.

"It's too obvious. She can come by once in a while, but to live here would draw too much attention. Trust me, Kate. There's more at stake than you're aware of."

Vidalúz said, "Sí, pues, Catarina. We must not stay together." She turned to Dixie. "For now I am all right at the hotel."

What they said was true. The offer had been selfish, and Kate felt justly corrected. She was sick of all roads leading back to her own desire, her own fear.

"I want Hector," Vidalúz said. "We need no more martyrs."

"Were you happy there?" Dixie said. "In Nicaragua?"

Kate was not prepared for such a question.

Vidalúz and Lino were gone. Lino had offered to walk her to her hotel. For twenty minutes Ginger had hunched over the kitchen table, smoking and memorizing verbs, then she had gone into her room and locked the door. Jude had arrived, declared her sleepiness, and gone straight to the bathroom to prepare for bed. Dixie and Kate had been sitting together with no words between them of their own. The words of Vidalúz hung in the night. A terrible echo.

"I had work I loved."

"Always a good thing," Dixie said, leaning forward, allowing Posh to step daintily up onto his forefinger. He brought the parrot to his chest; he cuddled him in one hand. He leaned back in his canvas chair to make a slanted surface of his stomach for the parrot to climb. Posh poked his beak into Dixie's buttonholes, into the pocket of his flannel shirt; he toddled upon his shoulder.

Kate said, "That kept me—"

"What?"

"Sane, I guess. In the face of—"

He watched her, waited. Kate pulled the afghan snugly around her shoulders. Wind slipped over the stucco wall.

124

Kate said, "You know—you see a lot of things that can make you crazy. Like Hector."

"I'm trying not to think about that right now," he said.

Kate let that pass. A balm, a silence. Then, "Vidalúz—what's her family like?"

"Her mother's all she has left. Here."

"Oh?"

"Her mother's Mayan. Her father was a union man. His picture's up on the wall of the Coca-Cola cafeteria. He died for the union."

"No brothers and sisters?"

"I never met them. They went into exile—in Costa Rica—before I knew her."

"Shouldn't she join them?"

"She won't."

Fireworks—what sounded like flares whizzing—went off in a neighboring yard. Kate grimaced. False forebearance.

Dixie said, "You want quiet—I go to the highlands once in a while. Maybe you'd like to come along." Posh had tucked himself into the crook of Dixie's elbow.

"I can't do that."

"They're usually quick trips."

She thought first of the business she should attend to: calling Paul, going to the bank, writing letters. She thought next of all the hours in his jeep, the coziness of road trips. "I can't do that."

"I just thought I'd try. To distract you."

The narrow wooden doors of the bathroom opened; Jude emerged, wrapped neck to toe in a chenille robe. She had swirled a towel turbanlike around her hair. She had scrubbed her face with Noxzema. Kate could smell it.

"Undeserved pain is redemptive," Jude said.

"That's one way to deal with it," Kate said. Actually, she thought she agreed with Jude, but the way Jude spoke—as though she alone were aware of this cosmic equation—elicited a bickering impulse from Kate.

"Where y'at, Jude?" Dixie said. Without waiting for an answer, he said, "Why do you reckon the lights went out?" He put Posh on the floor and the parrot flew in jagged flight up to the fern's leafy mews.

Jude came over to where they sat. She crossed her arms. There was something implacable about her. Passionless. As though her lack of passion could instill the same in others. A load she carried. A responsibility.

"No sé. But we're safe here," Jude said. And then pointedly, to Dixie, "Would you join me for a rosary tonight?"

They went into his room.

The light from his open door cast an orange shaft on the tiles of the colonnade. Kate sat out in the starry night. Marta was on her mind. Where did Marta end up sleeping every night? And she thought about Maggie. She got perspective, a little more perspective every day. She and Maggie had worked for eight years under adverse conditions. That was what really mattered to her when she thought of her life in decades. She felt almost steady under the afghan, its prickly woolenness. She had been sorry to see Dixie leave. The answers she gave him were puzzle parts that she was just beginning to realize fit together; some portrait would eventually emerge from the work she did to pry the answers from where they lay buried, in a place of dream and tenet, less mapped, less explored—a place he made her feel she had to go.

An evening sky, magenta with the smoggy sunset. Zone 2. All afternoon Dixie had wandered the parks, watching for Marta and Eduardo. It was not hard to wonder, Why search them out, in particular? Knots of street kids lived in every park or plaza, hustling money, glue, tortillas. But he had promised Kate and Lino. Now he walked the back streets. The attendants at the gas station waved. They remembered him.

At El Pacífico Sueño, Sunny answered his knock as though she'd been waiting. "Dix—" She took his hand. "Come in, come on in. I'm watching the China situation." Sunny—big-boned, nearly voluptuous—was still in her school clothes, a long denim jumper over a red turtleneck. She shut the door and locked it.

He kissed her cheek and breathed the scent of her long hair— spicy and suggestive of an elusive memory he could not quite conjure fully. He was glad to see her. Sunny stabilized him, oddly. She reminded him of Jude. Perhaps he was attracted to her friendship for just that reason; they related as siblings.

"Tea?" she said.

"Sure. Tea." She always remembered he did not want to be offered alcohol. He could imagine the clean bite of hard liquor on his tongue.

They went down the hallway and past the dim living room, where the television was on, past the workroom where Sunny and Vidalúz and Hector put out their monthly newspaper—*La Verdad de Hoy*. The workroom was the largest room in the house and lined with industrial gray-metal bookshelves piled with books and rolled-up maps. A computer, a fax machine, a phone, a printer, boxes of paper, many reams, piles of projects on the floor, bulging manila envelopes and files—a fluorescent tube bathed everything in its cool light. Blue pushpins dotted the relief map on one wall, each pushpin the death of someone they counted among their own. A journalist or union organizer or lawyer or teacher. Most recently, the owner of a bookstore where for a scant year they had been able to distribute *La Verdad de Hoy* and buy any book they wanted, in English or Spanish. She'd been shot in the head while driving near Lake Atitlán, on holiday with her cousin. The car of the marksman had sped away, dark and anonymous.

Dixie hung his rain parka on a wooden hook next to Ben's big, ratty Land's End parka and Vidalúz's plastic raincoat, the kind you could squeeze into its own pocket. They went into the kitchen and Sunny filled a kettle with water and set it over a burner on the apartment-sized gas stove. She opened cupboards, began pulling out tea boxes, a sugar bowl, a honey pot as she talked.

It was a shabby room, a utilitarian room, with faded melamine dishes, a few dented pans and skillets piled helter-skelter on the open shelves, cereal boxes and a partial loaf of bread on top of the pea-green refrigerator, whose motor growled and strained. Once Sunny had been a connoisseur of many things—wine, literature, handmade paper, fine ceramic pots, orchids—but he had not known her then. A bottle of Russian vodka with a gray bird on the label stood like a staple in the center of the table next to the strawberry jam and peanut butter.

She poured boiling water over the tea bags. Dixie doctored his tea with honey and a slice of lemon that lay withering in a bowl on the counter.

In the living room they sat down side by side on the sofa. The television was tuned to C-SPAN, with no voice-over, only the camera roving among a crowd of Chinese who were dwarfed by rippling red banners lettered in gold.

"How's Kate doing?" Sunny said.

Dixie sighed. He set his mug of tea on the coffee table. "Why doesn't she go on home? If that's what she wants."

Sunny said, "Maggie and she are a team."

His tea was a beautiful color, in a yellow mug. He sipped it, working on mindfulness.

He said, "She and Jude don't get along."

"Why, do you suppose?"

Dixie shook his head. "You know Jude."

On television there flashed an image of a woman sitting on the hood of an army truck, reading from a sheet of hand-lettered Chinese. She wore a white headband and her face was twisted, tearful.

"I bet you're good for Kate."

He said, "I don't know about that."

The C-span camera zeroed in on a pickup truck, its bed loaded with policemen in army-green uniforms, their pants creased sharply, their collars lacquer-red—these policemen stood and saluted the Chinese students. Their faces were joyful, though the faces of the students were pressed with fatigue.

"Amazing," Dixie said. He drank his tea, his soothing tea. Then he got to his point: "Vidalúz is talking about a vigil. Just her and a few witnesses. Outside the embassies of what she considers to be the free world."

"Where would she stay?"

"Not here."

"No."

A man's voice began commentary on the television. Sunny picked up the remote and turned up the volume. Sunny said, "Do you think Hector's dead? I know you don't want to think about it, but—"

He squeezed his eyes shut.

"Hey, hey, hey," Sunny said. She put her hand on his arm.

". . . can't help it."

"I know, Dix."

The room grew dim with night coming on, the blocky furniture fading into shadow. Dixie leaned forward, his elbows on his knees, and hung his head. Sunny took her hand away and waited.

"How're you feeling?" she said. "Physically, I mean?"

"Not very strong," he said, "but better."

Sunny said, "I guess we shouldn't assume the worst. But it's hard not to."

They stared at the Chinese students. Above Zone 2, a helicopter chopped suddenly overhead; he imagined it, a snaggly disruption in the sweet evening.

Finally he said, "Jude thinks Vidalúz should get out. For just a while. Go to the States. She needs protection. It won't be wasted time. We can set up interviews. That sort of thing. Ben can carry her across."

Sunny set her empty mug down on the tile floor hard enough to make a sound like a crack. She said, "I doubt she'll go for that." She stood and scooped up the day's newspapers, dumped them into a basket behind the sofa.

"What's wrong?" Dixie said.

"Nothing."

"Come clean."

She kept her back to him. Fiddled with some books on the end table, rearranged them. Neatened up whatever lay there. Matches. An eyeglass case. Forcefully she said, "I'd like Ben to stay here. At least a month or so."

In the light of all they thought about and denying where they'd come from materially and their friends disappearing and the weekly blue pushpins on the map, Sunny missing Ben was a relief to Dixie. It was so commonplace as to seem profound.

As though she were ashamed of missing her husband, Sunny turned around and punched her hands into her jumper pockets. She sighed. "We'll work it out. Don't worry."

Her face looked haggard from where he sat, in the long blue shadows of night. Her hair was silvering in long streaks; he had known her long enough to see that happen. On television the Chinese students were getting up to face the dawn in good cheer. Their blankets and bedrolls overlapped each other and necessities—toilet paper, water bottles, fruit—lay scattered across them.

"I'm not worried," he said. "Not about that." He drained his mug of cold tea. "I'm not." He got up to go. He had only intended to drop in for a few minutes. "If you want to know the truth, I'm envious. And worn out."

"It's killing you. Hector is."

He clenched his jaw, sucked in his breath. "Don't," he said. Then, "God bless, God bless."

She took his hand and squeezed it.

She would return to her work, to writing an inflammatory editorial or marking grade six worksheets or faxing a comrade in the States or mending socks so that she would not have to buy new ones or whatever else Sunny considered work.

He left her there.

He wanted home, the safety of that, however illusory. All the long dark bus ride through the mountains to Antigua he allowed himself an amorphous yearning, rich and secret and sinful, a feeling he attached in a fitful way first to one thing, then another. He fretted about mass. He missed it. He'd heard of underground ex-priests saying mass for bands of the radical faithful. What kind of life would that be? He missed the two moments of the mass he cherished most, raising the crisp ivory-colored Eucharist skyward, kneeling, surrendering, that's how he thought of it, and the invitation, Lift up your hearts, and his people answering, We lift them up to the Lord. We lift them up to the Mystery. We lift them up to all that we do not know. He did not believe that the people envisioned that lifting up of hearts the same way he did. They lifted them up to El Señor, to an anthropomorphic God, a cutout God in flowing robes above the clouds. Above the planet Earth. Sometimes he struggled to reconcile what he believed and what his people believed. Other times he allowed that every sentient being was evolving. There was no rushing. There was nowhere to go.

The women in his parish were eager to talk through these issues; close to magic and creation, they had their own ideas about God; he could only believe that this was so because they gave birth. The men were hard to reach. They'd been disenfranchised by the war, unable to support their families, forced to abandon their traje or risk dying. Though Lino was on the verge of some nearly inarticulate understanding; Lino was his hope for his parish. His longing circled anxiously around Lino. Where is he right now? Is he safe? Please keep him safe and out of harm's way. Please—

He felt a twinge, fear in his bowels.

He thought of all this. His plans. His own impatience and his own sadness. Doubts that had led him to ask for the leave of absence.

The Indians on the bus were quiet, tired, everyone swaying slightly in the curves. A dark bus ride was a good time-out. His selfishness could be excused for just those forty minutes. He pictured Sam in a Christmas snapshot, with his arms around his family. And his sweet-faced wife, who had become the mother of three children in her forties—boom! boom! boom! she always said when she described it, as though the babies had arrived of their own accord from somewhere outside her and Sam. Whenever he thought of them—often, for the photograph was right there on his dresser— he had to decide whether to go down the road of his usual temptation, the road of wondering what if—

He had not surrendered. This too astonished him. He could only assume that God did not intend for him to surrender; perhaps he would have to die to finally surrender to the celibate, solitary life. He who loved women had chosen the priesthood. He had not known when he was young that his love for women was extraordinary or that not all men loved women.

He loved the way women bent their heads together when they talked. He loved the way they moved, the way they easily expressed delight or sorrow. He loved the way their fingers and their hands could make the finest weaving or soothe a child or pat a tortilla or brush a vain eyebrow. They were always doing. The daily ease and consolations of home and community were made by women from almost nothing but their love. When he was in training, he thought that everyone in seminary probably felt toward women the way he did, that they were lovely and mysterious and interesting and dangerous. Not so. The issue was complicated; he struggled not just with the question of intimacy but also with pride: if he who loved women intensely could resist the comfort of sensuality, he must be strong. The bus shifted haltingly above the cliffs.

He marveled at how subtle sin becomes, surprised again by all its glittering nuance.

Dixie and I missed the Tiananmen Square massacre. We were making phone calls—arrangements—or looking for Marta and Eduardo, it seems to me.

By June 4, 1989, Vidalúz Rodríguez Terez had agreed to return to the States with Ben Hires. She had heard nothing from Hector and Dixie had convinced her that she would not last long in a vigil outside any embassy. The death squads would find a way to be rid of her without making a fuss. It was not difficult to imagine them killing her in broad daylight. At the end of May a political candidate was murdered, a former guerrilla who had come back to Guate and to his family life and to politics and to democracy. He came home to democracy. He wanted to believe the lies, and he was gunned down while walking his daughter to school. In a nice neighborhood. With expensive shops nearby, Gucci watches in the window. It has happened to thousands. The men who kill are called unknown men by the newspapers. Their gangs have names like Eye for an Eye and Purple Rose and the Hawk of Justice. Vidalúz would be more useful to her people in the States, Dixie argued, where she could travel and speak and educate others about the situation. I was not privy to the specifics. I did not know the extent of Sunny's involvement. But he had promised that Vidalúz would stay in touch and her reports from the States would be printed in *La Verdad de Hoy* and the people would know that they had more support from beyond the border. Their friends in Arizona would put her in touch with the press and there would be stories—big stories in big papers, Dixie told her—about Hector, about the civil patrols, about the night she was tortured.

The Chinese students died at the hands of their distant comrades in uniform or they dispersed to other countries and took up false names or they were imprisoned in China for treason, falling into the black well of political detention. Outside China responses varied. There was outrage, cliché of the network news, a tidy sadness, feeble attempts to slap the hands of authorities. Now I hear a trade war is about to begin between the United States and China. In China there is little or no control of the sale and distribution of U.S.-made videos and CDs and audiocassettes. That's a fine issue to cause enmity between nations. Who has the right to watch Rod Stewart perform in a three-minute MTV video? Who has the right to a slasher movie? They can smash the Goddess of Democracy but they can't steal our shabby underart. I don't have the right to call it ours, do I?

When I was a girl I kept a scavenged snakeskin in a shoebox under my bed. I loved that dry shed snakeskin much more than the living, muscular, unpredictable snake. The government authorities are like that. They say they kill students and demonstrators and writers and artists and union organizers because they do not want their countries to be plunged into chaos. But we humans are still in the messing-around stage, and what they call chaos is only form becoming more beautiful, more human. The Chinese students had a passion for form. They surged toward elegance and a new design for China, a completion of what has been in the making. They had the courage to imagine a new form.

Dixie and I followed the situation on television, first at Doña Luisa's, among the travelers and weekenders from the capital, then at the safe house near the jade factory, a house he had a key to, owned by a woman I never had the opportunity to meet. The

Guatemalans who sat in Dona Luisa's restaurant and ignored the China situation on CNN are merely keepers of their form, a democracy like a lost snakeskin bestowed on them by the United States and maintained by weapons sent to them from South Africa and Israel. The Guatemalans who envisioned new forms were not in that restaurant eating North American hamburgers and granola. A displaced people, they were in exile, speaking out in churches in Arizona and California or they were changing their names in Chiapas and trying to forget the bloodshed they'd witnessed or they were crowded into refugee camps in Campeche eating Danish pork from cans or they were living underground in Guate, fearful of every task, going out for a newspaper or watching a junior high soccer game. The silence of the grave perpetually threatens them.

There have been many martyrs.

Teachers.

Campesinos.

Factory workers.

Priests.

Union organizers.

Opposition political candidates.

Journalists.

Students.

Lawyers.

Some were massacred in their villages, some were picked up alone and left to die alone, in some ditch or field.

You still hear the stories, if you stay in Guatemala long enough you'll hear them. Some say it's the liberal press we have to blame. They say no massacres occurred. In the face of story after story, they say no massacres occurred. The people telling the stories must be suffering collective hallucinations. You hear about babies being torn in two for sport, you hear about an eleven-year-old boy castrated by soldiers. But don't rely on hearsay. Read the papers. It's right there in the daily papers. University students getting off a bus for classes and being gunned down in the daytime. The sunlight's like paradise, isn't it? Picture that. You hear about government soldiers being trained to drink the blood of their victims. You hear about someone holding a baby's feet over burning coals and noses cut off with machetes and villages burned to the ground. And so on.

"Touching Demise" is a parlor game I once played in Antigua, a twist on charades.

One Day of the Dead I'd gone to Santiago Sacatepequez to see the big kites flying in a cemetery. I sat with friends on a chalky-white mausoleum, watching the men and boys fly the paper kites that were as big as houses. The things we did in the cemetery. Right on the graves. Changing diapers. Listening to John Lennon. Eating ice cream or tortillas smeared with avocado. Playing tag. Flirting. Holding hands. Getting drunk. Waiting for love to be decisive. Helping an old man in a white dress shirt drape a pine garland around the next mausoleum over.

The kites were like patchwork quilts of tissue paper stretched over bamboo frames with long rag tails. How old does a piece of clothing have to be in Guatemala before it becomes a kite tail?

We were many hundred strong in the graveyard on Day of the Dead. We were Indians, ladinos, gringos, Europeans, wealthy, middle class, poor and dirt poor, and those pretending to be poor—world travelers making do for six months on a thousand dollars. We were teenagers in Guess? jeans from the capital, Indian mothers breast-feeding babies, campesinos in Sunday-best clothes, boys playing with fire on a stick. Steam from the volcano Fuego smudged the sky. Getting the kites aloft was a problem. They went up on the tentative wings of November wind before crashing or drifting down.

The cemetery was on a hillside. Above were the mausoleums of the wealthy and these were painted turquoise or blue or white with yellow trim. Below were the pauper mounds. The concrete pauper mounds were piled with dirt and strewn with the golden flores del muerto. Dust smeared the entire panorama of the cemetery. Clouds above, dust below. Behind us sturdy young trees flourished on the upper slopes, lucky with the decay of the land.

The kites were not the reason we had gathered there. We were there to look at the lie the flesh tells. It breaks your heart, doesn't it, when you can't remember the voice of a dead loved one? A laugh, a whisper. What you would give to hear that one more time.

Back in Antigua in the chill of the evening we rushed to the market for guisquils and tomatoes and onions and long soft pasta and butter cookies. Friends came over with bottles of red wine and we ate and drank our fill and then we played the game.

You pantomime the death of someone famous and the others guess whose death it is. You place stones in your jacket pocket and you walk into a sea and drown. You drink from a poisoned chalice. You stand slump-shouldered in round sunglasses and someone shoots you in your belly. The more recent the death, the less amusing the charade.

Far along in the red wine, we talked about the afterlife.

We talked about cremation.

We talked about death in many forms, but no one mentioned the stories of the disappeared blackening the newspapers every day.

Out of the blue Enrique, a kindergarten teacher, said, "Think of the difference between torture and death, the gulf between the two, the desire one induces for the other. Think of that."

"I will learn more English," Vidalúz said.

"Sí quiere," Dixie said. "But there will always be a translator with you. You'll know what to say."

"I will know what to say. The truth is simple and I am not afraid."

Kate thought that Vidalúz was afraid, but she understood the need to say otherwise. It could keep you on an even keel to lie to yourself about fear.

They were driving on the road to Chimaltenango, passing by a military base. The twenty-year-old jeep had habitual shimmies and rattles and thrums. It growled with gear changes. Kate sat in the back seat, hunched forward to hear their conversation. She listened; at the same time she anticipated seeing Ben; it had been the lure of Ben's presence in Panajachel, a couple of hours away, that had made her agree to go along. The checkpoint at the front entrance to the base had been built in the shape of a huge menacing army boot. Men in dappled camouflage wandered in and out of the boot, weapons at the ready.

"Sí, pues," Vidalúz said. "And what about you two?"

Dixie said, "I'm not sure."

Vidalúz said, "The evangelicos will steal your people."

They laughed. "You think?" Dixie said.

"And you, Catarina?"

Kate said, "I'm as good as gone. If Maggie were here, we could go with you—"

"I would like that," Vidalúz said. "You are my new friend and now I must say good-bye."

"Did you think about that?" Dixie spoke in English, urgently, to Kate.

"I couldn't," Kate said.

"I'd see that Maggie caught up with you. I could put her on a plane to Mexico City. Or Houston or Miami, for that matter."

"I know that. I can't do that."

Vidalúz said, "When will I be able to return?"

"After they know you are there, it'll be easier to come home. You'll be more safe. No one will hurt you after you've been in the *New York Times*."

"They are afraid of the *New York Times?*"

"They are afraid of the people who read the *New York Times*. They are the same people who send them guns and money."

"How will I know if they release Hector?"

"We will stay in touch. Our friends will help us," Dixie said. "Our friends in the States, and our friends in the capital."

He meant Sunny and Kate knew he meant Sunny. They conspired to help Vidalúz, to transfer her to Ben, but they never spoke of Sunny when the three of them were together.

"This is a beautiful road," Vidalúz said. "And I don't know when I will see it again. And Hector—"

That morning, in Kate's room, Vidalúz had dressed in clothes Kate had given her—clothes she consented to wear for safety's sake, clothes that made her look like a cousin of Kate's on holiday from Mexico City or El Paso, jeans and a pink turtleneck and sneakers and short white athletic socks—and she had talked about Hector. They had lain in bed one night, in their house in the highlands—

"Only one room, really, Catarina," she said, "and that was enough for Hector and me. You see, we had agreed to have no children. We were working for all children, and that meant we could not have a child of our own. This is my sadness now. If I had Hector's child I would have him, something of him—"

Vidalúz and Hector had held one another and discussed the worst that could happen. Now that had come to pass.

"I was pregnant once when I was very young and very innocent, and we had no farmacia in the village where we lived, and Hector's sister took me to a curandera who told me to eat the green pineapple. It was very hard to eat, sí, pues, muy difícil. And the baby came out of me. Do you think it is a sin to interrupt a pregnancy like that, Catarina?"

And before Kate could answer, Vidalúz had insisted, "Don't tell Father Ryan, please don't tell him—"

Don't worry, Kate had told her, and she hugged her. The bones in Vidalúz's back felt pliable; she was delicate. And Kate thought, This is how I feel when someone hugs me. Men don't know the strength in these pliable bones.

From the jeep's back seat Kate reached up and put her hand on Vidalúz's shoulder. She thought about how she had never wanted to have a child by Deaver.

"Here's Pana," Dixie said.

Panajachel. By 1989 the tourists were beginning to come back to Lake Atitlán. In 1981 the largest hotel had been bombed by guerrillas and the tourists stopped coming. From Sololá—where the faces of the Indians were sullen; they had their reasons, Kate was sure—they wound ten kilometers down the mountainside and ugly and visible from a long way were the two snaggly unfinished high-rise hotels, cement-block shells. But the lake in all its vagaries—blue-sky confection, stormy whitecaps, glassy silver—beckoned them and begged them to forgive the confusion and botched work, the empty swimming pools and high prices.

Dixie pulled to a stop before a rusty gate.

Kate had not seen Ben Hires in twelve years and she did not know what to expect. His hair had gone white and his long tanned face had worn down to essence of Ben—kindness, openness, weariness. His eyes were hazel and the leaves on his shirt made his eyes intensely green. He smiled when he saw her. Kate could not get over the sensation that Sunny was right behind him; she could not think his name without linking him with Sunny. He opened the gate and Dixie drove into the yard.

"Buenas tardes, buenas, buenas—" Ben said.

They got out of the jeep and Ben had a hug for each of them. Lastly, Kate. "Kate. It's been so long."

His greeting came over a month too late. She'd been humbled, somehow, by her aloneness. She felt shy, embarrassed to be singled out for an extra-long embrace. "What's different about you?" Kate said, looking up at him.

"No beard?"

"That's it. I don't think I've ever seen your face before."

He let her go. "The better to cross the border," he said, making eye contact with Vidalúz. Then he took her hand. "I'm sorry, Vidalúz—"

"I know, Ben Hires," Vidalúz said. "Gracias."

He closed and padlocked the gate. Clapped his arm around Dixie's shoulder. Led them through a square grassy yard, lined with four-foot-high poinsettias, to a white stucco cottage with a thatched roof. The colors—the grass, the poinsettias, the blazing stucco—were keenly vibrant.

Kate could think of nothing but getting Ben alone; on the long walk across the grass, with Dixie and Vidalúz murmuring beside them, she took his hand momentarily; his hand felt warm and solid in hers, and she said in a low voice, "I hope we'll have a chance to talk." Ben said, "We will, we will."

He brought them into the kitchen: a small room with big windows looking out on the garden. A table was set with flowers and cloth napkins. A woman at the counter stirred a crystal pitcher of iced tea that emitted sundogs, spools of rainbow, from the light streaming in the window. She was neat and prim—in ladino clothes—and wore an apron printed with onions.

"This is Gabriela," Ben said. "She runs the house."

Gabriela served them iced tea and delgados and fruit. Then she left them alone. After eating, catching up—Ben wanted to know about Ginger, about Lino, about the girls who cleaned the Antigua house, about Dixie's health, about Maggie—and making a brief plan—if the fog wasn't bad he wanted to leave by seven the next morning; he wanted to make San Cristóbal the first day and Monterrey the next—after all that, Ben said, "Will you two be content on your own? I haven't seen Kate in years—how long's it been? — I thought I'd give her a tour of Pana."

By then the shadows were long in the yard and Ben led her out the gate and down a steep and rutted lane toward the lake. He was tall and guided her lightly with a hand between her shoulder blades now and then. They passed a health food store and restaurants where foreigners lounged on patios; signs advertised massage and herbs and videos in the evenings.

"It's different here," Kate said.

"Than?"

"Antigua."

"Different worlds," Ben said. "Here everyone appears to be on vacation. Some of them permanently. Except the locals. You'll find the same thing in Myrtle Beach. It's a fantasy."

"That's it, isn't it."

"You could stay here for a few days. Until Maggie gets here."

"Ben—I don't have any money."

"Whad'ya mean you don't have any money?"

"I ran out. Maggie was supposed to be here. She has a credit card. I've been trying to contact Paul to send us a bank draft. We have a mutual account with him at home. But I haven't been able to get through—"

"I can lend you some money, Kate."

"Could we sit down somewhere?"

They had come to the windy lake; the tour boats bounced around at the lake's edge. Night was coming on quickly, with a round sky streaked orange. Boatmen tied their boats to the moorings; a light fog rose up around their silhouettes. A woman walked by, laboring under a netted load of beets the same dark red as her skirt. Mothers were calling home their children. A quarter mile away they could see the golden overlit hotels.

"A bar?"

"That would be good," Kate said.

They settled on the darkening porch of the Red Bird, protected from the wind by lush palm trees whose stiff leaves clattered dryly. Music was on, North American jazz, and a TV blared from the next room; a basketball game from the States. Comforting noise. Kate was emboldened by it; her words could get lost within it.

"Will you buy me a drink?" she said to Ben.

"Of course, Kate." He put his hand over hers. "I want you to tell me what's going on with you."

"You first," Kate said.

"Whad'ya wanta know?"

"I want to know about Sunny."

The waitress came—a young plump girl in a soiled white apron. She stood before them phlegmatically until they ordered. Kate thought a margarita sounded good; she hadn't had one in a long time but she thought she might get a more generous jigger of tequila if she ordered it straight up. "Con limón, por favor?" With a beer chaser. Ben ordered a beer.

He had taken his hand away. He unzipped his jacket.

"We're hardly married anymore."

"I'm sorry."

"That's just what's happening. Though it's not what I expected."

"What's going on with Sunny?"

"Look," Ben said, opening his hands, bidding for patience, "let me tell you what I can. I think you'll understand. And it starts with that—we've gotten on different tracks."

The waitress brought their drinks and Kate sipped her tequila. It tasted a little resiny, like turpentine. The tequila was hot going down; she relished the burn of it.

"When did we see you last?" Ben said.

"I thought about that," Kate said, "when I knew we were coming to see you. I saw Sunny on Roatán, two years ago." For Maggie's fortieth birthday they'd met on an island and sunned themselves for five lazy days. A bad girls' good time, they'd called it: snorkeling and drinking and dancing with the locals, pretending they didn't have a care in the world. "The two of you together—Fourth of July, 1977. Pier Cove. Lake Michigan."

"That's right," he said. "That's right." He closed his eyes and sighed. "You were with Paul—" He opened his eyes and grinned. "—and I think you were a bit bored."

Kate laughed, a cynical snort. "Why didn't you say so? You could've saved me years of back and forth, to and fro."

"Young and dumb, weren't we?"

"Sunny had quit her teaching job and you were getting ready to go traveling."

"We came here, bought the house—for the proverbial song—and we lived there quite happily, peas in a pod, and so on. We ignored the violence at first. We were actually able to insulate ourselves against it, in Antigua." He drank from his beer, then leaned in close to her. "But Sunny was cooking inside. She kept reading and thinking and when she got her chance to get involved—bingo—they came to the right woman."

"What—exactly—is she doing?"

"That's not for me to say."

"You're not going to tell me?"

"I'll tell you when we get home. You and Maggie come home and I'll tell you. But here—no."

They drank silently for a few minutes. Kate liked the feel of the first few minutes of drinking, the way a drink can bring you into the present. Ben seemed more alive than ever; yet paradoxically he glowed with an aura of the past and within that aura she saw their histories: Madison, all-night drunks, dancing, sweating on their knees in a community garden they had planted one year.

"Everything feels shadowy here."

"You've got that right. You want my advice, get your butts home," Ben said. "Why don't you just go on to the States and let Maggie find her way? Come with us."

Kate ran her fingers through her hair at the temples. She had for months envisioned such a straight trajectory home: mechanical, like following a string from Nicaragua to Guatemala to Mexico to Indiana. Here was a piece of that string, an easy section. But she said, "I can't leave without her. I promised." She adjusted her glasses, sipped her beer. "You know how hard it is to go back. I have a lot of what you might call unfinished business at home. Maggie'll ease the rough spots."

"I'm enjoying being back."

"Good for you." Then Kate said, "What about Sunny?"

"Sunny has gone off the deep end. She knows this is the last trip I'm making for a long time. I want to have a life again. A home. There, not here." He drained his glass. "I respect her, I do." He looked Kate right in the eye. "Sunny has made a commitment to live on the mean universal income—do you know how much that is? Something like eighty-four dollars a month. Dixie adores her for it. I do too. I respect that kind of . . ."

"Letting go?"

"That's what it is." He gently tapped the bottom of his beer glass on the table. "But I can't do it. Hell, I want life to im*prove* on the material plane. For everyone." He flagged down the waitress. "And it doesn't mean you do without. You just depend on other people. Your life is like a beggar's." Then abruptly he said, "So, me. Now, you."

"I came here fucked up."

"How so?"

"My love life—isn't that what we used to call it?"

"You were with Deaver."

"What do you know about him?"

Ben leaned back in his chair, folded his arms. She could see that he'd gone to fat, his belly sunk in a puddle above his belt.

He said, "Let me see—he keeps a stack of *Soldier of Fortune* beside the john. Likes guns. He's gifted. Difficult. A bit of a womanizer, am I right?"

"Was it all that obvious?"

"Mind you, this is secondhand. Thirdhand. Gossip was one of our leisure-time pursuits in Antigua. We had mutual friends in San Cristóbal."

"His mother lives there."

"Yeah, well, our paths never crossed. She's old-guard expat. Moneyed."

"I had hoped he'd go back to the States with me. Start over. I couldn't stay in Nicaragua any longer. I couldn't."

"So what happened?"

"I kept on with him so long. It was easier than finding someone new."

"You must've gotten something out of it."

"You go where you have the most to learn. Isn't that what they say?"

He waited. The waitress came over. They ordered again—the same. Ben said, "I'm hungry again." And he ordered pasta and French bread for both of them. They could hear the basketball game—Denver and Chicago in the playoffs.

Finally Ben said, "You're still a beautiful woman, Kate."

Kate sat up straight. "Are you out of your mind? I've never been a beautiful woman."

"You just didn't know it."

"Maggie's still beautiful. Wait'll you see her. We'll have to come and see you."

"Deaver wasn't right for you. I never met the guy, but intuition tells me—"

"Your intuition's right on the money."

"A year from now you'll laugh about it."

"It was eight years. In another eight years I might laugh about it."

"How's this—you're still a good woman. Now, that's harder for me to say with authority, because we don't know each other anymore. But beautiful—that I can see."

A couple got up to dance and then another. They were mixed couples: ladino men and gringo women with tans like tree bark. Kate said, "People have fun here."

"You could stay here. You could stay at the cottage. The gal who owns it's away."

"Who is she?"

"A benefactor who prefers anonymity. She made a fortune in the rock-and-roll industry." He sighed again; he admitted, "It's not all sweetness and light."

"How so?"

He turned his chair so that his cheek paralleled hers, though he faced the opposite way. "There've been—well—incidents. Gabriela tells me."

"Such as?"

"There're Gs in the outlying villages. There're black murders. Black raids. Perpetrated by both sides. Not in town—they're trying to hang on to the new tourist dollar—but don't stray too far. Two Indian women were killed on the trail. Ostensibly for consorting with the Gs. It was pretty grisly."

Finally someone was telling her. But Ben was the kind of man who sought the periphery of danger. He might be overstating his case.

"I don't want to stay here. I'm comfortable in Antigua." With Dixie, she admitted to herself. "Besides, Maggie said mid-June. We might beat you across the border."

"He's an ace, isn't he?"

"Who?"

"Father D."

"What're you saying?"

"You like it there because he's there."

"You really are out of your mind."

"I'm psychic, Kate. It's one of the burdens I bear."

"Come on."

"I see what others won't."

They watched the dancers thrusting their hips at each other.

He said, "You know what I want to do? Back home?"

"Tell me."

"Work outdoors. Toughen up my gut." He slapped his belly. "We've got a piece of property. An orchard near Kalamazoo. I want to start a business, be my own boss. Find a new woman. Maybe have a baby. Sit on the porch and play with my baby." He drank his beer, pursed his lips. "I coulda been in jail ten times over."

Kate thought he was trying to put a good face on the whole deal, but she saw tears in his eyes just for a second when she said, "I would really like to see Sunny."

He said, "I know that, I know that."

They sat there quietly for a few minutes. The jukebox had gone off. The game was in halftime. Next door to the Red Bird there erupted almost violently the sound of evangelicos singing and stomping. The songs they sang were songs of Kate's childhood somehow, though at first she could not place them. She and her mother and aunts had been Catholic through and through; at that time Catholics did not sing the rousing songs. Then she remembered going to Bible camp one summer with Maggie and Paul and their cousins, who were Evangelical United Brethren. She'd begged her mother to let her go; they had spent the weekend sleeping in a bunkhouse made of rough lumber; the dawn filtered between the boards every morning; the bunks smelled of musty weather and they took cold showers in a concrete-block stall; every morning, noon, and night there were those songs in the air, this little light of mine and I've got a home in glory land that outshines the sun. Kate longed viscerally for Maggie.

She said, "Did you ever go to Bible camp?"

"No, I never did," Ben said. His voice seemed to fade. He had his own reserve of memories.

The waitress brought their food and drinks; the pasta was overdone but they ate. They dawdled there.

After an hour Kate said, "I feel tipsy." What an odd word. She didn't think she'd ever used it before, as though she could actually tip over and be lost for good. Kate could feel the tequila and she did not want to be tipsy in front of Dix. He'd go to bed early; he needed his rest. She wanted to say goodnight to him and she had grown ashamed of him seeing her under the influence. By that time he'd told Kate that he'd been a drinker and she could see that drinking had cost him something though she didn't know how much. She only wanted to be sober enough to tell him goodnight. With clarity.

"You wanta go back?"

"Yes, yes, I do," she said.

Back at the cottage she saw Dixie from afar. He sat in a chair near the edge of the yard, empty-handed, in the dark. On the fence behind him wide moonflowers had opened like hearts in the night. She could not see his face. She wanted to go to him, but she could not think of any excuse for doing so. She wanted to go to him. She felt that physical fist of desire in her pelvis, hand of the mother magician drawing out her sensuality. Where does all the chemistry come from? Does it ever go away?

She and Ben stood under a dim yellow light beside a stone patio. A jasmine tree gave up its scent to the lake wind. Vidalúz had told her that a jasmine tea could relieve los aflicciones of the heart. Jasmine blossoms scent the full-moon night and make romance; the tea relieves you of the sorrow. She thought she might like to try it. With all the awkwardness of a man who'd been married to another woman for twenty-two years, Ben put his arm around her waist and cinched her close.

"Don't—" She freed herself and said, "That's not what I want."

"I'm sorry," he said sheepishly.

"It's okay. You'll get used to being single. You have to try or you'll never know."

"I still want Sunny."

"You probably always will."

"What do *you* want?"

"To sleep like a baby. I know it's early. But I want to see Vidalúz before she turns in."

Ben took her hand. "Come to Kalamazoo. I'll help you and Maggie get settled."

"That's a kind offer," Kate said. "We'll need all the help we can get, I'm sure."

And with that she went with disappointment to her room. Vidalúz sat up in bed, reading a newspaper Ben had brought from San Cristóbal. She wore reading glasses and a cotton nightgown.

"Catarina," she said, "I have decided not to go."

Kate flung her passport pouch onto a table. She sat on the bed beside Vidalúz. "What happened?"

"When I'm alone I hear a voice saying, Don't go, not now."

"Have you told Dixie?"

She nodded.

"And?"

"He fears for me."

"I'll help you any way I can," Kate said. "Until I go."

"I'm staying here in Pana. For a little time."

"That's what you want to do?"

"That is what I want to do."

"Poor Ben. He's driving back alone."

"You could go with him," Vidalúz said.

Kate said, "It's not quite time for me to go yet."

"Sí, I understand. I do."

When you tear yourself from the view of volcanoes and palm trees and mother hibiscus, you will see before you the abutment of malnourished women and children and Dobermans protecting the wealthy vacation homes, hotel linens laid out drying on the perfect grass beside a television satellite dish.

Not unusual abutments.

If you look, if you have eyes to see, these particular abutments can be found almost anywhere in the world. In Panajachel, if anything, they are more obvious. Resort town, few stone walls to lay the veneer of privacy over lives. There, where everyone has in common the love of the natural paradise, raw sewage flows where swimmers swim. At night when the lake wind picks up and a chill is in the air and you realize you need more than a sweater for warmth, when the colonels and their wives, the bankers and their wives are approaching the seafood buffet at the Hotel del Lago, oohing and aahing over the fruit sculpture, moving like mannequins through the museum-stillness of the lobby, the Guatemalan women and children of the street will grab your shirt or dress and beg the last quetzal you'll give. Or vendors get that desperate look, their dark mouths open imploringly, and you will want to be anywhere else but in the muddy lane of wooden booths full to the ceiling with weather-soiled goods, the rugs and woven place mats and bargain shirts no one back home will wear. There is that moment when they touch you, Señora, señor, por favor, when the experience can be distilled to its basic components. Have, have-not. Old hippies from the United States and Canada and Europe slouch about the streets, and you can imagine Haight-Ashbury, you can imagine Woodstock. They are the same people, still skinny from metabolic changes induced by speed, with gray hair, their skin sun-damaged. It is a place to be avoided. We seldom go there now, though that cottage was a safe and happy place.

I mark that trip to Panajachel as a turning point, but that's my hindsight, isn't it? At the time you turn and turn and don't really know that you've gone down a different road, that you'll never be the same. I kept thinking about what Ben had told me about Sunny, about her living on the mean universal income. The ride home made me love Dixie. Though I did not call it that. I was sleepy, it was late afternoon, and I had stayed up late with Vidalúz—I did not like leaving her—and by the time we got away from Panajachel that tropical stupor had come upon me and I wanted to sleep and he said, Put your head down, relax, and I bundled up my raingear and bunched it on the console between us and laid my head down and drifted, just drifted, and I felt his fingers wonderingly on my neck and I felt his warm hand on my forehead and I loved him for that, for the mercy in his touch. It was a touch that asked for nothing. When I woke up, or pretended to wake up, he said, Come with me. Where? I said. And he said, To the highlands. In a few days I'm going to my parish. And I said, I can't do that. I felt superstitious about leaving when I was expecting Maggie. If I kept watch, she'd be there soon, I told myself. And he did not know I'd been awake when he touched me. He never mentioned Jude. As though the sound of her name might have the power to disrupt what we felt.

At home we were confronted with Lino and Lino's anxiety. He had been in the capital looking for the children and he did not find them and that was upsetting to all of us. He said he was giving up. Why them, he said. When there are so many.

I did not like to picture Marta but I had been to a cobbler's shop that had the look of a worn black shoe, maw of a shelter, everything—the wooden counter, the dirt floor, the racks of broken boots, the cobbler in his leather apron—wizened and dark and wimpled. One bit of color had shone, a red Coke can on the counter. Eduardo might run an errand for the cobbler and return with tortillas wrapped in gray paper. The man would give him a measure of glue from a large metal pot. Eduardo and Marta would keep the glue in a baby-food jar. Instead of food.

Instead of food.

I could not eat. Dixie and Lino cooked and sat down together and said grace while I sat in the courtyard sorting through my visit with Ben and the bad dreams of Marta's life and once in a while thinking with relief of the fifty dollars Ben had given me, fifty U.S. dollars. Eventually Lino went to a friend's house where he often spent the night, and then we were alone.

A thin wisp of cloud strayed over the volcano we could see from our courtyard. As it got dark we did not turn on a light and we wrapped up in blankets he brought from his room and we sat side by side in separate chairs and we talked and then we were quiet. And then we would talk again. Something had changed. We had been on a journey together and we had been close and we had not come right out with what we were feeling, but I felt a physical softening—a hardness in me giving way I'd guarded fiercely until then—and when I looked at him the giving way would happen and I trusted him in spite of all we had not discussed and I wanted to be in his presence.

I like being near you, he said.

I said, I know.

Kate could hear the sling of wire hangers landing on the tile floor. Ginger was moving out. She took her time about it, wandering from her room to the kitchen and back to the courtyard, slowly filling up a sky-blue hard-shell suitcase and a shopping bag. Raccoon dark rings circled her eyes.

Once Kate went to her door and said, "Are you all right?"

"What do you mean?"

"We were worried about you."

"I've been staying with friends."

"You look sort of under the weather."

Ginger held up and critically eyed a turquoise rayon blouse. She rolled it up and stuck it in one corner of the suitcase, which lay spread open on the floor. "I had this icky flu."

"Are you sure that's all?"

Peevishly Ginger said, "What are you—my mom?"

With that, Kate left her alone.

It was June 20. Maggie was due, overdue.

Kate had been nervous. Strong-coffee wired. And waiting. She could not sit still. Could not keep from going out to the street to look up and down. She pictured Maggie struggling with her bags and she would have too many bags for a brigadista—too many clothes. It was one of those clean light days when the rain has washed the streets and washed the air and washed the leaves of all the trees and the hibiscus and roses seemed velvety and bright, all that color disguising the decay. Kate tried sometimes to imagine Guatemala without flowers and that was not a pretty thought.

She did not think of it as snooping. She wanted a U.S. stamp and she knew Dixie would not mind if she took one of his. She thought she could find a traveler heading to Miami or LA who would mail her letter to her mother. Her mother would receive the letter a week or so before she and Maggie arrived home.

She listened for Ginger.

Then she pushed completely open one panel of Dixie's wooden door and slipped in. A light had been left on. His bed was made up. Two shirts—one blue denim and the other crisp, starched, and white—hung on hangers from a loose ten-penny nail that someone had pounded into the plaster wall. On the dresser were photos in handmade wooden frames and a short metal crucifix.

She examined the photos. Dixie was in every one. His arms around everyone. She wanted to know who they were, these children, a family in Christmas sweaters, Indians, white-haired women carrying New Orleans Museum of Art tote bags. There was a brown leather address book. Kate opened it and there were the U.S. stamps, more than a dozen, inside a glassine envelope. She'd seen him tuck the stamps away after writing letters at the kitchen table. The stamps made her homesick for a moment.

His clock ticked loudly. It would be dark within an hour. She picked up Dixie's wool sweater—a dark green pullover with a shawl collar and one leather button—and she pressed it to her face unthinkingly. Thinking, actually, of Maggie. Wanting her to knock on the front door. Wanting her in order to have someone to embrace. Thinking it would be the end of an era when Maggie finally arrived and they faced the rest of their lives, moved on. Dixie's green sweater smelled of curry and cooking oil and something citrusy too, and the smell took Kate back to a restaurant in Madison, a place with flowered oilcloth on the family-sized tables, where she had felt at home. What was it—fault or virtue?—that she could so easily feel at home? A habitual café or restaurant, a friendly vendor at a news-stand, an old woman in the same apartment building who always asked her prying questions—it did not take much to make her feel at home. But the fact of interchangeability, the cafés with their local arts tabloids, the steamy squinch of the espresso machines, kept her from surrendering to a particular place. With each move she had given up the option of being at home, given up the accretion of experience in one place. That accretion was something of value. It was a loss you could never recover, like not having a child, a loss time stole from you. Curry and cooking oil and citrus—lime pickle, it was—she breathed in the smell of his sweater and thought it smelled like home.

"Qué pasa?" Ginger said from the doorway. Her voice catty.

Kate deliberately and slowly placed Dixie's sweater back on the chair beside the dresser. She felt caught—a flush crept over her jaw—but she did not want to concede that to Ginger.

"I'm looking for a stamp. I'll be out in a minute."

Ginger said, "So where's your friend?"

Kate wished she could slap her: an impulse she'd seldom ever had. "She'll be here."

"Stamp'll do you no good," Ginger said gleefully. "I hear the PO strike will last a long time." She started down the colonnade, saying, "Those bananas have seen better days, and if you don't mind . . ." Her voice died away.

Kate took a stamp. It was printed with a drawing of a vintage car, shiny and black with whitewall tires. She slipped the stamp into her shirt pocket. With her hand on the address book, its cover leathery rough, she realized she might find out Sunny's whereabouts if she didn't feel squeamish, guilty, about poking through his belongings. Not three seconds passed before she allowed herself to scan the scraps of paper stuck in the front of the address book.

In the kitchen Ginger turned on Billie Holiday: "Who loves you, ask yourself the question. Ask yourself the question, sweetheart."

She unfolded the scraps of paper one at a time. "Ayudame por favor. Necesito comida." Another said, "Write Sam." His brother, Kate knew that much. And the last piece of paper was a receipt for a printing job. She flipped to the Hs, to Hires. There was the Antigua address. And there was a penciled note in the margin: "El Pacífico Sueño/Calle Rigoberta nr El Jardín de los Niños. Zona 2." That was all, but that was enough, more than she'd known before. She would tell Maggie and together they would decide what to do. She hastily refolded the scraps of paper and stuck them back where he'd had them. She touched the front of the address book, the cross, the picture frames, just lightly, the way you might touch a table setting you had just put together, as if to say, There, all done. Then she left the room and closed the door.

In the courtyard the twilight breeze surrounded her and the neighborhood evening faded in and out, footfalls, children called in, music far away, barely discernible as salsa. Posh was perched on the lip of a hanging fern, shrieking, No way. No way. The Billie Holliday felt melancholy. Ginger banged around in the kitchen, getting out a skillet, running water.

"What're you doing?" Kate called.

"Warming up some leftovers," Ginger said. "I'm starving."

Kate sat down on the edge of the fountain and pulled out of the water one of the beers she had stashed there earlier in the day. Beers intended as festive. Just in case. The week before, to the day, she had finally gotten through to Paul, collect, and he had agreed to send the money to Lloyd's Bank.

"How are you?" she'd said. She knew he recognized her voice. He always had. Their first phone calls had been when they were in third grade, a life ago.

Paul said, "This is a surprise." He seemed caught in midgulp or -bite. "Hold on a second, will you?" And he had switched phones, picked up another, possibly, most likely, in another room, and someone—who?—cut off the first connection. "So—" Paul said. "Where are you?"

"Antigua. Guatemala. It's a small city in the mountains." Kate's voice quavered and she hoped he could not tell. The connection was crude, their voices gritty, with an annoying lapse of time: they interrupted each other. She reminded herself to slow down and wait.

"What's up?" Paul said.

"Maggie asked me to call. We need some cash."

He laughed, like a slap. Abrasively. "I should've guessed."

Kate hastened to say, "There's still plenty in our account. We need just enough to get home on. We're coming home."

"Let me talk to Maggie."

"Maggie's not here. She's not here yet."

"What's going on?"

"She's still in Nicaragua." Not to put too fine a point on it. She's out in the campo falling in love.

"Why's that?"

"She's fine. She asked me to call you."

"Why didn't she call me herself?"

"We need the money sent here. To Lloyd's Bank."

He was silent. The buzz crackled in Kate's ear. Then he sighed, long-suffering, and said, "Let me get something to write with."

She waited. Outside her booth a white-haired North American woman with a tennis tan read a newspaper, waited for her phone call to go through.

"Shoot," Paul said.

She repeated the name of the bank and spelled Antigua. Then she said, "How is everything?"

"Things are good—" She could feel him trying to decide how much to say. "The humidity's up already."

"And your mom?"

"She's a case. She's the same as ever."

"You like your new job?"

"I've been there over a year."

"Has it been that long?" Then, "Is there anything you want me to tell Maggie?"

"How much should I send?"

"How about a thousand?"

"Gotcha." He paused. "There is something."

"What's that?"

"I was going to write. To Maggie."

"What is it?"

"I've . . . I've met someone. I think I'm going to ask her to marry me."

Kate had missed one beat, but she caught up and said, "That's great, Paul. Who is she? Do we know her?" So calm, so smooth. But her heart pounded again.

"No. You don't. She's a woman from the lab. Carol."

Kate pictured someone in a white lab coat with a short contained haircut. She pictured someone like Paul, blond, broadly Midwestern, with a slight nasally twang in her voice that she had inherited from her mother and could not extinguish. For shame. She did not want to be nasty. She had no right. But that would take time. To sort out her feelings.

She said, "We'll have to celebrate when we get there."

"When'll that be?"

"By the end of July. How does that sound?"

"It's just you and Maggie coming?"

"That's right."

"What about . . . what's his name . . . Mark?"

She hesitated. She ran two fingers up and down her forehead as though to press out pain or a frown. "I can't talk about that right now."

"Who got dumped—you or him?"

"Paul—"

And without thinking, she hung up. She decided to pretend they'd been cut off. That was not unusual, to get cut off midcall. She leaned against the door. Someone had stuck a shiny pink bubble of chewing gum on the booth's Plexiglas window. He would send the money. He would send the money for Maggie. What a jerk. Instinctive response, but her heart wasn't in it. She felt mildly wounded, startled.

She had gone out to the street and then headed toward the central park. Toward the people of the evening. Families. Vendors. Kids of begging women. She stood in line to buy a chucho, a finger-length tamale with a pink sugar flower buried in its center. She took her chucho and retreated to a bench across from the vendors. The watery white streetlights gave off a weak light and the faces of the people were shadowed; she could not recognize anyone the way she might have in Managua. Though everyone was friendly just the same and she was not afraid to be at the park alone.

She drank her beer. From where she sat on the fountain's rim she could see Ginger eating at the kitchen table. They didn't have much to say to each other and that suited Kate fine. Paul had pissed her off. And made her sad. Too many memories crowded in, triggered by his voice. She wished she could file them away. She wished memory was not the separate animal it was. Always beckoning. Seducing. Cajoling. Begging.

Her birthday had come at the edge of early summer, in June. A date she had ignored for quite a while. When she was a child she could have whatever treat she wanted for her birthday, and she had always asked for chocolate cake with seven-minute frosting, the peaks of sugar like sea froth on waves; she would lick the bowl too; she liked it warm from the bowl. After that it would be full summer and she and Maggie and Paul would be inseparable.

It was nearly always the three of them. Brown-skinned. Their bare feet tough by the end of summer. Paul was the youngest, with a passion for tennis. No one they knew had played tennis. The men around there—a village, Winter Home—bowled or hunted or played softball. Once in a while you would hear them at the school playground hoop, razzing one another in a game of Horse. But Paul wanted tennis and his mother made arrangements. For three summers in a row she sent him to town for lessons. Kate and Maggie wanted nail polish and magazines and clothes. "Girlygirls," Paul called them derisively. But he needed them; their houses were on a gravel road and the road arched away over hills to places they could not see or imagine very well. Paul was lonely; even though he resisted many things they wanted to talk about, he was stuck in the company of women and girls. Maggie. Kate. Their mothers. Kate's Aunt Dodie and Aunt Mary Lou.

Paul and Maggie's mother, Ruth Macon Byrne, had been accustomed to a finer life as a girl. She had expected to marry a man who would care for her and better her life. All the mothers they knew had expected that. "It's just as easy to marry a rich man as a poor man," Ruth would say to Maggie and Kate. Memorial Day until Labor Day, Ruth Macon Byrne wore white cotton gloves to church on Sunday. She had lost half of her fingernails from the perm and color chemicals she used at Debbie's Shear Shop, where she worked five mornings a week. White cotton gloves concealed her red cracked fingers. White cotton gloves concealed the knobby fingertips, where the nails looked as though someone had tried to quilt them or sew them inexpertly, the way the flesh grew up and around the leftover nail. She took some pleasure in other people's scandals. Whose common-law wife had run off. Which child had been caught stealing. Ruth Macon Byrne. Femme fatale of their road. Her schoolteacher husband had left her for a senior girl when Maggie was in kindergarten. After that she showered twice a day and had a stable of perfume bottles and nail polish on her bedroom dresser. She had a slight gap between her two front teeth and she called that sexy and Maggie and Kate believed her. Paul retreated in the wake of the frills and colors and hemlines and baubles. Maggie blossomed, so said Ruth. She dressed flamboyantly to please herself. And Kate—Kate retreated too. She said she detested the phoniness of always worrying over clothes and fussing over faces, but Maggie would not let her go. Maggie held on. Maggie was a solid friend who did not care what you looked like dancing next to her on the high school stage at noon hour. Stop in the name of love, before you break my heart. What Maggie cared about was talking, confessing, and if you were good at that, she loved you fiercely. Ruth would suggest to Kate a French braid or a shade of lipstick called Poppy or Spice and Kate would squirm and Maggie would say, "Kate doesn't need those things, Mom. She's a natural beauty."

A natural beauty. Once she had had good skin—creamy brown and fine-pored, like the skin of a plum. And nails with perfect half moons. Eyes that spoke of longing, eyes that spoke of delight. Small breasts without a crease on the underside at all and nipples the color of freckles, a kind of sun-rose. And thighs with a long lean muscle visible when she knelt over a man, her knees on either side of him, astride what she wanted most. How could she have wanted them so badly? And shoulders, they had often mentioned her shoulders. Round, petitely muscled, brown. She knew her strengths and weaknesses. What used to be. Her hands were oldest now. Loose brown skin sagging in pockets above each knuckle. Gone the way of all flesh. Unable to resist gravity or the sun's warp. Her hands had served her, her body had served her, and she told herself she did not care about all that now. She had grown tired, more than anything, of comparing herself to other women while she was with Deaver. She could feel him doing it. She did it too and nearly always felt the slight and thought she knew that in his eyes she did not measure up. That was one freedom of solitude. She did not have to measure up. She did not have to prove anything. She was relieved of the terrible burden of failing to be prettier.

She remembered Paul, his nervous kisses, his gulping, his sweet sighs, honey-voiced Johnny Mathis—

It is so easy to fall in love when you're young and you don't know who you are. Where had Maggie been? Somewhere, sometime, she had begun leaving them alone in the attic. Or they had begun going without her. To the wine-colored velvet sofa that slanted because one claw foot was missing. She was afraid of getting pregnant and he was equally afraid of getting her pregnant and they rubbed themselves raw in other ways of coming and coming and coming on the dusty sofa. An endless train of orgasms; it wasn't work at all.

That had been the best time with Paul.

Later they grew bored. They broke up, got back together, broke up. All over the course of years and many moves and graduating from college.

Whenever they made up and moved back in together, within a week Kate would wonder why. Was it the orgasms? He knew how to make her come. Or how to be there while she made herself come. Did all those moves and fights and reconciliations and apartment leases broken and long-distance telephone bills, did all of that depend on those five or ten seconds when she would lose herself in front of him?

Ginger came to the kitchen door. She said, "I'm leaving some clothes in the bodega. Do you think Sunny'll mind?"

"I'm sure not," Kate said, on automatic pilot. In that moment, with the cold wet bottle in her hand, she knew with conviction that Maggie was not going to arrive. She wondered how long she would have to wait. She looked forward to Dixie coming home. Two days before they had watched the news together, at Doña Luisa's, and now she wanted him to come home and say, Let's go watch the news. The news was horrible; the news was usually horrible; but there was something humble and companionable and safe in that invitation: Let's settle down together and see how the world has fared today and usher in the evening.

Maggie not arriving signaled a new phase. Everything up to that point had been easier than she had thought. She would have to gear down emotionally and that was not the same thing as lightening up, not the same thing at all. Lighten up, Deaver would say whenever he wanted to weasel out of talking with her, about her, about them. Gearing down was about endurance or patience. It was about walking uphill. With a heavy load. Maybe Maggie had fallen truly in love with Bob Elliott; maybe she would give up everything they had planned for the true love of an engineer from New Mexico.

Billie Holiday was singing "Pennies from Heaven."

The stars were out, so soon, so soon. At that altitude, above the clouds of industrial waste, the stars crackled in the blue-black sky.

Three days later.

In a flowered kimono, feeling more female, more physical, than she had in a long while, Kate wrung out her shirts at the sink near the bodega. Posh squawked and darted from fern to clothesline. Victoria and Juanita giggled in the bodega beside the ironing board, standing up to eat their lunches and poring over a comic book, a soap opera. It was a nice day. Sunny. Fragrant with hibiscus and laundry detergent.

She looked forward to writing another letter to her mother. She had written her twice, paving the way to go back, making less work of their reunion by writing letters, asking her forgiveness. Kate was finding strength in asking forgiveness and that seemed oddly a gift. She would go down to Doña Luisa's and try to find a traveler returning to the States to mail the letter. Dixie had gone to the market and they would cook together later in the day. They had made a plan: meatless lasagna, salad, crusty bread, and a walk to the ice-cream stand later in the evening. She might even make a quick trip to Lloyd's before it closed to check on her bank draft.

She had four shirts, all mens' made of oxford cloth with button-down tab collars except one, a pale yellow sleeveless tank top printed in fleurs-de-lis. She might even dry the tank top by hand with a hair dryer if she had to. She wanted to wear it with a skirt and thought about shaving her legs and under her arms. She hadn't done that in a long time—and only for a man.

Some things she could not change: the money and waiting for Maggie and Paul's meanness and Vidalúz. And her thoughts were moving away from what had gone wrong to what might work. Ben's offer meant much; she kept turning his words over, piecing together what helping them get settled might mean to him. She felt a shift taking place almost physically, as though her sight had improved. As though windows had been opened.

Sometimes the girls giggling in the bodega irritated her and sometimes she felt lenient, almost pleased, with what they brought into the house, the adolescent fervor and secrets and hope. She wished she could feel that again.

Regret split her embryonic sense of well-being at least once an hour. She harbored much that she did not want Dixie to know, especially the shabby things she had done with Deaver. She wanted to tell him she'd snooped in his room and she was afraid that if she did confess—that's what it felt like—he would no longer want to be close to her.

Soapsuds ran twinkling in the sunlight down her wrists and forearms. A rooster crowed.

Dixie came in the front door, and for just a moment street noise crammed into the foyer with him. Wheeze of a diesel truck. A man shouting, greeting someone. He shut the door deliberately. Quietly.

The girls stopped giggling. They scampered out of the bodega, mops in hand.

He was not carrying groceries. "Kate, come here," he said.

"What is it?"

He went into the kitchen and she followed him, wiping her damp hands on her kimono. He slapped a folded newspaper on the counter. He poured a glass of water from the agua puro bottle, drank it down, took off his glasses, and laid them on the table. His face sweaty and pink and contorted.

"Sit down," he invited.

"What's wrong?" Kate said, sitting down at the table. He pulled out another chair and it scraped peevishly. He took the seat next to her.

"This is very bad news," he said, reaching for her hands.

"*What?*" Kate said, frowning. She thought first of Lino, then Sunny.

"Something's happened to Maggie."

Kate reared back. "No!"

"It's the worst thing."

"What are you telling me?"

"She's gone, Kate."

"Are you out of your mind?"

"She died in Ruinas."

She whimpered and a furious quaking began inside her.

"Not Maggie, please—not Maggie—"

"Kate—it's in the papers."

He opened the paper and she cried out. She scanned the article in the *Miami Herald*. North Americans Killed by Contras on June 14. Robert G. Elliott and Margaret A. Byrne. Found with shovels in their hands. Near a creek. A State Department investigation is pending. The remains were returned on June 16 to their families in the United States. Over a week, a week, a week had gone by.

"Fuck, fuck, fuck." She flew up and pounded the counter, bruising her hand. She swept a pile of grocery sacks to the floor. She bawled, "Jesus fuck."

The two girls had come to the kitchen door. They stared inside. Dixie said, "They were doing the work they were called to do."

Kate fumed at him, "What? What—do you—fucking—know about it? What do you know about her? You—"

She beat her chest with her fist. "Listen to me. They were out there strictly because, because they were hot for each other. That's all." She crumpled to the floor. "That's all . . . that's all—"

She tore the newspaper in two, with great effort. Her hands blackened with newsprint ink. She pounded the floor with her fist.

"Dix oh Dix oh oh oh. I can't do it, I can't . . . I just can't. . . ." Kate sat up, weeping. She trembled from within. "God, I can't lose Maggie. I can't lose Maggie. I just can't. . . ."

"Kate, Kate," Dixie comforted. He knelt and tried to put his arms around her.

Kate yanked away. "They were only putting in a water system." Then, "Leave me alone. Just leave me alone. . . ." She wiped her face; she wiped her tears. Ink smeared her cheeks.

He crouched beside her. He hung his head, relenting. "If that's what you want." Then he rose as far as a chair and sat down.

"Oh my god my god my god oh my god." She fisted up her hands and hit her temples.

"Let me make you a drink."

"I have to call Paul."

"The phones are down." Then, to Victoria and Juanita, "Maybe you'd better go home, girls."

The two girls stood there, mouths agape. Finally Victoria said, "Ahora mismo?"

"Sí, ahora mismo. Por favor," Dixie said. "La señorita está muy triste."

Kate dragged herself up and tore out to the courtyard, her kimono flying. She jerked a clean wet towel from the clothesline. Swatted at plants and Posh. She thrashed. She screamed. She clutched up a potted red geranium and flung it at the wall; it broke and the pot shards fell neatly into four sections.

"There! There," she yelled.

Over and over.

He let me storm around.

It was the blackest time I had ever known. That kind of grief is a monster that holds you down and it's very strong and you might as well give up wrestling, you don't have a prayer, you have to endure it, and all you know in your heart of hearts is that life is one fucking loss after another. You don't know that for the first forty years or so, but then it dawns on you. Oh, this. Okay. Oh, that too? Then you lose something really big. And the monster grins at you. A god you have confronted. He holds all the power. You're at his mercy. But mercy's not the stuff he's made of. Maggie Maggie Maggie Maggie Maggie Maggie Maggie Maggie Maggie Byrne—

In her darkened room, lying spent on the bed. Maggie's name a weight on her chest. It was night. She did not know how late. Her door was open a slash. To moonlight. Starlight. She could hear the water in the fountain.

"I want to die," she cried out.

"I'm here," Dixie said. His voice just outside her door.

"I can't stand it. . . ."

"If you need me, let me know."

She listened for his footsteps. He did not leave her doorway.

All night long waves of grief broke over her, took her out to the sea of sorrow.

Los Cuartos de Sangre, Los Cuartos de Amor

Days she spent in her room gray as night and the nights themselves smothered Kate. With fireworks and the inexplicable cheer of people in the neighborhood. Going on with their lives. Helicopters blackened the sky over Antigua, a pared sky, its borders the up-and-down horizon of deep folded mountains. Helicopters chopped overhead, hanging peeringly, spinning away. At first Kate would venture only as far as the kitchen but she heard them beating their wings, miracles of machinery. What did they have to do with her? Nothing, her rational voice said. Her rational voice: issuing from a cave in her torso. She located it, listened for it. Nothing has anything to do with anything, she reiterated unceasingly. That was God's honest truth: Maggie dying did not mean anything to the Sandinistas or the Contras. She'd been used for target practice.

Sunny had visited while Kate was in bed, weeping. The middle of the second night. Sunny had come rustling through the bedroom door, saying, "Kate. Kate. May I come in?" She sat on the edge of Kate's bed. In a smear of yellow light from the colonnade. She looked jaundiced in that light. Kate felt like a prisoner Sunny was visiting. Fated. They whispered, though there was no need to whisper. No one was home but Dixie. A day later Kate could not remember what they had said. Sunny had placed a caring hand on Kate's back and left it there, circling lightly, never losing contact, until Kate had finally fallen asleep. When she woke up Sunny was gone.

For a week she did not eat more than a slice of toast now and again. The food would sit there on the kitchen counter, glistening obscenely. Pasta salad under plastic wrap. Potato rolls and butter. Melons. Hunger was a dream she might have had once. Her appetites had been sucked from her. Dixie laid out the food and he put it away. Kate would come to the kitchen and sit at the table and drink while he had dinner. He had gone out and bought her a bottle of Gordon's. It was what she wanted; she could make herself sick on it if she liked.

Finally she gathered her reserves to go to GUATEL. Dixie had gone to the market. She moved through the house as though her flesh were weighed down with disease. It took a long time to get dressed. To braid her hair. To make sure she had everything she needed in her denim pouch. She wrote out a list of numbers she would try. A list of lifelines.

Dixie came in the front door and set down his string bags. Long stiff egg noodles stuck out of a narrow brown sack. He said, "Where you headed?"

"Out. I have to get out a while."

"Don't go right now, Kate."

"I have to," she said, moving toward her room. "I have to get out. It's been a week."

Dixie followed her. "Stay for dinner. You can go after. I'll drive you."

Her room was dark with narrow slats of weak evening light coming through the shutters, cutting across the paisley bedspread. She sat on the soft edge of the mattress. Bent over her sneakers to tie them. Hair curved over her face. She did not look at him but said, "This is important."

"Don't, Kate."

She peered up at him. He stood in the light just outside her door. Posh flew up to his shoulder and clawed obeisantly at the wool stitches of his sweater. He said, "I think someone was watching. As I came home."

"Like who?"

He hesitated. He plucked the parrot up and set him on a nearby table. He put his hands in the pockets of his chinos. "I don't know. Their windows were dark."

"Well, who would want to?"

He shook his head. "Don't get involved."

"Believe me, I won't. I have to make some phone calls. I have to." She pressed past him.

He grabbed her hand. His hand felt warm and padded; she felt a slight keen surge. Touching.

"What?"

"It's safer inside."

She pulled away from him. "You're paranoid."

Kate strode toward the front door. He tried to block her way.

"Eight years in the lion's den and you're still naive."

"Leave me alone."

"I think Ben's coming back." He put out one hand, offering her this last bribe.

"None of that matters now."

Dixie turned away from her, rubbing the back of his neck, exasperated. He blocked the doorway with an outstretched arm. "I'm trying to look out for you."

"I have to talk to someone who knows me." She slipped under his arm. "I'll be back."

She lifted the iron latch of the front door and stepped over the door sill into the early evening street; an opaque coppery light coated the sky like the inside of a bowl. The pastel colors of the houses had deepened. There were people on the street: two plump women talking by a short doorway, their dark heads tucked urgently near each other, a boy on a ratchety motorbike, three men moving a large piece of furniture into the house across the street, a wardrobe or an armoire. Two dogs circled a wad of garbage, yelping tentatively. Plucking and yanking at it with bared teeth.

Kate caught a glimpse of the car Dixie spoke of—she could see that its windows were tinted almost black. New and boxy, a Cherokee or something like it. She would not look long at it directly; she did not want to lend it credence. Instead she set off walking forcefully, purposefully. Toward the center of town. The volcano. The volcano lit by the sunset.

Her heart pumped—a fierce lub-lub. So this is what it's like, she thought. She had been followed before, but that time she had been accompanied by Sandinista soldiers and had felt protected. She had been on her way to the mined school bus where the children were waiting in shock, covered in blood like birthmarks. This time she did not know her enemy. This was different and she felt her bladder pressing inside her and her stomach contracting and it was a sick feeling and she kept saying to herself, I'm lucky, I'm lucky, worse than this has happened to me. She thought of the times she had lied to Mexican soldiers when she walked past their checkpoint on the way to the refugee camp. Once they grew accustomed to her she did not even have to lie. She had been dark-skinned and growing darker every day, with long black hair, the hair she had not cut more than an inch or two in years. She had taken to wearing it in a long braid to keep life simple. She learned to be deferential to the Mexican soldiers, to speak a minimum of Spanish, and they actually let her pass. So many times. Not once did they ask for her papers. In Chiapas she had been pumped full of the adrenaline of lust and the adrenaline of subterfuge. She had almost always felt this pressing in her bladder as though she had to pee but couldn't.

At GUATEL she called collect.

She heard Paul come on the line. The operator asked him to accept the charges. "No," he said, "I don't think so."

Kate's throat constricted. Her tear ducts were dry and swollen. There was that click at the other end.

Her hands shook. She went out of the telephone booth and gave the clerk her mother's number. It was busy. Just to talk, to honor Maggie—all the hope she had mustered washed away. She wished she could lie down.

She went out to the park stood in line to buy a chucho, out of habit, not hunger. She stood in line to buy the chucho. To have something to do. Tears stung her eyes.

She did not know if she could eat but she wanted to try. She felt hollow from not eating. She'd swallowed the sound of Paul's voice saying no. A dark raw no. She took her chucho and retreated to a bench across from the vendors. She ate; it was hard to swallow. Paul said no. She looked at that from every side. Paul who had loved her said no. The thought was like a box right in front of her that might explode. Emotional detonations were likely.

Kate got up and tossed her corn husk in a trash can. When she returned to her bench, a portly man in a tight business suit sat down on the opposite end. He ate an ice cream cone and a slight brush of pink ice cream ran across his mustache. The streetlight shone down, casting a lavender splotch on his bald head.

"Buenas noches, señora," he said quietly, without looking directly at her.

"Buenas noches," she said, with not one shred of good will.

"You are a friend of Sunny Hires."

"Who wants to know?"

At that moment someone in a car, his car, it must be, shone its headlights directly on Kate. Pinned her there. In piss-yellow foglight.

"My friends want to talk to Sunny."

Kate got up and walked away.

"We know who you are, Vidalúz," the man called. Or did he call, "Do you know Vidalúz?" Kate did not trust her own ears.

Her knees shook. Vidalúz. She kept walking until she got to the shadowy edge of the park where the taxi drivers squatted, across from the cathedral. At the highest cathedral step, a lone drummer banged a big mournful drum.

She found Alberto on a curb under a broad and leafy tree, in the tree's shadow, with two other taxi drivers, their cigarette tips brass pins in the dark. The three men looked up startled from their desultory talk. Alberto's face was slim; an athletic sleekness cloaked his body; he leaped up and graciously opened his taxi's door.

Once inside he said, "What is wrong, señorita?" He leaned over the seat. His elbow nearly touching her knee.

"I don't know, Alberto."

He spoke very softly. "Where do you want to go?"

"Take me to the Mexican restaurant," she said. "Near the Church of the Merced."

"Pronto." He started the car and worked his way around a clump of revelers at the corner of the park. One woman glowed in a white dress.

"Can you come back and get me later, Alberto?"

"A qué hora?"

"Two hours from now?"

"Sí, sí." He glanced up at her in the rearview mirror. "You will be safe there?"

"I'm sure I will be. I'm just going to have a glass of wine and visit with some friends. But I do not want to walk home that late."

"I will come for you. Don't worry."

She did not turn around to see if the bald man had trailed after. She looked ahead and all Antigua was out, it seemed, in the streets and on the steps, amid the golden lights and white lights, amid the pearly black shadows in the middle of the blocks. Engines gunning. Babies crying. Salsa music erupting from the gardens and the restaurants. All their bridled energy released into night, into a few hours of freedom. She did not think she should feel afraid but she did feel afraid. Her body was afraid, shivering.

The Mexican restaurant had floor-to-ceiling shutters opening onto the street. The bar sparkled—opaque iridescent glass lit from inside. Music from the States reached the street, rock and roll she did not recognize. There was probably plenty she would not recognize when she got home. If she was able to find her way home. Eight years in the lion's den. She paid Alberto and wished him a good night. Inside she made her way to the inner patio, a sheltered place with stars overhead. She felt she did not breathe a normal breath until the waiter had taken her order and she had the chance to simply sit for a few minutes, among other North Americans. It made her feel more safe to sit among them.

There were many places a woman could not go alone but this place was all right. Sometimes it was called the Texas Spur, sometimes it was called the Lone Star. For an hour Kate took refuge on the patio, dim exile of drinkers, nursing a glass, and then another, of bitter red Argentinian wine, examining the cloudy detritus in the bottom of her glass. Now and then a stench like rotting chicken skin rose over the patio wall. The music never changed: a country twang the origin of which she could not quite put her finger on. The round metal table wobbled. Kate folded a matchbook cover and tucked it under one table leg. Hands trembling. She held the opaque glass in both her hands to steady them. A wind portended a cool night, possibly rain. A chill tingled unexpectedly up her back and arms. She wished she'd worn her only wool sweater. The people dining or waiting to dine were inside. She could see them through an open window where gauzy curtains belled out, the wind inside the curtains persistent as flesh. Waist-high terra-cotta olive jars lined the patio; ivy curled and twisted up one stony wall.

"Kate?"

There slouched Ginger, boyishly slender, her skin chapped around her nose and mouth, her clothes—a wool poncho, loose slacks—stinking of patchouli and cigarette smoke and cardamom chewing gum. On her feet she wore only sandals.

"Ginger," Kate said. "Cómo le va?"

Ginger leaned close and stage-whispered, "Do you believe in God's will?" Her fine hair brushed Kate's cheek.

Kate laughed, more harshly than she intended. "You mean everyday chaos?" she said.

"Can I sit down?" Without waiting, Ginger pulled out the other metal chair and folded herself into it, arms straight out on the table, hands clasped.

"See those people in the dining room? By the palm tree?"

The woman's hair was falsely red: red cellophane. The man wore a dark suit; he hovered over a calculator; he had a bald spot the size of an egg.

Kate struck a match and lit the stubby white candle in the center of the table. A curl of flame lit up Ginger's face. Her crucifix earrings bobbed in the candlelight. Kate felt a warmth established by the light: a potential but slight and undesirable connection, as though they'd found themselves seated side by side on a bus. "What about them?"

"They want me to have their baby."

"Are you out of your mind—"

"Shh—"

Kate said, "They look . . . like they don't belong here."

Ginger smacked her lips, slightly irked. "I think you're reading them way wrong."

The woman straightened her skirt and cupped her hand protectively over her leather clutch lying on the table. The man had a recent haircut, with his sideburns trimmed shorter than Kate had ever seen sideburns, even with the tops of his ears. His face was freckled and guileless but Kate thought it was a studied guilelessness. The woman's makeup—a coppery sheen—concealed whatever emotion a face might possibly register. Her face was small, foxy. The man placed his hand over hers. They made an effort not to glance Ginger's way.

Ginger flipped up the hood of her poncho. "She thinks I look like her. She can't get pregnant." She reached tentatively for Kate's glass. "Can I have a sip? They only let me drink juice."

Kate nudged the glass across the table. Ginger took a gulp of wine.

"So, did your friend finally show up?" she said.

Kate closed her eyes; she covered her mouth with her hands. She tried to treat herself gently. She had noticed a tendency toward roughness when she touched herself, punishment of a sort.

She shook her head. She couldn't form the words to tell Ginger.

Ginger shot a sly look toward the couple. "So—are you staying?"

"God forbid," Kate said. Then, "Tell me you're putting me on."

"Listen. They're paying me. They'll put me up in a nice place, cable TV, pay all my expenses—" She made a fist as though she'd caught the brass ring on the merry-go-round. "I'm like, wow, I could actually *not* go home and sponge off my folks. I could relax—"

"Having a baby's not a temp job."

Ginger peered at Kate from beneath the hood, squinting, irritated. She whined, "They have a right to be happy." She drank from Kate's glass once more, then grinned sheepishly. "And—at the end—after—I'll have ten thousand dollars. Clear."

Kate hung her head, squeezed her temples. Adjusted her glasses. "Ginger, Ginger." She reached out and Ginger relinquished her wine glass. "Does Dixie know about this?"

Ginger said, "What's Dixie to me? I'm Methodist. Sort of."

"He cares about you."

Ginger said, "That's his job."

"What about school?"

"School's over."

Kate frowned.

"For the year, it's over for the year," Ginger said. "I passed everything. I did."

"I thought you had a guy here?"

"Figment of my imagination," Ginger said.

"This is a cold way to bring another life into the world."

"You have a better idea? Like love?"

Kate took that in. She had nothing to counteract Ginger's cynicism. Then she asked, "I'm not sure I want to know, but what's their story?"

"Simple story. They're from California. San something or other. He's a banker. He has a laptop computer with him. He's *starting* a bank. In the capital. She golfs and grows zinnias and stuff like that."

"I'm stunned," Kate said. "Though I don't know why."

"I had to see what you'd say. You're like the first person I've told."

"You don't have a clue what you're getting into. Your hormones'll change. It's not a joy ride."

Ginger shyly glanced down. "No big deal," she said.

In that moment Kate intuited—suspected—that she was already pregnant. And worse, she had a premonition: that somehow, somewhere, she would be called upon to deliver Ginger's baby. She pictured it: the crowning of the big red head, Ginger terrified and screaming.

The waiter went to the couple's table and left the check.

Kate leaned close to her across the table. She slid the wine glass in Ginger's direction. "I am absolutely freezing. If you're going with them—they do have a car, don't they?—could I borrow your poncho? Just till tomorrow. You could come by for it, or I could meet you at the park."

"What'll I wear?"

"This," Kate said, stripping off her cardigan. "If they have a car—"

"They do. It's really cool."

Kate shrugged.

"Sure, okay," Ginger said. "That's cool. You can just put it with my stuff in the bodega. I'll stop by for it."

They traded cardigan and poncho. Kate stood up, slipped into the poncho. "That's better, much better," she pretended. Like pinpricks, the woolen fibers scratched her bare arms and neck.

"I'm not afraid to do this," Ginger said.

"If you say so." Kate thought some encouragement was called for, but she did not have it in her. Then she faintly mustered, "It's okay if you are afraid."

"I'll probably be, like, nervous, when the time comes. But I'm not now."

Ginger got up and looked at the couple and smiled. They smiled back at her—cordial, phony, meant-to-be-reassuring smiles. Ginger pressed her palms on the back of the chair she'd been sitting in. Her nails were bitten down to the quick. "You can tell Dixie. Tell him not to worry about me."

Tell him yourself was on Kate's lips, but she said, "If you want, I will."

"I'd better go," Ginger said. "They're waiting."

"Wait. Please. I wondered . . . did you know Sunny very well?"

"Sort of, I guess. I moved in before Christmas."

Kate stepped closer to Ginger. She could smell her chewing gum. "Do you have any idea what was going on for her?"

Ginger stuck her fists in the cardigan pockets. "Look. I gotta go." She turned and walked proudly, head high, sandals squeaking. The hem of her slacks had come undone in the back.

The man and woman sighed with relief, exchanged glances. He laid a pile of wrinkled quetzales on the check. They hurriedly scooped up their things—a tan umbrella, her purse, his calculator—and hustled Ginger out of the Texas Spur.

Kate tried to imagine Ginger's mother and father, somewhere in Washington State, having an ordinary life while their daughter was out of their reach, making mistakes. She was old enough to be Ginger's mother: that was a shocking thought. She didn't dwell on that. She paid the check, said, Pase buena noche, and flipped up the hood of the poncho.

At the open front doors, between the dark green shutters, she waited for Alberto. From beneath the poncho hood she scanned the cobblestone street for the men who had followed her. She watched for Alberto's yellow taxi; he would squire her home. At her back the music wound its way among the drinkers, filament of nostalgia: she finally recognized it: the Allman Brothers. Paul had liked that. For a moment she could almost taste shots of tequila at someone's kitchen counter on New Year's Eve. Paul had worn a paper king's crown and she had worn a paper fool's cap. The memory muddied after that, blurred. She recalled the music and the tequila and the paper hats; the feel of the night was lost. The wine she had drunk made hazy all that had gone wrong that day: the argument with Dixie; Paul's refusal to accept her phone call; the man in the park.

She stepped down onto a sidewalk made long ago of blocks of granite like modest gravestones laid end to end. Under an archway across the street a policeman in a royal blue uniform held a chubby baby in his arms; the baby wore a lacy ivory dress; the baby's mother looked on approvingly. People strolling home took their sweet time. A gringo strode around the dawdlers, into the street. Kate would have called him a boy, about nineteen, in a tam-o-shanter made from recycled tipica. He could have been a basketball player from the Midwest. Strawberry blond. Clean-shaven. Well fed. He sang out, to no one in particular, "Te amo y solimente tu! I love you and only you!" He seemed a little drunk, a little lonely. The Guatemalans nearby laughed at him, with him. For that moment there was good will among everyone on the street.

Except Maggie. Maggie did not laugh or sashay down the street or kiss Kate's cheek. Maggie did not exist anymore and that knowledge was too big to see, too enormous.

An almost imperceptible earthquake tremor snaked under Kate's feet. No one else seemed to notice. She folded her hands beneath the poncho; brushing Ginger's hand as they traded garments had made her feel all over again the scarcity of touch. She had taken to falling asleep at night holding her own hand under the pillow; there was closure, a circle, comfort, in that. Across the street a woman sold steamed corn on the cob out of a zinc washtub. Children crowded around the tub. She thought of all the corn she'd eaten as a child. The nubby kernels. Butter running down your wrist. Shingly salt and silky butter. And the sigh of night, the visible humidity over rosy-tasseled cornfields, the unending sizzle of insects during summer, during the fall. Lupita liked to say that when you get older you live in memory more than not. Memory had heft; available imagery. But what lay ahead dissolved, disappeared. The iridescent cries and laughter of the children lit up the darkening street.

I don't believe the dead can dance.

Or hear the music. Not now or ever. Think of resurrection, heavenly equations. Me. My body. My family. In heaven with me. The priest crosses your forehead every Ash Wednesday with fine grit. His words are the literal truth: dust to dust. The cheating hearts and faded loves are trashy compulsions, aren't they? In the face of that.

My mother and my aunts listened to country music, they sang those songs. They belted them out. My mother and Aunt Dodie and Aunt Mary Lou. They would sit in the dark on the screened-in summer porch when the bugs were bad or they would sit on the patio when the lilacs were coming in or when the catalpa leaves were falling and they drank syrupy drinks, cocktails, they called them. The music would be blaring from the hi-fi inside the house and they would giggle and sigh and long for—men, I suppose they thought that's what they longed for. "Empty Arms" was a song they loved, and I felt deeply embarrassed by them and I would go into the house and turn down the volume on the hi-fi, notch by notch, in case the neighbors could hear. They gossiped always about the past, that was their obsession, the past. They never talked about what lay ahead, and Maggie and I did not understand that then. They talked about

betrayals, evil motives, the carelessness of men, and I swore I would
never be like them. Left drinking on a humid Midwestern porch,
the steel glider squeaking, the mildew creeping into the seams of the
glider's cushions, with piles of cut fabric circles or skeins of yarn on
a bridge table. They were always making something, covering bottle caps with fabric and sewing the caps together to make a trivet or
crocheting Christmas ornaments in August. Idle hands are the
devil's playground—there's a lesson Maggie and I took to heart.
Aunt Mary Lou had been married and had two boys—my cousins,
where are they today? We are not a family that keeps track of
cousins, we are scattered—and then John Williams left without saying why or where he was going. He just lit out for parts unknown,
they always said, and there were those stories of the deserters, the
men who went out for a pack of cigarettes and never came back, who
went to work in the canneries in Alaska or the oil rigs off the Texas
coast, who went to live in anonymous high-rises near Pimlico to be
able to play the ponies, who worked as bill collectors and repo men,
pots calling the kettles black, Aunt Mary Lou would say. You could
take a man to court for desertion and failure to support, if you could
find him. That was the trick. When I was a skinny kid hanging
around that porch, learning my love lessons, Aunt Dodie had been
in love with a married man for twenty years or more, and every year
he promised her that he'd leave his wife after the holidays. She liked
to sit on the darkened porch in her slip. I always wanted a slip like
that. Satiny. Champagne-colored. Always—when I was ten or
eleven. My mother would wear her robe or a sundress printed with
lemons like kitchen wallpaper or, in fall, a downy corduroy shirt and
jeans that zipped up the side and bobby sox. Aunt Mary Lou had
permed blue-black hair and she always wore red. Their hair smelled
like menthol smoke and Evening in Paris they bought in boxed sets
at the five and dime. The Evening in Paris bottles were blue glass—
cobalt blue—and they couldn't bear to throw them out, they kept
them stashed in a cupboard in the basement, thinking they might be
valuable someday. "Empty Arms" was a song Aunt Dodie could play

on the upright piano and Mary Lou could sing. Her torch songs, she called them. You remember those songs? I've got your picture, she's got you. Sweet dreams of you. I'm crazy, crazy for feeling so blue. If you've got leavin' on your mind, get it over, hurt me now, get it over.

Those songs determined my course in ways kept hidden from me. Some wise man said that sin consists of enslavement to what you don't know about yourself. I can think about that now, I can, in spite of being at the crossroads, I have taken the time to mull over what I'm telling you. Dixie told me, and I believed him, that looking deeply into everything is a spiritual path you can follow anywhere, anytime. That's contemplative prayer. Just looking deeply, travel on the dark side, a journey once you begin you cannot stop. But then, in Antigua, sin was a word I hadn't spoken or thought in years, a word I'd left outside the attic door when Paul and I were kids. We didn't know we were only kids, what a sweet time that is, when you think you will always be the way you are. The priest tried to spoil that, but I just quit going to confession, that was how I solved that problem—and Paul and I lay down together on the dusty sofa in the attic. The song would be over, the needle would scratch and wobble and scratch on the forty-five, you really got a hold on me, we loved that song, we gave ourselves up to it, we called what we did dancing, but we stood there, leaning into each other, swimming in the motes of attic dust, finding out how we fit together, you really got a hold on me would be over, you really got a hold on me. And somehow we would end up on the slanting sofa, and we would not get up to change the record. We would not let go, we would not stop our mouths, which became one mouth. If that was sin I could not speak the word and mean it.

We were young together.

After all that. He said no.

The sound of his voice solid.

Later I would think of that no as a bell ringing, clarity calling me to another window. But that night my feelings blew up and wailed from the four directions.

Ten o'clock. It seemed like the middle of the night. So close to the equator the night and day were nearly of equal length year round. There was some lesson in that, Kate thought, when Alberto dropped her off at home, some template to be borrowed for balance. No one was about. A wafer of moon shone on the windshield of the jeep. Latched shutters creaked. Alberto did not drive away until she was safely inside.

Two lights lit the otherwise darkened courtyard, a candle fluttering just inside the front door and a pad of lavender fluorescence from the bathroom down the colonnade. Kate slid the bolt lock over. Iron on iron, a secure sound.

"Blow that out, would you?"

Dixie appeared beside the bathroom door, a length of dental floss wound between two fingers. He was barefooted.

Kate said, "I hope you're not waiting up for me."

"What happened?" he said.

She had to pass him to get to her room. Key in hand, she stood close enough to whisper, "You were right. I saw them."

"Did they say anything?" He stepped into the bathroom, dropped his dental floss into a basket. Waiting.

Kate waved one hand over her head. "It was a bald guy. In a suit. He asked for Sunny, then . . . he said something about Vidalúz."

Dixie said, "You're okay?"

Kate took a deep breath. "They got my heart rate up."

"What'd you do?"

"Walked away."

Dixie put his hand on her shoulder. "I'm glad to see you." Then, with a glance at the poncho, he said, "You saw our friend? Ginger."

"She's in deep trouble."

"How so?"

Kate went on to her room, fiddled with her lock, and said, "Can we talk?"

"Come on to the kitchen."

In her room Kate stripped off the poncho, picked up her bottle of gin by its neck. There wasn't much left.

Dixie waited in the kitchen beside the stove, arms folded, a question in his eyes. He'd put on his sandals and a sweater. Kate began by making a drink—ice from the fridge; you knew you were in a civilized place if there was ice for a drink; a clean glass from the shelf above the sink, a tall glass corny with Christmas decals; a can of grapefruit juice, the size they serve on airplanes, with a bluebird on the label. The preparations for drinking felt, if not good, consolingly familiar, particularly late at night.

She told him about Ginger.

He said, "She's got a long way to tumble before she wakes up."

"Do you think we can do anything?"

"I doubt it. But if I run into her, I'll try. If you see her again, let her know, let her know—that we're here for her."

Kate drank a long sip. The gin cut a pleasant swath down her throat and into her empty stomach. She had not eaten much in a week; she would have to eat; hunger was finally evident. She was coming back to her body.

"How're you feeling?" Dixie said.

"I tried to call Maggie's brother," Kate said. "He refused to accept the charges."

"I'm sorry." He arched one eyebrow. His eyes were not to be avoided.

Kate sat down at the table. She did not want to cry. She drank again. It was good, the tart juice, the edge of gin. She waited. His kindness made her feel like crying.

"Who are those men?"

"No one knows for sure," he said.

"Sunny's really in danger, isn't she? It's not just her protecting someone."

Patiently, to cut the sting of his words, he said, "I can't believe you lasted as long as you did in Nicaragua."

Old rage flared up. "The Revolution was over. There."

"The war wasn't. Obviously."

"I did my job in Managua." She did not like hearing her own defensive tone. Somehow they had gotten on opposite sides.

"I'm doing mine here."

"How do you see that? Your job, I mean." Before he could answer she spat out, "Oh, I can imagine. You're moved by Vidalúz's effort the way you're moved by the Chinese students. So what're you doing to help them? They need weapons, not your self-indulgence."

"You don't mean that."

"You don't know me."

"When you talk about armed struggle, that's not you. It's Mark Deaver."

"You didn't know him."

"You're not going to defend him, are you?"

"I was in love with him. I thought I was."

"You're upset. Not about that."

Kate did not know what demons filled her mouth. She shook her head and began to cry.

Dixie went to her. He put his arms around her, cradled her head against his belly. Kate said, "I don't want to be like this."

"Is there anything I can do?"

"I wish I had a cigarette," she said, not to him but to herself. She wiped her eyes on her shirt sleeve.

Dixie sat down across the table from her. Gently he said, "Kate. You need to go home. I'll be sorry to see you go. But don't you think—"

"I'm stronger than you think." She got up and rummaged in a basket on top of the refrigerator. The basket held bulbs of garlic, matchbooks from dance clubs in the capital—Manhattan, El Optimista—and a crushed pack of Winstons with one cigarette left. Ginger's remains. "Pay dirt," Kate said, wiggling the cigarette out of the pack with her forefinger. She lit up and leaned against the counter, her hips pressing into the formica. "But right now everything's an undertaking. I don't feel up to it. I don't feel up to going yet. Do you understand that?" She tapped her ashes in the sink. "Did they know Sunny was here? To see me?"

"I don't think so."

"You still want me to go with you? To the highlands?"

"If you want to go."

"I do."

"I'm not going to my village after all. I'm taking some fruit and other things to Xamamatze, a relocation camp."

"That's fine. There's nothing holding me here."

Then she cried again. She thought she had no tears left, but they kept on.

The wine she'd drunk, feeling on the spot: these made her rasp, "I can't deal with how . . . defeated I feel."

His arms opening were no different than his arms opening at mass: The Lord be with you. Kate moved into them. He smelled clean, soapy, and felt invincible. Her cigarette was in her way and she reached beyond him to the ashtray on the counter and placed the half-smoked butt on its lip. He wrapped his arms around her and let her cry. Better to drink alone, she thought. Drinking primed the pump and she brimmed with all she could not say to herself sober. But drinking with company somehow distorted her feelings. She did not know if what she wanted to say was the truth so she said nothing. Was there anything true she could say except that Maggie was gone? All other news of the world or the heart paled in comparison to that.

Dixie was holding her. She thought she could not stand it; it was all she wanted and needed. Don't give in—

He crossed his hands on her back. She heard his breath in her ear.

He said, "Feeling defeated's not the worst thing. You've allowed so much in. And it's hurt you. There's strength in that willingness."

She stopped crying and pulled back.

"Am I making things worse?" He sat down.

Kate rescued her cigarette, picked up her drink. Her props; having her props shored her up. "Look," she said, "I'm just not in very good shape. I'm better. I am. You've . . . I've . . . been grateful. But I need to handle this alone."

At the door, in a faint voice, she said, "Sweet dreams. Really."

She turned away, onto the colonnade, the slippery waxed tiles like a stream whose wavelets she rode to her room. A truck rumbled over the cobblestones beyond the foyer; a drunk—a kindred wraith, she thought—went by singing in Spanish at the top of his lungs, his song some sloppy ballad. And before sleep's vertigo the church bells rang, not celebrating anything, just the simple notation of time passing, life gone.

The house was emptying out.

Lino had gone to the highlands by chicken bus.

After that night, three rainy days passed before they managed a truce. They avoided each other. Only once did their eyes meet across the courtyard. A clap of thunder had shaken the house. Kate opened her bedroom door and stood barefooted, staring out, her hair unbraided; she wore sweatpants and a T-shirt, wrapped in a scratchy wool blanket, with the rain walling her in, the birds-of-paradise blowing about as though their flowers might break. Dixie stepped to the kitchen door with Posh a green shiny blur on his hand and even with the steely cadence of the rain Kate could hear that he was soothing Posh, saying all the comfort love he could to keep the bird calm, for Posh hated rain. Their eyes met through the rain and Dixie's broadcast a question and hers closed in response.

She had to cut her losses. Close down.

Once or twice a day she went out to the corner store to buy a carton of yogurt or a few bananas. The Cherokee that had followed her was never in sight, though she watched for it. A chill came over her whenever she turned to the spot on the street where she'd first seen it, the way your body shivers at the place where you've once been burned or cracked your shin. She would return wet from the rain and light the gas oven and open the oven door and stand in the kitchen drying her clothes and listening to the BBC. By the light of the sixty-watt bulb in her room she read biographies Sunny had left behind, bits and pieces of musty paperbacks whose pages bloomed damply and contained the rain of many rainy seasons. She read until her eyes ached but sometimes she would find herself reading the same block of type over and over while her thoughts wandered farther and farther away. Paul would send the money. She wanted to feel sure of that. He was efficient and responsible that way; he did not want to talk to her, but money, that was a different story, easier to give than love buried in sorrow. She imagined the crisp bills she would receive from Lloyd's. Her thoughts turned to one woman after another whose babies she had caught in their slippery birth grime. And to Maggie, all mental roads led back to Maggie, her greatness of heart. Kate had been less at war with herself when living with Maggie; she had been more whole.

Jude returned on a rainy morning and packed a plaid suitcase. She was going back to New Orleans on business, for how long she could not say. She sat in the kitchen with Kate, waiting for Dixie to come home from the market so she could say good-bye. Kate made her a mug of coffee. Jude kept one eye on the foyer.

Posh screamed, a sound like a tormented child, when the rain rang down hard from the red tile roof like thick gray cords into the abandoned courtyard. And Dixie was not there to console him.

Out of the blue, Jude said, "What do you want in your next life?"

What a peculiar phrase, your next life.

"Ordinariness," Kate said. "Time to think about myself instead of others."

Those answers seemed to bring Jude some relief. She couldn't wait any longer. She shook Kate's hand and said, God bless, have a good life, and it was obvious that Jude thought they would never meet again.

On July 4, Kate and Dixie managed a truce.

He invited her out to Doña Luisa's to watch the news. They told each other Fourth of July stories: the worst and best. Watching fireworks over the Wabash. Making homemade ice cream. Humidity so thick you thought you could drink it. Too much drinking. There was always that, the longing for a change of mind, a dilution of what you could not confront, whatever troubled you. She said she was sorry. She said she was going to quit drinking and suddenly that seemed a possibility. Easy. Not a big sacrifice. He did not press her to talk about that; he did not scold or instruct.

Kate waited. Once she had waited for her best friend; now she longed for congruence. A galvanizing.

People crowded into Lloyd's Bank. The soldier guarding the bank wore black wraparound sunglasses, a gold chain, a beret. A Sacred Heart tattoo on his arm. Fuzz on his upper lip. Kate guessed he was seventeen or eighteen. What did he think about with his weapon slung there at his hip? What adolescent cravings swept along like little boats behind those eyes?

She had been frugal but money was beginning to matter. She stood in line and the woman in the teller's cage said, No. No money for Katherine Banner. That did not mean he hadn't sent it. The system was a mystery to her; she had heard stories of money being sent bank to bank—Athens to Tegucigalpa or Chicago to San Miguel—and finally arriving weeks later.

On a bench among the roses she opened the denim pouch in which she kept her passport and her money. She wore the pouch's strap across her chest and it fit snugly under her left breast. She took out a red change purse stuffed with bills. Twenty U.S. dollars and one hundred quetzales. That was still plenty of money. She could flick through it without taking it out of the change purse. Looking at the money, counting the money, and putting the money safely away made her feel less strapped.

GUATEL was closed again. She had wanted to call her mother. How accustomed she had grown to doors being locked, inaccessibility. On the way to the market she checked the post office, where the strike was still on, the heavy wooden doors shut.

At the market some vendors had covered up their produce, their grains and beans. It was not a big market day. They were away from their stalls, running their own errands. The concrete aisles were slick in spots and an almost rotting odor hung over everything. She bought beans and rice, a half kilo each. Garlic and onions. Candles. She bought a shriveled orange to flavor the black beans.

On the walk home sunlight cut into the narrow street. She passed an optometrist's shop where a pregnant clerk in a wide pink dress helped a customer. Tourists lingered at a restaurant doorway, struggling to read the handwritten menu in a glass display case. Deaver was on her mind; he came and went. Something about the day, the way the weather had changed at last, some cue she couldn't even clearly see had tossed her into memories of Deaver, his voice when he pounded out his unshakable belief in armed struggle or the way he stood over the cardboard stage when he made his puppets speak or his charm—he could be charming. In the beginning he had been playful, flattering, validating glance for glance her own lust for herself. What she thought about, what obsessed her walking home, was a pastiche of memory. A kind of totalitarianism reigned when she remembered Deaver. She had been ruled by him for eight years, ignorant and craving. The fragile realization shamed her, humbled her.

She arrived at El Petén #3 without knowing the streets she had taken.

"Hola," Lino called. He sat in the shade of the courtyard, a book open on his lap.

"Hola," Kate said.

"Qué tal?"

"I'm okay," she said, willing that to be so. She set her purchases down on a table. Sweat dripped into her eyes. She wiped her forehead with the sleeve of her shirt. "Where's Dix?"

"Father Dixie—he's at the doctor's."

"Is he all right?"

Lino closed his book and kept one finger at his place. "I think he's all right. But the doctor wants to see him." In English he said, "To check him up."

"To check him out."

"To check him out." He cleared his throat. "Catarina."

"Yes?"

"I am so sorry about your friend. I wanted to say that I was sorry, but you were in your room when I left."

She did not want to talk about Maggie. She did not want to go over it one more time. Talk of what had happened cut into her privacy, an erosion that left her depleted. In four more days it would be a month since Maggie had died. She was anxious about facing that day. "Thank you," she said stiffly. Then, "It's hot today." She moved a lawn chair to the shade and sat down, not far from him.

"We have lemon-grass tea. Would you like?"

"Yes, I would. Thank you."

Lino laid his book face down on his chair and went into the kitchen. There was a balance about him, a physical symmetry, as though he had not been scarred too much, Kate thought. She picked up his book. *Where There Is No Doctor.* It was open to a chart of skin problems—diaper rash, eczema, pellegra, bedsores.

"Real ice for the iced tea," Lino said.

"For joy," Kate said. "Thanks."

"What is joy?"

"Alegría. Regocijo."

"Joy. Por joy." He lifted his glass in a toast.

They drank their tea and sat together quietly for a few moments. It was the first time they had been in the house with only each other. Posh wandered aimlessly around the courtyard, his green feathers dusty, pecking at a dead fly or a seed or a crumb here and there.

"Did you see the helicopters?"

"I heard them," Lino said.

"GUATEL is closed," Kate said.

"This happens."

"And the postal workers are still on strike."

Lino got up again and started for the kitchen. "Do you want to hear the news?" He brought the yellow radio to the courtyard and plugged it in just outside the kitchen door. Rose petals had fallen on the floor beside a bookcase from a day-old bouquet Dixie had made. Lino fiddled with the dials.

Rock and roll in Spanish blurted from every station. "No news," Lino said.

"Let's turn it off," Kate said. "Please. It makes my head hurt."

Lino came and sat down with her again. "We will hear about it. Whatever it is."

"So. Why're you reading this?" Kate said.

"My cousin—Angelina—she has a problem. Like this, I think—" Lino laid the book on the floor between them. He pointed to the chart in the book: a line drawing of the blisters called shingles. Posh toddled over to the book, pecked at its edges.

"Where are they?"

"Here," Lino said, raising his arm and rubbing.

Kate flinched. "They hurt, don't they?"

"She is in terrible pain."

"Where does she live?"

"In the mountains. Where I was visiting. She does not know what is wrong."

"Is there a doctor there?"

"Yes. There is a Belgian doctor. But she was away at another village."

"The doctor will know what to do. There's a cream you can use for that."

"Why does this come?"

"Everyone has that, inside—" Here Kate waved both hands from her head to her feet. "It stays dormant, asleep, most of the time. Hard times—you know what stress is? Stress makes it wake up."

"Stress?"

"Temor. Inquietud."

Lino was silent. He shook his head.

Kate said, "What?"

"Yes. I see."

"And what do you see?"

"We pray every day about these things."

"What things?"

"Fear y anxiety."

"What is Angelina fearful of?"

"Her life has not been easy. If you go there—to the mountains—you will see many women like Angelina. They will run from you. They have no trust."

"What happened to her?"

"She lost her family, Catarina," he murmured in Spanish. "One day she went to another village to buy tipica from a weaver in that village. Angelina has a store, you see, in her front room. While she was away the rain washed away the road, and she waited for the rain to stop. While she was away the soldiers came and took away her daughter and her husband. They took twenty-nine people that day. They took them to the bridge and they hung them over the water and they cut them with machetes until they fell part by part into the river. The river was muddy with the rain." Out on the street firecrackers went off and almost drowned his words. "But people say that after that the river was red with blood."

"God help us," Kate said.

"Angelina is sick now. It has been seven years. She has this—" He pointed to the book again. "In the month of her daughter's birth."

"What is going on here?" Kate said.

"It is plain to see. If you want to see."

"How can you just keep going?"

"What choice do we have?"

"Resist," Kate said.

"Many have resisted." He drank from his glass. "Many do."

The tea in his glass was jewel-like and pale, pale green. The shade surrounded them. Sunlight was out there, beyond where they sat, and at one time she would have experienced the sunlight as pleasant and enjoyable and drowsy, watching the sun move across the courtyard. A buffer, a wall, stood between Kate and the sun. They talked of many terrible things. She learned all that he would tell her about his family and la situación in the mountains. She told him all that he wanted to know about Nicaragua. The humming-birds trembled above the hibiscus. He had seen his brothers stabbed and killed by a soldier. The soldier had made the sign of the cross before he struck the first blow. Clouds too slight to threaten them puffed along the horizon. She had seen the children damaged by Contra mines. She had seen mothers giving birth while guarded by soldiers. Posh fell asleep on Lino's shoulder, his green head drooping. Lino wanted to know the cost of food in Nicaragua—beans, rice, corn. He wanted to know what made the people joyful. Did the Revolution make the people joyful, as he had heard? She had seen too much suffering to call it that. Still, they had forced a change. At what cost? Then Lino said, "My mother is a weaver, and her weavings tell the story of all that has happened. Blessed corn. Lords of the hills. Saints. The skulls of children float-ing in the river."

The courtyard contained a stillness like music, broken only by the music of their secret voices and the fountain water tinkling cleanly. Music over music. A gracile breeze, hummingbirds. While he talked, she forgot her particular pain.

Finally Kate said, "I can give you medicine for Angelina. If the pharmacy has it." And she went to the pharmacy. She paid for the Zovirax with quetzales from the red change purse. It was all right to trust that the money would come. That would be soon enough to decide whether to buy a one-way ticket to Indianapolis.

Back at home she put her black beans to soak in a red plastic bowl. No one else was about. Lino had left a note for Dixie: he promised to come for his lesson in the morning. He was going to his friend's house; his friend's mother would make dinner for them.

The little gin she had left she poured down the sink. She knew she would miss it, if not now then later, and she laughed, her first laugh since finding out about Maggie.

The vegetables she washed in a solution of water and chlorine bleach. She laid them out on a clean towel and admired their colors—the pale watery cabbage, the bright carrots. She concocted a salad, covered the salad bowl with a tin plate, and stashed it in the refrigerator. She had made enough for Dix.

He nearly always left his room open and unlocked. The house hung heavy with silence like funeral crepe. She stood before his slightly open door; her heart drummed. She nudged the door; he had left a lamp on, clipped to his headboard. His bed was made up, covered with a wool blanket: yellow stripes and gray birds. Books in disarray slipped down from piles. At the foot of the bed, where she could read the titles without entering, were *The Gnostic Gospels* and *Love in the Time of Cholera*.

Hammers pounded next door, across the stucco wall, arythmic banging, irritating, threatening. Whine of a saw, lumber clunking: the noises dispelled her reverie. She had always prided herself on not being a sneak, for any reason. But she could not undo her mistake. The hands on Dixie's clock clicked as each second unwound, a life undone, undone, in waiting.

Dixie said, "Saint John of the Cross called it the lucky dark. That was my lucky dark—during the fever."

Kate asked, "How so?"

They were eating dinner in the highlands, where Dixie had taken her. In the Cuchumatanes Range at nearly two thousand meters above sea level. They had risen, switchback by switchback, into a new ecosystem—subtropical, lush, wet. Above the world, she thought. But not above what tore at her.

Dixie said, "My defenses were down. I hallucinated. What strange and beautiful times. You don't think you'll feel that being sick. But I did."

"And?"

"I came out of it questioning language. The church's language."

"So what happened?" she asked, pushing food—rice, some unnamed meat—around on her plate. She still could not eat much.

"Dogma fell away. Like scaffolding you build to do the work you need to do."

Rain fell lightly in the dirt courtyard just beyond their table. Down the corridor a large lightbulb—stippled with dead insects—burned dimly. Rain gleamed in the dark from elephant ears and ferns and begonias in rusty syrup cans. It had been dark for over an hour. Dark and wet and cold. Kate could see her breath.

After dinner Dixie lit a candle. Between them was a pot of licorice tea. Kate's mug was plastic, with a border of white flowers around the rim. She'd bought it in the market in San Cristóbal, so long ago; how silly that this mug was one of the few things she'd kept; she had been careless with possessions; they hadn't mattered to her in the long run. One thing that exhausted Kate whenever she imagined going back to the States was the weight of all those things, organizing them, labeling boxes, sorting through the garage shelves, the clothes closets.

Dos Tías. The two proprietors, their graying hair pinned up in buns, shuffled from kitchen to patio in black dresses and greasy aprons. The older one seemed sick. During the day she had coughed near the pila while baby chicks the color of cream stumbled and wandered in the mud at her feet. She had been the one to register them, watching them sign their names with a fountain pen in black ink. The thick nub creating a rough pleasing script. Their signatures looked ancient in the green ledger. The ledger had grown moldy around the spine. Dixie said he was certain the proprietors had taken their names to the commandante at the army base. The commandante had to know everyone who visited the village. They had told most of the truth: Dixie wanted to visit his former parishioners who had come home and been placed in a relocation camp: Xamamatze. Kate had come along in case she was needed. No one knew—they had hardly said so to each other—that she was not her usual self, that Dixie was all that had kept her stable those first few weeks.

After dinner the two aunts disappeared into the kitchen, a smoky windowless room where they cooked over an open wood-fired grill. The flirtatious girls who had led Kate and Dixie to the hospedaje also disappeared, after much giggling and many offers to take Kate to back rooms where bargains, handmade purses and sashes and blouses, could be had. No one was about. The front gate was still ajar; from somewhere nearby a radio played music from the capital; rainwater tapped against the pila water; once in a while a dog barking raggedly broke the quiet.

Dixie read. He had a penchant for Neruda and Yeats. He pushed his book up close to the candle and leaned on the table. Candlelight flickered on the lenses of his round wire-rims.

Kate sighed and wrote July 15, 1989, Nebaj, at the top of a yellow sheet of paper. Her wool poncho smelled of sheep's oil and tortillas; comfort could be had from smells and warmth. Basics. She did not know to whom she wrote; she had only the urge to speak, to explain herself to someone. It might have been a letter to Maggie. There was a tone—most intimate and trusting and authoritative—that she and Maggie had always taken when writing to each other.

"This place is calm," she wrote. "Out of time. You start a fire to heat the water for a bath. The bath is a concrete trough, kind of like a grave vault. Here is the difference a decade makes. Eight years ago I still thought the world should—could—be improved. Now I wonder why we tried so hard."

A skinny straw-colored cat rubbed up against her leg, startling her. Kate felt Dix's eyes on her.

Quietly, as though it didn't really matter, she said, "What're you looking at?"

"You."

"Don't do that."

He laid his book face down on the table. Its paper cover was stained, as though often read. "Who're you writing to?"

She placed the cap on her pen, set it precisely at the base of the candle. She pulled up the hood of her poncho, set her feet on a chair, folded her arms. Half hidden from him. "Writing letters might be a cheap cure."

Dixie pinched a wad of soft wax from the candle and shaped it with his thumbs and forefingers. He sat there, saying nothing. Waiting.

Kate reached out from her poncho, took a sip of warm tea. Her knuckles looked pink, chapped. A fresh wave of rain blew over the yard. "I just want to sit here."

Kate's voice was low and Dixie matched her, speaking quietly, and if you'd heard them, almost out of earshot, their voices—his kind, hers melancholy—might have sounded like a dance. A ritual murmuring. Two people diminishing the distance between them.

"Sure you don't want to talk?"

"I'm not like you, Dix."

"I keep thinking it might help."

"I'm not so sure."

"Not just for you," he said. "For me. I want to hear about her."

She thought she did not want him to know her that well yet. "I can't."

"Suit yourself," he said, without impatience.

He picked up his book and leaned back in his chair and began reading again, twirling a lock of his hair. It was a habit he had. She could imagine him as a boy reading and fiddling with that one lock of brassy blond hair. He had no need of shields against the world.

Not like her.

Kate was only beginning to notice herself again, to shower and brush her hair with attention, to eat. The telegrams had come, from her mother, from Paul. Paul sent the money and a terse telegram: "Don't come back." Her mother's read: "Come home. Don't waste another minute. I'll buy the ticket from here, if you'll let me." When the phones were up she had called Frank and María and grieved with them as well as she could over the telephone. No one mentioned Deaver and she did not even notice that until the calls were over. Bitterly she thought, People like Deaver fall away.

"I look forward—every day—to seeing you," Dixie said.

Kate swallowed a lump in her throat, ducked her head. She said, "What about Jude—when she comes back?"

He laughed. "Now, that's a hornet's nest. Jude's been scared of my falling in love since—"

"Since when?" Kate said.

"Sixth grade."

Fall in love. The words echoed. He had said them with ease.

"Tell me about it."

"Her name was Melissa. She was good at marbles. Not too many girls played marbles in those days. She had . . . fluffy blond hair and wore gold sandals."

"Okay," Kate said, with the slimmest underpinning of tease. What a surprise, to feel repartee come back. "There was Melissa, and?"

"Are you asking me how many times I've been in love?"

She nodded.

"You want God's honest truth?"

"Father Ryan, what else?"

"The potential has been there several times, my dear. But I couldn't afford it. Emotionally or spiritually."

She didn't want to hear about that. That was a direction she didn't want to go. What could she afford, really?

He looked at her over the top of his glasses. "And you?"

She squirmed inwardly. "You know. Just Paul. And Deaver." That felt almost true. She wasn't going to tell him about the others, the ones she didn't know for long, the dead-end streets. She thought she might have to tell him eventually, and she was worn out at the prospect.

The night was almost still. Their old chairs squeaked whenever they shifted. Radio music from the kitchen had been turned down, a mournful ballad, fuzzy-sounding and banal.

No one knew where she was but Dixie. They were far away from everything and there was solace in that. Or there should be solace in that. There had been, in other times. She tried to think of the most remote place she had ever been: it must have been in the UP in Michigan, skiing with Paul. He had said they were twenty miles from the nearest road. She had still been a girl—in her late twenties, but a girl at heart. Now she had passed over into being older; it had happened without her taking the time to notice. So many things she wished she could undo. Words and deeds. Things she pushed over there—dark files she kept in a dark place.

She tucked her hands inside the poncho; she closed her eyes, willing herself to feel better.

A rifle fired—rapid, solid, rhythmic.

Neither Dixie nor Kate budged; they lifted their eyes to each other.

One of the aunts hurried into the courtyard, toward the gate. "Madre de Dios, Madre de Dios," she muttered, pulling a shawl about her shoulders. Her felt house slippers moved soundlessly down the brick corridor. She rattled the padlock at the tall front gate.

They had seen a man in the custody of soldiers earlier that day, between the gravel road and a copse of birch trees. The leaf in his hair, his stubbled cheeks, his torn shirt. She knew—thought—he had been killed and her heart beat harder. There was another spurt of gunfire.

The proprietor stopped beside their table. She whispered, "No se preocupen. Don't worry. Sometimes this happens. In the night." A pearl rosary dangled from one of her hands. Her shawl was black wool. Her eyes black. Her opaque stockings lay in wrinkles around her ankles.

"Should we go in our rooms?" Dixie said.

"Buenidea," she said. "Go to bed. We are going to bed."

"Pase buena noche," Dixie said hushedly.

"Y usted, también," she said, straightening a chair at the next table. She disappeared into a hallway.

The candle sputtered. Nearby: loud knocking on a door, staccato banging.

"We should try to sleep. Are you all right?"

"I guess so," Kate said.

She imagined her room, the one at the end of the corridor, nearest the gate, the framed picture of the thorny Sacred Heart above the single bed, the horsehair mattress. A two-Q room—about a dollar.

"Why don't you let me walk you to your room."

"I'd like that."

He tucked his book into his hip pocket.

At her door she handed him her things, her pen, her pad of paper, a packet of envelopes, a tattered address book embroidered with a Chinese landscape on its cover—she thought of those students in Tiananmen Square—and unlocked her padlock. It felt flimsy in her palm. She went into the room and pulled the string so that a harsh blue light pushed inward from the corners, as though the room were not large enough to contain the relentless light.

He laid her things on the trunk at the foot of the bed. "Will you be okay?" he said. His chinos were muddy along the cuffs, the collar of his sweater unraveling. But his face was ruddy, healthy-looking; he'd gained weight.

"I guess so." Kate walked back to the door, the padlock in her hand. "I'll lock up when you leave."

"In the morning we'll go out to San Gabriel. We'll stop at a waterfall. It's secluded there—" He stepped out of her room into the corridor. The rain had let up. The light from her room lit him up like statuary. "If you want to bathe there, you can. The bath here's pretty swiny."

"I saw that."

"If I'm not here when you wake up, I've just gone for a walk."

Kate closed one half of the wooden double door. "What time's breakfast?" she said.

"Seven to nine."

"Well. Good night."

"Kate—"

She waited.

"Thanks for coming up here. I know it's not an easy situation."

As though there had been a choice. She had not wanted to be left alone. She could bear to be alive when he was around, when she could hear her name spoken by him—

"I've seen worse," Kate said, though she could not think of many. "Sleep tight." And she shut the door and locked it from the inside.

She had the feeling that he stood outside her door for a few minutes. Her heart still beat hard from the gunfire. It wasn't even eight o'clock. She imagined people all over the village. Holding their breath. Hearts racing. She wished she had a window she could open in defiance. Her room was a cell, a grotto, painted sky blue and so damp that the plaster flaked in streaks where the wall met the floor. Her pine bed had been hand carved; she stripped back the wool blanket and examined the coarse muslin sheets and tried to figure out how many people had slept on those sheets before her. She had never felt so tired of her life but there was no escaping her own skin. She untied her sneakers and set them side by side under the bed. Her glasses she folded and laid on the trunk. She pulled the string that turned off the light. The darkness was dense and endless. To give herself room to breathe she unbuttoned her slacks and then with a sigh lay down on the hard bed and the hard pillow. Prison pillows, Maggie would have called them. Sleeping in her clothes would protect her; no one would walk her away in her nightgown; no one would touch her. Not without resistance.

The next morning Dixie knocked on her door. She opened it to the glare of sunlight and the mug of coffee he handed her. The courtyard seemed in a flurry—with children running by, craftswomen haggling with travelers who had just checked in, chickens squawking, darting, and beguiling music. Live music, someone playing a flute, Kate thought. She took the mug and motioned Dixie inside.

"I'm eaten alive with something," she said. She set down her mug and scratched between her shoulder blades, grimacing.

"Oh, man."

"Did they get to you?"

"I think I'm immune after living up here."

"Look. Will you tell me what this looks like?" Kate turned her back to him; she unbuttoned her shirt and lowered it, revealing her back.

"They're bumps. Bright red."

"Bedbugs." She flicked up her shirt, buttoned it without turning around. "They're driving me crazy."

A silence came between them. She turned around. A shim of sunlight from the courtyard barely lit the room. He had been up a while—she could tell—and he looked rested, pulled together. His clothes were clean—pressed chinos, a white polo shirt, boots with rubber soles. He had shaved. His lips were full. His lips were healthy, sweet, a color that made you consider kissing.

Dixie gently touched her face with the palm of his hand. He held her cheek. "Morning, merry sunshine," he whispered.

"Good morning," Kate whispered back. Then she withdrew. "There's an ointment we can buy. I'm not sure where, around here. It's for cattle, but we can mix it with Vaseline—"

"Sunshine helps too," Dixie said, stepping back to the door. "Let's get over to Xamamatze, then go to the waterfall, what do you say?"

"Yes, yes," Kate said, and she shooed him out the door.

When she came out, ready to go, he had started the jeep and crept outside the gate, waiting. Kate glimpsed from the corner of her eye a gringo family eating breakfast at one of the tables: a burly man in bib overalls, a woman in a dress flowered with sprigs of mint, and a girl, about sixteen, the flautist. The girl scrunched down in her chair, sullen, bored with her parents. Her flute hung in a bamboo case on her chair back. She had short tawny hair, a woman's body she hadn't gotten used to yet, and a tomboyish manner.

"Who're they?" Kate said.

"Missionaries," Dixie said. He handed her a fresh white roll drenched in butter and jam, nesting in a paper napkin.

"Her music's beautiful."

"That's Debra. I didn't think she'd come along this year. They come every summer to build houses. They're Presbyterians."

The jeep moved haltingly through the muddy lanes, around the dogs and children. A big brown pig lay in a mud puddle in the road. Dixie inched around him, scattering chickens with glistening feathers.

Kate said, "What was it last night?"

"Hard to say. But it's not unusual. We're close to what the State Department calls low-intensity conflict."

"With the tourists and missionaries right here?"

"Life goes on, Kate. Life goes on."

The dwellings at Xamamatze were like tractor barns. Low wooden structures around three sides of a mud pit the size of a high school football field. Indigenous people lived there, people who had been living in the jungle for eight years. They had no privacy. They lay at night on plank shelves. They covered up with felt blankets, blankets stiff and never long enough or wide enough. The teacher in the cell they called a school said that when the people came down from the jungle to Xamamatze their children had no clothes. The children were very much afraid, she said. The walls were covered with children's drawings on foolscap. Helicopters. Bursts of gunfire. Leaflets falling from the sky. The army leafleted the people and urged them to return, and when the people finally did return, they were placed at Xamamatze for ninety days of reeducation. We did not see a single armed soldier, though they must have been there, beyond the trees. Women ran from us, in fear or shyness, I could not tell, around the stacks of UN rice and beans in fifty-pound bags.

This is such old news, isn't it? Picture the earth, almost eight thousand miles around at the equator, picture the pockets of refugees. Maps are available. You can purchase such information. Demographics creates such order, knowledge, pattern, security of a sort to the onlooker. While down on the ground, down in the mud, we heard a woman singing a lullaby in Ixil. She knelt at a backstrap loom, her baby nearby in a makeshift hammock made of cotton sacks. She had rigged a stick and swing to rock the baby in his rag cradle. Never missing a stroke of weaving.

Dark, it was dark in there, no windows.

The men stood around outside, talking, crocheting. Crocheting bags is the work of men, you will see them other places, men who've been reeducated to their patriotism, men who've gone back to villages and built new villages, and now they serve as civil patrol, carrying heavy World War I Mausers around the village all day long and crocheting, with the rifles in the crooks of their arms. And if they refuse to serve in the civil patrol, if they lay down their arms and prefer to grow corn, they might be disappeared. They might be found with their mouths burned from the sticks of fire, what we call cattle prods. But at Xamamatze the men had no weapons yet. They might speak to you of Gandhi. They might speak of Vietnam. And at Xamamatze what they had learned of the wide world had to be cast out like devils. They saluted the Guatemalan flag several times a day. They recited the army's vow of friendship toward them.

We visited, delivered seven crates of mangoes and piñas, delivered bundles of yarn and thread, and I treated a woman who had been bitten by a pig that had wandered down to Xamamatze from the army base. We found her lying on a ragged tapete on the dirt floor, her gathered skirt pulled up above her bitten calf. Circles of flesh the size of two nickels had been torn away around the teeth marks. The skin was swollen and bruised. A trickle of blood had dried all the way to her ankle. There was no doctor that day, but a doctor did come around, three days at a time, every ten days, and there was a padlocked clinic. Dixie talked the man in charge into letting me in. I felt capable for the first time in a while. The woman had been given a tetanus shot upon arrival at Xamamatze. Her husband had the wrinkled vaccination card to prove that. In the one-room clinic I found what I needed, penicillin in the fridge, potassium permanganate, Neosporin, bandages. I knelt down beside the woman, and she had the brownish stains on her teeth from not eating right for a long, long time. She had pellegra, patchy, scalded-looking flesh on her legs, from lack of niacin. I knelt down and treated her and all my molecules that had been scattered with my sorrow to the winds, all my molecules caught up with me, and I felt that I was where I was supposed to be. Kneeling down before an injured woman.

We did not stay there long. Dixie bought a crocheted bag for thirty Qs from a man who had been a teacher before the violence. The man's wife was pregnant and he made Dixie promise that he'd come back soon, very soon, to baptize the baby and Dixie said he would do his best to return. That bag's overpriced, Dixie said, but I knew him. Antes.

What I remember of that day is this. People loved him.

After Xamamatze, after the many tugs on Dixie's hand, the blessing he gave anyone who asked, they drove out of the village.

"I'm not supposed to do that—bless people. I'm not supposed to perform any priestly functions while I'm on this leave."

Kate fed him fruit and cheese as he drove.

She had not thought they could climb much higher, but they did, winding around a mountain with deep valleys in three directions, verdant valleys, quilted with red tile roofs and corn milpas, the smoke from morning fires curling in and about the draws and foothills. At a muddy Y in the road they took the left fork. In three kilometers they arrived at the waterfall. A high and noisy shine falling from a limestone cliff fifty meters above a meadow. Whitish boulders—silvery in the sun—lay at its bottom in an oval, and within the oval a pool eddied, the water in the pool a clear glass green. Pine trees grew out of the boulders, gnarly-barked, secluding the pool.

He shut off the engine. The water clattered.

"It's idyllic."

"I'm glad you think so."

"So—what's the procedure? Will anyone see us?"

"I'd leave on some clothes if I were you."

She made her way alone, carrying a rucksack of clean clothes, a towel, a comb, shampoo, an empty kids' sand bucket Dixie had handed her at the last minute. Through the long green grass and down the footpath to the pool. Cold wafted from the fall. Her skin turned to goosebumps but she was determined. She took off her sneakers and socks, slipped out of her slacks, folded them neatly, laid them on a rock. She put her glasses on top of her slacks. The water's rough noise surrounded her. She tied her shirt tails in a knot above her stomach, rolled up the sleeves. The bottom looked stony; she slipped back into her sneakers to protect her feet. Maggie's spirit was there; she could feel her in the way she tied up her shirt. They'd done that when they were girls, thinking it was sexy, and it was, their smooth flat midriffs bared for the boys as they rode their bikes down gravel roads. Remember when, that's all she wanted, to have someone say, Remember when—

The forge into the pool took all thought away; the cold clasped her legs and thighs as she walked in. She squealed in shock.

She floated, her hands circling to tread water, her feet out in front of her. Dipping her head back and in, her face up to the sky. The cold water felt good on her bug bites. When she stood up, dripping wet, Dixie was not far away. He sat on a boulder as big as the jeep, his skin pale, sunlight glinting in the hair on his chest. In watch-plaid boxers.

"Pretty snazzy there, Father Ryan," Kate said.

"Stop." He closed his eyes, put up one hand.

"Have you been saving those for a special occasion?"

"For years," he said, climbing down and entering the water.

He came to her. They did not touch, not yet.

"Let me teach you something."

He still wore his glasses. She said nothing, waited quizzically.

"Repeat after me." He shivered. "I don't know how long I can stay in."

"I don't know how long I can stay in."

"Be serious, now."

"Well, what?"

"Bang go shash."

"Bang go shash."

"That's hello."

"Bang go shash."

"Orash."

"Orash."

"That's good-bye."

"Bang go shash. Orash."

"Now—tan-tish."

"Tan-tish?"

"Please," he said.

"Tan-tish?"

"Tan-tish what?"

"Tan-tish . . . will you help me wash my hair?"

"Can I get out?" And he waded out of the water. He waited on a sunny boulder, his arms folded, watching her. Rubbing in shampoo, trying to work up a lather in the hard water. She brought him the sand bucket full of water.

"Let's go a little farther," he said. "People drink from this."

"You always try to do the right thing, don't you?" Kate said.

"Do I?"

"Or is this a virtuous front you're putting on for me?"

"You'd see through that."

She sat on a flat rock with red wildflowers bobbing around her, the warm sun on her shoulders. He set down his bucket of water and stood over her. He slipped his hands into her sudsy hair.

"That feels good."

"You relax, now."

Dixie massaged her scalp. The cool air left her almost breathless. Her shirt clung to her. She felt like a cat being petted; he used the padded tips of his fingers, tugged and pulled, gently, gently, as though making something. The nearness of him, that kindness, did make something. Tears welled in her eyes, tears of loneliness abated.

"Maggie had the most gorgeous hair," she said. She caught her breath. "Is that the wrong thing to talk about? Right now, I mean."

"It's okay. I want to hear what you want to say."

"I would've never stayed in Mexico if not for her. She lived what she believed."

"Which was?"

"From each according to her ability. To each according to her need."

"What else?"

"Treat your lover like a friend. Don't be an armchair adventurer. Work builds character. Do whatever—whatever—you do in celebration. And you won't go far astray. To her that meant to the hilt. Nothing halfway."

"I'm washing your hair in celebration—"

A sob caught in her throat. Her chest was hot with tears, hot with holding back.

"There, there," Dixie said. "Let's get you rinsed 'fore you get soap in your eyes."

She stood up in the long grass; she bent over from her waist; her long hair hung in ropes. Dixie carried bucket after bucket of bracing cold water and with each bucketful, she screamed, "Tantish!" He rinsed her hair until no trace of shampoo remained; it squeaked; it shone wetly in the sun.

He wrapped her head in a towel and held her. He said, "I am overwhelmed by you."

Kate whispered, her lips against his ear, "I'm not sure I can take that right now." She could feel him pressing against her; she felt her body press back.

"I'm falling in love with you."

She said sadly, "You don't know the things I've done."

"I see the way you are."

"I'm not pure like you—"

He laughed. "Don't be so hard on yourself."

A shepherd girl came into view, following a string of black sheep. She wore a tinkling bell on her wrist. Her skirt was turquoise, her lace huipil white as a cloud. Kate and Dixie fell apart. The girl pretended not to see them.

"We'd better go," he said. "I want to make haste. I don't want us staying at Dos Tías tonight. After what happened to you—"

Kate had momentarily been distracted from her bug bites.

"Give me ten minutes," she said. And that is all she took, hidden among the trees, ten minutes to wash her face and rinse it, comb out her hair, slip into dry clean clothes.

She met him at the jeep. She chucked her things into the dusty back seat. When she got in, she said, "Dix—I can't, can't, afford this."

The shepherd girl crawled up on a rock and opened a pouch. She laid out a lunch for herself, a bruised banana and tortillas. The black sheep grazed nearby, their golden eyes dumb.

Dixie patted Kate's hand. Once. Twice. Staring straight ahead. "I understand," he said. "I think I do."

" 'What were you doing while the poor were suffering, their humanity and their lives consumed by flame?' Do you know that?"

Sunset had faded to a close. They stood at an overlook above the lights of Panajachel, with the lavender-shaded volcanoes in the distance across the lake.

Kate shook her head.

"Otto Rene Castillo. A Guatemalan poet."

The day had been a good one after all; she had not found the ointment she needed, but the cold water had relieved her bites somewhat; they had talked and eaten at a market and driven slowly down out of the highlands. They speculated innocently, wondering what might happen to Ginger, Lino, Ben, Sunny, though when they spoke of Sunny, there was always that missing piece, their secrets. Dixie had his best hopes for everyone.

There had been only one bad moment. Around three in the afternoon, in the heat and thirst of the day, they had driven into a village to buy orange Fantas. An army transport truck had been parked in the central plaza, a dirt hexagon with an adobe red fountain in the center. Only a trickle of water ran in the fountain. Kate took in with one glance that soldiers were rounding up young men—boys of fifteen or sixteen—and shoving them up into the truck. She would not forget the round face of a boy perhaps ten years old, watching, his eyes alert in terrified rehearsal. Women stood nearby, helplessly, with bundles of laundry or baskets of masa on their heads. Dixie had done a quick U-turn and taken them back out to the highway. "Guerrillas do it too," he said. "It's common practice. Young soldiers—the things they've confessed—it'd break your heart."

There had been a hastily hand-lettered sign on the tailgate of the truck: *Only he who fights deserves to win. Only he who wins deserves to live.*

Kate said, "Castillo's question is a good one."

"He was killed by the army for asking."

"When was that?"

"The '60s. He was thirty years old."

The wind blew up in gusts. Kate folded her arms inside her poncho, shivered, tucked the wool around her elbows. Dixie hugged her from behind, linked his hands at her collarbone. Their cheeks brushed, silkily, warmly.

He said, "It's a question, once you ask it, you have to ask it every day—"

"Where do you draw the line?"

"I haven't figured that out yet."

Vidalúz sat on the terrace under a yellow light, reading. Her huipil like a beacon. Mosquito coils burned nearby. As soon as she saw them, she strode to the gate and opened it.

"Buenas noches, buenas noches, mis amigos," she said. "I am not expecting you—hear my English, Father Ryan? Catarina—bienvenidos."

Kate hugged her. They laughed for no other reason than pleasure at once again meeting. It felt good and peculiar to laugh. She felt a tug of guilt about laughing, about being alive. Dixie parked the jeep while Vidalúz and Kate walked arm in arm toward the cottage.

"Como está? Como está?"

The two women sat down on a bench, the jasmine tree low about them, its white blooms like scraps of cotton in the dark.

Vidalúz took Kate's hand. "I am sorry to hear about your friend, Catarina. Very sorry. This is bad news."

"Gracias. It's been hard."

"Sí, muy duro. I understand."

They sat in silent companionship.

Then Vidalúz said, "These are difficult times."

Dixie walked from the jeep toward them on a flagstone path.

"May we stay the night with you?" he said.

"Sí, sí. Estás en tu casa. I am glad to see you. I may return with you. To Antigua."

"Why's that?" Dixie said, sitting down beside her. The three of them faced the grassy yard, the stars above, the palm trees lining the fence, their trunks painted white and glowing.

"Father Ryan, I have prayed. I have written a letter to the president of Guatemala. I have talked with our friends. I believe that I must sit down on the street in Guate and insist that they let Hector go. This is what I must do."

"Ah, Vidalúz—"

"Believe me, I know what God is calling me to do."

"Have you talked to any reporters?"

"Reporters are coming here—there has been trouble in a village across the lake." She lowered her voice; she spoke with gravity. "Soldiers killed a man who was studying the village. A sociologist. The reporters will make time for me as well as that situation."

"Did we know him?"

"Señor Solano. He was from the University of San Carlos. Did you know him?"

"No." Dixie hung his head dejectedly. "I didn't know him."

"I spoke with him a week ago. He was a good man. Muy inteligente. He told me a story, which I will tell you." She cleared her throat. "If you want to hear?"

"Sí, sí. Por favor."

"Not long ago, in Africa, anthropologists discovered the perfect remains of a woman's body. These bones are the oldest bones they have ever found. This woman broke her thigh bone somehow. What the anthropologists believe is wonderful is this. Her broken bone healed perfectly—what do you call it, the word for that?"

Kate said, "Knit."

"Yes. The bones knit perfectly. And this is proof, he tells me. Proof of compassion long ago. Someone put the bone together. Someone took care of the woman. For at least six weeks, he said, while she healed."

Dixie sighed a long sigh. "That's a good story," he said. "I wish I'd known him."

"It is not just for Hector that I go to the capital," Vidalúz said.

Kate wished she felt as secure in her own decisions.

Vidalúz said, "And you, Catarina? Now—"

"I'm going home. To my mother's."

Vidalúz said, "When?"

"Soon," Kate said. She took a deep breath, as though to under-score her decision. She did not look at Dixie; she watched the stars instead. "There's Orion," she said, almost to herself. "Orion's still up there." Paul had taught her the stars and Orion was all she could remember.

"Vidalúz," Dixie said, "we must talk."

"Many things will happen in the morning," Vidalúz said. "The reporter from the *Miami Herald* is coming. A friend has already made this arrangement." Vidalúz patted Kate's hand. "You will share my room with me again? Sí?"

"Me gustaría mucho," Kate said.

Vidalúz said, "We must talk before you go. And this may be our only opportunity."

Dixie said, "You need witnesses with you. Everywhere you go."

"I know that," Vidalúz said patiently. "We can work out the de-tails in Antigua. But for now, pasa buena noche."

Vidalúz excused herself; Kate promised to join her.

When Vidalúz had shut the door to her room, and her light be-hind the striped curtains had come on, Dixie said, "Come walk around the grounds with me."

"Not tonight," Kate said. "Please. It's too hard." The senti-mental odor of the jasmine condensed around them.

He touched her knee, met her eyes. "I want to be near you."

"I can't do this. . . ." Kate stood up.

Dixie said, "All right." He too stood up, jingled the coins in his pockets. "Sweet dreams, my dear. God bless."

"Likewise. Sweet dreams."

Kate retrieved her rucksack from the jeep and went to the whitewashed room she shared with Vidalúz. A fire crackled in the corner fireplace. Vidalúz had made the room homey, lived-in, with a vase of wildflowers, her embroidered and ironed huipils hanging in the open closet. She sat up in her narrow bed, under rumpled rosettes of sheets and blankets, where she had nested, gotten up to tend the fire, nested again, surrounded by her books and papers. She had taken her hair down. She read in the burnished lamplight.

Kate changed her clothes and got into bed. Vidalúz turned out the light. They lay awake beneath the stout dark ceiling beams. Kate spoke in a pliant probe, her voice quiet, suggesting that Vidalúz did not have to respond.

"Are you afraid? You must be."

"I have no choice. When you have no choice, fear goes away."

Kate did not believe that. She thought of the boys on the transport truck, where they might be, their mouths, their eyes, gashes of fear. "What do you think will happen?"

"I do not know. Terrible things have happened. The Harvard University was here—did you know that? They were studying the criminal justice system of Guatemala. They have gone. They have given up. Because they say tenemos las leyes. We have the laws. But there is no will to enforce the laws. No will. Publicity is what we need. No more hiding."

"How has it been, hiding here?"

"I do not like living like this, like a nun, but spoiled. While my husband—sí, pues, who knows, only God knows."

The firewood had fallen; no flames arose; there were only fierce coals. No one said anything. A dog barked from beyond their environs, not close enough to be a nuisance. The kitchen was not too far from their room. Kate thought she heard Dixie in there. Filling a kettle. Keeping his own vigil.

Think of the difference between torture and death. The gulf between the two. The desire one induces for the other.

Think of that.

Vidalúz said, "Where have you been?"

"Nebaj. Xamamatze." Kate scratched her upper back, then the small of her back. She squirmed.

"How were the people at Xamamatze?"

"All right, I guess. Alive. I could not tell if they had much hope."

"My ancestors were slaves there in the highlands."

"Slaves?"

"The Spaniards made them slaves. They branded them."

"Sweet Jesus." She scratched, rolled her shoulders.

"Is something wrong?"

"I am eaten alive with bedbugs."

"From Nebaj?"

"Yes."

Vidalúz sat up on the edge of her bed in her long cotton gown. Her feet did not touch the floor. "Let me see."

"I'll be all right."

"Let me see."

Kate sat up and in one motion turned around and untied a ribbon, allowing her nightgown to slip down around her shoulders. Vidalúz switched on the light and perched on Kate's bed. "How do they look?" Kate said.

"Angry."

Kate smiled.

"I know what you need," Vidalúz said.

"What do I need?"

"Wait here."

She slipped out the door and was away no more than two minutes. She returned with a vial of amber oil, a blue Chinese bowl, a white washcloth. She had run water into the bowl. "This is menta. Mint. It will give you some relief."

"How do you know?"

"My mother taught me to do this. She picks the mint near her house. This is the oil of mint. I noticed this the other day—this will be useful, I thought. And here you are, with such a problem—"

"Menta."

Vidalúz made a wash in the bowl with a few drops of the oil and the water. She daubed the wash on Kate's bug bites. The mint wash stung and that felt good. Vidalúz worked caringly, talking as she ministered to Kate.

"My grandfather was a leader. His father también. They went up to the sacred mountain. They made our ceremonies."

"Where is your grandfather now?"

"My grandmother is a widow. My mother is a widow. Two of many."

Vidalúz pressed the mint wash against Kate's skin.

"This moving I do," she said, "we have been forced to move many times. We are easier to control if we live close together."

Kate said, "In Chiapas, I worked in a camp of Guatemaltecos—Casa Buena."

"I have heard of Casa Buena."

Music started up, an intricate net of feeling, from a room far away from theirs: saxophone, no words. Vidalúz said, "I do not think Father Ryan is feeling well."

"Perhaps not," Kate said.

Vidalúz set the bowl on the nightstand between their beds. She folded the washcloth. Kate covered her bites, tied up her night-gown. They turned out the light and went back to bed.

"I could see him, down the hall. He was sitting in a big chair in the dark."

Kate said nothing.

"Catarina—why did you not stay in Chiapas?"

"The army attacked the people. It was dangerous. And North Americans were not allowed to be there."

"Where did you go?"

"Nicaragua. I went with a man I thought I loved."

"Love is a luxury."

"You love Hector."

"My love for Hector cannot be separated from our work." Vidalúz rose up on her elbow and stared in the dark at Kate, her face velvety in the shadow light. "Was your love of this man like that?"

Kate shook her head, almost violently. "No." Then she too came up on her elbow and faced Vidalúz across the narrow space between their beds. "But I can imagine love like that."

"Sí, es dulce, es terrible," Vidalúz said.

"I admire you."

"Don't admire me. I don't have a choice. To whomever much is given, much shall be required."

They lay back in their clean narrow beds.

"Are you better?"

"Yes, thanks."

"We will do this again in the morning. Before I go to the dock to meet the reporters."

"Muchas gracias, Vidalúz."

The saxophone music had swelled and faded. "Your mother," Kate said. "What happened to your mother when your father died?"

"She lost the land we had. My father's papers were not in order. She wants to start a market shop, a stall—she wants to sell sewing things. She loves lace and thread and ribbons. But she has no money to begin. She lives with her sister's family in Sacapulas and dreams of this." Vidalúz yawned, a delicate giving up.

Kate tried to enter the sleepy breathing of Vidalúz, the way you change your stride on a walk to be in synch with a friend. She wanted to rest that peacefully. But the thought of Dixie and what Vidalúz had said of him kept rearing up before her in the dark. She was accustomed to a nightcap every night, or almost every night, to soften her bones, to make them relinquish the day, the struggle. At night she thought about drinking more than any other time.

"Vidalúz?" she said in a hushed voice.

There was no reply.

Kate swung her legs stealthily over the side of the bed. She put on her glasses, groped into her rucksack for her hairbrush, and brushed her hair—three, four strokes—and decided against wearing her sneakers, though she knew there were scorpions about. She didn't want to feel that clunky, with sneakers on under her nightgown. She felt modest enough; her gown was gathered at the bodice and yoke, made of creamy flannel, worn soft with washing. She slipped on a pair of clean socks. And she was out the door, closing it with exaggerated care.

She stood outside the room, getting her bearings. She was at the edge of the patio, with a bathroom right next door. The main rooms of the cottage lay around the corner to her left. She turned the corner; a light was on in the kitchen at the end of the courtyard. Corn and squash grew there, as well as many flowers, marigolds and pansies, lobelia and snapdragons. On a wooden column a string of miniature white lights—oddly Christmasy—lit her way.

The kitchen, electricity, sky-blue ceramic tiles in a design someone had planned quite carefully, mums in an Italian flowerpot, fruit in a bowl—the night was still possible, interesting.

"Hey, where y'at, kiddo?" Dixie said.

"Are you all right?"

"I'm just awake," he said. He stood at a large window of twelve panes, framed with blue plaid curtains. "Watching this dog." He nodded toward the yard. "And he's watching me."

Kate went to his side. A black mongrel looked eagerly up at the window, his eyes so black you couldn't tell them from his fur. "See his tail wagging," Dixie said. "He wants to be taken in."

"Does he belong here?"

"I think he's Gabriela's watchdog. She lives over there." A servant's house the size of a one-car garage was situated not far away. A floodlight lit the yard between.

He took her hand. Gave her a sidelong glance. Arched one eyebrow questioningly. His hand felt square and compact, warm and padded. He said, "You smell like herbal tea."

"Vidalúz washed my back with mint."

"Did it help?"

"Uh-huh." Her knees trembled.

"This feels good, doesn't it?"

Kate watched the dog intently. "It does."

He patted her hand and let go. He said, "I'm hungry, are you?"

"I might be."

They left the window; Dixie rummaged in the refrigerator; Kate sat at the table and lit a novena candle. The clock on the wall above the sink ticked loudly. Dixie slapped tortillas, a slab of cheese, a plastic bag of grated cabbage, on the counter. He opened the cupboard and took out an ornately decorated can of olive oil. "This won't be fancy." He set a cast-iron skillet on the stove and lit the gas with a long kitchen match. "There's wine."

Indeed, there was a half-full bottle of red wine on the counter, behind other bottles, sauces, vinegar, honey. Whoever owned the place had real wine glasses, neatly lodged in a slotted wooden rack overhead. Kate said, "I meant what I said about not drinking."

"Well, then. All right. I won't offer again." Then he said, "Juice?"

And she took the glass of orange juice he offered.

"It's hard to be cheerful," she said.

"That's the best time to aim for it," he said. "When it's hard." He grated cheese over four tortillas. "Besides, you're out of here. On to the rest of your life."

"That's true."

"Tell me what it'll be like—where you're headed."

"Michigan?"

"You don't sound so sure."

"First of all I'll go to my mother's. In Indiana."

"What will that be like?"

"I imagine they'll fuss over me. My aunts and my mother."

"Describe the place."

"It's where Maggie and I grew up." Ordinarily she would have said, Maggie and Paul and I. But she found herself leaving out Paul. "It's green right now. It's so lush that the weeds grow over the roads if the county doesn't trim them. And my mother's roses will be blooming. Climbers. White ever-blooming climbers. Used to be there wasn't anything much out there—it's seven miles from town, but I hear they've built a McDonald's."

Dixie made a face.

She said, "That's progress."

"The low road of Western civilization." He poured oil in the skillet and eased one quesadilla into the sizzle.

While he cooked she told him about her mother and her aunts, the three of them living together in the house they had inherited from their parents; painting the gingerbread trim a different color every few years; Aunt Dodie knowing all the news from Saint Ann's, where she worked in the parish hall; Aunt Mary Lou keeping house for them all and selling her crafts at every crossroads craft fair in the summer. She described their summer place, a fixer-upper on the Blue Star Highway near Lake Michigan. But she left out how difficult she found them, how she dreaded becoming them, how her moves and decisions had been a lump-sum revolt, so much, against them.

"And your father?"

"Never knew him. He left before I arrived."

"I'm sorry."

"Fact of life."

"And Maggie's family—they live there too?"

"Her mom lives down the road. She runs a beauty shop."

"And Paul?"

"He lives in town. He works at Eli Lilly. In a lab. He's a chemist."

"Was he your childhood sweetheart?"

"Mmm. You might say that."

"How do you feel about seeing him?"

"Not so good. His telegram was pretty mean."

The grainy corn smell made the kitchen more like home. She had gotten used to watching him wield a spatula. "Is he generally mean?"

Kate thought that over. She sipped her juice. Then she said, "I don't really know him anymore. It's been a long time."

"That's a generous way of looking at it."

Kate smiled. "I'm putting on a virtuous front for you."

When he finished grilling the quesadillas, he dimmed the light, then bowed his head for just a silent few seconds, and she did too.

"What did you say? For grace?"

He said, "It's short and sweet. 'Feed my spirit. Make me whole.'"

Dixie watched her eat.

Kate carefully spread a teaspoon of salsa over her quesadilla. "You are making me self-conscious," she said.

"How's Vidalúz in there?"

"She told me about her mother."

"She's a wise old gal."

"She wants to start a business—did you know that?"

"A hundred bucks'd get her started. That's the work Jude's doing. Setting up a bank for low-income women."

Kate thought of the money she and Maggie had saved and lived on for years. They had been frugal even in high school, always saving back a portion of whatever they made waiting tables or babysitting.

"I didn't know that."

"She doesn't talk about it much." Then, "I know people at home who spend a hundred bucks on a bottle of wine with dinner."

"How do you support what you do here?"

"Like that," he said. "Money from friends mostly. I go back—to New Orleans. Or Cleveland, near my last parish. And someone'll throw a party, a fund-raiser. The liquor flows. There'll be food like you wouldn't believe. Homemade everything. I might show some slides. Then the checkbooks come out. It's usually enough to keep on with things six months or so. It doesn't take much to keep me alive. The rest goes for supplies. And Vidalúz. And Lino. And various projects." He put down his knife and fork. "Let me tell you what's up with that. Since you won't be here. To see with your own eyes—"

"Tell me." She had finished her quesadilla and witnessed his headiness, the way his voice warmed to his subject. He had a kind voice. She watched from lidded eyes and thought, How providential, just this night, to be here with the comfort of him.

"I'm buying an old dairy farm, a goat farm, not too far from where we were this morning. Mary's House it's to be called. It has a lot of potential. There's space. For maybe a clinic. And a library."

"The church is doing this?"

"Not exactly. It's being funded by friends. At least the initial purchase. They've agreed to buy the place, deed it over to me, no matter what I decide."

"How good of them."

"Kate," he said, leaning across the table, "I wish you could see it. It's up on a hill, with the mountains right there. It has a fairly new hacienda—the old one was burned down during the violence—with new stainless steel cheese-making equipment."

"Do you know how to make cheese?"

"I'll learn."

"Will you write me? Send me photos."

"Sure. I reckon I can do that."

A silence ensued. He searched her eyes frankly, put out his hand across the table.

Kate looked down, ignored his hand, and tucked hers under her thighs.

"I'm happy here," he said. "I don't want to go back to the States. I don't much like the choices there. So I don't do Mary's House out of some heroic love of the Maya. I do it because I want to find a way to live here once the pope and I part ways. Though I wouldn't mind at all if some Cajun chef set up shop in my neighborhood."

"You could be that Cajun chef."

"I've got other fish to fry."

"Is that a blender on top of the fridge?"

Dixie got up and brought down the blender. It was made of heavy chrome-plated steel and glass. "Prototype."

"Is there milk?"

He opened the fridge and brought out a tricornered carton of milk. "What else do you need?"

"Platanos—" She pointed to the blackening bananas in the fruit bowl. "An ice cube—"

Dixie opened the freezer and nudged one ice cube from its blue tray.

"Who owns this place?" Kate said. "Is she famous?"

"She works for someone famous. Her uncle worked for the State Department. This was his."

"Ah, the mystery of it all."

"I do it that way to protect you."

Kate got up and started for the counter.

With one imperative finger, he sent her back to her chair. "Now, you sit there and let me make this for you." He peeled the bananas and plopped them in the blender. The blender growled. They could not speak above the noise. He leaned against the counter, arms folded, and he watched her, smiling, and she felt the lack of anything protective between them. She went to the window. The dog had disappeared.

Dixie poured her drink into a tall glass. He watched her take a big gulp.

"It's good."

"I do believe you're starting to feel better," Dixie said.

She wasn't ready for that. She wasn't sure it was fair.

"Oh, you don't have to feel better," he said, as though reading her thoughts.

"No, I am." She thought about what she could say that was true. She went to him and let him hold her. She cried.

From his back pants pocket, he took out a clean cotton hand-kerchief folded into a square. "Give me your glasses," he said. She did what he said. He folded the temples of her glasses carefully and laid them on the counter. He lightly stroked her cheeks and under her eyes with the handerkerchief. "You're okay, you're okay," he said. "You've seen the worst of your lot for a while."

She reared back, tried to smile. Her face felt quizzical, exposed. "You think?"

"I do."

She wanted him to hold her again, but she was afraid.

"Have you ever," she said, "made love with a woman?"

"I'm makin' love with one now."

"That's not what I mean. You know what I mean."

He put his arms around her again. She could feel his heart beating. He held her tightly; they trembled. "Right now that'd be more than I could bear," he said. And then he let her go, a slow release. He patted her cheeks, checked her eyes, patted her shoulders, smiled.

She went to the five-gallon agua puro bottle, poured herself a glass of water, and drank it down. The clock buzzed: it was ten o'clock. She felt drowsy, cleansed. She thought about home—her original home, her mother's home—and she thought about the pleasure of turning on the tap and drinking water right from the spout. She thought about hot water, all the things she hoped she would never take for granted again. Dixie began doing the dishes, humming, filling the dishpan, squirting dish detergent.

"I like this," he said. "Being with you in the kitchen late at night."

They were on different tracks, she thought; her feelings did not go by in an orderly parade; they seemed to wreck within her. A pile-up. Damage done. She felt panic at all she could not undo.

A storm blew up in the night, tearing palm fronds from the trees, battering corrugated tin roofs, upending boats that lay moored at the furious edge of the lake. And stirring sleep, and dreams, whipping prayers skyward in weathercocks of dread. Kate and Dixie and Vidalúz prayed together at the break of day, though day was dark, sooty, with the corpulent cloud settling in the caldera. They could not see more than ten feet ahead, pressed upon by the dim alley of shacks and boarded-up market stalls they had to traverse to arrive at the dock. Smells funneled together, married: copal incense burning, human excrement, fish. In the rain, the reporters waited. They stepped into a thatched-roof café and Vidalúz took off the plastic raincoat she wore and she was radiant in her traje; she stood up ramrod straight and spoke in fluent Spanish; she had taken great pains with her hair, lifting and pinning it in smooth coils secured by her headdress.

She told them why. She spoke of all the disappeared. She opened her heart to the reporters, telling them of Hector, of Hector's devotion to justice. She said she had decided to go hungry—that she would consume only liquids—until she learned what had happened to Hector. She described the torture of that night, her night of clandestine detention. Beginning August 1, she would wait on the steps of the cathedral in Antigua until she was given the truth. She answered their questions and then she told them the story Señor Solano had told her, the story of compassion at the dawn of human time. Dixie had talked her into staging the vigil in Antigua, where she would be surrounded by foreign students and tourists for protection, and where he and other witnesses could care for her. They had made a plan. She would not sleep at the cathedral; he would find her a safe place to sleep where no one would ever think to search for her; she would have a witness with her day and night.

To travel, Vidalúz wore the clothes Kate had given her when she had first come to Pana, the pink turtleneck, the jeans, the athletic socks. As a Mayan woman in traje traveling with them, she would not fade into the stream of travelers; but in the pink turtleneck, a smudge of lipstick, her indigo hair in a single practical braid, Vidalúz might be a ladino from the capital; she might be a Mexican student; she might be someone like Kate.

The drive was muddy and grim. Rain poured down unyieldingly. Kate's jaw would not relax; she did not speak again of going home; the privilege of it felt gluttonous, though she imagined going to the travel agent above the bookstore in Antigua; she would sit at the desk and behind the desk would be glorious travel posters of the Mayan ruins at Tikal or the white sands of the Cayman Islands or Miami—yes, lush art deco hotels in Miami, those pastel grande dames—and yet, underneath all that she hummed with Dixie's nearness.

In Antigua they went to the safe house a few doors away from the jade factory, where tourists even in the rain wandered in and out all day, buying black jade or green jade or gold laid out on velvet racks. It was the house where Kate and Dixie had watched the China situation. Dixie pounded on the door, soaked by the rain. He spoke with the woman who answered—Kate could not see her, but she saw her hands reach out, the shiny red nails, jewelry in coils around her wrist—and Dixie motioned Vidalúz out of the jeep.

"Adiós, Catarina," Vidalúz said with her hands on Kate's shoulders.

"Good luck," Kate said. She squirmed around in the cracked leather seat; she kissed Vidalúz's cheek. "I hope we will meet again."

"Si Dios quiere," Vidalúz said. She handed Kate the vial of menta. "I took it from the medicine chest. I know our friend wouldn't mind. She would be happy for you to have it."

"Muchas gracias, mi amiga." Kate held her smooth brown hand. She did not want to let her go.

"I must go," Vidalúz said. "I must prepare myself." She had to step over a croaking frog as big as a tortilla to get to the door. She ducked inside.

Back in the driver's seat, Dixie said, "Where do you want to go?"

"To the house," Kate said. "I'm worn out."

"I know." Still, they sat there in the gray discordant rain, with the motor on.

"Listen. When I leave," Kate said, "I want to give you some money to give to Vidalúz. For her mother. To start the market stall. I want it to be a loan. She can pay me back bit by bit. As she gets it going."

"That's good of you."

"It seems like a lot of money here. But at home—"

They made their way around and through the narrow back streets, which the rain like a live and constant threat had cleared. It was late afternoon. No one was about.

Dixie said, "You know what I've an urge to do?"

"What's that?"

"Get porch-crawlin' drunk."

"But you won't."

"No. I won't. But you're the only person I can say that to who'd understand."

"The urge to be unruly."

"Turn up the boombox. Go back in time. But—"

"You can't afford it."

"Right."

"Well, what could we do? To satisfy that urge?"

"You're an incorrigible flirt."

Kate laughed, embarrassed. Her body and all her body's nerve endings keened toward him. But she stayed deliberately on her side of the jeep. She absentmindedly wrote KB in the dust on the glovebox. She did not know if he too thought of the days they had gone to that same safe house to watch the China situation; side by side in a darkened living room; the mildewed books behind them on the shelf; the tabby cat that leaped into Dixie's lap the minute he sat down; the way they'd concentrated on the C-SPAN broadcast as though entering a slow-motion nightmare, in quiet complicity and awe and apprehension. She had thought life was miserable then. Lovelorn, her bones had ached with all that stupid pain.

"Where does compassion come from?" Kate said. Now that she knew she was leaving, she had things she wanted to talk about.

"I thought you had that all figured out."

"I'm asking you."

"I think it's something you learn through practice. Like a muscle you train."

They sat in the jeep outside the door of El Petén #3, in a sweet suspended place before entering, before Kate's packing, whatever lay ahead in the evening. They would have the house to themselves.

Kate said, "A discipline."

Someone rapped on Dixie's window. Through the wash of dirt and rain, through the cracked glass—there was Lino, his white shirt soaked to the skin, and he carried a child on his hip who clung to him. Dixie rolled the window down.

"Mire! Mire—I found Marta!"

Marta turned around, looking worse than ever. Muddy from scalp to toes. Her lips cracked and dry and sore. Her nose runny. Eyes crusty. She put out her arms to Kate.

Dixie hustled out of the jeep and unlocked the door to the house; they clambered inside and stood in the foyer, dripping wet. Posh was screaming, terrified of the rain. Marta leaped from Lino to Kate. She hid her face against Kate's neck. She pinched Kate's arms, hanging on. The bony heels of her bare feet dug into Kate's hips.

"Where on earth did you find her?" Dixie said, stepping lively to the clothesline.

"In Guate," Lino said. "At a park. Not far from where I first—"

Dixie fetched four towels and brought them back; they wiped down; they shivered. "And Eduardo?" He bent down and picked up a pink envelope someone had slipped under the door: Miss Kate Banner. He handed it to Kate, but in Marta's grip she could not pay attention.

She knelt and wrapped Marta in the first thing that came to hand, an afghan on the back of a chair. It was only peripherally that she saw Lino put his finger to his lips. He shook his head.

"Well. Well, let's get inside and get warmed up," Dixie said.

They went into the kitchen, closed the doors. Dixie lit the oven and left the oven door open for warmth. They sat around the table. Posh still cried chillingly, and finally Dixie brought the parrot inside. He perched on Dixie's shoulder.

"Marta, Marta," Kate crooned.

Dixie put out food: bread and cheese, mealy apricots, milk. He ran water into a kettle and set it on the flame for tea. Lino ate ravenously, as though he hadn't eaten in a while. Marta had to be coaxed, but once she began she took her fill while cuddling on Kate's lap. Kate had leaned the pink envelope against a vase of roses in the middle of the table. She did not recognize the handwriting. Rounded, unhurried script, quite feminine. She was distracted by Marta, by the envelope, and only gradually did she begin to listen to Lino, who was talking, talking, imploring—

"Yes, certainly," Dixie was saying. "I'll take you—but first I have to tend to Vidalúz—"

"What's going on?" Kate said.

"A man from my village," Lino said in a rush, "un hombre con buenideas, muy buenideas, un maestro, he found some land near the volcano Fuego, land the government will sell to us, and he has the idea of starting a new community there, legos del ejército, legos de las guerrillas, away from the army, away from the guerrillas. Solamente cincuenta familias will go. This man is an educated man. He understands the way to get the best from the land. He's studied modern farming practices. I want to go with him!"

Kate watched for Dixie's reaction. She thought she saw him flinch, but he could not resist Lino's passion. Lino wanted Dixie to return to his village with him and help him move to the volcano. As they talked, Marta fell asleep in Kate's arms. Dixie made a pot of tea. He took great care. He poured Kate a cupful and served it to her on a saucer, with a teaspoon and a sugar bowl nearby. He covered the teapot with a quilted tea cozy and sat down with them. Only then did he say, "What happened to Eduardo?"

Lino did not say anything. He closed his eyes; he swallowed the bite of bread he had in his mouth. "This is only hearsay—" he began. "From boys. In the park."

"Well?"

"The police in the capital swept through the park. Night before last. They were cleaning up the streets. To make a good impression on visiting dignitaries." Lino paused, his chin dimpled in repugnance. They waited questioningly. In a voice Kate could barely hear, he said, "It is enough to say they got rid of some of the boys."

Dixie said, "I see."

"Mother of God," Kate sighed.

Dixie put his hand on Lino's shoulder.

Lino bowed his head, shook off the bad news.

Marta lay in Kate's arms. The tablecloth was wrinkled, the table strewn with crumbs. Posh chittered peaceably now that he had been allowed indoors; he groomed between his turquoise wing feathers with his shiny beak, like an amulet of old ivory. The warmth from the oven flushed their faces. They did not speak for a while. Kate drank her red hibiscus tea without sugar. Dixie met her eyes and there was no need to speak; she thought he felt looted by all that was happening: sadness, powerlessness—these were in his eyes.

He stood up and came over to Kate, put his hand on her shoulder. "Let me lay her down," he said. Bending low, low enough that she felt his breath on her cheek, he tried to scoop Marta up, but she was like a barnacle against Kate's ribs. She clung to her, even in sleep.

"It's okay," Kate said. "I'll put her down in a bit."

Lino talked about the land at the volcano, the fuchsia trees. He had not seen the land, but he had heard descriptions of it. The land had not been depleted like the land around his village; it had lain fallow for thirty years. He would need a new machete. He brandished an imaginary machete. His happiness could not be forestalled by Eduardo's death. His face was the animated and handsome face of a man inspired; his white teeth shone; he smiled, seeing in his mind's eye a new life, a bright opportunity.

Kate managed to slice open the pink envelope. She slid out the matching note paper, opened it, and strained toward the light to read it. At the top the note paper was engraved in gold with "Mrs. Earl Clark." Below her name was a gold fleur-de-lis. Written in black ink from a fountain pen was the message:

Dear Miss Banner,

Ginger is not feeling well and she is asking for you. I've taken her to the Canadian doctor at the hospital. But she would like to see you if you could manage to come. We are staying in a suite at La Sombra Hotel near Doña Luisa's.

Sincerely,
Mrs. Earl Clark

"What is it?" Dixie said.
"Ginger."
"Is she all right?"

Kate handed him the note. "I wonder how long that note's been there?"

"It's not dated."

"No."

"I'd better go see about her. She might be scared."

Dixie took his keys from his pants pocket; they were on a ring attached to a silver cross. "Take the jeep."

"Where shall I put Marta?"

Lino had been leaning back in his chair with the front feet off the floor, lost in the future, but he said, "I'll take care of her," and he plunked his chair back to the tile floor. He reached for Marta.

They attempted to transfer her. Marta woke up, looked around, startled, and grappled between them to stay with Kate. Mute but determined. She smelled very bad; Kate wanted to bathe her, as before. She did not want her to disappear again.

"I'll take her with me," she said. "We won't be gone long."

Carrying Marta, Kate went into her room and found her rudimentary medical bag, her fanny pack, and a blood pressure cuff in a box under her bed. She felt ready. Inwardly ready.

The street ran like a river. In the jeep Kate settled Marta beside her, wrapped in a windbreaker Dixie had left in the back. Marta pinched her thigh to hold on.

"Hey, hey, sweetie pie," Kate said, disengaging Marta's tight fingers. "Don't hurt me." She opened her hand, tried to show Marta how to pat instead of pinch. And Marta did all right. They drove to the central park, where the wind blew the fountain water sideways and the rose bushes bent back pliantly. Soldiers stood sentry at the door across from the park where Kate had first seen Vidalúz. Under a tarp at the cathedral door a man beat the big drum. They drove down the side street, past Doña Luisa's, where she could glimpse bright bits of expensive clothing, travelers and students waiting out the rain.

Kate parked right in front of La Sombra. She gathered up Marta, the blood pressure cuff, her pack, and clumsily made her way inside to the wooden booth at the back of La Sombra's courtyard. No one was about. She pushed a buzzer. She waited. A North American woman—Mrs. Clark, Kate recognized—appeared in a doorway on the other side of the courtyard. She opened the door and looked helplessly out at Kate, her hand at her throat, at her pearls. In a frilly white blouse under a smooth sweater, a plaid skirt. From a distance her face wore the longtime lines of a woman who expected little. Kate did not wait for her to speak. She went over.

"I'm here for Ginger," Kate said.

The woman stood aside and let Kate and Marta in. Kate took in the place with a glance: a sitting room with a loveseat and a chair and a bookcase of *National Geographic*s, a bedroom beyond, not really separated from the sitting room.

"She's . . . in the bathroom," Mrs. Clark said, unnecessarily, for Kate could hear the sound of someone vomiting, harsh, unremitting coughs and retching.

Kate set Marta down on a pristine white bedroom chair. "Now, you sit still," she said. And something about her tone, the circumstances, put the fear of God into Marta, for she did not cling to Kate or make a move. She stared wide-eyed at Mrs. Earl Clark, who returned her stare with obvious distaste. Marta scooted back in the chair, planted herself there more firmly.

Kate knocked on the bathroom door. "Ginger? May I come in?" She went in without waiting.

The bathroom was enormous, tiled in black-and-white tiles, with a high clawfoot tub. Ginger knelt on a towel at the toilet. She wore a slinky robe through which her pitifully thin flanks were revealed. Her limp hair hadn't been washed in a few days.

"Kate!"

"What in the world's happened to you?" Kate said, bending over her.

Ginger sat down cross-legged on the floor. She wiped her mouth and face with a wet washcloth she'd been gripping in one hand. Kate squatted in front of her.

"I've got this stupid fucking vomiting thing." Her lips were wet.

Kate put her hand on her forehead.

"It's not just morning sickness," Ginger whined. "It's making me, like, anemic."

"What'd the doctor say?"

"Oh, him—"

"Let's get you back into bed," Kate said. "Are you through? For now?"

"I think so," Ginger said.

She limped, Kate at her elbow, back to the bed. Mrs. Earl Clark had not made a move. She stood beside Marta, looking bereft, concerned. There was rigidity in her pose; her face was slim to the point of gauntness; her mouth turned down habitually. Ginger climbed back into the high bed. Kate helped her, brushed her bangs aside, patted her.

"Let's take your temp," Kate said. She stuck a thermometer in Ginger's open mouth, under her tongue.

Ginger mumbled, nodding, past the thermometer, "Who'th that?"

"That's Marta," Kate said. "She's from the highlands. But she's been living on the street in the capital."

She held Ginger's hand and Ginger let her. "So, how's your appetite?"

Ginger cast a malevolent glance at Mrs. Clark.

"Mr. Clark prefers that she eat here," Mrs. Clark said. "At the hotel."

"Why's that?"

"He has his preferences."

Marta had begun scratching mosquito bites on her leg. One began to bleed.

Mrs. Clark said, "She's going to bleed on that chair."

Kate shook out the thermometer. "No fever," she said. "That's good."

Ginger smiled diabolically, falsely sweet. "There's nothing wrong with me that nachos wouldn't cure."

Kate said, "You want to get dressed and go out? I haven't had dinner yet. And I'm sure Marta could eat again."

Ginger said, "I don't have any money."

"My treat," Kate said.

She picked up Marta and eased past Mrs. Clark, who wrung her hands, saying, "When will you return?"

"Don't worry," Ginger said, flinging open a chifforobe and surveying her clothes.

Kate waited in the courtyard. The rain had finally ended and all that remained was the heavy gloss afterward, slowly evaporating. She thought that by nightfall there would be that cleansed feeling over everything. Roses. Cars. Cobblestones. And the people would wander out to the park, relieved. Marta smelled so bad; Kate felt a push-pull toward her because of the smell, part urine, part rotting food, part glue. Marta patted Kate's shoulder.

"Let's go," Ginger said.

Out on the street, Kate said, "Let's drive."

"Hey, Father Dixie's ride."

"On loan."

Ginger laughed. "We could run away."

They made their way haltingly to a restaurant Kate knew where the food was purely prepared, jazz played on the stereo, but she didn't think they would mind Marta's grubby presence. El Jardín de la Música.

Inside, she said, "Are they keeping you prisoner there?"

"It feels like that."

"Where do they stay?"

Ginger smacked her lips. "Next door to me. But Mr. Clark's hardly ever there. And she's such a worrywart."

"They're going to be the parents of your baby."

"Don't let's talk about it."

A waiter took their orders: enchiladas, ensalada, limonadas. He brought them a basket of greasy corn chips and a bowl of salsa. Coltrane played, lovingly. The street grew dusky beyond the long open windows. Kate could see a narrow strip of sunset—yellowish, lavender—over the municipal building.

"You call them Mr. Clark–Mrs. Clark?"

Ginger blew her bangs up with a sigh, rolled her eyes. "They want me to. They've just—like—changed!"

"Since?"

"Since we found out—for sure—that I'm pregnant."

"When did this intense vomiting start?"

Ginger rolled her eyes. "A week. Or so—"

"What are you doing with yourself all day?" Kate unfolded a paper napkin in front of Marta, laid a few corn chips before her.

"What's there to do? They promised me cable TV."

"I think you need to stay busy. It's not good for you or the baby."

"Why'm I throwing up?"

"You're not happy."

"Is that all?"

"I think so."

Marta reached for the chips; she ate delicately, smiling.

"How could I be?"

"If you keep on, you'll get malnourished. You're too thin."

Ginger did not want to talk about that. "How's Father Dixie?"

"He's okay," Kate said. "There's a lot going on."

"And Lino?"

"Lino's moving."

"Did your friend get here?"

Kate was in the middle of a sip of limonada; her throat clutched up; she could not swallow for a moment. When she was able to, her throat hurt with the burn of it. She only shook her head.

"When's she coming?"

"She's not."

"What happened?"

"She's not coming. She died there."

"*Oh* my God."

"That's what I don't want to talk about right now. Okay?"

"Okay, okay, okay. Let's talk about something else. *Jesus.*"

The waiter brought their food. Kate had lost her appetite by then. Marta squirreled herself into Kate's lap and ate from her plate. Bathed in serpentine jazz. The lights low. Couples drifted in to the candlelit tables.

"Look," Kate said, watching Ginger, taking a medical interest in her eating. "What do you want to do? Do you want to get away from them?"

"Are you kidding? What would I do?"

"What do you mean?"

"With—" She gestured toward her belly.

Kate said nothing. Marta patted her face. Marta, even as she gripped Kate and smiled, had the eyes of an animal who expected to be struck. Or shunted aside.

Ginger said, "Please. Come back to see me again."

Kate nodded. "But right now—"

"What?"

"I need to get Marta back. Clean her up." Kate laid twenty Qs on the table. "Can you get back okay?"

"It's not that far," Ginger said. "I'm fine. She'll be waiting." Then, "Kate?"

"Yeah?"

"Did you see that picture of him—Mr. Clark?"

"What picture?"

"In his uniform. It was in the sitting room. He's real young in it. He was a Green Beret."

"Great."

"He's weird."

"I bet."

Kate picked up Marta. She rushed. She needed to be safely back at the house.

"I'll come again. Don't worry," she said to Ginger.

And it was with urgent relief that she faced the street, the night, the drive back. Marta's hand on her thigh did not pinch. She could smell the woodsmoke of the evening fires. The streets were convivial. Four Mayan girls in black cortes jumped rope under a street-light. A band in red cummerbunds—a fiddler and two guitarists—opened their instrument cases near the fountain. Every night, every day, so much joy.

Dixie had made Kate's bed with clean sheets that smelled wind-dried, sunny. He did not press her for news of Ginger; she offered none. She took Marta into the bathroom, stripped her down, bathed her, catalogued to herself all that was wrong with Marta's body—the impetigo, the infected scratches, pinkeye, her hair turning rusty and dry—and she washed the sores, soaked them in warm water until the crusts came away, then, as a last step, she daubed on antibiotic cream with a Q-tip. Bandages were necessary to keep the bacteria from spreading. When she wadded up Marta's filthy corte, with its unraveling hem, she found a secret pocket at the waist into which someone—Marta's mother, no doubt—had sewn her birth certificate: Marta Elena Hernández de Salam. 9 de Julio 1981. This Kate folded back up and placed in her own passport pouch. Eduardo had been wrong about Marta's age; she had just turned eight.

Marta submitted soundlessly to Kate's ministrations. The morning would be soon enough to go to the farmacia and buy meds and vitamins, a toothbrush. Whatever else it might take to get Marta started healing. She dressed her in a too-big T-shirt that came down to her feet. She remembered seeing hair barrettes and faille ribbons tangled in a clay bowl in the bodega, left by Juanita and Victoria. She poked around until she found two kitty barrettes and clipped them in Marta's damp hair. She held her up to show her what she looked like in the medicine chest mirror. But when she saw herself Marta did not hold her own gaze for longer than a second or two. She watched Kate in the mirror. And when Kate coaxed her to stay with Dixie in the courtyard, Marta held tight to her hand. She sat on the toilet lid, waiting, while Kate took a short hot shower. Then a snack. Then to bed. The both of them.

A lamp was on in Kate's room. Dixie had set up his boombox on the floor beside the bed. Kate got into bed with Marta. She tried to get Marta to say good night. Marta heard her, watching, on guard. Listening. But Marta would not speak.

Dixie came to the door. "Can I tuck you in?"

"That'd be nice," Kate said. Who had ever done that?

He sat on the edge of the bed. Marta lay between him and Kate, her sore eyes closed. She sucked on the ends of her black hair. He ritually tucked the covers around them.

"Be careful," Kate warned, "she's contagious."

He laid one tender hand on Kate's shoulder. Wonderingly, it seemed. Then he said, "I wish we had a fireplace in this house."

Kate murmured, "Fire's nice." She felt the wear of the day. She drifted.

"The house in the highlands has a fireplace."

"I can't go now, can I?"

"Go where?"

"Home," Kate said.

"I wish you couldn't." Then he said, "Jude's coming back. Tomorrow."

Kate felt a beam of resentment rouse her, like a light in her eye. But she held her tongue. Finally she said, "Where's Lino?"

"At his friend's. He's higher than a kite."

"And you?"

"It's fine, it's fine for him. It's what he wants."

"What a good soul you are."

"Listen to this," Dixie said. He reached down and pressed the play button. A flute made music like a loon's call across a darkening lake. "Debra. Remember her?"

Kate murmured yes and plummeted toward the delicious lure of sleep. Dixie bent and kissed her temple, and then Marta's. That was the last thing, his kiss.

Time got crazy after that. The first two weeks passed in a blur.

Marta was with me, she was always with me, and she needed special care, she needed an ally, a girl needs an ally, her sores needed to be cleaned, she needed medicine, she had a bad spell of dysentery, she needed clothes, and all of that took energy and money. The money from Paul arrived just in time after all, a godsend given Marta's needs. We bought sturdy shirts and pants. We bought huipils and cortes from vendors who sold their goods on Sunday at the park. No one seemed to recognize her, no one claimed her.

Most of all she needed touching.

Touch, adoration, the adoration face to face. Some authorities, baby doctors, say that past six months it does no good, the die is cast, and perhaps Marta's mother did adore her, perhaps she stared into those eyes and said, you exist, I adore you. But Marta had been damaged. And she hung back. She pinched my hand so tight, I had to teach her over and over not to pinch me, that I would be there without her pinching me.

So much of that time runs together. I remember Marta's grip on me, Dix's eyes. Being tired to the bone.

Jude had come back. She was on her way from Chimaltenango to Guate to renew her visa. She stopped off in Antigua at breakfast one of those mornings after Marta had arrived. Marta was still asleep and Dix and I were having coffee in the kitchen. We were sitting without talking. There is a kind of intimacy in silence. I had Sunny's address in my mind and I wanted to tell him, such a forgettable transgression, but it mattered to me, what he thought of me, too much already, even then. He had been up early and gotten the *Miami Herald* and fresh eggs and butter and he'd made biscuits, perfectly browned, perfectly risen, and by then whenever we were in the same room a sensual thicket grew around us.

Jude came to the kitchen door and had to cut through that.

We didn't even see her standing there until she cleared her throat. She asked him to haul some things from the capital to Chimaltenango and he went off with her. For days, it seemed. Though knowing what I know now, he must have spent some of that time with Sunny.

I hardly saw him after that until day five of the vigil, when he said, Would you look after Vidalúz today? And I said, yes, yes, and Marta and I went to the cathedral. My presence was that impromptu. It began with that one yes.

And we went to the cathedral and sat with Vidalúz. The tourist buses would arrive. A man sold snakeskin belts at a table right beside us. Ginger would come by and talk. She'd squat on the cathedral steps, she'd bring us the newspapers. She was starting to show the way skinny women do, a compact bulge. Vidalúz would make a shrine of Hector's photo, flowers, a novena candle burning, whatever well-wishers brought by, more photos of the disappeared, messages written on paper sacks, dried bundles of los flores del muerto. She kept her strength up with the broth a kitchen boy from a restaurant would bring and juice and limonada. She never complained of hunger. Rosaries were left there. Every night we gathered up the elements of the shrine and carefully placed them in a rucksack and every morning we laid them out and waited to see how the shrine would change that day. Always Hector's photo was set up first, a grainy eight-by-ten in a punched tin frame.

You might wonder how we passed the time. It wasn't hard. We laughed and visited and prayed. I was beginning to get an inkling of the way the repetition of prayer cloaks you in surrender, the way the language changes consciousness. And we told the stories of our lives. We visited with the passersby. Marta would sit with her elbow on my knee, her chin in her hand, listening intently. A human rights attorney would come and keep Vidalúz informed. There was nothing to do but file a writ of habeas corpus and wait.

It was all of one piece. Life at the vigil. On the south side of the park, above and in front of the Palace of the Captains-General, the soldiers would pace with their weapons, weapons from the United States, weapons from Israel. They would not meet our eyes.

At night we slept in a secret place. Right before dark we would gather up our things and with Randall, a high school biology teacher from Corpus Christi, and a phalanx of witnesses from an international organization, we would go into the cathedral and wait, sometimes for ten minutes, sometimes for fewer, sometimes for twenty minutes, then we would take a passageway that ordinarily only celebrants used, through the sacristy, past the dusty cruets and the tarnished incense boat and the vestments hanging on an iron rod, and out the back of the cathedral onto a dark street. We would walk together for several blocks or perhaps into a different neighborhood that allowed us a loop through darkened streets. We tried to avoid the well-lit streets, and then we'd scatter for a few blocks, and sometimes Marta would go with me and sometimes she would go with Vidalúz, and we never took the same route twice, we never did. Our witnesses would peel away and Vidalúz and Marta and I would meet on a corner a few doors from our destination, the cloisters that lay in ruin from the eighteenth-century earthquake. The watchman would be waiting to let us in. Our last two witnesses would leave us there. When Randall was one of the last to say good-bye, he'd give a treat to Marta, a pocket-sized box of Frosted

Flakes or a stick of gum. In his Southern drawl he'd coax her to say gracias. To no avail.

The stone columns of the courtyard were as thick as old-growth trees. Vidalúz and I could not hold hands around those columns. Well-established bougainvillea grew there and in the watchman's light the blooms were perhaps more vivid than in the afternoon. He was a fat good-natured man with curly black hair. He couldn't button his shirt at the belly. His baseball jacket was satiny and someone had embroidered Our Lady of Guadalupe on the back. He sat all night in an overstuffed chair that'd been left out in the rain at one time or another. He had a portable TV he'd rigged up to a car battery and every night we'd pass his room and see the TV on, a wavery picture of *I Love Lucy* or *The Love Boat*. The watchman took us down an ivy-laden passageway into a deep empty room, a stone chamber in the shape of a pentagon. There were no windows. It was a room that could be sealed quite shut and we could have a light. He'd seal us shut. And Vidalúz would strike a match and light the lantern Dixie had sent there, and we had cots and we had blankets and we had a short-wave radio and we could listen to the BBC. We had a chamberpot to pee in. We knew that once he sealed the door we would not go out again that night, the stars were lost to us, the night, but we felt exceedingly safe. Dixie would have sent someone with food from street stalls or food he'd prepared himself. There would always be a note. I always watched for the note. Sometimes it would be carefully written out on lined school paper, sometimes it would be hastily scribbled on whatever was at hand, the gray wrapper from tortillas or an old receipt. I did not like to eat in front of Vidalúz, but Marta needed to eat and as she grew more fleshy, Vidalúz and I did not. We did not feel deprived. We had water and juice in a picnic cooler. We had the radio. We had books and newspapers. We had light.

I would read the note to Vidalúz—it was for all of us. We learned that Jude was still in town but that she planned to leave soon. I tried to read between the lines, but finally there was enough right there, he would be honest, he would be straight. He didn't like the way he had to stay away. But he'd been warned.

We had kept the vigil on the steps of the cathedral for twelve hours and talked to many people. And we would lie down, blow out the lamp, sing a lullaby to Marta, whisper, whisper, the talk of women who have nothing left between them that has not been gone over. Like searching in a field for what you lost, we searched, we talked, comadres we were in the cloister. Vidalúz knows all there is to know about me. If I could not recall the word in Spanish we worked around that word.

In the mornings we would leave when it was still dark, that crystal-blue dark of mountains. The moon might still be up, circled by a red ring, and two witnesses would be waiting, sometimes Randall and a Quaker woman named Carol, sometimes an older Quaker couple from Philadelphia, sometimes others, I forget them now. We would separate and find our way to nearby homes where it had been arranged that we would shower and dress and meet again to start the day at the cathedral. Someone would walk Vidalúz to the cathedral. Or they would find a taxi for her. We used the cover of night and she was never alone on the street.

And during that time, if I glimpsed Dixie in a crowd I would remember what had passed between us, holding hands in the kitchen in Pana, the day at the waterfall. But that seemed like another life, the way up north you can recall summer in the dead of winter, the way you might search for color in a wintry landscape.

The twelfth night of the vigil. Cool night. She could see her breath. Kate stood alone for a few moments outside a tienda, eating a chucho, licking her fingers. Randall had ducked into the tienda to buy cigarettes. Traffic bumped along—a black sports car, trucks. Across the street in a restaurant, beyond the potted palms, a waiter in a short black jacket bent down. Lighting the coals in a brazier. Wind stirred the crystals of the chandelier above him.

"Hay Frosted Flakes?" she heard Randall ask.

A van door slammed open. Men gripped her arms above the elbows. Shoving her in, banging her knee.

The van crept along the street. The man whose arms she'd been thrown into deftly pocketed her glasses and jerked a cotton hood—smelling of tobacco, pipe tobacco, stale and vanilla-like—over her head. He tied the hood at her neck. He held her down. She struggled against his arms. He pressed her to the carpeted floor, twisting her breast to restrain her. The carpet abraded her cheek.

Around her wrists he tied a rope reinforced with wire.

A radio was on. Big-band music. *When that deep purple falls over sleepy.* A two-way radio sputtered. She made out three voices, talking over each other. Rapid-fire Spanish she could not decipher.

"Están equivicados!" she said.

Wire cut into her wrists.

"You are mistaken! Soy ciudadana de los Estados Unidos!"

He twisted her breast.

She went limp. The van trundled along the cobblestones. Soon she felt smooth blacktop beneath the tires.

In a mean purr, the man beside her said, "Bien. Bien. You can sit up now. You must do what I say. Or your friends, your mother—"

Kate righted herself, clutched her knees to her chest. She surmised that he was settled in a seat against the side wall of the van, behind the driver's seat. He kept one meaty hand around her upper arm. Her heart raced; it pulsed into her head, her arms and legs. She took deep breaths. Marta, Vidalúz—she kept their names too close to the surface. Afraid of calling their names.

She could not think straight, not where she was. From beyond the van, someone—something—mocked her: luck! What do you know about it?

In slow deliberate Spanish, a man in the front seat said, "They will be sad. They may never see you again." A match was struck. A pipe lit.

"We need your help. You have the security of knowing you are doing the right thing. You are a patriotic woman."

The road whizzed by beneath the van. Uphill. Around curves. *Breathing my name with a sigh—*

In a trembling dignified voice, muffled by the hood, Kate said, "A dónde vamos?"

No one said anything.

Dixie found a parking spot only a few doors down from the orphanage, a relief. He didn't want to walk far; he'd been feeling drained, as though the breakbone fever might be reasserting its sway, as though his legs might go out from under him if he walked more than a block or so. The Canadian doctor had scolded him for not resting enough. Such inertia was hard to imagine. He longed to be in the highlands, though mass would be celebrated by a new priest. The bishop would no doubt eventually send someone new, young, perhaps a Guatemalan or a Salvadoran who would ride the circuit on horseback while Dixie would live in the hacienda above the road and teach reading and make cheese and when he'd mastered making cheese he would teach the older children to make it. You make plans, then you find out what's in store. Doors open. You can wrestle at the door or yield.

Fresh bundles of *La Verdad de Hoy*, tied up with waxy brown twine, lay in the back of the jeep under a tarp. Sunny's mood when he picked up the newspapers had been somber; as they talked she had offered him a carefully calibrated hope, a pretense, but everyone they knew waited for the worst. It was all there in the newspaper, a fortnight's news.

Salvador César Solano, forty, internationally recognized sociologist, shot through the heart as he tried to escape abduction.

A mass grave discovered near the village of P—, containing the remains of fifty Mayan villagers. Many of the skulls still wore blindfolds, which had not rotted away with the flesh. Beveled round bullet holes revealed the cause of death.

Rosa María Gonzales Castellanos, ten, a street child attacked by police who poured glue on her head and burned her legs with cigarettes. One of a gang of girls who had tried to steal from a bakery.

The door of the orphanage creaked. Once a fine door, with intricate carvings like ancient stelae, it had been neglected, worn away into splinters. He buzzed.

A nun in simple dress, a straight black skirt, a modest white blouse, opened the door almost at once. Toddlers swarmed around her. Young, with a smooth bland face and heavy black glasses, she braced one hand against the door frame to maintain balance in the surge of children.

She nodded obsequiously, sweetly. "Bienvenido, Padre. Buenas tardes."

"Buenas tardes. Estoy aquí para mi hermana."

"Ah, sí, sí. Está aquí." She admitted him.

The toddlers like a herd of small animals followed this way and that, wherever the new and enticing drew them. Several put their arms up to him and said, "Papá, Papá—" He could not choose. He sat down on the floor of the courtyard and let them climb on him, let them take off his hat, let them untie his shoelaces, let them push into his arms for hugs. There must have been twenty of them. Beyond the courtyard was a TV room. Older children sat there on plastic chairs, watching TV, with the blank faces of the almost adolescent. Aware of their misfortune, their losses. He hoped to take them to the farm. He wanted to see them in the healing mountains. Fretful babies squalled somewhere beyond. The courtyard was roofed in whitish glass reinforced with wire; night could not enter, nor day. The floor was concrete, the early evening light opaque and tinged with the brown paint used on every wood surface within; no plants or ornaments were about save an austere cross on one of the pillars. The sister smiled at him until one of her superiors came to the courtyard door and said something that made her jump. He couldn't make out what she said; it was a sly remark. Then Jude arrived.

"Well, well," she said.

That was for his tardiness.

She pulled on a gray cardigan and picked up two tote bags. She'd been at the orphanage for several days, visiting friends and working and running errands in the capital.

"Where y'at, Jude?"

"Please let's not get waylaid here," she said. "I'm eager to get back to Antigua."

And out they went, without much of a good-bye. He reckoned she had already said her good-byes. Jude was not one to linger at the door. She had agendas. He allowed her that. She accomplished much in the world. But sometimes he wanted merely to play in the courtyard. In the tug of the children, he nearly forgot the malaise of the afternoon, his low energy.

It grew dark as they left the capital. Smoke and exhaust poured from the vehicles next to them, honking before and behind, zigzagging in and out of what might have been true lanes of traffic. There were no lanes. Traffic like schools of fish in a wide toxic ocean went amok. People in fatigued throngs waited for buses. Lights came on, yellow points of refuge, tiendas, parks, homes, fruit stands, cantinas, evangelical temples, brothels. Yes, there was refuge in the capital, however rough, however crowded and foul. But there had been no refuge for Eduardo Gaspár Hernández de Salam. To know you have a safe place to lay your head at night: that was too much to ask.

They wended their way past the shopping plaza, past the McDonald's, past the road to the airport. Jude was unusually quiet until they emerged from the capital onto the dark open road headed up into the mountains toward Antigua. A back-seat driver, she liked to warn him of errant drivers entering the flow without signaling. Or buses running red lights. Or people on foot crossing where you might not anticipate them. She had been that way since high school. Though she was a year older, she'd been the navigator and he'd been the driver when they were out on a Friday or Saturday night in their parents' second car, a car he'd been grateful for, a light tan Chevy sedan from the '50s. That had been a time of dreams. Where they would go to school. What they'd do to change the world.

"Hey, let's call Sam sometime soon. Want to?" Dixie said.

"We could've stopped at the airport and dialed direct."

"Want to go back?"

"Ni modo."

They rattled along, past the political emblems of chickens and circles and flags painted on the mountainside, past entrances to outskirt villages. He thought she had something on her mind and he was waiting for it to come out. He didn't know if it would be better to bring it on by asking—friendly probing—or to wait. He did not have the energy for Jude.

"When you move up to your farm," she said without preamble, "what'll you do? If you turn your back on your vows?"

"You think the work I do is about vows?"

"That's not what I meant."

Patiently he said, "I thought we'd gone over this. There's not a shred of difference between the secular and the sacred. I used to think so, but now I don't. I'll work. The place has great potential. We could have a school. A clinic."

"We?"

"You're welcome to join me there."

"I'm not called there."

"Well, whoever is may come."

"It's Kate, isn't it?"

"You're simplifying things."

"What do you see in her?"

"Be careful."

"No. I really want to know."

"What do I see in Kate? There's a mystery at its core."

"That's not good enough."

"All the best things are mysterious. Don't you think?" Then, almost to himself, he said, "She's not the reason I'm going through what I'm going through."

"She's changed you—"

"You're out in left field—"

"Just like Sam—"

"Sam's okay. He doesn't have any regrets."

A long silence ensued. Dixie drove. He enjoyed the driving, the way he knew the road, its bends and potholes and climbs. Sam was not sorry, he was sure of that. Sam with his children was a man totally in his element—advising, loving, holding, teaching.

"People leave marriages the same way you're leaving the church—"

"How's that?"

"Thinking they need to grow and that they can't grow in the marriage. They don't realize what they're relinquishing. Until it's too late."

"My lesson to learn—if that's the case." He chopped the steering wheel twice with the side of his hand. "Have you given a thought to this? Why're you so upset about what I'm doing?"

Jude plucked a tissue out of her cardigan pocket.

He let her cry. That wouldn't last long. Might do her good.

"A point of clarification," he finally said. "I'm thinking about leaving the priesthood. Not the church. I want to stay here. I don't want another tour of duty in the States. You know that story, don't you, Jude, of the young man who asks Jesus what he has to do to have eternal life? I don't want to walk away in sorrow."

"That's just part of it. For you. There's pride driving you."

"I'm looking at that. That's mine to stare in the face."

"Everything's changing."

"Give me your hand." He took her hand across the darkened cab in the green glow of the dashboard lights. He squeezed her hand. "I'm sorry to be making you feel bad. Bear with me. Okay?"

He took his hand away to shift gears. They rode in silence up the mountain; a kicker of lightning coiled inside a visible thunder-

cloud to the northwest. Dixie fell into his inner habit, silent instructions to himself, meanderings. Purge out the old leaven. Make
clean the habitation of thy heart. Purge out the old leaven. Make
clean. Make clean. The habitation of thy heart.

In Antigua he drove directly to the market. Evening was a good
time to drop off the newspapers. He parked behind an aluminum
door that rolled up noisily when he knocked. Jude stayed in the
jeep. A woman let him in, a vendor in a soiled apron. She went back
to her work, sorting rotten tomatoes from the ones she thought she
could sell the next day. The market was closed. The lights had been
turned down and the commercial decorum maintained during the
work day fell away in tiredness. Friends gathered in front of stalls,
smoking cigarettes or listening to a man strum a guitar or standing
over a quick bite to eat, a tortilla smeared with beans or a plate of
grilled plantains. Children squealed, chasing after each other. Dixie
spoke to a couple of men he knew. One man sold machetes and
knives; the other sold cassette tapes and watches. He left a bundle
of newspapers with each of them; he left a bundle with a butcher.
Someone offered him a glass of rompompe, a thick eggy liquor,
guaranteed to thin your blood and give the evening room to
breathe.

"Sí, sí. Salud! Padre!"

But he said no and went on out to Jude.

At the house they went their separate ways. The postal strike
had ended and Jude had letters to catch up on. She was leaving for
Chimaltenango in the morning; she needed to be there for crucial
negotiations concerning the women's credit union.

Dixie went into the kitchen and made a pot of tea. He toasted
bread and ate the toast with butter and jam. He had a penchant for
jam and you could get good jam in Guatemala, strawberry or
mango. He tried not to think about the pesticides. He sat at the
table and read the poems of García Lorca, with Posh chittering on
his shoulder, Van Morrison very muted on his boombox. *Give me*

my rapture today. He wanted to play that song for Kate. And others. He wanted to let her hear the final instrumental, the alto sax wrapped around such sentimental moments. He could not indulge himself with thoughts of Kate, thoughts of a simple pleasure like sharing a song, without brooding about Hector. He did not want to give himself such temporary pleasure until he could see Hector. As if his thoughts could make a difference.

He read "The Faithless Wife." He didn't like looking at the word *faithless.* He didn't like the empty feeling that blew like wind through his heart when he looked at the word *faithless.* But the poem—the starch of the petticoats, the horizon of dogs barking, the hollow in the earth they lay in, the thighs like trout—

The knock startled him. Jude did not stir. Someone knocked again.

Dixie got up and hustled through the courtyard. "Hold your horses."

He opened the door. Randall stood there, grimacing. He took a deep breath. "Kate was picked up—"

"Get in here," Dixie said. "What in God's name happened?"

Randall stepped over the sill. His silver hair was pulled into a ponytail. He cringed and had trouble looking Dixie in the eye. "We went to a tienda—she stood outside—I don't know why—it happened so fast."

"Tell me exactly what you saw." Dixie's heart beat hard. A pain reached like a diabolical hand into his upper back, a pain that he had to endure sometimes for days on end when he could least cope with it, the pain of burdens.

"A van. They carried her off in a van."

"And Vidalúz?"

"She's all right."

"And Marta?"

"Marta's with Vidalúz."

"Who else knows?"

"The other witnesses. The local police. We tried to get through to the U.S. embassy—we couldn't."

He gave Jude the bad news and grabbed his keys. After dropping Randall at his hotel near the market, instinct led him to the safe house not far from the jade factory. There was a phone in the safe house. He parked and knocked politely, though he felt desperate and his back ached as though he'd been stabbed. No answer. He decided to use his key and hoped the woman who'd given it to him was out of town rather than in the shower or asleep.

No one was about; the courtyard was still. A cut of moon rose overhead. Mail had piled up just inside the door below the mail slot. His thoughts scrambled, paralyzing him. His contact at the Archbishop's Human Rights Office had fled the country. He sat beside the black telephone, numbers flying inside his brain, as well as the faces of the human rights attorney and the undersecretary he knew at the embassy, but it was night and anyone with any sense would be at home, safe, perhaps with a cocktail or watching the news. Those numbers were not available to him. Vidalúz would have the home number of the human rights attorney, but he could not go to Vidalúz. He dialed the U.S. embassy. The line was busy.

The telephone rang. Loud, shocking. He hesitated, then answered in a formal voice.

"Dix? Is that you?" Sunny said.

"Mother of God, I'm glad to hear your voice."

"She's here. Kate's right here. With me."

Dixie inhaled sharply and sank onto the sofa. "Thank God."

"She's all right, she's all right," Sunny said. "She's kind of shaken, though. They took her glasses."

"Can you put her on?"

"I don't think that's a good idea," Sunny said.

"But she's all right?"

"She's got a couple bruises. She's dazed."

"How did she find you?"

"She wants to tell you that."

"I hope she acted alone."

"That makes two of us."

"We'd better not talk."

"That's for the best."

"I'll come and carry her back."

"No. We'll come to you. Remember that place where we had Ben's birthday that time?"

El Mirador, she meant a restaurant near El Mirador, a steak-house in the suburbs that had a good reputation. Ben had wanted a treat. He said he hadn't had a decent steak in ten years.

"I remember."

"She wants you to get word to Vidalúz. She's worried about Marta."

"I can do that. I can have a witness go there."

"We'll take a taxi—"

"I'll bring some money—"

"We'll leave soon—"

"Tell Kate—"

"What?"

"I'll be there. Just tell her I'll be there. Waiting."

"You don't have to talk," Dixie said, starting the engine.

Kate said, "I will when I can."

It was the same road. For Kate the road unwound like a bridge of praise. For Dixie the road felt malevolent, the road that had carried Kate to the capital while he argued with Jude. The dashboard lights washed upon their hands, which met at the edge of Kate's seat. She thought her fingers felt cold and bony in his. He let go to shift gears. But he came back.

Finally she said, "There were speed bumps. Where they took me." Her voice still shook; she could not control her voice or her hands. "I counted the speed bumps."

"I want to get you home."

"And there was a garage. I heard the overhead door opening. The room smelled like blood."

"Kate, Kate."

"I know the smell of blood."

Dix squeezed her hand.

"I could hear marching, soldiers—I'm sure of it."

"I'm not surprised."

"A North American man was there. Where they took me."

"Are you sure?"

"I'm sure."

"Reporters would find that mighty interesting."

Kate said, "I can't talk to them."

"You don't have to. Right now. Let's just get you home."

"I have to see Marta."

"You don't want to go back there."

"Yes, I do."

"You don't think she'll be all right? For the night?"

"That's not enough."

"I sent word."

"Thank you. Thank you." She started to cry but stopped, with effort.

"I saw the address. In your address book. When you weren't there—"

"Ah," Dixie breathed. "When was this?"

"Ages ago. Before."

"Why didn't you tell me?"

"I've been trying to. I was—ashamed."

"I was trying to protect you. As well as Sunny."

"I know that."

"It's okay."

"It's not okay."

"Then I forgive you."

Kate burst into tears.

She cried while he patted her back. "There. I know," he would say. She would cry and then draw into herself, her face in her hands, and then she would cry again, until she felt the cobblestones of Antigua beneath the tires.

Dixie said, "Can we go somewhere? For just a few minutes?"

Kate squeezed his hand. She caught her breath. "I guess."

He drove to the house by the jade factory. He knocked, tentatively, then used the key. Kate felt relief to be standing on the street; she felt relief to be entering the house. Her impulse was to stay there forever.

The moon had passed over the courtyard. Stars were out. Dixie held her hand. He seemed uncertain where to settle.

"They want Vidalúz," Kate said from out of nowhere.

"I know," Dixie said, wincing.

"What's wrong?"

"It's my back. A stress reaction."

"I could—you know—" Kate said, offering her hands. Her voice still felt unreliable, trembling from within her chest.

"You think it'll help?"

"I think it'll help."

They stepped into the living room where weeks before they had watched television. Dixie lit a lamp; it gave off a rusty tint. They sat on the sofa. Kate could smell the musty books on the shelves behind them. The room bespoke a leisurely, appreciative life; woodcuts on the walls, the books, a phonograph in a mahogany case, a rack of phonograph records in leather albums: Debussy, Haydn, Mozart. There is in certain houses the sense that what has been acquired is of great value, has been there for a very long time, and that it satisfies. Kate had never had that feeling. You must live in one place a long time; you must be concerned with the pleasure and work of choosing things. But right then, she wanted it. She wanted to move in and take over that life. She wanted the security of the yellow Italian teapot on the shelf, the books, the silver candlesticks, the antique huipils.

"Let me see," she said.

"I should be doing this. For you."

"You can. Sometime," she said.

He wore his chambray shirt; his blond hair lay in curls on his collar. She put her hands on his back and said, "Up high? Or down low?"

"Right between my shoulder blades."

Kate got up on her knees for better leverage. She used her thumbs; she worked the knot she could feel, glad to be touching him. Attending to someone else calmed her.

"I want you to think about this, Kate. You don't have to go back there. There are people standing in line now to be her witness."

"Hush."

"It's a terrible risk."

Kate pressed into his muscles to silence him.

"And doing no good. She should end the vigil."

"You don't know her very well, do you?" Then Kate said, "Why didn't we go back to the house?"

"Jude's there."

"She's going to have to know."

"She knows. She knows about us."

Kate pressed. She put her weight into it. He had to brace his foot against the floor. She worked him over and he responded with almost inaudible grunts and ows, and then, within a few minutes, with sighs of respite.

"It helps," he said. "But stop, please."

She eased her hands away, laid them on his shoulders.

He turned to face her, took her hands in his. Her braid was coming undone. She glanced away.

He held her chin in his fingers.

"What do you want?"

"To hold you. If that helps."

Clumsily, uncertainly, he eased her down on the sofa and lay beside her. She had her back to him. She faced the sofa and its dusty swirls of wool and the scratchiness if she allowed her face to brush against the wool. The length of him was there; how intimate, to lie length to length. She sighed a deep sigh. She pressed against him slightly. On the threshold of a lawless place.

"Too good to be true," he whispered.

"What's that?"

"The way we fit."

His words brought tears to her eyes. She thought he must never have spoken those words before. She was sad the same could not be said of her. But she gave herself five minutes. Of sighing. His hand tenderly holding hers. His knees against the backs of her knees. Her breathing ragged. Her sweet low center of gravity between her thighs reacting within, pulsing.

"I have to get to Marta," she said.

"Kate. Please."

"Alberto will take me there."

"All right. We'll go whenever you say."

She made moves to sit up. He stood up. She rose as if leaving a trance or sleep long needed.

They gathered their things, locked the door, and went out to the jeep. Kate breathed long deep measured breaths, gathering her courage. She watched the street as he drove to the cathedral, where the taxi drivers loitered between fares. She was afraid that if she looked at him she'd stay.

"Are you sure about this?" Dixie said. "You want to get Randall to go with you?"

"This'll be quick," she said. Then, "I think I see Alberto."

"I'll come tomorrow," he said.

She smiled. A smile tempered with exhaustion.

"I'm going to need my sunglasses. They're in a green case on my dresser."

"First thing in the morning I'll bring whatever you want. Give my love to Vidalúz. Tell her—"

"What?"

"Tell her I'm praying for her."

He let her out at the corner and watched with his window rolled down. She approached the taxi drivers, who squatted in a circle, talking and smoking.

Alberto said, "Señorita Catarina, buenas noches, I am at your service. I am at your service." He snuffed out his cigarette. He opened the back door of his cab for her.

She saw Dix wave, his hand a blur under the street light. Alberto turned the corner into the dark side of town.

She rapped sharply but lightly on the cloister's door. The night watchman came right away and let her slip in. He led her down the stone passageways and opened the sealed door just wide enough for her to pass through. Marta leaped on her. She pressed Kate's face with her fingers as if testing to see if Kate were really there. She stared into her eyes. Kate had hoped that Marta would speak this night of all nights. She had hoped that the reunion would bring a word from her. But no. A metal plate of food covered in tinfoil waited there for Kate. Famished, she ate cold rice and a garlicky stewed chicken leg. Marta held her hand. She did not want to speak the truth until Marta fell asleep. Once she did, in the dark Kate told Vidalúz the story of what had happened. Vidalúz offered her hand between the cots. "Gracias, mi hermana," she said. "Mi gemela. My twin."

And then Vidalúz said, "You know that Father Dixie wants to call the farm Mary's House, but Catarina, you must not let him. Venga lo que venga. Come what may. It should be called Hummingbird House. Hummingbird House was one of the first women created by the gods. That is the better name."

Kate said, "You have to let him know."

"What you think is very important to him. Will you speak up with me?"

Kate said, "Sí, sí. It is the better name." Kate held her hand until Vidalúz moaned sleepily and pulled hers back.

How greedy were her thoughts of love.

I counted the speed bumps.

Though later, when someone asked me how many there were, I couldn't say. A garage door ripped open. We drove up a slight incline and got out and they took me to a place that smelled like blood. They sat me on a low hard stool, and I was fixated on my glasses, I wanted my glasses back, as though everything would be all right if only I could see clearly, and Marta, I thought about her, not in any coherent way, but just her presence, what that had felt like, and what it felt like to be torn from her, and Randall, I willed him to tell the right people, to get me out. I am a citizen of the United States, I ranted silently, I am a citizen of the United States. It's hard to tell the kinds of things that rush through your mind, the stories you've heard, at a time like that, and you're waiting in unholy dread, nearly shitting your pants, you understand about that then. Your body goes one direction, your mind splits into too many grooves. And right before you there is that smell and the menacing velvety prattle of men conferring in the next room and from somewhere beyond a man begging for mercy, and from outside the huffing and shouts of soldiers, it must've been soldiers drilling, cadent responses given in time to a superior. They left me sitting there. And finally I raised my voice and said, Aquí está mi pasaporte. My hands were tied, aquí meant nothing, I could not indicate my pass-port pouch. Por favor, I said. And someone opened my denim pouch and took out my passport. The next thing I heard was the voice of a North American man. I will never forget it.

Jesus Key-rist. Get her the hell out of here.

I will never forget that voice. And as it turned out I heard it again. I came nearly face to face with my redeemer and my enemy. Jesus Key-rist. Get her the hell out of here. My passport was shoved back into the denim pouch. I was shoved back into the van. I did not count the speed bumps.

They took me where a putrid smoke saturated the air. We drove into it, a rotten burning, and onto a dirt road, but not too far, the trip took maybe fifteen minutes, and what happened next hap-pened all at once. We stopped, the hood was plucked off me, my wrists were freed, and I was rolled out the door. I stumbled, but not too hard, and I was afraid, I was afraid because I did not have my glasses. I was at the head of a mammoth ravine and up and down the ravine were cardboard boxes and lean-tos and sheds and some of them had tin roofs weighed down with old tires and broken ce-ment blocks and candlelights and fires lay in a crooked string like beads on a rosary down that ravine, hundreds of lights. The first thing I did was stick my money in my pocket. My passport and Marta's birth certificate I stuffed inside my underpants against my belly. The smell, part rubber smoldering, part plastic melting, and food rotting, and human flesh discarded, hospital leavings, the waste in shallow latrines and ditches, that smell stung my eyes and nose and I thought I might vomit, but I didn't, I held that down. I saw a gang of rats as big as housecats roving over a pile of trash. These are the events of my life that Paul does not want to hear about, he can't listen, he says it makes him sick, he works around whatever the horror, he says, Don't, please—

The mercury-colored glow of Guate hovered beyond the place where I was. Black shadows stirred within the dwellings. And when my ears would let me hear I heard their voices, I heard their music, an out-of-tune guitar and singing, and I heard children crying and

I heard a man howling and I heard a laugh and I heard the urgent sound of sex, all the human voices being lifted up beyond that burning.

I wandered down the path and I'm not sure how long that lasted. I passed a pile of bones and the partial carcass of a dog. And midden piles, unrecognizable trash, whatever was left after the first trash had been scavenged and recycled and used up. Banty hens cackled and scattered before me. Deeper I went and as I did, the shit and sweat and walls closed in on either side. A girl in a shiny blue dress came out to the path and said, Puta, puta. She spat at me. A black bird landed in the mud. Good God, good God, I said under my breath, and when I spoke a man emerged from a refrigerator box and said curiously, Cómo le va? And I said, I am lost. Estoy perdida. Estoy perdida. He took pity on me. He came up closer, not so close as to be threatening, and he looked me in the eye and said, A dónde va? A dónde va? He was a short man, an older man, with a pitted brown face streaked with grease and a red kerchief around his neck. He took off his straw hat and held it at his chest, almost a sign of chivalry and I saw that one of his ears was gone and left in its place was a mass of scar tissue. And I said, I need to find a taxi. He said, Ah, sí, un taxi. There are taxis, but they are a long way. I will take you there. And I let him take me. He chased away the mangy dogs who bared their yellow teeth and plunged at us. I let him take me across a metal bridge and down into a poorly lit street where eventually we came to a gas station, that raised my hopes somehow, the ordinary gas station, the pumps, the dirty cracked windows where the attendants watched and waited. There was a grocery store across the street and he, Gaspár, my guide, happened to know that there was a man who drove a taxi who stopped at the store to see the woman who ran the store. He knew all this. The woman said, Sí sí, he will be here soon. She eyed the clock above the curtained door that led into the back room. She did not take the least bit of interest in me once she knew what it was I wanted. She watched a grainy-looking TV show, a game show in Spanish. They were giving away baby goods, a year's supply of disposable diapers.

I tried to pay Gaspár. We had talked all the way to the store and I remember hearing the hushed and musical sound of our voices in the walking, but I cannot for the life of me remember what we said. The whites of his eyes were red from the smoke. I remember that. At first he said, No, no, you do not need to pay me, but I insisted, it was all a dance we were doing, he knew he would take the money and I knew he would take the money. I said, This is not much, you saved me, and he took a ten-Q note and the woman behind the counter looked at me with disgust. She thought I was a fool. I bought a soda from a cooler, a warm lemon-lime soda in a green bottle. I will never forget how it tasted. How good it tasted. And when the taxi driver came I asked him, How close is Zone 2? He said, Not such a long distance. I can take you there for twenty Q. And we went speeding through the streets to Sunny's. I asked him to wait for me.

I knocked on Sunny's door and called her name. She came to the door in her robe and I paid the taxi driver and fell into Sunny's arms. Right there. In the foyer of El Pacífico Sueño. Among the baby coffins.

From far away, women heard about the vigil and they came to the cathedral and left photos of their loved ones who had been disappeared. Women came to them and left written messages and prayers. Rosaries tangled in a pile upon their tapete. Vidalúz's cheeks took on the glow of hunger. She lost weight. Reporters from the *Economist* and the *Miami Herald* would visit them and take their pictures and go their way. A drummer monotonously banged a drum near the cathedral door behind them, nearly every day for hours on end. No message ever arrived from the president. Vidalúz waited for a message from the president. Dixie came down to the cathedral early every morning. He passed notes to Kate and she hungrily read the notes. He wrote that Sunny had received a phone call warning her that she had gone too far. She was thinking of quitting her teaching job and going to Ben in Michigan for a while. They would sell the house. He wrote that Jude too was going home for six months. He wanted Kate to think of leaving. He wrote that the deal had gone through on the farm. He had the deed in his possession. He loved her dearly. At night he remembered holding her. He wrote that she was brave. He never signed his name. Kate would read the notes, once, twice, three times, and then she would crumple the paper and burn them on the cathedral steps. Dixie prayed with them. He was one of many who came to say a prayer, to lean their heads together, to kneel, to hold hands. Such strength in holding hands.

The voices would mingle—Our Father, Padre nuestro, who art in heaven, qué estás en el cielo, sanctificado sea tu nombre . . .

One day someone unfurled a home-painted banner above them: Y libranos del mal. And deliver us from evil. The women cried sometimes, swaying above the flickering candles. They wailed, When will God deliver us from evil?

Marta cried without vocalizing. Her mouth would be open in a dark O. The tears would flow like ribbons down her cheeks. Times like that, nothing appeased her, not zapotes or Frosted Flakes, not the gift of a red bead rosary around her neck, not Kate's soothing lullaby or holding her in her arms and lap. The seventh night after Kate's detention, Marta cried for over an hour on the steps of the cathedral. Silvery lightning above the volcano portended a rainy evening.

Vidalúz said, "Let us go early." She spoke quite softly. Words from just inside her mouth. Dwarf birds from a cave. The liquids she drank, the chicken broth and tea and juice, were not enough to keep her from failing.

They packed up everything. A Quaker couple from Chicago—youngish, in nearly identical Goretex rain parkas and boots—were to accompany Vidalúz in a taxi. Randall took the rucksack. He usually wanted to go with Kate; he felt such remorse about the night he'd been in a hurry to buy his cigarettes. In the momentum of packing up and leaving, Marta's tears subsided. They said good night to the women who regularly came to keep them company. A gray cloud had descended.

With their witnesses they went in and out the cathedral. Kate and Marta and Randall strolled out a block or two past the Church of the Merced, past its huge dry fountain, past the restaurants full of travelers waiting out the impending storm on stools, with cigarettes at hand and wine glasses smudged with lipstick. Kate caught sight of them while walking by. Once she might have been among them. She and Maggie might have lived like that for a few weeks in Antigua. On the swashbuckling surface of the night.

They met with yet another witness—Randall knew her, Kate did not—and the four of them walked up an alleyway and detoured back, past the place where AA meetings were held. A gang of shirtless boys kicking a black-and-white soccer ball in the street. Lovers kissing in a doorway. A toothless woman hawking her last tortillas. Dogs and policemen and beggar kids. Marta had stopped crying. She laid her head upon Kate's shoulder; she patted Kate's back. They might have been a family out for a walk after dinner or they might have been travelers from the same hometown rendezvousing for a nostalgic evening, a show of photos from the Mayan ruins, a plan of meeting on a beach in Belize a week hence. Kate missed for a moment all that might have been. She resisted melancholy. Melancholy like a sore muscle.

Their witnesses turned them loose about a half block from the cloisters. Randall settled the rucksack on Kate's back and bade them good night. She and Marta met up with Vidalúz outside the cloister door.

The night watchman opened the door and lurched there, his big face sweaty and flushed. Contorted and bloody. He waved his flashlight wildly. Its narrow shaft of light cut up the walls.

"Yo quiero romper con ustedes, es necesario, it's necessary, do not come in," he wheezed, his voice thick with something—not drunkenness, as she'd first assumed, but fear. He swung his flashlight like a sword. A big gash—a cross—on his forearm bled down to his wrist: a machete wound.

"We must," Vidalúz said.

He tried feebly to push the door shut. "Do not come in," he said.

Kate laid her weight against the door and it creaked open. They entered.

The watchman leaned against the wall and slumped to the floor. "No vengan," he rasped, "no vengan, no vengan!"

Kate set Marta down. She shrugged off the rucksack. She knelt beside the man and examined his wound. It was nasty. His arm was black with hair, and hair and sweat and dust contaminated the wound. It lay open, a fatty split that would require stitches. He crawled away from Kate, terrified.

"We must go to our room," Vidalúz said.

The watchman cried, "No, no!"

Kate's stomach clenched. Her scalp tightened in a prickly cap. She had to choose between accompanying Vidalúz and tending to the watchman. She decided he was not in danger of anything but his terror. A few more minutes would not matter. She thought that if she could boil water she could clean him and sew him up. In due time, in due time.

With Kate carrying Marta and right on her heels, Vidalúz went rapidly down the passageway and beneath the cherry-red bougainvillea that hung in old and weighty boughs over their doorway. She pushed the door open. Stale blackness wavered there like stage curtains. She reached in her pocket for matches. With trembling hands she lit a match. Right away it went out. The lantern stood beside the door. Vidalúz bent down and raised the globe. She lit another match and stuck it under the globe to the mantle of the lantern: in a burst of light as she stood up, the lantern in one hand, the stone room was illuminated shockingly in a wide yellow bloom of light. They gasped and Vidalúz let out a cry—she cried out Hector's name.

Kate said, "Sweet Jesus."

His body lay on Vidalúz's cot. He wore no clothes. He'd been thrown there on his stomach, his face turned toward the door. His skin was whitish blue. Strips of skin had been peeled from his shoulders. One hand dragged the floor and his fingers had been cut off that hand. His face was black with bruises, swollen. A cardboard hand-lettered sign lay on his back:

AHORA TU SABES

VER ES CREER

Vidalúz collapsed on the floor.

Kate set Marta just outside the open door. God only knows, she thought, what Marta has seen, but she wanted her to see no more.

She knelt beside Vidalúz; she gave her water from a canteen. Vidalúz fell apart; she spat away the water. She wailed. The shock seemed to infuse her with the power to wail. "They are madmen, sin duda, sin duda, without doubt," she wailed, "they are the work of the devil, the devil, I tell you, Hector was a good man, he was pure—"

And Kate held her. She held Vidalúz and let her cry out. She felt watched. As though whoever had dumped his body knew every word that had passed between them in the cloister, every thought, every move. But there was no way to stop Vidalúz from wailing.

Kate looked up.

Marta stood in the doorway, her girl's face frowning in empathy. Kate thought she could see the woman Marta would become—and all too soon. Her huipil fell off one shoulder; her shoes had come untied.

Marta cried, "Catarina!"

Tears flooded Kate's eyes, but she could not give in to that. "Come here, Marta, come here," she said, opening one arm to Marta. "I am here, don't worry."

In the foyer at El Petén #3, a candle flickered fitfully in a copper candlestick. They had gone to El Petén #3 out of a homing instinct, though they knew they might be watched. Alberto had driven the three of them from the park. Vidalúz was strangely quickened, telling Alberto where to turn, working out vehemently what she thought they should do. Dixie had rushed them back to the cloister and they had tossed their makeshift camp into the jeep—cots, reading matter, bags, everything incriminating. Only Hector's body had been left in the cold stone room. The watchman was calmed by Dixie, who told him what to say: the partial truth.

Dixie took the women to the house, put on his Roman collar, and drove the night watchman to the hospital; he would pay for his wound to be sewn up by the Canadian doctor. He would accompany him to the police, to the lies we tell with lives at stake.

At the house, the women raged. Vidalúz and Marta and Kate were there alone, and they raged at the world, at God. Vidalúz said God had forsaken the poor and the just. Marta clung to Kate. There was no calming Vidalúz. Kate did not try to contain her for Marta's sake, for the sake of anyone.

There were many tears. Kate put up the black cotton wreath she'd hung when Maggie died. Vidalúz ate, mechanically. A bowl of rice, a pot of tea, bread and butter: simple foods she thought her system could bear without becoming ill. Breaking such a fast could make her sick and she needed to be strong for travel. She slept for a while, worn out, the lucky sleep of mourning when you can plow under sleep what you cannot forget.

While she slept Kate wandered the house, holding Marta by the hand, talking to Marta, eliciting responses that never came, showing her baubles or a photo of an animal in a magazine. She was split between what she knew she had to do for Marta and what she felt herself. Her revulsion at seeing Hector, his knucklebones exposed, his face tortured. Her impotence. Her love of Vidalúz. Her desire to rest, to do nothing, to allow maintenance details to become her life. She could not think straight.

Sunny had been to the house. The bedroom she had shared with Ben for years was vacant, its doors flung open for all to see. There was the faint smell of mothballs, a trace of cedar. She had cleared out clothes and taken down art and emptied dressers, and all that was left was a queen-sized-bed with two lumpen pillows covered in a cotton bedspread—a sky-blue bedspread printed with wild horses. Sunny and Ben had put the house on the market. They wanted everyone out by November 1. Kate could not puzzle her way so far ahead.

Later, nearly ten o'clock. Dixie and Kate and Marta and Vidalúz sat in the courtyard. Kate drank a glass of wine. It felt like the best way to cope; it felt deserved. They had sat there for over an hour without talking; if a cry seeped from one of them, the others would say brokenly, "I know." The fountain had been turned off. Posh slept among the fern fronds.

They expected Randall and the Quaker couple who were to drive Vidalúz across the border into Chiapas. Hector's sister and her husband and their two boys lived in San Cristóbal de las Casas; they had taken on new names; they had put away their traje; they lived deceitfully as Mexicans now.

"They fled in 1982," Vidalúz said, suddenly talkative. She seemed to take some refuge in the details of their lives. "Before the violence they were students. De negocios. Y teatro. Now they labor. For the first three months they ate nothing but tortillas. They could not sleep."

"How do you know?" Kate said. Marta lay in her lap, sucking the ends of her hair and dozing.

"A traveler spoke with them and sought us out. If not for that, we might not know they are alive. But I will find them."

Not once had Vidalúz and Hector been able to visit them; they lived in torment when they thought of returning to their native land. Now she would go to them. Eventually she would go to Mexico City and ask for asylum and talk with reporters, but first she wanted only to sit down face to face with Hector's sister, to be Hector's spouse in mourning, to nurse her private sorrow.

Though they had not seen it happen, Hector's body had been taken to the morgue in the capital. He had only one relative left in the country who would claim the body for a funeral, an uncle from Huehuetenango, a honey farmer. And that would not be possible until the forensic doctors were through with Hector. His body must be subjected to still more scrutiny.

"Time will pass," Vidalúz said. "You will be safe." Then, "Alma mia es solamente en dolor. But someday—si Dios quiere—the farm and what you do there may be my comfort."

"Si Dios quiere," Dixie agreed.

Marta flung her arms about suddenly, irritably; she made no noise. Kate carried her into her bedroom. She laid her down and turned on the music, meadow music of flutes.

"Mi hijita, mi hijita," Kate murmured, tucking Marta in. "Someday you will be comforted too. Someday I will take you to the highlands. Si Dios quiere."

She did not speak again until the middle of September.

I began to think that I had dreamed her voice, that the sound in my mind was the girl at the hospital in Comitán, calling Catarina, Catarina—years before, long ago. But no—Marta had called my name. And once we settled down, she was to speak again. And again. Her needs were easy for me then, though at the time I wondered if I'd have the strength to carry through her mute days, her nightmares, her tantrums.

I would try to recall what my mother did for me if I cried like that, as though from some lost pain. But Marta was inconsolable, and I'm not sure I ever cried like that where anyone would know, it wasn't allowed, you had to have a reason, a skinned knee full of gravel or a splinter under your thumbnail or a bad name another child had lodged right in your heart, and even then the message was to toughen up, your face'll freeze like that, you'll look that way forever and you are not a pretty sight. But Marta taught me patience with her crying.

Dix was the only man I've known who would let you cry yourself out. When you live alone or when you live with other women you can cry through whatever it is. A cry is like a storm, it passes, it takes time but it passes. A cry can have at its core what you may never articulate, old wounds, old desires, sins of omission, impossible reasons, if a cry can have reasons. Paul wants to fix the cry. He offers solutions, answers he cooks up on the spur of the moment, or he tries distraction, the way you do a kid with a toy, and Deaver, Deaver would say, What the fuck are you crying about now? But Dixie said, The Holy Spirit has taken you over when you cry. You're being healed.

Marta is a woman now, almost sixteen, and other people think they know exactly what she needs—

Marta herself makes the silver flute call like the loons.

Though she has never heard a loon, that was my time, the time of loons, when I would ski with Paul in the frozen birch woods of the north, the blue sky a blessing. We were strong and could ski for days and sleep out in the cold. Once we made a snow cave, more like a box, and we laid our sleeping bags inside, and that was the perfect place for sleep in winter, windless, hushed, clean, smooth. It is almost impossible to imagine snow now. The loons would be calling. The loons were all we would hear, that and the slap of cards, our game of hearts. We'd go to sleep so early. After the Drambuie from the bottle, the coil of heat it made inside. Paul says he can remember every conversation, every wish and lie, every protestation, every adoration, every confession. Paul says your first love can be your true love. The love that transformed you most of all, he says that's what love is, he has ideas about love, he's been to workshops where they talk about it, teach it, endlessly. Some people return, like migrating birds they go back, they go back in time, they marry the same person twice, or if they never married, they move in together again, into habits or black magic like the song says weaves a spell, and if he's right then Marta would hear the loons and understand the way her music in all its mystery completes my sense of loons.

The life Paul wants for us is achingly familiar.

Hummingbird House

Marta gained weight.

Kate went to the market on the big market days, maneuvering through the stalls and among the vendors, right at sunrise, assessing the market through a mother's eyes. The Mayan farmers would come down from the foothills and the mountains, some on mules, some on buses, some on foot. The ramshackle buses would be loaded down with nets of fruits and vegetables, whatever was ripe and in season. The children of the vendors would be sleepy-eyed, dragged from sleep in the wee hours of the morning, and they would sit and comb out their hair or tend a baby or run an errand while their mothers and fathers set up the mounds and pyramids of food. New white potatoes with paper-thin skins, gigantic lemons and limes, pearly onions, tough green squash. Fifty-pound burlap bags, open invitingly and filled with dried beans the colors of dirt and clay, red and black and brown and creamy white: kidney beans, black beans, pinto beans, navy peas, chickpeas. And the platanos, the papaya, the piña. Brown eggs and nearly black eggplant. All the while Kate thought vitamins, she thought minerals, she thought carbohydrates, she thought complete protein. She envisioned meals of avocados and wheat germ and mangoes and oatmeal and honey and whole milk and good stout bread and peanut butter. And when she had contented herself with the food for the next few meals, when she was loaded down and her arms that ached from carrying Marta ached from carrying the string bags, she would stop and buy a bouquet of roses. A dozen short-stemmed roses, pink or yellow or almost white. She knew they would not last more than a day. Still, for two Qs they were a bargain. And with these parcels she would return home, where Dixie and Marta waited for her. For her. Someone waited at home for her. This never ceased to amaze.

Her solace was Marta. The songs she sang to her. The sweet pad of Marta's hand in hers. The kitchen was Dixie's. The flour flying. Chopping piles of garlic or onions or green peppers. There was so much food and still there was so much hunger. You could not help but think about that.

Inevitably, she and Dixie gained weight too. Dixie's clothes seemed to fit him differently; he was bearish again; he looked younger: a grizzled blond bear, the way he'd looked when she first met him. He grew a beard and kept it neatly trimmed. Kate lost the hunted look she'd had during the vigil. Her hair grew lustrous and she left it long and out of braids and brushed it frequently, teaching Marta to brush her own. She taught Marta to care for herself and in the process taught herself again. They brushed their hair one hundred strokes at night. And Dixie looked on.

Still, they did not touch.

After Vidalúz left there was the first tier of trauma to work through, each day weighted with relief and sorrow. That was a little like mining; she hoped clarity lay embedded in the deep. They managed a week trying not to mention Maggie, trying not to mention Hector. She saw the ache in Dixie's eyes if Hector's name arose on the edge of a conversation. Then they began acquainting each other with what they did not know. Kate would tell Dixie stories of Maggie, their exploits. Tentatively at first, and then, when she saw that he enjoyed the stories, enjoyed the way she told them, she searched her memory and gave him stories to see him smile. And he would speak, more haltingly, of Hector. The forensic doctors had not yet declared the cause of death; they knew his body lay in the morgue, and this they did not discuss.

When she put Marta down at night she played the flute music. She would whisper, "Necesita la música?" And Marta would drift away to sleep, listening.

Lino would come in the mornings for his lesson and he and Dixie would talk at the kitchen table. It seemed to Kate, overhearing them, that Dixie's voice took on new urgency with Lino, knowing he was soon departing for Fuego, that Lino was a man going off to seek his dream. He wanted to be a farmer and a teacher and a catechist; he talked about later on getting training as a health care worker; he had big ideas. It was good to know someone who had big ideas.

Nearly every time he left the house, Lino would verify, "We are going, yes, to Fuego? You will help me move?"

And Dixie would say, "Eventually we'll go, but I'm still not well. Besides, the Hungarian's waiting for a part."

Lino would smile eagerly. "Gracias, muchas gracias." And he would go to his friend's house where he stayed.

They walked everywhere. The jeep was in the Hungarian's garage. The repair had been held up; the Hungarian was sick in bed with an ulcer, and they were waiting for a connecting-rod bearing. Yet when they left the house each day, for the market or the nearby tienda or the playground or the church, no one followed them. At first Kate had started at every knock on the door, every erratic firework, her body wrought in antipathy of the street, the neighbors, strange cars. She wore her sunglasses—she was waiting for her new glasses to arrive from a lab in the capital—and those helped her feel invisible beyond the safety of the house, dark glasses and a floppy straw hat. Gradually fear slipped away.

She called her mother from the GUATEL office. She did not know what she would say until she heard her mother's voice: squeaky, putting on a chipper front. Kate said, "I'm sorry—"

"You're safe and sound. That's what matters—"

"I'm not . . . not coming back right now. I know I said I would. But things've come up—"

Marta perched just outside the booth on the plywood bench. A soldier nearby, bored. Early evening light still dappled the GUATEL garden, where orange-and-blue birds-of-paradise pressed up against the Plexiglas window separating the garden from the waiting room.

"Well, we're just coming down there. We looked it up in the atlas, and it can't be more than two hours from Houston."

"Don't come down here—"

"It's safe, isn't it? Where you are it's safe."

"Relatively speaking."

"Dodie and Mary Lou want to come too—"

"I didn't think you ever would. Come here."

Silence. Kate tried to picture home: corn twice as tall as she was, the mosquitoes swarming by the creek, the bats diving. Labor Day just past.

"People change, Kate. People change."

More silence. Kate's palm sweated on the dirty receiver. She smiled at Marta, who kicked her heel rhythmically against the leg of the bench. She eyed a man with a candy bar.

Her mother said, "When they buried Maggie it was hard."

"I . . . can imagine it was. . . ."

"Ruth took to bed—sedated—for two weeks." She lowered her voice. "She's just a shadow."

"It was hard here too. It still is."

"Honey, why weren't you and Maggie together? Why wasn't she with you?"

"She'd met a guy. I'd broken off with Deaver—"

More expensive silence. You get rusty when you don't call home habitually. You forget what to say; you forget the lulls and the pacing.

"Do you want to tell me what happened with him?"

"Do you want the long story or the short story?"

"Whatever you want. I like the sound of your voice."

Kate's throat closed; tears threatened. She did not want that.

"It's hard. On the phone."

"I know."

"Listen. Mom. Don't come down here. Not yet. I'm just not ready yet."

"Will you call me again soon?"

"Yes. Yes, I will."

"I'd like that. I'd like to hear from you." She waited. "Is there anything I can do?"

"Yes. There is. Would you send me something? Would you send me a photo of me when I was a kid?"

"Give me the address—"

And then Kate got off. She had called collect. It would turn out to be a very expensive call, but a necessary call.

Later that night she told Dixie, "My mother and my aunts, they're thinking about coming down here. To visit."

"That's gutsy."

"But I told her to wait."

"Why's that?"

"Well, you know," Kate said. "Until we're up at the farm . . ."

Dixie smiled, really smiled. So many of his smiles of late had seemed forced, intended to make her feel better. Rain, light and even and cool, fell on the courtyard floor. She sat down beside him under the colonnade. Posh nervously flew from the fern to Dixie's shoulder.

"He's getting ready to cry out," Dixie said. "I'm certain this poor bird was traumatized during a rainstorm."

Kate said, "Who're you reading?"

Dixie held up the book. "Neruda."

He pivoted slightly in his chair, held the book to the yellow bodega light. He read, "'We came by night to the Fortunate Isles, and lay like fish under the net of our kisses.'" He put the book down against his chest, still open. Posh pecked at the book's pages. "That's where I want to go," he said. "The Fortunate Isles."

And he began to weep. His shoulders shook, his chest heaved with all he had held in check. Posh toddled down Dixie's shirt, hopped to his knee and then to the floor.

Kate put out her hand. "I'm here."

Dixie took her hand. He checked his weeping. "Whatever we do, I want it to be the honorable thing."

No man had ever spoken to Kate of honor. She took back her hand, a protective manuever, as though another Kate, an inner Kate, could not help herself.

"What's wrong?" he said.

Kate frowned. "I don't know—"

He said, "I'm happy with you here—"

"You are?"

"Of course. Can't you feel it?"

"I think I can feel it."

He reached for her hand again. She slipped her hand in his. "But one thing at a time. I'm working on letting go. Of—"

Kate said, "Everything that went before."

"Yes."

"Necesito la música!" Marta keened. At last.

Kate and Dixie stared at each other, astonished. They got up and made their way to the room Kate shared with Marta. On the way there, Kate said soothingly, "Qué pasa? Qué pasa?"

And Marta spoke again, insistently: "La música!"

Kate switched on a lamp beside the bed. Marta rubbed her eyes; she sat up. She wore pajamas scattered with rosebuds. Dixie and Kate sat down on the edge of the bed. The covers trailed the floor.

"Quiere la música?" Dixie asked, reaching to flip the tape.

"Sí," Marta said.

Dixie punched the play button. Meadow music.

Marta pulled at Kate's sleeve. "Y Catarina."

Kate lay down beside her, tucked the covers up around Marta's shoulders. She pointed to the lamp and Dixie turned it off. Kate whispered questions, just to hear Marta's response. Le gusta la música? Quiere agua? O ir al baño? Dixie sat in silent company for a long time on the edge of the bed, watching over them. Marta sucking the ends of her hair, Kate nesting beside her.

La Verdad de Hoy had folded. Sunny had stored their equipment and their supplies in a friend's back bedroom. She did not know if she would return or if she would sell or give the equipment to others who would come up, up from hope and anger, to take on the yoke and risk of telling the truth. No one knew what would happen with that. But they had heard stories of other newspapers and photographers' darkrooms that had been broken into, equipment destroyed, people detained clandestinely. Sometimes you would not know you had stepped over the line until that first warning; she did not have to be warned twice. Ella fue, fue. Sunny could go—she could flee so readily. Kate knew her visit to El Pacífico Sueño had been the last straw. She felt regret at that, yet she took heart knowing that Sunny was not in danger, that Vidalúz was not in danger. Vidalúz was all right. She had met Ben in Mexico City and he had taken her to a place of sanctuary in Arizona. There had been one :icle about her in the *LA Times*. For a while Kate did not want to id newspapers; she wanted to purge herself.

At night they talked of these things, of what had transpired. What was possible.

After dinner Kate would bathe Marta; she would lie down beside her in the double bed they shared; the flute music would be playing and she would speak the titles of the pieces to Marta, in Spanish and English: "Evening Star, La Estrella de la Tarde." "Canyon Reverie, El Ensueño del Cañon." Marta repeated the titles, gleanings from the natural world, pieces the Presbyterian Debra had learned from a Navajo teacher. Debra's music in the house became as constant as the fountain water percolating.

When Marta fell asleep, Kate would get up again. She would make herself a pot of chamomile tea and she and Dixie would talk for hours. Of Vidalúz and Hector and how he'd become involved with them. Of Sunny and Ben. Of Jude and Dixie's family. Of God and all the wisdom traditions of the world. Of love and what that was. Of drinking—oh, they had stories of drinking. They'd both been drunks, though Kate was a crisis drinker and could stop after one if she wanted to. Dixie could not stop once he began. He could not drink at all. He had given it up, he said, to be able to see. For clarity.

He told her the Jews thought mystics should marry. He told her Islam meant peace and surrender.

They talked of what they loved and missed about the States: the efficient and reliable postal system and art museums and blues bars and pizza and state parks and the health department's restaurant standards and the vastness of it and the stupid innocence—

They sat facing each other in the canvas slingback chairs, under afghans, with Posh on the lip of the fountain cocking his head as though listening. Dixie would read aloud to her, would pause sometimes to point out the constellations above them, constellations she would learn anew. He would show her Polaroids of the dairy farm: the black-and-white goats browsing at the foot of the hill, the hacienda with its new pine porch and lace curtains in the windows. Their feet would almost touch, his well-formed lovely statue's feet. But no. Neither made the move. She wanted to. Kate would be listening for Marta, who would sometimes stir and thrash in bad dreams. She and Dixie did not touch all those nights. They wandered in the language and stories and revelation each offered the other. It was as though they took the time to notice the fine veins on a leaf, the striations of quartz in a rock, cirrus clouds in a bony whirl. Each other's nature. To know. The days unfolded slowly, beautiful fans of cosmic dancers. They could not resist a return to what was good. In spite of everything.

Marta speaking marked a turning point. What nectar of brevity, the time they had remaining in the house. With the girls—Juanita and Victoria—giggling once again in the bodega. Glorious sun. Fuchsias in abundance. Time letting them be indolent, letting them take a minute or an hour to talk or cry or pray or laugh. When laughter finally came, they let it.

Yet there was no ignoring monthly anniversaries. The day she'd left Nicaragua. The day Maggie had died. The day Marta had come to live with them. The day they'd found Hector in the cloisters. Shifts in direction. God makes demands.

Four months after Maggie died—October 14—Kate awakened with a cold, stopped up, her bones achy. Her head felt heavy. And she'd slept late; Marta was already out of bed; her voice drifted down the colonnade from the direction of the kitchen. "Naranjas—o—" Kate barely heard. And Dix—the two of them quiet so as not to wake her. Kate started to roll out of bed, then relaxed, turned over, sighed back into the covers.

"Knock, knock," Dixie said.

"It's you," she said.

"Catarina?" Marta said.

"I'm not feeling so good," Kate said.

Dixie came to the edge of the bed, sat down. "What's the matter?"

Marta crawled up on his lap. She'd gotten dressed all on her own; Marta had her choice of ladino clothes or indigenous clothes and that morning she had chosen pink pedal pushers and a white T-shirt. "What'samatter?" she said.

"I think it's a cold—"

Dixie put his hand on her forehead. Kate brushed against his hand like a cat petted. She was not so sick that she didn't relish his touch.

"You feel a little warm," he said. Then, "Marta and I'll do the marketing. You want us to fix you brekkie and bring it in?"

"I'm not so hungry—"

"Tea?"

"Tea would be nice."

"Aspirina, también?"

"That's a good idea."

"Catarina está un poco enferma," he told Marta. "Let's take care of her."

Dixie brought a tray to her room, a pot of hibiscus tea, her favorite mug, a packet of soda crackers, two aspirin, and set the tray on a chair beside the bed. Marta stood at the door, waiting. A string bag looped around her wrist.

"Wear your hat, sweetie," Kate said.

And Marta ran to get her hat.

The front door ka-chunked when they went out. Kate sat up against the hard pillows, went to the bathroom, came back, and weakly drank her tea without much interest in it. She knew she needed liquids. Then she sank back into bed.

Voices awakened her. She did not know how long she'd slept; it might have been ten minutes, it might have been an hour.

"This stuff's like important stuff."

Ginger.

"Whatever you can leave behind, leave behind," a woman said.

Kate thought it must be Mrs. Clark. "We can go shopping when we get there."

"You don't understand. I'm attached to this stuff."

"All right, Ginger." Exasperated, as though the conversation were an old one.

Kate got up and went to her bedroom door.

"Kate!"

"Ginger. Mrs. Clark—hello."

Ginger said, "Did we wake you up?"

"I'm not feeling very well." Kate buttoned the top button of her nightgown.

Ginger looked bloated and pale. She had on a man's shirt over mouse-gray leggings. Her hair was bedraggled; she'd pulled it back in a beaded barrette. She wore mismatched silver earrings, one quetzal, one quarter moon.

Mrs. Clark said, "I'm sorry." She wrung her hands. She had her traveling clothes on: a lavender linen pantsuit. Her makeup was the worse for wear, as though she'd put it on slapdash.

"For what?"

"We didn't know anyone was home. I really didn't think we should just come in. But Ginger—"

"What's up?" Kate said. "I didn't know you kept your key."

"We're going to the States—" Ginger began. She dangled the key.

Mrs. Clark looked at Ginger as if to silence her. "It's just that the medical care we'll need will be easier there, and Mr. Clark—his work is nearly over. For now."

Ginger said, "What happened to that box I left here?"

"It's in the bodega," Kate said.

Ginger went into the bodega at the back of the house. Mrs. Clark stared at Kate for a moment but said nothing. Then she raised her voice a notch and called to Ginger, "I'll wait outside." She left without so much as a backward glance. Ginger came out of the bodega bearing a large cardboard box.

"Is it heavy?" Kate said.

"Not so heavy," Ginger said. She set it down at Kate's feet. "Where's Father Dixie?"

"Out."

Ginger took a deep breath. "Tell him I said good-bye. Okay?"

"I'll tell him." Kate took the key Ginger offered.

"I didn't think I'd leave so soon."

"Where are they taking you?"

"Maryland. They're moving to Maryland."

"Are you—all right?" Kate said. She didn't feel all right herself; her stomach was queasy.

"I guess I am. The Clarks are nice enough. But—" She sighed.

"What?"

"Being pregnant makes me feel like—"

"Like what?"

"Like things are out of my control."

"Do you want to sit down? Do you want to talk?"

"Our flight leaves at noon." Ginger looked around at the courtyard, the house. "I lived here for six months."

"Sunny and Ben are selling the house. We're moving next week."

"Wow." Then she inched closer to Kate. She said, "Do you think my baby'll look like me?"

"I'm sure."

"Do you think he'll—I think it's a he—do you think he'll have my toe?" She lifted her sandaled foot to make sure Kate understood. The pink polish on her toes had peeled away in spots.

"He might," Kate said.

"Then they'll never be able to forget me."

"You're right about that," Kate said.

Ginger picked up the box and started for the front door. Kate said, "I'll open the door." And she followed.

But Mrs. Clark had left the door ajar. Just as Ginger stepped across the door sill, just as she turned to say one last word, Kate heard a bossy drone from out on the sidewalk: "Jesus Key-rist. Let's just get the hell out of here."

Jesus Key-rist.

His voice was unmistakable. Mr. Earl Clark.

Kate's heart pounded. She was in her nightgown and weak; she had every excuse to simply shut the door and not go out.

Good-bye, she said, good-bye, Ginger. Good luck. They never heard from her again. She was absorbed by the great sponge of comfort to the north.

Their last day in the house dawned muggy. Grizzled clouds passed over all morning. Dixie sorted through the kitchen shelves under the counter, with Van Morrison singing: *Tupelo Honey*. Sunny had said, Take anything you want. He was tempted to take it all, but of particular interest to him were the cast-iron skillet and a copper-bottomed saucepan he knew Sunny and Ben had been given as a wedding present all those long years ago in Madison. And there were various knives the house had accumulated—a paring knife he favored, its handle repaired with duct tape, a serrated bread knife, a chef's knife for chopping onions, peppers. He'd gotten attached to Sunny's things. He wrapped his favorite mugs in newspaper and packed them in a laundry basket. He neatly folded the table linens, frayed and spotted though they were, and laid them in a box on top of silverware and baking dishes.

He still had not figured out how to get Posh up to the high-lands. They did not have a birdcage and he was afraid it would upset him to be cooped up in a box for a long day's drive. Kate and Marta had gone out to look for something to transport him in. Dixie stopped for a moment, went to the kitchen door, looked out. The courtyard was topsy-turvy with boxes half filled and suitcases and duffels and piles of books. His mind sprinted ahead to the mo-

ment when he would take Kate and Marta up the steps of the hacienda and see their response. It was a country house and in his way
of thinking a country house had it over a city house any day. Brick
floors. Rough pine tables and chairs and beds. And with the mountains always right there, in view, and the bright-eyed goats chewing
their cud in the yard.

Posh groomed himself on the lip of the fountain. A bird, a child,
a woman—all these companions had come into his life while he
lived in this house. The day he'd arrived—last Day of the Dead—
that day he had been sick, feeble, and he had cared about nothing
but rest. He had slept twelve hours a day for the first few weeks.
Sunny and Ben would come from the capital for the weekend and
there had been rumblings of their discontent: Ben sitting up late
into the night in the courtyard, ice melting in the glass of whiskey
beside his chair; Sunny spending her days out on strenuous walks; a
kind of bright and false cheer whenever he would come upon them
in the kitchen at the same time. A cramped kitchen, better for those
who got along.

Now they seemed to have weathered whatever had been happening. They were moving to Madison again. For now, Sunny had
said. Vamos a ver.

Marriage and its labyrinths of trial and error mystified him. He
thought of it every day. Words kept twinning up with his feelings:
wife, *nurture*, *love*—weighted words that changed his course. He
wanted to wake up every morning and see Kate's face before he saw
anything else. That's what it came down to. He had not said so. To
her or anyone.

Jude might never understand. He had to let that be. Her life
was all this back and forth, making arrangements, moving money,
cajoling people into cooperating. The women's bank was a beautiful project—he gave her that. An important project. Jude's work re-
lied on her own iron will. His work was not about will; it was about
ease, about peace. He wanted no filter between him and his work;
he wanted to cleanse himself of the church's arrogance.

The tape clicked off. He went back inside, flipped it over. The music made him feel thirty again, though when he was thirty life had not been as good as now. Everything had seemed more predictable.

He had started his letter to the bishop. That letter was the honorable way; he had to tell the bishop why he wanted simply to be a householder, a dairy farmer, among the people of his village.

It was a hard letter to write.

He heard the door opening. Kate and Marta came in chattering. "Tenemos una juala para Posh, tenemos una juala—" Marta sang.

He went to the courtyard. Kate carried an ornate brown wicker cage.

"It's an antique," she said.

"Where'd you get it?"

"We have to bring it back. We're only borrowing it. Renting it."

"Such a deal," Dixie said. "I can carry it back when Lino and I come down."

"That's what I thought," Kate said. "What's this?" The music, she meant.

"Packing music," he said. "Want to dance?" He slipped his arms around her.

Kate laughed. He loved the sound of her laughter. They two-stepped around the courtyard, around the fountain, among the geraniums he hadn't found a home for yet. They'd probably have to take the geraniums along, bouncing in the cargo rack. He could remember the basics of dancing. Marta set her hands on her hips, mesmerized. Kate's back curving against his hand felt alive and muscular and responsive. Her hair smelled like tangerines, a new season.

They left the next morning under a pink sky.

Lino had only a knapsack. It was on the return trip that they would be loaded down with Lino's belongings. His eyes were puffy and he promptly fell asleep in the back seat with his baseball jacket folded up like a pillow against the window. He said he'd stayed up all night talking, saying good-bye.

Marta squeezed in the front with Kate. She'd chosen to wear her corte and plastic sandals and a blue huipil embroidered with black and red animals. The top of the jeep was loaded with boxes and odds and ends, all of it secured with bungee cords. Posh in his cage was stashed beside Lino, who slept until Chichi, where they stopped at the market and had lunch and bought fruit to take along. Fruit was hard to come by in the high mountains. You rarely saw a piña, Dixie said, but they would make trips to the closest market; they would make lists—don't worry, he said.

"I'm not worried," Kate said.

And he did not think she was. He appreciated that about her, that she didn't worry. She took hardship as it came.

At nightfall they arrived at the farm, the jeep straining and bucking up the muddy hill as far as a spot that had been leveled for parking. And then there was the walk, not far, a few hundred yards. Lino carried Marta, who had fallen asleep. Kate carried Posh in his cage and Posh chittered nervously. The sky green-blue, a halcyon gem. Smoke in the air. The hacienda was lit up, each window a chunk of yellow light. The caretaker came out of the cheese room and waved his straw hat.

"Bienvenidos!"

They shouted, "Buenas noches, muchas gracias!" Dixie was glad for the chance to shout.

The caretaker, who had been tending the goats, gave them a tour. They had to taste the cheese; they had to see the spindly-legged kids who had been born only two days before; they had to drink the water, which was pure, the caretaker said, from the best well in the village. And when he'd gone and Lino had been settled in a room and Marta had been fed, kissed good-night, and given her música with which to fall asleep again, eventually, at long last, Kate and Dixie were left alone in the kitchen of the hacienda.

It was a big kitchen. Fit for big meals. "Cooking extravaganzas," Dixie said.

"Yes. I love it—"

"Do you?"

"Yes." Kate sighed. "We can feed so many people here." She ran her hand over the smooth pine counter. She said, "The silence, that's what I love."

He took her hand and they went down the hall to the last bedroom. A carved wooden door hung partway open. He switched on the light. It was an austere clean room with a double bed. Red rugs woven with cream-colored crosses lay on the floor. They could imagine nights to come in that room, sun-drenched mornings. He held her. To hold her was enough for now. He cupped her head in his hand, fingered her fine hair, kissed her temple. They lay awake for hours, whispering or not whispering. Out the window they could make out the black curve of the mountains against the night sky. The metallic smell of geraniums in a windowbox. The half-heard chiming of a bell on a goat shifting in sleep.

Kate experienced the move as she had no other, through Marta's eyes.

The first morning they ate breakfast on the porch, early, before Lino and Dixie were awake. Smoke from morning fires rose in tendrils across the valley. In his cage Posh made his happy gobble. Posh le gusta, Marta said, shivering in the mountain air. Kate wrapped her in the old afghan, brought her a mug of steaming hot chocolate. Goats browsed not far away in a tawny field. One caramel-colored, one black and velvety, with two identical kids nudging her udder. Kate realized how much she had to learn; she would become personally acquainted with goats.

That day she kept Marta by her side, and sometimes Marta led the way, first exploring the barn and its seven cats, then the pastures, then the village where other children played or carried wood for fires or—the girls—knelt beside their mothers learning to string a warp on a backstrap loom. Sí, recuerdo, Marta would say. They went to the homes of neighbors and introduced themselves. They found out when the mail came in; they asked about the nearest market. Kate knew Dixie had all the answers to her questions, but she and Marta wanted to discover for themselves; they wanted to talk with the women. And to face any rumor head-on. The women asked her outright, How is the health of the padre? When will he say mass? Kate told them the truth, that the bishop was sending a new priest soon. That Dixie wanted to live and work among the people with her. The women would smile knowingly and say, We want him to be happy.

During the first few days Marta and Kate found a rhythm of their own while Dixie and Lino learned from the caretaker. They wandered the muddy lanes, talking with anyone who wanted to talk. They watched afternoon rain from the shelter of the porch. They unpacked and organized the kitchen. Sunsets and twilight would linger. Dixie and Lino would be done with the milking, and after dinner they would sit on the porch and relish the peace.

On the third night Dixie showed them the deed and abstract, whose pages were yellowed, held together with brass rivets. The history of the land had been recorded in large black script. The Czech man who had come before World War II. His wife, whose father was a coffee farmer. Vidalúz had been named the owner now. Kate wondered if the time would ever come when Vidalúz would feel safe enough to live on her own land.

"This is what the families will have at Fuego," Lino said. "Our own deed to our own land."

"Yes, you will," Dixie said.

"When will we go?" Lino had been patient and helpful, but Fuego, his own dreams, were on his mind.

"How about tomorrow?" Dixie said.

Lino beamed. "I will be ready."

That night, lying with Kate in his arms, Dixie said, "When that priest comes we'll marry, won't we? Immediamente?"

"Immediamente," she whispered.

The next morning, while Marta slept in, Kate wandered down to the cement-block post office. She would not feel entirely settled until she knew for certain that their mail had been forwarded. The clerk handed her a packet secured with rubber bands. She could not wait to open it but sat on a wooden bench outside the municipal hall. Wind gusted and she held tight to the mail.

There was a large manila envelope from Managua—addressed in María's handwriting—and a letter from her mother. She opened that first. A photo slipped out of the one-page letter: a grade school picture of Kate in a red plaid cotton dress, her smile shy. She had one front tooth missing. Kate remembered that dress and how happy it had made her to wear it. She had thought her mother might have forgotten about the photo. It had taken so long. She scanned the note—busy, on our way out the door, Dodie and ML send love—

A neighbor woman hastened by, balancing a tub of masa on her head. She called, "Señora Catarina, buenos días!"

"Buenos, buenos," Kate called. Then she smoothed the manila envelope from María on her lap, postponing it as though she had to ready her heart for whatever lay inside. She took a deep breath. With a sense of ceremony she peeled open the envelope.

Inside were three smaller envelopes.

One, a wedding invitation printed on rough brown paper: a rustic woodcut, Brueghel-like, a peasant man and woman dancing. She slit the envelope open with her thumbnail. María and Frank. It seemed right. Looking back, she could see that they had waited for a private moment to declare themselves, for space. Romance takes space. They would marry on December 31. In Managua. There was a letter from María, written on lined school paper.

Dear Kate,

I hope by now you are feeling better. It has been hard for all of us. We loved Maggie very much. The clinic prospers, in spite of no money. The women who come say gracias every day. They learn from the videos over and over. Frank and I want you to come to the wedding. Please. Mamá says you must. Between Frank and Mamá, it will be a grand party. I am very happy, Kate. Life goes on. As well as the fighting. I am sorry for any unkind words I spoke to you.

Your campañera,
María

Next an envelope of photos: Cecelia! Cecelia walking in a seersucker sunsuit; Cecelia trying on sunglasses way too big for her; Cecelia eating a cupcake. Kate had silently noted her first birthday, a date inextricably twined with hard memories: the hurricane, Consuela dying, Deaver. María had not mentioned Deaver and Kate was glad of that. Cecelia was a sweetie pie, with a wispy shock of black hair, big brown eyes, pudgy hands and arms. There was a photo of a grinning Lupita in her comedor, at a table with customers. And one of María and Frank in Hawaiian shirts, holding hands in a garden. Kate shuffled through the photos, delighted.

The third envelope was sealed, bulky. She opened it gingerly to the smell of money, like sweat. Money and the credit card she had left in Managua for Maggie. The credit card embossed with *Margaret Ann Byrne*. Money that hurt her heart. Tears sprang into her eyes. She wiped them on her shirt sleeve.

"Qué pasa, Catarina?" Lino stood before her, his hair slicked down from his shower.

"Nada," Kate said. "Only letters. Letters from friends."

"Qué bueno," he said. "It's a good day."

Indeed, the wind had died down and the sky was clear. Kate came back to the present. The red clay roofs lay like patches across the land. Hummingbirds dipped into milky pink roses that grew near the post office.

"Necesito ver un hombre, un amigo de mi padre," Lino said. "Father Dixie has coffee for you."

"Qué bueno," Kate said.

And Lino sauntered away around a corner past the municipal hall.

Kate carefully put away the mail and walked up the hill to the house, among the curious goats. Dix had set an overnight duffel on the porch.

He patted his knee when she walked in.

"Where's Marta?" Kate asked.

"Still asleep." He patted his knee again. "Come sit here a minute."

Kate put down the mail, slipped off her shoes, and sat on his lap. He hugged her. Then he said, "Are you going to be all right? Just for a couple days while I carry Lino down to Fuego?"

"I'll be fine."

"I'll miss you."

"I know," Kate said soothingly. "But we'll be here. When you get back." Then she got up and took a seat at the table. He had poured her coffee; he must have been watching for her to return. "How far's Lino's village?"

"Thirty clicks."

Kate leaned into the table, the wood warm on her arms. A fire crackled in the fireplace. Out the window she saw the caretaker at the barn, the faded gold blooms of los flores del muerto around the barn door. She said, "Do you think we can make yogurt?"

Dixie put his hand on hers. "Yogurt. Yes—" He squeezed her hand. "I'm having a hard time going. It doesn't feel right to leave you."

"I know." To cheer him up she shared the mail with him, the school picture, the snapshots of Cecelia, the wedding invitation.

"Maybe we'll go to Managua for their wedding," Dixie said. "Maybe—"

A woman wailed, a plea. Men's voices clashed.

Dixie went to the front window. Kate joined him, slipped her arm around his waist. "What's up?" she said.

A transport truck had pulled to a stop in the village square. Its exhaust pipe had broken off and the racket it made could be heard from a long distance. Women at the community fountain moved as one body to the far side of the square, their striped plastic water jugs still balanced on their heads. Men in ragtag uniforms leaped from the bed of the truck, rifles in hand. Eight or nine men.

"Guerrillas," Dixie registered. "See the shape that truck is in."

The men darted warily to the pastel houses, slammed against doors. One soldier dragged a boy from a corner house, a terrified look in his eyes.

"I wish Lino hadn't gone—"

Kate said, "There he is—"

Lino strode toward the foot of their hill, carrying a brown paper bag.

A soldier waved at him, an imperative. Lino kept to his path. The soldier yelled again, stalked him. He overtook Lino, twisted his arm behind his back. The brown bag and its contents—yellow squash—spilled to the ground.

"Mother of God—" Dix said. He bolted from the hacienda, pounding down the steps. The soldier and Lino struggled at the bottom of the hill. Blinding sun rose over the cliffs.

"Mijo!" Dixie shouted.

The soldier looked up, frightened. Young himself, a young beardless soldier.

"Hombre, no—por favor—" Dixie begged. Out of breath. His hand against his chest.

The soldier jerked high his rifle.

Kate ran from the house in her stocking feet, her muscles lax with fear. She plunged down the muddy hill. Goats scattered, bleating. Dear God dear God how can they how can they how can they rushed urgent and clamoring don't take him how can they and pleading don't take him not him and roaring over and over and over don't take him, don't, no don't, no, no, no, no, no—

From the porch Marta cried, "Catarina . . ."

The soldier fired at close range. He and Dixie stared at each other. Birds glazed with sunlight flickered into the pine branches. Dixie held open his arms, a puzzled look on his face. He fell, his glasses half crushed under his skull, the mud sticky on his cheek.

The soldier shoved Lino up into the transport truck. He prodded him into the middle of a gang of boys.

Dixie's heart raced. That would not last long. Kate knelt beside him, ripping open his shirt. She cried out harshly through a dark veil.

Kate knelt in the first rough pew. Marta silent beside her.

A European Christ above the altar. With pale skin, a cropped head of black hair. His robe ornamented, green and leafy. A chunk of plaster broken away from his cheek. Three spears entering his torso from different angles emerged from his neck and shoulders.

Dix's face was in her line of sight. Candlewicks burned in tiers behind the coffin, brushes of fire warming the church. The dank church. Without a glimmer of gold or satin. But what odors there were: pine and wax and rain and the grassy stems of flowers piled at the feet of the Christ.

Kate felt she had no flesh left. Her bones glowed incandescently, hard and sharp as knives. Someone tapped her shoulder.

She stood and faced two men from the village. Beyond them the church doors opened to fair weather: a trapezoid of blue sky. They clutched straw hats against their chests. The young one, who had a smooth compassionate face, fixed his eyes on the fresh pine coffin. His big silver belt buckle, two crossed guns, gleamed in the candlelight. The other man was ancient, with red-rimmed eyes. He straightened his striped sash, vestigial traje.

"All of the people are sorry God has taken him," he said.

Kate nodded. She put out her hands. The old one took them.

Stoically, the young one spoke. "Sí. Pues. He was a good man."

The old one said, "The people want to bury his heart behind the church."

Kate caught her breath, stifled a moan. "No tengo el derecho decir. Sí o no. You will have to ask his sister when she comes."

Kiddo.

I remember you.

It was the rainy season, wasn't it. The zócolo in San Cristóbal would get that greenish glow from the rain. There was a guy there reading Mayan astrological charts. For next to nothing.

You thought your story was a love story, didn't you?

Careful what you wish for.

I remember your khakis. Your braids. And your knife. You had a red Swiss army knife. I thought you wouldn't last long. I thought you'd skedaddle back to the Midwest.

Fooled me.

What a dream—

Before the refugees. Antes de la violencia.

The Sandinistas killed plenty of people. They'll find mass graves there by and by. Deaver probably didn't tell you about that, did he?

No army's innocent.

I remember you.

Good morning, merry sunshine.

The Fortunate Isles. I want to go there with you—Kate Banner—

Listen to this: What were you doing while the poor were suffering, their humanity and their lives consumed by flame?

Do you remember when the refugees first came across? I heard it from a photographer. He said they had no food. Mexican soldiers confiscated his film. Acting on instinct. Nobody had developed a strategy at that point. There were just all these people streaming across the border. Those trails are like a sieve. You would've never gotten into the refugee camp later on. They kept internationals out of there. Kept a lid on things. The Mexican government didn't want to offend the Guatemalan government. They might've lost some roadwork contracts in the deal.

Good morning, merry sunshine. What makes you wake so soon? You scare the little stars away and frighten away the moon.

You know what Blake wrote about passion? The Treasures of Heaven are not Negations of Passion but Realities of Intellect from which all the Passions Emanate Uncurbed in their Eternal Glory. I like that. But I don't know if I believe it.

Uncurbed in Eternal Glory. We can never know what uncurbed passion would look like. There'd be an innocence to it. An end to duality.

I got used to living in the highlands. You might have a village of ten thousand people. And only four vehicles. That makes for a silence you might not know about your whole life in the States. It's a silence that won't be disturbed. Except by gunfire.

Eight years is a long time. Long time in the lion's den.

The wheels slipped in the mud. The jeep groaned and rocked. Rain exploded—that's how it felt, that violent, that hard. Marta lay asleep in the passenger seat under a sweater of Dixie's. That curry smell assailed Kate. She did not exactly remember his voice; no, it was not like that. It was not the way you lie awake combing through your evening for sweet things to remember or wonder to be had. No, it was not like that. His spirit grafted to hers.

The road was something to be tamed. And the night. Vidalúz always said, Don't drive at night. You might not see anyone—who would be out on a cold wet night?—but you might run into a liquored-up civil patrol, sick and tired of carrying their heavy wooden Mausers in the rain. Or bandits. Or worse, some would think, you might run into soldiers.

There were things Dixie wouldn't have said to her right now, things he knew she would not be able to stand, things he'd said to her while he stroked her hair with infinite care. Care she had hoped was infinite. She had begun to think that: This man will be with me always. Grief, tears, hot truth in her chest, grabbed at her like barbs on a barbed-wire fence. She drove on, she had to—

She would never know what he felt like. Inside her. Uncurbed.

She came down a long grade, past a house where one weak yellow light glowed, probably a lardy candle stuck in a bottle. A house that was a home, however grim it might seem at daybreak. An Indian woman would rise before her husband and children. In the dark. To build a fire and pat the masa into tortillas. Then Kate was on a straightaway. Pine trees on either side. Rain sissed on the long pine needles. She knew that sound from home, from a long-needled pine outside her girlhood window where Steller's jays had squabbled.

A fresh wave of rain washed over the hood. At Casa Buena she had known that sound, the pine trees, the rain. There had been a few pine trees among the cacti. And cockroaches. But in the dry season, parched dirt blew up as white as talcum. Even in dark glasses you had to avoid the sun's glare on the ground. Insects whirred all the dry day long. Every daily act had seemed like a subversive gift. A piece of luck she found and added to her store. She had tried not to think of the worst thing happening. Her mother had taught her to think of the worst and she had defied her mother by rarely dwelling on what could go wrong.

Catarina, Catarina!

Just come with me, Deaver had said. They need nurses everywhere.

Sweetie, sweetie, Maggie had said.

He's really a nice guy. He's really a nice guy.

What're you doing with him?

I don't want to get into it.

Pet. Sugar.

I love you, Kate Banner.

Brigadista. You do not belong here.

Kate had been groomed to be somebody else. She had not been groomed to drive a twenty-year-old jeep down from the muddy highlands to Guatemala City. With a child, in the middle of the rural night. She had not been groomed to meet Father Dixie Ryan's sister and brother at the international airport, where their flight from New Orleans was expected at four in the morning. They were coming for the body. For what was left. She had not been groomed for so much loss, but she could feel that bullying her, a numb weight like a pitiless thief stealing her—everything—

Hard rain pulsed on the roof of the jeep. She heard rushing water. The red taillights of another vehicle wavered ahead. She pump-pumped the brakes. Her knee trembled. Someone lunged toward her, stepping high out of water, swinging a lantern, yellow ball of light within a rainy curtain. She rolled down her window. The creek rushed by.

A man's face appeared, the lantern light shining up on his angular cheeks. He had an old friendly face. His mouth fell open when he saw her, revealing a gold front tooth. His Lakers T-shirt was torn at the shoulder, soaking wet.

"Buenas noches, señora," he shouted. And then, holding high his lantern, gesturing toward the creek that poured across the road, he shouted again, "The bridge is gone." He shook his head, frowned. "La enseñada esta muy profunda. Very deep."

The steering wheel felt worn beneath her hands. Rain lashed inside the jeep. Up ahead, in water up to his knees, a tall thin boy wearing only boxer shorts danced around the bumper of the vehicle that was stuck. Her headlights seemed to illumine his every ligament, every sinew. She thought of the puppets beside the kitchen door of their house in Antigua, white wooden skeletons from Day of the Dead that went clackety in the courtyard wind at night.

Kate shouted back, "Is there another way to the capital?"

"Ah, sí, sí—pero, it is a long distance."

"Shit." She knocked her forehead on the steering wheel. "Shit."

"Perdón, señora—you can cross, you can cross!"

"I don't think so."

"You can help us."

"Señor, no—" she began.

She knew that was wrong. To have a task at hand was exactly what she needed. The man waited, question in his eyes.

"Sí, es possible," Kate said, nodding. "I'm going to get out."

The first step to take to get home again.

The man scuttled around to the jeep's push plate. He held high his lantern. Dark rain molded the cast light. Kate could see him smiling.

"Ah, sí, sí," he said. "Gracias, señora. Un torno, a winch, qué bueno, qué bueno. Tiene un torno—"

He called his son from the creek.

What I remember is being wet to the skin.

Chilled. Worrying about getting sick. Not for me—for Marta. I was afraid I would get sick and she would have no one to take care of her. Again. And I dreaded seeing Jude at the airport. I was insane, no one could understand what I was going through, we'd been so secret, no one really knew. Oh, Jude knew, she understood—and feared—that Dix loved me, but what that meant to her I did not know.

None of that mattered, none of it really mattered. You hear the same worn-out inner voices at a time like that, what you want, what you need, and then you come right up against what's happened and you know your paltry whining for what it is.

A day had passed before Marta and I left for the capital, and his body had been laid out in the church, his church, in a fresh pine box, and the people had been coming around to pay their respects, and men of the village came to me, and one said, We are very sorry God has taken him. We want to bury his heart here in the village. He loved the village and we want his heart to remain here. I could not answer for his family and I told them this, I told them that they would have to ask his sister when she came, and Jude and Sam did say yes, yes, that would be right, let them have his heart, and a doctor came, a doctor from Belgium who was working in Nebaj, and she cut out Dixie's heart—they took his heart—and they buried it with a proper ceremony behind the church, and he is there, I can see the very spot where his heart is buried, we marked it with a granite stone that came all the way from Antigua, a stone carved with David Dixie Ryan . . . en las Islas Fortunadas para siempre . . . and sometimes I forget to look, but other times I sit here on this porch and meditate on just that place, and hear his voice—

We got across the creek all right.

It has been years—

Hummingbird House is high on the hill above the village, and Marta plays her flute for us in the evening after all the chores are done. Work is our practice: cleaning the stainless-steel water buckets and trimming the hooves of the sweet-natured La Manchas and milking and kidding and making cheese and keeping the brick floors clean and stretching the lace curtains on pine frames to dry in the sun and vaccinating the children the mothers bring to our house and caring for each other, there's always that, listening, asking after feelings, asking after bodily needs. We understand that our bodies are temples of the Holy Spirit, we understand that now. Debra, with her silver flute in the bamboo case, still comes with her parents every summer, and it was Debra who taught Marta to play. Like the loons calling.

And Marta speaks.

We have come far enough to talk about Eduardo. She fills in her life with memory. Marta is not afraid of memory. She has been loved at last. We sit on the porch and shell peas and talk. In the work room we shape the chalky rolls of goat cheese and we talk.

She speaks Ixil, she speaks Spanish, she speaks the English slang that Debra teaches her, she reads the English poems in Dixie's books. Still, this isn't reason enough to send her to the States for school. Sunny and Ben are generous, but I worry that she would fall in love with all I left behind. That seductive life. Antigua seems too far, but there at least I can visit her for a weekend or she can bring her homesick self back to the mountains on the bus—

We serve the women of the village. We teach reading, we sell our cheese, we have two rooms we rent when women travelers pass through.

Vidalúz does not live here, though she visits. She tells us, Hummingbirds are found only in the Americas, did you know? And they fight, they fight to protect their young, they're tiny but fierce. And they build beautiful nests. They build their nests of caterpillar filaments and spider silk just as the Mayan women wove their huipils centuries ago. Vidalúz has traveled as far as the Inuit villages of the far north and the southern realms of Chile, learning the healing wisdom of the women who live wherever she goes, and every few months she comes home, home to us, home to her mother, who lives nearby. She makes the creams and ointments, the tinctures and decoctions. She knows the uses of garlic and cypress, that yarrow stops a nosebleed. She tells us that verbena—what indigenous women call locab—was a sacred herb of the Druids. She will make a tea of rosemary if you have a stomachache. She knows that quil contains a bitter oil similar to quinine and that is what she recommends for flu or inflammation of the throat.

Someday perhaps it will be safe for her to live with us in peace. Without fear. We all have fear. Like weather it comes and goes. Still, the people of our village have banded together and insisted that the army leave the village and that the guerrillas abandon the foothills to the north of us, they have insisted, and for now, they have their way. They want one generation of children to live without so many weapons in their faces.

We have company, we have plenty of company—

My mother comes, and with her my aunts. They sit on the porch and talk and giggle and have their cocktails as if they were at home.

When Jude left Guatemala with Dixie's body, at the airport she said, I'll send you home, Kate. My brother would have wanted that.

That was kind of her. I knew how much that cost her.

And I said, I am home.

It hasn't been long since Paul traveled here to coax me back. He'd forgiven me long ago, he felt there was a need for forgiveness.

After he visited the farm, we rented a hotel room in Antigua for three days. We stayed there like brother and sister while he made his case. How odd it is I've never married. You grow up thinking that you will. Someone gives you a bride doll when you're five years old and after that you never doubt it.

The woman Paul thought he loved, the woman he planned to marry—she left him for an inexplicable reason, she took a job in another state. And now he thinks I'm the one, he has so much to say about love, he's a late bloomer, he says, and though I can recall those times in the attic dancing to Smokey Robinson and in our bed with the magnolia tree blooming in creamy tips just outside the window and though he's a pleasure to see standing on our porch with the goats coming up curiously behind him to figure out who's here and though I like to remember Maggie with him and all those years we measured ourselves by the mayapple leaves, desire is not what I feel. Something happens to desire. You think you'll always feel it. That charged and honeyed longing you can't master. It controls you. Then time, time takes you over.

Up here we have let go. We never listen to the love songs.

We are told that the commandante at the nearest army base lays our cheese upon his bread. And the children and the mothers come. We do what little we can for children with emphysema who since birth have breathed in woodsmoke from the indoor cooking fires. Soot hangs like moss in the rafters of their houses. We deliver babies. Los milagros. We scold the mothers about too much sugar, too much soda pop. We have the BBC on short-wave. We know about Bosnia, the way the women were treated there, we know about the child soldiers in Africa, we know that in the States if a girl dies and she's not yet four years old, she won't die from disease but at the hands of the person she depends on. We see with quite clear eyes the war beneath the wars. If you pass this story along, make sure you get it straight. What little balm we have, we have against all odds. Do not walk away in sorrow. Do not be consoled.